Amanda's Room

Chuck Miceli

A note from the author: Each chapter of this book begins with a factual quote about the weather. It is not necessary that you follow or completely understand them. If they detract from your enjoying the story, feel free to skip them. Note, however, these quotes are not just about the weather. Like any good forecast, they anticipate what will happen in the story and the lives of the characters, and many readers have found making these connections a rewarding experience. Enjoy.

This is a work of fiction. All of the characters, organizations, and events portrayed in this novel are either products of the author's imagination or are used fictitiously.

Amanda's Room
Third Printing - August 2013
Published by Hitchcock Lake Publications

Copyright © 2012 by Chuck Miceli
eBook available through Amazon.com

All rights reserved. Except for use in any review, the reproduction or utilization of this work, or portions thereof, in any form is forbidden without written permission of the author.

ISBN-13: 978-1475291971
Library of Congress Control Number: **2013915827**

Cover Design by Michael C. Miceli and Jenn Blessing Miceli,
Miceli Productions, LLC
Printed in the United States of America

A portion of the proceeds from this book are being donated to Every Dollar Feeds Kids, (**http://www.edfk.org**), a non-profit organization that raises money to feed hungry children in the US and abroad.

For Judy

More than Yesterday, Less than Tomorrow

Each of us makes his own weather and determines the color of the skies in the emotional universe, which he or she inhabits.

Bishop Fulton J. Sheen
From The Way to Happiness

Prologue

Weather: The state of the atmosphere at a given place and time.

The blackness was absolute. Thick clouds blanketed the Catskill sky as Gareth and Cynthia Reynolds continued the longest night of their lives. The car's headlights illuminated tiny stretches of the winding mountain road until a single lamppost appeared in the distance. At the light, Gareth turned his new 1990 Bentley off the road, passed the open wrought iron gates, and up the long driveway to number 34. Cynthia roused from her sleep and sat up in the back seat as the car rounded the circular driveway. The house was dark except for the Christmas tree illuminating the large center window on the second floor. The stately mansion was always imposing to Cynthia with its three-tiered fountain and columned entry, but now it felt terrifying. Saint Michael, locked in battle with Satan atop the fountain, looked impotent; this time, the demon had won. Even the Christmas tree appeared mocking and grotesque. Gareth exited the car but Cynthia remained frozen in her seat and wouldn't move.

"Gareth," she insisted, "I can't. I can't go back into that house. I can't stand the thought of seeing the room, the bed. I just can't."

Gareth leaned over and placed his hands on the hood of the car. He closed his eyes, lowered his head, and shook it from side to side. Then he gritted his teeth and responded, "All right. Enough! We'll get a room for the night and come back for our things later."

"No!" The word came out as a command rather than an answer. "You're not hearing me. I can't, I won't go back into that house, Gareth, not later, not ever."

Gareth didn't say a word. He looked away toward the

house, and for the first and only time that night, he smiled. He returned to his seat, adjusted the rearview mirror, calmly buckled his seat belt, and then slammed the door shut. As the car made its way down the long driveway to the street, Cynthia looked up to the second floor of the house and focused on the right corner window. Gareth turned onto the street and the car moved off into the night. Cynthia's gaze remained fixed on the window until the house was consumed by the darkness. What she did not see, could not see, was that inside that darkened window, Amanda's room lay peaceful and still, and bathed in a perfect pink glow.

+++

The sky was just beginning to brighten when they checked into two separate rooms at the Friar Tuck Inn. Later that day, Gareth went alone to the mansion at 34 Sunset Terrace and packed two suitcases, one for Cynthia, and one for him. For the next several days, they met repeatedly with Harry Weinstein, their personal attorney, and doctors and administrators of the Hudson Valley Medical Center. There were accusations of malpractice and threats of lawsuits but in the end, even with the Reynolds' considerable resources, it amounted to nothing.

A week after the funeral a moving company arrived at the mansion. According to detailed instructions from Gareth, the crew carefully packed selected clothing, dinnerware, electronics, and personal belongings. They labeled each box listing the contents and the name, Gareth or Cynthia. They took nothing from Amanda's room. The other furniture and items remained behind. Gareth had the Christmas tree and its decorations burned. He donated the unwrapped Christmas presents, including a diamond tennis bracelet and a European vacation, to charity.

Weeks later, another crew arrived. They cleaned and dusted the house, covered the furniture with drop cloths, and placed loose articles in plastic storage bins. In accordance with Gareth's instructions, the door to Amanda's room remained closed and the workers did not enter it. They turned off the electricity to everything but the alarm and heating system and set the heat just high enough to prevent the pipes from freezing. For a time, other crews arrived to mow the lawn, trim bushes, and clean away leaves and snow. The Reynolds did nothing to maintain the home's interior, and they never reentered the massive mausoleum.

Several months after the funeral, Gareth and Cynthia divorced. In the settlement, neither of them requested the property at 34 Sunset Terrace. Four years later, the east gutters clogged and overflowed, soaking the wood soffits behind them. The following spring a pair of squirrels ate through the rotted wood and took up residence in the attic.

Birds built nests atop the accumulation of leaves, twigs, and dirt. A young robin, attempting to leave its nest too soon, faltered and fell down between the wall studs. For two days, it fluttered helplessly trying to escape. On the third day, a stiff westerly breeze developed and blew constantly against the house. The resulting updraft aided the chick's efforts, but not enough. The bird died, the breeze faded, and for weeks after, all that remained was the stench of death.

For the next fifteen years, the house decayed, musty and dirty, bitingly cold in winter and stiflingly hot in summer. And throughout that time, oblivious to the outside world, Amanda's room remained immaculately clean, peacefully quiet, continually comfortable, and constantly illuminated in that perfect pink glow.

1

Climate: The aggregate weather conditions for a long span of time over a large area.

Nestled in the Hudson Valley, surrounded by rolling hills and low-lying mountains, Nadowa College's setting was magnificent. Spring turned the hillsides a lush green and autumn exploded in vivid colors and textures. But the valley was a bowl that trapped weather and held it tight. In midwinter, the icy winds were relentless, and the temperatures of a late summer heat wave could blister paint.

"Hey, Chris," Drew Richardson's words were slow getting through to Chris Matthews, "are you grabbing the other end of this crib or what?"

Chris's unresponsiveness was odd. Everything about him was spontaneous and smooth. His baby face, soft blond hair, and transparent blue eyes complemented his easygoing personality. He stared at the closed window a moment longer, frowned, and then responded.

"Sorry, Drew. How about putting this other stuff inside the crib and taking it all down at once?"

Drew surveyed the room's contents: a Winnie-the-Pooh lamp atop a nightstand, a wicker hamper, an animated cat clock on the wall, a dozen children's books, and the crib.

"No thanks. I don't feel like backing down the stairs with that much weight. You take the nightstand, I'll get the rest of these things and we'll come back for the crib."

"Sure thing, Hercules," Chris handed Drew the lamp and started to lift the nightstand. From the strained look on his face, it was heavier than he expected. Drew smiled through his wiry beard but said nothing. He placed the books and lamp in the hamper and reached for the clock.

"Hold on, Drew. I'm keeping the clock."

"You've got to be kidding." Drew examined the black plastic cat for a moment. Its giant eyes moved slowly side to side as its tail wagged lazily beneath it. "It's a kid's toy."

"It's an antique. Haven't you ever heard of the Kit Cat Clock? Besides, it's got lots of personality."

Drew looked at his wristwatch: 9:20. "It doesn't even keep the right time. Its hands haven't moved in the last hour." Drew pointed to the clock's hands displaying 10:07.

"Of course not, genius. There's no electricity, remember?"

"Oh, yeah, then what's making his eyes and tail move?"

Chris looked at the clock and frowned. "Batteries. Damn!" The battery operated models were more recent and considerably less rare. "Leave it anyway, I still like the way it looks."

Drew exited the room, but had to stop because Chris was standing in the hall. Chris had put the nightstand down and was staring back into the room again. "Now what?" Drew asked.

"I'm drenched again." Chris's blond hair was limp and his face was flush. Both men were in their early twenties and physically fit, but even in their lightweight T-shirts, they were soaked with sweat.

"And you're surprised why? It's only about 95 today and we've been carting stuff outside all morning. Or did you just discover that you have sweat glands like the rest of us?"

"No, listen, I'm being serious here. Didn't you notice how cool it was in the kid's room? I didn't sweat the whole time we were in there."

Drew realized Chris was right. "Maybe it's air-conditioned."

"Sure thing. No electricity, remember? Great trick."

"All right. So it's on the shady side of the house or maybe there's a breeze or something."

"Wrong on both counts Sherlock. The window faces south

so it's been getting sun all morning long and look there," Chris pointed to the room's window, "it's shut."

"Listen, can we finish this outside? I'm getting dizzy from the heat in here." Drew's heavy-rimmed glasses were steamed and his curly black hair was soaked through with perspiration.

Chris picked up the nightstand and smiled, "My point exactly."

2

Most weather phenomena result from the uneven temperatures of the Earth's surface and the resulting processes that reconcile those differences through the transfer of heat.

"Here you go, Katie." Drew laid the items on the lawn next to the table and wiped the sweat from his face. A white film of pollen muted the scorched brown hue of the lawn. "That's the next to last load. Just the crib in the kid's room, and we're all through. Is there anything cold to drink? I'm dying of thirst."

"There are plenty of Cokes in the cooler," Katie Jarvis answered. The first term junior class president looked remarkably cool and composed for such a sweltering day. The huge beach umbrella she stood beneath helped, as did her airy white blouse and tan shorts. Even so, heat was never much of a problem for her. She was thin and athletic. Growing up on a Kansas dairy farm had accustomed her to hard work, long hours, and plenty of sunshine.

Katie had a natural look about her. She never wore makeup, had barely noticeable freckles, and a tanned complexion. She radiated an outward calmness that made her approachable and easy to like. She was excited by the success of her first major fund-raising effort. The banner hanging from the table she stood behind announced:

TAG SALE–All proceeds to benefit the 2010/11 Nadowa College Student Activity Fund.

"This is going to be great," she said. "Even before we started tagging things people started buying them up. We've made over $200 already."

"And what's this?" Drew examined the delicate looking

object in front of Katie and then answered his own question. "A thermoscope!" He admired the tall liquid-filled cylinder. Glass globes filled with brightly colored liquids sat at the bottom. Each had a shiny gold tag attached to it. "It's beautiful."

"Thanks, Drew," Katie smiled. "I'm buying that for myself."

Drew returned the smile, gratified at the opportunity to have something to focus the conversation on. He was a gifted math major but was also painfully shy and in awe of Katie. "If I recall correctly, it works on density. When the temperature increases, some globes sink lower while others stay afloat. You just look for the lowest floating bulb, read the number on its tag, and that's the temperature."

Katie nodded, "I've seen lots of these before but never one this big. Normally there are only about six or seven bulbs that cover a temperature range from about sixty to eighty degrees. This one has ten bulbs that go up to ninety-six degrees. It must have cost a fortune."

"Well, don't charge yourself too much for this one. It must be broken; all of the bulbs are resting on the bottom."

Katie peered inside. "I'm certain it works fine, but that means it has to be at least ninety-seven."

"I'll tell you exactly what the temperature is." Drew reached under the table and withdrew an instrument cluster mounted on a highly polished mahogany base. Separate brass-encased instruments measured barometric pressure, relative humidity, and temperature.

"Drew, that's gorgeous."

Drew smiled, happy that Katie appreciated his find. It verified for him that she and Chris weren't the only ones with an eye for treasure. "Whoever owned this house had outstanding taste. Now, Chris has his toy cat clock, you have your thermoscope, and I have my weather center."

Katie eyed the temperature, "A hundred and one degrees: can it really be that hot?"

"It wouldn't make sense to put cheap instruments in such expensive cases, and they've been in the shade all morning. I'll bet you they're absolutely accurate."

Katie's cell phone interrupted their conversation. She opened it to a text message:

HI K T CAT
R U NAKED?

Drew glanced away when Katie noticed him staring over her shoulder. As he did, he saw Chris closing his cell phone. He threw Katie an inquisitive glance.

"It's a long story," Katie returned with a Mona Lisa smile.

"That's OK. I've got all day."

More cars arrived and parked along both sides of the house's quarter-mile long driveway. The air rippled above their hot metal hoods. Nevertheless, as soon as they stopped, the occupants bolted from the comfort of their air-conditioning and crisscrossed through the displayed items. Katie returned to the tag sale topic, "See what I mean?"

"This tag sale idea was pure genius," Drew answered. "I knew that running on your slate was a smart move."

Katie smiled appreciatively. She was satisfied that with Drew as class secretary and Chris and Tess as officers, her job would be easy.

"I've got to give credit where it's due." Katie's words displayed the kind of honest humility that drove Drew's admiration. "It was really Chris who discovered this."

"You mean stumbled on it." Drew wasn't about to let Katie give away all the credit. "It wasn't something he went out and researched. The administration handed the announcement to him at the broadcast station. If they didn't need this house cleaned out for construction, they would never have offered to pay students to do it, and Chris would never have thought to ask. It's just lucky he mentioned it at our meeting before blabbing it over campus media."

From Drew's perspective, if Katie hadn't thought of the tag sale idea, they would have spent all weekend making runs to the dump or Goodwill for a couple of hundred dollars. That would have barely paid for their gas. They had made more than that already and, thanks to Katie, by the time they finished, they might pull in ten times as much for half the work.

"Now that's leadership," he ended.

"Wow. Thanks Drew. That's sweet."

As Katie smiled, two distractingly attractive dimples formed on her cheeks. Drew stammered something unintelligible and then started looking around. He spotted Chris making out with Tess DiNardi under a shade tree. "Hey, Chris!" he shouted.

Chris looked up and pulled his hands out of Tess's back pockets. Tess did likewise. As they walked toward Drew and Katie, Chris's arm was draped over Tess's shoulder. They had been an item since freshman year.

Tess was tall with cappuccino skin. With the exception of her long firm legs, she was all curves. Whereas Katie had the look of a high schooler just emerging from puberty, Tess had the body of a fully matured woman, and her braless halter top and skintight shorts strategically accentuated every curve and crevice. However, her most beguiling feature was her smile. When Tess smiled, her whole face beamed. It wasn't the asymmetrical look typical of most people. There was no hint of restraint from any muscle trying to hold this or that line in place. The look was disarming. Whatever Tess lacked in sophistication, she more than compensated for in sensuality. Drew resumed talking as they arrived.

"I can't believe you two could smother each other in all this heat."

"A word of advice, Drewski," Chris announced, "don't knock it 'till you've tried it."

"The heat doesn't really bother me much at all," said Tess. "It's all this pollen that gets me. I've taken three allergy pills already and my head is still pounding." During the conversation, a woman approached Katie and inquired about the master bedroom set.

Drew asked Chris to help him get the crib out of the baby's

room, but as they turned to go, the woman and Katie finished their negotiations. Katie interrupted the men mid-stride and asked them to load the furniture into the woman's pickup.

That was how it went for the rest of the day. People arrived, negotiated purchases, and then asked for help loading things into their vehicles. It was late afternoon before the last car pulled away.

"Can you believe this?" Chris asked. "We must have had a couple hundred people. It never stopped. I'll bet we made a thousand bucks."

"$1,581.10 to be exact," Tess reported.

"Prompt and precise as usual, Ms. Treasurer," said Katie. She was fond of Tess.

When Katie transferred to Nadowa, Tess approached her on the first day, guided her around campus, and then helped her settle into the dorm where they both lived. Katie talked her friend into running for student government but the person most surprised by Tess's victory was Tess herself. When it came to money, however, she had a natural aptitude for finances and she knew it.

"And ten cents?" Chris asked.

"That was mine," said Tess. "A lady wanted a snow globe marked a dollar but she just wasn't about to pay that. She offered a nickel, I counter offered with quarter, and we finally settled on a dime." Everyone laughed until Drew broke in.

"Is it just me, or is anybody else starving?" Katie suggested that the student fund pay for pizza and beer but asked that they eat it at the house. She didn't want to leave things unattended for too long before dark. Drew offered to make the pizza run while the others reorganized and covered the tables with tarps.

"Just one thing," said Drew, "this heat has really gotten to me. Maybe when I get back, we should just eat in the car with the AC on?"

As hot and sticky as everyone was, no one was thrilled at the prospect of trying to balance food and beer in Drew's VW Beetle.

"Hey, wait a second," said Chris. "We've got our own little walk-in fridge right on the premises." He pointed up to the right corner window on the second story of the house. "Let's eat upstairs in the kid's room."

3

Heat is energy transferred from one body to another because of a temperature difference. It always flows from the hotter object to the colder one.

By the time Drew returned with the pizza, the others had retreated to the upstairs room. He wished the ride from the pizzeria was longer. The air-conditioning had finally started to take effect. As he exited the car, he propped two six-packs atop the pizza boxes, wedged a bag of potato chips between his chin and the beer, and headed for the house.

The sun had dipped behind the mountain but the air was still scorching. It worsened when he entered the front door. The house was an oven. By the time he reached the kid's room, his shirt was soaked through. Everything changed, however, when he walked through the doorway.

As Chris predicted, the room was cool and comfortable, perfectly so. Sitting on the rug, the others looked remarkably relaxed after their sweltering afternoon. Drew tossed Chris the bag of chips.

"Salt and vinegar," said Chris. "My favorite - perfect!"

Drew shook his head, "You've got one weird sense of taste."

"You haven't lived," answered Chris, "until you've had potato chips with your pizza, and pepperoni pizza with salt and vinegar chips is the ultimate combination."

As Drew opened the pizzas, everyone grabbed a beer. Chris raised his bottle and gestured. "Madam President, I propose a toast: to a brilliantly conceived, thanks to me, and brilliantly executed, thanks to you, class fund-raising effort."

"Thank you, Mr. Vice President," Katie and Tess raised

Drew frowned at Chris's self-serving gesture ...d for his beer.

...dd," Drew closely examined the bottles. "I was ... these just before coming in and I could swear that they ...e dripping with condensation, now they're bone dry." He hadn't noticed that the same was true of his shirt.

Katie interrupted to say that when Chris talked about coming into the house to eat, she thought he had lost it, especially once they entered the front door. "It felt even hotter in the house than outside, but he was right. It's wonderful in here."

"Yeah," Tess added, "it's like air-conditioning. Even my sinus headache has disappeared."

Fifty minutes later the quartet had finished both six-packs and most of the pizza. "Whew," said Tess, teetering somewhat as she spoke, "three beers in less than an hour. That's got to be a record for me."

"Four," said Katie. "You also had one of mine."

Then Katie got an idea. "As the incoming student government officers we're going to be working very close together for the next year. I think we should get to know each other better."

Katie suggested playing a couple rounds of *Favorites* Trivia. Each person would share a favorite book, play, or movie, and explain why.

"If you want us to get to know each other," Chris offered, "we should get a couple more six-packs and play Strip Beer-Pong."

"Wow," said Drew sheepishly. "Then we'll really get to know each other better."

"Boys," Tess protested. "Katie's being serious."

"And you don't think we are?" volleyed Chris.

Tess glared at Chris, "Play nice."

"All right, all right," Chris caved. Drew shrugged his shoulders.

"I'll start," said Katie. "Mine is the musical 'Rent.' I loved the concept of a bunch of Bohemian squatters taking on the establishment, but mostly I loved the song, 'Seasons of Love.'"

"Why, Miss Kansas," said Chris, "I never would have guessed that from a nice country girl like you."

Tess jumped in. "This is easy. Mine is a movie: 'Fifty First Dates.' It was soooo romantic and I love Drew Barrymore and Adam San...," Tess hiccupped, "Sand…," she hiccupped again, "Sandler!" she shouted, then giggled. "Especially Adam Sandler; I think he's cute."

"Mine is a book," said Drew, "'Pillars of the Earth' by Ken Follett. I loved everything about it. It made me wish I'd been born in the Middle Ages. At first, I wondered if a book with that many pages could hold my interest. Later, I could hardly put it down. Finally, I purposely stretched out finishing it because I didn't want it to end."

"What about you, Chris?" Katie asked. A wry smile wiped across Chris's face.

"Mine is a movie," he paused, "that greatly underrated 1972 cult classic," he paused once more, "'Deep Throat.' Who would have believed at the time that you could get such great camera close-ups on…?"

"Chris," Katie interrupted with false sternness, "you're such a pig!"

"That's it, Chris," Drew added. "You're cut off. You're not allowed to play anymore."

"No, seriously, Chris," Katie pleaded.

"I was being serious!"

Katie frowned.

"All right, all right," Chris continued. "Then it has to be the movie, 'The Ring.'"

"Oh!" Tess gasped. "That was really creepy. I had to sleep with the lights on for a week after seeing it."

"That's what made it so great. You almost felt like it could really happen. And I loved the idea of that girl living on through an electronic medium. She could be everywhere and anywhere – even here!" Chris reached over and tickled Tess who screamed in terrified delight. After a pause, Chris changed the subject.

"Isn't it amazing how cheap some people can be? I still can't believe that old lady arguing over a quarter."

"It's got noffin' to do with being cheap," Tess slurred. "She was just following the rules."

"Rules?" Katie asked.

"Yep," Tess hiccupped and then giggled quietly. "The tag sale rules. My stepdad taught them to me. We went tag-saleing most every Saturday, even in the rain. There were ten of those little buggers. I can't remember them all just now, but let's see; I know one: Never look too anxious, no, no, no. No matter how bad you want something. Yep, that was one of them.

Another one: if you really want something really, really bad, don't even look at it. Ask about something else instead, then sorta back into what you really want. Yep, that's another one.

But I still member the big rule, Numero Uno, because if he said it once, he said it thirteen thousand trillion times: NEVER, EVER, PAY THE ASKING PRICE. Period, stop, end of story! Yep, that's what he said all right." Tess's face beamed as if she had just recited Hamlet from memory.

Chris reached over and put his arm around her, "I love it when Tess gets buzzed."

"Imagine that," murmured Drew. "Your stepfather took you tag-saleing every weekend. That's something. My foster father was some big shot corporate consultant. He was always flying off somewhere. When he came home, he'd always have some cheap souvenir for me. I got a chest full of that junk from all over, but when it came to time, I couldn't even get him to stick around long enough to play catch. I must have asked him a hundred times. He always found some excuse to weasel out of it. Can you imagine a father who couldn't even take the time to toss a ball around?"

"Yeah, well," Tess interrupted, her drunken smile suddenly transformed into a cheerless, sober expression, "be careful what you wish for; you just might get it."

"What do you mean, Tess?" Katie asked.

"I remember this one day in grammar school, I came home and told my mom that some older kid on the bus gave me a quarter as payment for a job he wanted me to do. He and his friends were all laughing. I didn't know why but from the way they laughed, I figured they were making fun of me.

"Now, my mother was strict Baptist. When I told her the kind of job he wanted me to do she made me wash my mouth out with soap, but she wouldn't tell me why. I hadn't said any cuss words that I knew of. My mom was terrified about talking to me about sex and stuff like that, so my stepdad proposed that he do the teaching for her and my mother jumped at the offer. Only thing was, when it came to sex education, stepdaddy's method was show and tell." The other members of the group cringed but forced themselves to continue listening.

"Over the next four years I got one hell of an education, and my mother just pretended it wasn't happening. Whenever I even hinted at it, she just changed the subject or left the room."

Tess paused for a moment and rose to her feet, "Speaking of leaving the room, I gotta pee," and she bolted out into the hallway. Everyone else sat, stunned.

"Wow," Drew broke in. "I never saw that coming. I guess maybe I shouldn't have tried comparing fathers, I mean, how do you top that for creep of the heap?"

"It's not your fault, Drew," said Katie. "You had no way of knowing. Maybe Tess just needed a way to get it off her chest."

"Well, if that's what she was looking to do," Chris's face was pale, "she sure as hell succeeded."

As Tess reentered the room, she blurted out, "Hey guys, I don't know what made me say all that. I've never shared that with anyone before, not even my minister. I was always too embarrassed." She paused for a moment. "Please, you can't repeat what I told you. If it ever got back to my mom, it would just kill her. You've got to promise me you won't say anything to anyone."

"But, Tess," Katie protested, "don't you think it would be better…"

"No," Tess stopped her. "It wouldn't. My stepdad's a dead man. All it could do now is bring my mother more pain. And, believe me; she's had more than her share of that." Everyone reluctantly agreed, then dropped into stillness again. Chris finally broke the silence.

"Listen, why don't you girls clean up all of this stuff while Drew and I bring the crib downstairs? We've got to be back here early again tomorrow morning."

4

Climate is how it should be...Weather is how it is.

Katie and Tess started cleaning up the bottles and trash as Chris and Drew moved the crib through the doorway. Chris went through first. As Drew crossed the threshold, Katie shouted.

"Hey, guys, don't kill the lights yet; we're still cleaning up in here!" Drew stopped and turned around.

"What are you talking about, Katie? We didn't touch a thing." Engrossed in their conversation, none of them had noticed it getting darker outside. The late afternoon had faded into evening. Drew looked for the light switch. As he did, he inadvertently moved the crib back inside of the doorway and the room's pink glow immediately returned. He frowned, then scratched his head and moved the crib past the threshold as the light disappeared again. He moved the crib back and forth through the threshold a few inches at a time. Each time he did, the light vanished or returned accordingly. He took a step back, folded his arms, and smiled.

"Now that's different!" Suddenly, the crib jerked violently. Drew looked up to see a barely visible Chris having a temper tantrum in the hallway. Chris was yelling wildly, but Drew couldn't hear what he was saying. It was as if there was a soundproof barrier between them.

"Stop fooling around, damn it!" Chris shouted at the top of his lungs, but he was inaudible to those inside the room. Drew couldn't understand why Chris wasn't completely engrossed with the light show. Meanwhile, Katie and Tess stood and stared at the bizarre goings on between the two fellows.

Chris pushed hard on the crib, driving it and Drew back

into the room. He said, "Now maybe you can tell me what the hell is going on." He had intended it to be a bellow or at least a grunt, but it came out as an objective, controlled statement.

"Couldn't you hear us?" asked Drew.

"I couldn't hear or see a thing, at least not until you put the lights back on." The other three looked skeptically at Chris.

"Chris," said Drew, "just stand to the side for a sec." With that, Drew wheeled the crib through the doorway. Once again, as the last of the crib cleared the threshold, the room plunged into darkness.

"Awesome!" Chris looked surprised. "How'd you do that?"

"You didn't see that happening over and over before?" asked Drew.

"There you go talking all crazy again."

Drew brought the crib back into the room and, once again, the lights returned. "Do me a favor, Chris, push the crib in and out of the room after I step out into the hall."

"Wait a second," Katie sprang for the door. "I want to check this out, too." Once she and Drew had stepped out into the hallway, Chris did as instructed. Moving the crib through the doorway, Chris and Tess sank into darkness but were able to talk clearly with Drew and Katie. As soon as the crib reentered the room, however, the pink glow returned, but it was impossible to hear across the threshold.

"Holy shit!" Chris finally understood what caused all the commotion. A similar exclamation came from Drew and Katie out in the hallway, but their words didn't carry into the room any more than Chris's words escaped from it. While Chris and Tess had plenty of light, Drew and Katie could barely see them. It was apparent that as long as the crib was at least partially inside the room, neither light nor sound could pass through the doorway. Drew and Katie reentered the room.

"Hey, guys," Katie looked around as she spoke, "where's the light coming from? I don't see any lamps in here, do you?" Surveying the area, they quickly concluded there were no light fixtures anywhere in the room. Other than themselves, the sparse furnishings and the dinner trash, the room was vacant.

"Even if there were light fixtures, it wouldn't do any good," said Chris. "No electricity, remember."

Drew looked at Chris's cat-clock. "Chris, how long did they say this house was abandoned?"

"At least fifteen years. Why?"

"Don't you think fifteen years is a little long for a clock to run on batteries?"

Chris walked over to the clock and took it off the wall to expose the electrical cord and outlet beneath it. "So there is electricity in this room." As he unplugged the clock, the room went dark. He replaced the plug and the light returned.

Tess rubbed the goose bumps rising on her arms, "This is getting way too eerie."

"Not really," said Drew, "Just some awesome technology."

"So, Edison," Chris chided, "you think this is all just some sort of technical wizardry?"

"Well, Doctor Frankenstein," said Drew, "if it's a choice between that or eerie..." Drew raised his hand while wiggling his fingers and mouthing the 'Twilight Zone' tune.

"Listen," Katie interrupted, "before you two start unzipping and pulling out rulers, I know how we can find the answer for certain."

The rest of the entourage looked at her doubtfully.

"Monday, Drew and I are in Professor Myers' last afternoon lab. If there's anyone who could explain what's going on here, it's Doctor Myers."

"What?" Chris asked. "Uncle Weatherbee? He teaches meteorology. What would he know about stuff like this?"

"Katie's right," said Drew. "I've had him for physics, too. Before he came to Nadowa, he was at MIT. He's one of the most brilliant physicists in the country. He's also published books on paleontology, botany, and microbiology. The guy's like a human Wikipedia. He just teaches meteorology for the fun of it."

"Well, if he's such a hotshot," said Chris, "then why isn't he still at MIT?"

"I heard they offered him a boatload of money to come here," answered Drew.

"There's got to be more to it than that," Chris returned. "He's not some football star. Someone with those credentials doesn't just switch from the Ivy League to the Poison Ivy League for money."

"It doesn't matter why," said Katie. "What matters is that he's probably the most qualified person within a thousand miles to help us figure out what's going on here."

"I've read several of his research papers. He seems fascinated by anything out of the ordinary. I'd bet he'd jump at the chance."

"Yeah," Tess added, "and he's cute, too." Everyone stared at her with confused expressions on their faces. "Well, for a professor."

Katie smiled, then addressed the group, "There's also this," she pushed the crib out of the room. Everyone stood silently, scanning the interior of the darkened room.

"Forget what you do or don't see," she instructed, "What do you feel?" Immediately the rest of the group knew what she meant.

"It's hot in here," said Drew.

"Hot as hell," added Chris.

Katie pulled the crib back across the threshold. "Not any more." In an instant, they were perfectly comfortable again.

"You know," said Tess, "it seems odd that with something like this going on, we're not totally freaked. In my head I know I should be, but somehow I'm just not."

"Now that you mention it," said Chris, "stumbling across something like this, I should be about a seven on the Richter scale by now, but I don't feel at all antsy. That's too weird."

"It's getting late," said Katie, "and we've still got a full day ahead of us tomorrow. Can we agree to keep this to ourselves until we know what's going on?"

Everyone nodded.

"Good. Then on Monday, Drew and I will have our talk with Professor Myers."

5

Weather forecasting uses science and technology to predict changes in the atmosphere that will occur over a defined area in a specified amount of time.

Monday afternoon Katie and Drew were in Professor Myers' 3 p.m. meteorology lab. Of all the places on the Nadowa campus, this was Katie's favorite, partly because of the subject matter, partly because of the room itself, and largely because of Professor Bertrand Myers.

At thirty-seven, Myers was the youngest department chair on campus, yet no other faculty member could match his credentials. Bert was a prodigy.

By the time he graduated from high school, he had earned a fully paid scholarship to Yale and had already completed half of his first-year credits. He finished his undergraduate degree in three years. Before his thirtieth birthday, he held multiple doctorates from the most prestigious universities in the country and authored half a dozen books on a wide range of topics.

As part of his move to Nadowa, Bert negotiated a dedicated work space and supervised the reworking of the lab according to his personal specifications. Walking through the door of his classroom was like entering a time machine.

With its cream-colored walls, black chalkboards, and tin ceiling, the overall effect was that of a high school science lab in a 1950s movie. Incandescent bulbs washed the room in a soothing yellow glow. The scent of chalk dust hung in the air. As with most movie sets, however, what the viewer saw was only a facade. The real magic lay behind-the-scenes.

With the flick of a few switches hidden in his desk, Bert transported his students from a nostalgic past to a Spielbergian future. The front chalkboards slid open to expose a wall of high definition displays. Responding to voice commands, the displays linked to the professor's computer, student workstations, Nadowa's central computer system, or directly to any of 300 top colleges and universities nationwide. There were direct links to the National Oceanic and Atmospheric Administration (NOAA) and the Department of Energy (DOE), not only to their web sites, but also to their administrative offices.

Bert helped to create the college consortium that supported the joint weather research conducted by DOE and NOAA. That gave him unprecedented access to academic and government meteorology experts throughout the United States and abroad. He brought his credentials and his connections with him when he made the move to Nadowa, which in turn made its program one of the most sought after in the country.

A NASA-like console hidden in cabinets at the rear of the classroom contained real-time feeds from weather satellites and Doppler radar installations worldwide. There were links to mountaintop instrument clusters from some of the highest points on Earth and ocean-based ones from some of the lowest. The data displayed on a digital map of the entire planet, which could be zoomed instantly to virtually any point on the globe. Severe weather reports updated the map in real time. The entire installation cost more than the gross domestic product of many small countries.

Most freshmen, however, never saw the magic behind the panels. They spent much of their first year studying the nature and origin of weather phenomena and the history of weather research, from the earliest cave dweller to this morning's weather forecast.

Students like Chris Matthews found Myers' curriculum and his fixation on the basics exasperating, which led to a significant freshmen dropout rate. That was not a problem, however, given the list of students waiting to fill those vacancies. It was also not a problem for Katie, who found both the man and his methods exhilarating. She was distracted this particular afternoon by the subtle streaks of gray in the professor's dark hair and the lack of a ring on his left hand.

A bell sounded signifying the end of the session. It was another of Bert's alterations.

"That will do for today people," he shouted. "Remember next week will be a review quiz on chapters one through seven. Papers are due on Tuesday, outlining your analysis of Hurricane Camille's trajectory, variables, and dissipation factors." As most students exited the room, Bert fielded questions from hangers-on while packing texts and materials into his worn leather book bag. Katie and Drew waited until the last of the students left before approaching him.

"Excuse us, Professor," Katie said. "Have you got a few minutes?" Bert smiled at the sound of Katie's voice. She stood out as one of the brightest and most inquisitive students he had known, and Drew's math and computer skills were unmatched. He finished packing and answered Katie without looking into her aquamarine eyes.

"I was just going to put these things in my car and grab a cup of coffee. Would you two like to join me?" Katie and Drew followed the professor out to his parking spot.

Sitting just below his classroom windows was Bert Myers' pride and joy: his 1968 canary yellow GTO. Its black leather interior matched the vinyl-covered hardtop. As Bert opened the passenger door to put his materials in, Drew gazed at the chrome four-speed Hurst shifter. Katie thought the car looked cute; Drew was transfixed.

"Professor," he said, "that's got to be the most beautiful thing I've ever seen."

"Why, thank you, Drew, I think she's kind of pretty too. I bought her from the original owner and restored her myself. She's always acted like a lady to me, so I try to repay the favor." Bert's care was evident. The paint finish gleamed and the vinyl top glistened in the late afternoon sun.

"What's it got under the hood?" Drew asked.

Bert's face lit up. "It's got a 400 cubic inch engine and a Ram Air II carburetor. The engine peaks at 360 horsepower. With a manual transmission and rear wheel drive, she can be a bear on slick roads even with the Positraction rear end, though that's never been a problem - I put her up every winter. I've chromed out most of the front-end components. I could pop the hood if you'd like to see."

While Katie sympathized with the man-car relationship thing, right now there were more pressing matters to discuss. She said, "If you don't mind, professor, maybe you two could continue that some other time. If you're ready for that cup of coffee now, we've come across something bizarre and we need your advice. If what we've experienced is real, it might just make predicting the weather look easy."

6

Clouds are made up of water droplets or ice crystals. Most of the particles are so small they stay suspended in the air or descend very slowly and evaporate before reaching the ground. It takes about a million cloud droplets to make up a typical raindrop.

It was after dusk by the time Bert Myers' GTO and the Volkswagen Beetle he followed rounded the circular driveway of the dark, decaying mansion. The four mile drive from Nadowa's administration building seemed long and tedious in the relentless deluge. From the description Katie and Drew had given him over coffee, however, Bert had to see this phenomenon for himself.

Bert barely made out the four figures inside the Beetle's fogged windows. As soon as he cut his headlights, the quartet bolted from their car and raced under the covered porch. Once he saw the large entrance door swing open, he ran to join them.

He hadn't brought an umbrella, nor was he dressed for the torrential downpour. Despite the short distance to the house, he was soaked through by the time he entered the front door. His clammy, wet shirt stuck to his skin. A sudden breeze snuck by as Katie closed the door, sending a shiver up his back.

"Professor Myers," said Katie, "I think you know everyone here."

Bert scanned the group. "So Mr. Matthews and Miss DiNardi, you're also part of the mystery house team. Should I read anything into all the secrecy surrounding this meeting?"

"You don't have to worry about being played by us, Professor," said Chris. "If somebody is pulling a fast one here, then believe me, we're all vics."

"All right then, lead the way."

Chris turned on his flashlight and led the group up the darkened stairway to the second floor. At the top of the landing, Katie halted the group. "Professor, I think you might want to note this before we continue. Look down to the end of the hall. What do you see there?"

Chris turned the flashlight off. It took Bert a moment to adjust to the darkness. "A faint light coming through the doorway at the end of the hall," he said.

"Why don't you take a closer look, Professor?" Katie motioned Bert toward the doorway.

"Miss Jarvis, I never realized you had such a flare for the dramatic." Bert made his way down the hall and peered into the open door, "Through the window I can see a street lamp in the distance."

"Good," said Katie. "And would you say that it appears to be the source of the light that's spilling out into the hallway?"

"Y-e-s-s-s." Bert started tapping his foot. The wet sock sloshed around inside his shoe. "To be honest Katie, this 'Twenty Questions' game is getting old very quickly. I'm cold, wet, and hungry. Would you please drop the 'Ghost Hunters' routine? I'd really appreciate it if you would just show me what we came here to see."

"Sorry, Professor," Katie and the others joined Bert at the doorway. "If you'll just step inside the room I think you'll find that all of your questions will be answered."

Bert started to move but before he took a step forward, Chris added, "And all of your answers will be questioned."

Bert cast a cynical look toward the group. Then he stepped out of the damp, dark hallway, through the doorway and into the room.

Even in the dim light of the distant street lamp, the students could see the astonished look on the professor's face, but they couldn't hear the words he said once he entered the room. "Well, I'll be damned!"

7

Snow crystals form when tiny supercooled cloud droplets freeze, and then grow larger in the cloud's supersaturated environment. As larger crystals fall through the atmosphere, they collide and stick together, forming snowflakes.

John Thompson's giant frame nearly spanned the breadth of the picture window in his spacious office. He stood looking out at the snow-covered campus and contemplated the kind of problem his predecessors could have only hoped for: where to put all the new students applying to his school.

It wasn't so long ago that Nadowa College was developing contingencies for its own demise. But that was before the casinos. The local Nadowa Indians had been running high-stakes bingo games forever without much impact in this sleepy section of upstate New York. When they won tribal recognition, however, the casinos soon followed. The slot machines came first, then the gaming tables and ATMs. The hotels followed and with them busloads of tourists anxious to give their cash away. Fortunately, the founding fathers of tiny Nadowa College had chosen the tribe's name for its title; a tribe suddenly flush with money and desperate for land to expand its growing enterprise. Moving the college to its new, expansive location was just the beginning. The real windfall came from retaining the College's name.

For many years, the Nadowa tribe had faced crushing poverty, alcoholism, and heartbreaking suicide rates. With prosperity came a renewed sense of pride, a desire to reclaim the tribe's heritage, and a goal to establish its own legacy. Tribal leaders saw investing in a college with their own namesake as a way to insure historical immortality. Now, with a broad curriculum including specialty tracks like broadcast journalism and meteorology, a top-flight faculty, and a sports program rivaling the Ivy League, the biggest problem was accommodating the increasing student population.

Unlike many colleges, time was more of a problem for Nadowa than money. Even cookie-cutter brick and glass dormitories took several years to go from concept to completion. Thompson had convinced the board of directors to use a portion of the school's endowment to purchase homes adjacent to the campus and convert them into temporary student housing. He was now under pressure to demonstrate results. On this particularly cold March afternoon, he spent several hours reviewing records for three houses on Lakota Drive, formally Sunset Ridge. Concurrent with its relocation, the college renamed all of the enclosed streets after Indian tribes. The three large houses were slated for renovation in early fall. Numbers 17 and 21 were already housing two dozen students each. Number 34, however, remained "under construction." At the same time, it oddly listed four student residents.

Repeated calls to the contractor from Thompson's delegates got the same terse response, "Listen, we were ordered off the job and we've got it in writing." Dean Thompson decided to review the work orders for the houses personally.

While initial requisitions called for similar materials for each of the houses, the work on number 34 stopped about six weeks into renovations. Since then, the work orders attached to the job showed little resemblance to the other two dwellings. Instead of sinks, bathtubs, beds and cabinet installations, he saw obscure requests for demolition and unspecified equipment installation.

He opened another folder labeled "Physics Department." It contained purchase orders for a long list of standard test equipment like sound analyzers, light meters and weather instruments, and exotic instrumentation that he had never heard of. While the purchases were within the approved range for the department, the delivery address, 34 Lakota Drive, certainly was not. If his suspicions were correct, someone would probably go to jail.

Thompson would have called the auditors had it not been for the signature on the purchase orders: Bertrand Myers. John considered Myers and his wife, Evelyn, friends. If there was anyone whose work and personal ethics he trusted, it was Myers. Bert was one of the most gifted members of the faculty. John personally recruited him from MIT at considerable cost. The investment was a lucrative one. A significant number of students transferred into Nadowa specifically because of Myers' reputation for teaching and research. He also attracted many times his salary in grant money, enough to equip a dozen new labs.

So what business did the physics department chair have with student housing anyway? As Thompson reviewed the records, he noted that Myers' signature started appearing on the suspect purchase orders just as the normal renovation work stopped. He picked up the phone and called Bert's cell.

"Professor Myers, it's Dean Thompson. I need to talk to you. Are you available?"

"Actually, Dean, I'm in the middle of something right now. Could we meet sometime tomorrow?"

"No Professor, I'm sorry, it can't wait. We need to talk right now. Are you on campus?" Thompson nodded as Myers' answered and smiled.

"Good, stay right there. I'll come to you."

It was unusual for the college president not to simply instruct a faculty member to meet him in his warm, spacious, and intimidating office. However, John Thompson didn't want Bert Myers to come to him. He wanted to meet him where he was - not in Myers' office or in his classroom - but where he said he was currently working: at 34 Lakota Drive.

8

The amount of heat absorbed from the sun's radiation varies widely from place to place. A forest will absorb 90% or more of the sun's radiation. Fresh snow will reflect 75 to 95% and retain very little heat.

The last light of the winter sun was quickly vanishing as Thompson rounded the top of the circular driveway. If Bert had not said he was there, Thompson might have thought he had stopped at the wrong house. He saw two cars parked along the driveway, but the windows were all dark and the building looked deserted. The house stood by itself at the end of the road, more than a mile from its nearest neighbor. Beyond the road's end, a dirt trail continued and then disappeared in the thick underbrush that covered the steep mountainside slope. Across the street lay 1,500 acres of state-owned forest, which was frequented more by black bears and whitetail deer than people. A single street lamp alerted visitors to turn into the concrete pillared entrance.

Beyond the 12-foot high wrought iron gates, the quarter-mile driveway led up to the three-tiered fountain in front of the mansion. To the right of the driveway was the large greenhouse that once cultivated the flowers and shrubs that adorned the property. Seventy acres of dense, downward sloping woodland separated the back of the house from the lake-sized pond below.

Thompson surveyed the outside of the property. What he saw pleased him. The exterior looked nearly finished. The roof, siding, windows, and trim looked new with the possible exception of the second story window in the front right corner of the house. Its weathered appearance was out of character with the new renovations. Even under the light snowfall, the landscaping looked neat and trim. The walkways were clear, and the driveway was shoveled and dry. Perhaps, he wondered, the reports were wrong. His opinion changed as soon as he opened the front door.

The house was getting dark and felt even colder inside than out. Stacks of hardwood flooring lay where there should have been finished floors. He flipped the light switch with no effect. Through the fog of his breath, he could see that the thermostat was set at 55 degrees. Working his way around the left side of the house, he moved from room to room with similar results in each. Scraped walls waited for paint. Stacks of hardwood sat atop unfinished floors. New moldings leaned against the walls from which the old ones had been removed. New light fixtures remained in their corrugated boxes, and the old ones still hanging didn't work.

It was as if some cataclysm had struck and the workers suddenly abandoned their stations and never returned. The kitchen and downstairs bathroom were even worse off—gutted and then abruptly stopped. As he entered a room in the back of the house, he felt something crunching underfoot. White powder and pieces of gypsum board surrounded the muddy snow that covered his boots. Looking up, he saw the watermarks and cracks in the badly damaged ceiling surrounding the fallen section. He could also make out the snow that rimmed the perimeter of the hole. The greatest shock, however, came as he entered the room in the front right corner of the house.

"What the hell?" There, the skeleton of what should have been the room's ceiling greeted him. Mountains of plaster, lath, and insulation filled the corners of the room. Gypsum dust covered the floor and stuck to Thompson's wet boots. Looking up, he glared at the bare beams supporting the floor above. Wires of different types and sizes hung down like the tentacles of a giant jellyfish. His mind raced from one scenario to another, but he could not conceive of any plausible explanation for what he was seeing. He loosened his tie and unbuttoned the collar from around his perspiration soaked neck.

"Professor Myers!" boomed out from deep within his gut while treads and banister railings creaked violently under his mass as he bounded up the stairs.

9

Shangri-la: An imaginary place, remote and beautiful, where life approaches perfection.

Nothing that Thompson observed on the first floor could have prepared him for what he experienced at the top of the landing. After more than two decades of education, "Oh, my God," was the only sentence his mind could assemble. To his left was a posh but typical floor configuration. Doorways punctured the wall of the main hallway and led to the rooms on that side of the house. To his right, however, he found only a dark, gaping cavern where there should have been walls, floors, doors, and ceilings. The lone exception was the remains of a single room still standing in the front right corner of the house. As with the downstairs ceiling, all that remained of the room's exterior walls was a skeleton of studs. Once again, tentacles of cut wires hung suspended from outlets and switch boxes. Thompson refastened his overcoat, bracing himself from a sudden chill as he realized that it was even colder upstairs. Then he noticed that all of the windows on the second floor were, open, and a stiff, steady wind blew across the icy landscape. Looking toward the rear of the house, he saw snow that had piled against the inside of an open window, except for where it had broken through the ceiling to the floor below.

As Thompson prepared to issue his next shout, Bert Myers stepped out of the skeleton room wearing jeans, a short-sleeved shirt, and a tooled leather belt. He looked better dressed for a summer rock concert than the dark, frozen interior of the bombed-out shell of a house. His bizarre appearance only added to Thompson's confusion and deepening concern.

"Dean Thompson, it's good to see you," Bert smiled and

extended his hand. Thompson didn't return the gesture.

"I can't say the feeling is mutual, Professor Myers. Can you offer any plausible explanation for what is going on here?"

"Plausible?" Bert smiled. "Now that might be a bit of a stretch."

Thompson was not amused. "Don't toy with me, Professor. If it were anyone but you here, you'd be talking to the police instead of me. Misappropriation, fiscal malfeasance... I have purchase requisitions and work orders with your name on them. Your position's at stake here and I don't see any..."

Thompson stopped in mid-sentence as the image inside of the darkened doorway came into focus. His eyes followed the bundle of bright orange extension cords that ran through the doorway. Midway in the room, he could make out the young woman kneeling on the floor. Like Professor Myers, she looked grossly underdressed for the frigid temperatures. Behind her, he saw the open bedroll against the back wall. He looked back at Bert.

"Good God, man, have you lost your mind? You have no idea what you've done here. Professor Myers, losing your position is the very least of your problems. Gather your things. You and the young lady are leaving this house, right now."

"Professor Thompson," Bert reached up and put his hand on Thompson's leg-sized arm, "I know that this looks impossibly bad but believe me there is an explanation, and if you'll just step inside this room with me for five minutes, I promise I can address all of your concerns."

Thompson removed Bert's hand, "Professor, right now God would have difficulty addressing all of my concerns."

Bert looked directly into Thompson's eyes, gestured toward the doorway, and instructed, "Please."

Thompson bristled, "Don't presume to order me around, Professor."

Bert lowered his hand, and his voice, "Please."

"After you," said Thompson. As Bert started to turn, Thompson reached out and squeezed his shoulder, "Five minutes."

Thompson followed Bert into the doorway. As he did, he made out the figure of another man standing in the corner of the room nearest to the door. His mind raced. Could he have been so far off in his assessment of Myers? None of this made any sense. The other man looked big but he was nowhere near Thompson's own size. Anyway, if he needed to, he could flick Myers like a bug. His confusion deepened exponentially as soon as he entered the room. John Thompson suddenly found himself blinded, completely disoriented, and utterly helpless.

"Dean Thompson," said Bert, "I don't believe you've ever met Drew Richardson." Thompson's eyes cleared, He saw Drew's outstretched hand and bare arm extending out of his Star Wars T-shirt. "May the Force be With You" underscored the graphic.

Thompson returned the handshake.

Bert interrupted, "I believe you already know Katie." Thompson turned as Katie rose to greet him.

"Hello, Dean. It's nice to see you again." As Katie spoke, Thompson became aware of the soft pink glow that enveloped them.

"I wish I could say the same to you Miss Jarvis, but under the circumstances, to say I'm concerned right now would be an understatement."

"I don't blame you a bit, sir." She smiled. Like Myers and Richardson, her short-sleeve button-down blouse seemed discordant with the environment, and yet she looked comfortable. Behind Katie on the floor were several electronic instruments with small wires attached. The wires were bundled around an extension cord that ran along the wall and out through the door. Thompson asked what she was doing.

"I'm taking vibration measurements. We have sensors running along the beams and…"

"Katie," Bert interrupted, "let's not overwhelm the dean with too many details just yet." Thompson continued surveying the room. He noted a second bedroll directly under the open window and in the opposite corner of the room, equipment racks on both walls. They were filled with instruments from floor to ceiling; some were familiar, many were not. The more he took in, the less it all made sense.

"Can I take your coat?" asked Bert. As Thompson removed his coat, he realized that the room was not cold at all. In fact, it was completely comfortable. He gazed over to the open window and then to the open door. There was no discernable breeze. That's when he noticed it was almost fully dark outside. Once again, he scanned the room. There were no light sources other than the screens and tiny panel lights of the electronic instruments. Nevertheless, the room's lighting was sufficient and comfortable. Thompson raised his hand in front of the adjacent wall. There was no shadow. There were no shadows anywhere. Light seemed to come from nowhere and everywhere at the same time. "All right, Professor, you've got my attention. Now can you tell me what is going on here?"

"Actually, I can show you much more simply than tell you." Bert walked over to the window as Thompson followed. "Put your hand through the window opening and tell me what you see and feel." Thompson did as instructed. The bite of the winter's air was unmistakable. The stiff wind chaffed at his fingers. He recoiled from the shock and almost withdrew his hand, but then suddenly stopped when he looked down at his tingling limb. He could barely see the outline of his own hand just outside the window. He moved his arm slowly in and out and noted how the light stopped abruptly at some invisible pane. Inside the room, every detail was clearly visible. Yet outside the window, even his white dress shirt almost disappeared completely in the wintery darkness. There was no spillover of light whatsoever. He drew his hand back into the room and shook it to release the effects of the cold. "Impressive, isn't it?" Bert asked. "We've been studying the effect for the last five months in virtually every kind of weather and it's always the same. The environment of this room appears to be completely independent from that of the outside world and vice versa."

"Vice versa?"

"Yes," Bert started for the door. "Just step out into the hallway for a moment and look back into the room. You may want your coat." Thompson ignored Bert's theatrics, stepped out into the black hallway, and turned around. Had he not been immediately outside of the room, he might have had difficulty returning. The room was almost completely black except for the glow of the panel lights and screens from the instruments. Through the open window, he could make out the dim light of the distant street lamp as he had described it to Bert. As fascinated as he was at the effect, he did not want to linger much longer in the frigid hallway without his coat. The wind was chilling, and his feet started aching inside his snow-covered boots. He stepped back into the room.

"Like diving into a pool, isn't it?" Bert asked. The description was as accurate as any Thompson could imagine. Wetness, temperature, light, air, everything above is clearly demarcated from what lay below. However, Thompson realized that even the pool analogy had its limits. Water doesn't distribute itself vertically without a container and light and air temperature have at least some influence. In the absence of a better analogy, however, it would have to do.

"Did you want to wipe your boots?" Bert asked. Thompson looked down at his boots and squinted at what he saw, or rather didn't see. They were clean and dry. Moreover, the off-white rug beneath them showed no signs of wetness or soiling. In fact, the entire rug was clean and dry.

"When you step into the room," Bert explained, "any dirt or wetness remains outside; that is, until you leave, at which point you immediately pick it up again."

"Why?"

"Oh, I can give you volumes of what, but as to why, I could only guess."

"In that case, Professor, give me your best guess. What's going on here?"

"My best guess?" Bert paused a moment, then looked toward Katie and Drew and smiled before answering, "Dean Thompson, welcome to Shangri La."

10

Thermal comfort: When a person wearing a normal amount of clothing feels neither too cold nor too warm. It occurs only when the air temperature, humidity, and air movement are within a specified range, often referred to as the "comfort zone."

Over the next couple of hours, Bert and his students reviewed their five months of research with Thompson; readings of internal and external temperature, humidity, light, sound, vibration, wind velocity, and a dozen other parameters that they had painstakingly measured, recorded, compared, contrasted, and analyzed every hour of every day. The results were striking in their consistency.

"No matter what it's like outside," Katie explained, "the internal environment of this room remains steady. More than that, virtually every reading falls within the range of what most people would describe as 'comfortable': it's never too hot or cold, too dry or sticky, too glaring or dim, not even too loud or too quiet."

"And it's not just the external environment," said Drew. "The room seems to have its own built-in regulator for virtually every parameter." He could see that he was losing Thompson.

"Let me demonstrate." Drew walked over to the instrument rack and flipped a switch. A row of a dozen halogen work lights on the top shelf came on simultaneously.

"Each of these work lights is 500 watts. That's 6000 watts total light and heat. In a room this size, that should drive you right out of here in a matter of minutes. We can leave those on all day and night and the temperature and light level of this room won't budge." Thompson approached the lights and stared directly into one of the lenses.

"Normally, at that range," Drew continued, "you should be blinded by that halogen bulb, and you'd never try this at home." Drew reached up and placed his hand on the ribbed metal casing. Thompson knew the ribs were there to radiate away the intense heat, but Drew's face remained placid as he spoke, "It's as though the light and heat are trapped within the unit."

"Or how about this," Bert moved over to a CD player. "This is one of my all time favorites." He picked up a CD of "In-A-Gadda-Da-Vida" by Iron Butterfly and inserted it into the player. "We've hooked the player to a thousand-watt sound system." He set the volume to full and hit the play button. While Thompson was unimpressed by the acid-rock music and lyrics, he didn't experience the pain in his ears for which he had braced himself.

"Once again," said Bert, "it doesn't matter how much sound we pump into the room. The decibel level always stays within a perfectly comfortable range. In addition, if you eliminate all sound whatsoever, a peaceful white noise remains that can almost lull you to sleep."

"Speaking of lulling you to sleep, Dean," Katie interjected, "I think you'll find this interesting. If you wouldn't mind, please close your eyes for just a second."

Thompson did as instructed. Katie smiled at Bert and then spoke again. "Good. Now just relax and take in slow, deep breaths."

After a few breaths, a broad, peaceful smile crossed John Thompson's face, "It's delightful, almost imperceptible, but it's definitely there. Just the slightest hint of..." Thompson opened his eyes, "baby powder?" Katie smiled and nodded.

And then there's the other thing," said Bert.

"The other thing?" Thompson questioned.

"I'm a physicist," Bert responded. "As crazy as all this may be, at least it's in the range of the physical world. I can get my mind around that. I can measure it, analyze it, and at least try to make some sense of it. However, there's something else going on here, something much less tangible—something going on inside of us."

Katie saw Bert struggling for words and intervened, "Dean Thompson, do you remember how you felt just before you walked through the door tonight?

"I'd have to be dead not to. I was mad as hell. Then seeing you on the floor next to that bedroll, well, it certainly didn't seem like you two were up here conducting research. I hadn't even noticed Mr. Richardson until I started into the doorway. By that point I was almost ready to come up swinging."

"But you didn't," Katie interjected. "Can you recall what you felt immediately after you entered the room?"

Thompson tried to reconstruct those first few moments, "After the initial shock and getting acclimated, I guess I just felt—calm."

"Precisely the word I use to describe my own feelings when I'm here," said Bert.

"Actually," Katie added, "that's pretty much the same word all of us use to describe how it feels." Drew nodded in agreement.

"All of us?" Thompson asked. "How many people know about this?"

"A half dozen now," Bert answered. "There's me, Katie, Drew, Chris Matthews, Tess DiNardi, and now you."

"Chris Matthews?" Thompson pondered the name. "Doesn't he run the student broadcast station?"

Bert nodded. "He's majoring in communications and journalism."

"And he's been in on this since the beginning?"

Bert nodded affirmatively.

"How did you get a journalism major to sit on a story like this for over five months?"

"I asked him not to tell anyone until we finished our research," said Bert, "and he gave me his word he wouldn't."

Thompson looked skeptical. Katie continued, "That seems to be another aspect of 'the other thing.' The longer you stay in this room, the more difficult it becomes to lie or hide the way you feel about things, and once you make a commitment, it becomes impossible to go back on your word. At least, that's been our experience. Somehow, this room seems to be its own little universe—a kind of paradise on earth."

Bert added, "We haven't come up with any reasonable explanation as to why. The best we can do is to document what we've studied and experienced."

"And why all the demolition?" Thompson asked.

Bert explained the team's methods for ruling out potential causes of the anomaly, by segregating the room from its surroundings, by removing adjacent structures and obstructions, and by eliminating potential contributors such as heating systems and electricity.

"I think we came as close as we could to isolating the room, short of suspending it in midair with a crane."

"And I assume you've adequately documented your test results by now?" Thompson's question caught Bert off guard. It seemed as though he was taking the conversation in a new, potentially dangerous direction.

Thompson read the concern in Bert's face. "Listen Bert, I understand that you're on to something enormously important here, but your methods for going about it have left you vulnerable. I've been asking questions and so have others. If you don't change direction and fast, your activities won't be a secret much longer. I can appreciate the need to be discrete, but for that to occur, this project needs to become invisible again, and the only way that's going to happen is to start normalizing it. I have some ideas and I need you to come by my office first thing in the morning to discuss them. This isn't a request."

Thompson stood to leave, "It was nice meeting you, Mr. Richardson." Then he turned to Katie, "And it was good to see you again, Miss Jarvis. You're very fortunate that Doctor Myers chose to involve you in his research." Katie smiled and looked at Bert.

"Actually," Bert said as he handed Thompson his coat, "it

was the other way around."

"You'll have to tell me more about that tomorrow." Then Thompson glanced over to the pile of clothes from which Bert had just retrieved his coat, "At the same time, I'm dying to know what that crib is doing here."

11

Change of State: A process that causes a material to change from one state, e.g. solid, liquid, or gas, to another.

As promised, Bert met with John Thompson the next morning. "So you see," Bert explained, "it was the students who got me involved and not the other way around."

"And you say the crib is still there because it acts like a switch to the room's environment?"

"One of them."

Thompson poured himself a third cup of coffee. He handed Bert his refill, "One of them?"

"Removing the crib interrupts whatever it is that powers the room's environment, but it's not just the crib. Almost any change to the integrity of the room's interior has the same effect. When we were investigating the electrical, for instance, we started to remove the outlet covers to check the connections. As soon as we removed the screw from the cover, everything shut down—light, heat, sound suppression, everything. When we replaced the screw, it all came back. We had to make all of the electrical disconnects from the outside."

"You never removed the covers?"

"No. We were concerned that if we did, we might break the paint seal and lose the environment forever. We tried to replace the screw with another identical one, but the environment didn't return until we put back the original screw."

"Fascinating." Framed by his university degrees, his team's Rose Bowl photo, his MVP award, and pictures of himself with the governor and two U.S. presidents, John Thompson was the personification of power. Nevertheless, that power seemed dwarfed by the mysterious, inexplicable aura of a baby girl's room. "What about the rest of the room's contents? It seems very sparse."

"The students had already cleared everything else out at the tag sale. The only other items left in the room were the clock and the rug. The rug doesn't seem to have any effect but it provides a nice cushion for the bed rolls so we left it. As you've seen, it's always perfectly clean. And then there's the clock."

Thompson recalled the clock. It brought back a childhood memory of one hanging in his grandmother's kitchen. He hadn't seen another like it since. "The clock?" he asked.

"If we unplug it, the animation stops and so does the room's environment, even though there is no electricity in the outlet. Even with it plugged in, if we move the hands to anything but 10:07, the same thing happens."

"Do you have any idea as to why?"

"I wish I did."

Thompson leaned back in his chair. "Thank you for the explanation, Professor Myers. I think I now have a fairly complete understanding of the situation." His expression took on the stoic look of a military leader and his speech was clipped and authoritative. The sudden change alarmed Bert. He feared this might lead to the conversation he was hoping to avoid, the one in which the project was terminated or transferred out of his control. Thompson leaned forward again and rested his arms on his oversized desk. He stared directly into Bert's eyes and spoke in a tone reflecting the full authority of his office, "Professor Myers, it's time we got to the matter at hand."

Bert swallowed hard. Maybe he should have come to Thompson earlier. In retrospect, it was easy to see how the secretiveness of the project could appear suspicious, maybe even criminal. Regardless, this was no ordinary research project. Nothing from Bert's experience came anywhere near the potential of this find. No, this was much too significant to let a bunch of bureaucrats scrap it because of some errors in judgment. He was so entangled in his own thinking that he was unaware Dean Thompson was still speaking, "... so we'll have to find a way to protect the site in order to allow you to continue your research."

Bert's mouth engaged before his brain could catch up, "It would be shortsighted and downright stupid to allow this research to stop now. There's no telling where these findings could lead. And if you stopped to think about the benefits it could have for the college, you wouldn't even...." He paused. "I'm sorry; did you say 'continue the research'?"

A grin wiped across Thompson's face. While he respected Bert's intelligence, he didn't think the squirmy little geek had that much fight in him. "That's what I said, professor." Thompson stiffened again as his voice boomed, "What in blazes did you think I called you here to talk about?"

Bert was too embarrassed to form an adequate rebuttal, "Well, I didn't...did you want to...Maybe you could just share your thoughts on how we might go about it."

Thompson explained his plan. The most important aspect was to lower the project's visibility. He would address the fiscal improprieties first. Too many people had already been involved in the investigation, and it would look suspicious if he did nothing. He would generate a memo to all department heads noting that some members of the faculty were skirting the purchasing rules. He would then emphasize the proper procedures and institute an additional review signature. That would appease the business office, which had been lobbying for tighter measures anyway. Making it look like he was slapping Myers' hand would also send a signal that he was preventing any future reoccurrences. That would keep the auditor types at bay. Bert would route future requisitions directly to the Dean's office, where Thompson's secretary could handle the purchases discretely.

Construction had to be fast-tracked but to insure the integrity of the project, Bert needed to remain directly involved. Thompson had that covered, too. The student government offices occupied portions of an older, smaller building on campus. The officers had been asking for better quarters for some time. He would have the student government offices moved to the Lakota Drive house under the direction of their new faculty advisor, Professor Bertrand Myers. Then the dean would have the previous location renovated for student housing. Thompson would also include some additional meeting rooms at the new location to fill out the remaining space. As part of his new duties, Bert would oversee the renovations to accommodate the new offices. For efficiency, the student government officers, who just happened to be on Bert's research team, would also be housed there.

Once work on the house resumed, it progressed faster than Bert was prepared to handle. Maintaining his full course load was demanding enough. The research on the room had placed added demands on his time, but he had managed that without much difficulty. However, Bert was a scientist, not a contractor. Making decisions regarding bathroom fixtures and kitchen countertops were not his field of expertise, and he had no interest in wall colors, carpeting or drapery patterns. At home, he had always left those decisions to Evelyn, something for which they were both grateful. Bert was relieved to the point of euphoria when Katie Jarvis volunteered to handle the task.

12

About 1,000 tornadoes strike the U.S. each year. They have occurred in all 50 states, in every month, and during both day and night. On average, they kill 70 people and injure another 1,500.

Katie was one of those students who had transferred into Nadowa specifically because of Bert Myers. Born and raised on her parent's farm in western Kansas, weather was an integral part of her life. Her family owned one of the largest agricultural and dairy farms in the country. Long before she studied the science of weather, Katie could sense an oncoming storm hours before it arrived.

Even with the farm's sizable workforce, there was always plenty of physical work to do. Katie's small stature made her look younger than her years and disguised her significant strength, a fact soon realized by any boy who tried to move too fast, too soon. Not that Katie was prudish; she was just selective. Surrounded by farm animals, sex was as natural and normal for her as sleeping outdoors or having biscuits and grits for breakfast. Katie also had a close, loving relationship with her parents. As she prepared to enter her senior year in high school, Katie felt satisfied, self-confident, and secure.

"Now, Katie," Elizabeth Jarvis addressed her daughter who was sitting in the back seat of their Buick Century station wagon, "remember, we're looking for school supplies today, so please don't go dragging your father into the clothing section to look at those designer jeans."

"Dragging me?" Jim looked at his wife with feigned indignation. "You make me sound like some sort of pushover."

"Really, Jim," Elizabeth answered, "all Katie has to do is say please and you fold like a house of cards."

"What can I say? I have a weakness for Jarvis women." Jim smiled and squeezed his wife's hand. Then he turned his attention to Katie.

"So are designer jeans all the rage now Kitten?"

"Daaad," Katie shook her head, "you really have to get a life. Everyone's wearing them."

"Maybe so," Elizabeth interrupted, "but I don't understand how they justify charging three times the price for them. After all, they're just a pair of overalls with a little extra decoration." Elizabeth faced away so Katie couldn't see her smiling. She and Jim had already planned to surprise Katie with the jeans for her return to school. Elizabeth decided to drop the subject and hoped she hadn't been too obvious. She didn't have to worry. Her words had barely registered. Katie was much more preoccupied with surveying the city streets.

While the farm was always bustling, Katie loved everything about downtown: the traffic, the streetlights, and the buildings sandwiched one against the other. There were so many signs in the store windows that Katie couldn't read them all, except when her father stopped for a traffic light. Pigeons filled the town green, pecking on the lawn and lining up on the granite statues and gazebo roof. Then there were the ice cream shops, hot dog vendors, and stores for every imaginable taste. And everywhere there were people; weaving in and out along the sidewalks, running across the streets, strolling hand in hand on the green, carrying armloads of shopping bags, and eating lunch in their business suits in the restaurant windows.

The theater marquee advertised a rerun of "Twister." When it was first released, Katie's parents were critical of the movie for romanticizing something that was a stark reality for people in the Midwest. She loved the special effects. Anyway, Bill Paxton and Helen Hunt were great together. Maybe she could talk her parents into an early show before they headed back home. She didn't know that her parents had already made other plans. If she had, she wouldn't have given the movie a second thought. After picking up Katie's school supplies, they had an appointment at the local Buick dealership. John, the owner, was a member of their church and had known Katie all her life. Jim and Elizabeth had arranged for Katie to test drive several used cars and pick the one she liked best.

"Jim," said Elizabeth, dangling her hand outside the car's window while resting her head against the headrest, "on days like today, I wish we had a convertible." Elizabeth looked up at the billowing white clouds drifting lazily across the deep blue sky and then took in a breath, "And that breeze is just wonderful."

"Strange," Jim replied, "I hadn't really given it much thought, but now that you mention it, it's pretty nearly perfect today." Jim recalled the oppressive heat spell they had just endured for four straight days, "I guess it finally broke."

"There's a parking spot," Elizabeth pointed to an empty space in front of Sears.

Once inside, Jim headed directly to sporting goods to check out the latest fishing rods and tackle. Elizabeth went to the fabric aisle. She loved to sew and wanted to look up the latest McCall's patterns. Katie started for the stationery aisle but stopped short when she spotted Steve Nylen. He was handling a football, turning it repeatedly, and squeezing it while he did. Growing up together in a small community, he and Katie had been friends for most of their lives. He played quarterback on the high school team, and during the previous semester, had shared Katie's third period chemistry class. Katie always considered Steve handsome but after a summer working at his father's lumber mill, he had changed considerably. His chest was as broad as his waist was narrow, and straight lines and angles replaced his once rounded facial features. Steve's arms bulged with new muscles, and he looked bronzed from the summer sun. As Steve turned toward her, Katie quickly looked down toward the shelves, trying to disguise the fact that she had been watching him.

"Hi, Kate," he said as he walked up to her. She pretended not to have heard him. Steve waited for her to recognize him for a moment. When she didn't, he asked, "Do you favor any particular style, or are you just comparison shopping?"

Katie looked up, "Oh! Hi, Steve. I'm sorry, I didn't see you there."

"Obviously," Steve said while looking toward the shelves. A broad smile crossed his face. "After all, you have much weightier matters on your mind." Katie's eyes narrowed as she looked at Steve. When she looked back at the shelves, she saw what he meant. She had been so distracted that she hadn't even noticed where she was standing. When she did, she was mortified to discover that she had wandered into the pharmacy section and was staring directly at the condom selection.

"If I were you," Steve said impishly while placing a package in Katie's hands, "I'd go for the ribbed." Katie looked down at the box. The broad text boldly proclaimed, "For Her Pleasure." Katie's face was crimson. Fortunately, Steve was already walking away from her, twirling the football in the air, and whistling to himself. Katie lowered her head and struck off in the opposite direction toward the stationery aisle. When she realized she was still carrying the box of condoms, she bounced it from hand to hand like a hot ember until she unloaded it on a shelf directly in front of the booklets of daily inspirational quotes.

Twenty-five minutes later Katie's basket was brimming with school supplies: writing pens and paper, a portfolio with a three-ring binder, a daily organizer with a built-in calculator, and a canvas backpack with enough zippered compartments to hold all of her essentials. Katie had accumulated most of those items in the first few minutes. She spent the bulk of her time selecting her personal notebook.

Katie had been keeping a journal every year since sixth grade. Each one, carefully written in her best penmanship, contained an entry for every day since she began, even if it simply said, *"Too tired to make an entry today--will catch up tomorrow."* Together, the eleven volumes chronicled Katie's journey from childhood through adolescence to young adulthood. They documented the exploits of her Barbie and Ken dolls:

Barb and Ken aren't talking this week. Barbie is convinced that Ken secretly likes Jenna.

They chronicled her transition from grammar to middle school:

Wow, is this place big! I can barely make it from one class to the other before the bell rings.

They memorialized the loss of Kippy, her pet turtle and the more traumatic loss of Pepper, her black Lab/German shepherd. Pepper was a constant companion and protector since Katie's first birthday:

Today, I lost my best friend. I just can't stop crying. I guess this is what real loneliness feels like. I don't think my life will ever be the same.

In some cases, they contained only vague or cryptic references to things she was not anxious to recall, like her first period:

OMG!-- Today I wish I'd been born a boy.

The diaries also contained detailed accounts of other of Katie's "firsts," like her first crush on her freshman gym teacher, her first kiss from Anthony Krupchuck, and her first time with Jarrod, the muscular hired hand, during the autumn of her sophomore year:

Today I'm definitely glad I'm a girl, or should I say woman?

The journals became Katie's sounding board after the terrible fight she had with her mother and father when they found out about Jarrod and sent him away. They also captured the slow, painstaking process of rebuilding her relationship with her parents:

It rained today. Dad was away at the agricultural convention and Mom and I sat in my bedroom talking most of the day. I really lit into her for sending Jarrod away. I thought she was going to yell a lot and tell me that I was too young to understand and all, but she didn't. She just sat there and took it. Then she got all teary eyed and said how Jarrod was so much older than I was and how she and dad were so scared, and that they didn't want me to get hurt. We both cried a lot. I'm still really mad, but not so much as I was. I guess if I were a parent, I might be scared and overreact too, with everything that could go wrong and all. Maybe I've been too hard on them.

Most importantly, her journals captured the deep love and affection Katie felt for her parents, friendships made and lost, and Katie's hopes, plans, and dreams. Katie ended each journal at a significant milestone, usually her birthday, which coincided with the end of summer vacation. Occasionally, she would end at the close of some crucial event that indicated a passage into the next phase of her life. She always ended with the same three words: *To Be Continued…*

Katie lovingly stowed the completed diaries away for safekeeping and began a new journal at the start of each school year. Her first few diaries were simply extra copies of the cardboard covered notebooks that she used in class. As the years went by, Katie came to treasure these quiet confidants and became more selective about their look and feel. She carefully examined the color and texture of the cover, the ruling and feel of the pages, the quality of the binding, and even features like bookmark ribbons, gilding, and key clasps.

The stationery department was in the corner of the store next to the large windows looking out on Main Street. Katie was so deeply engrossed in her research that she didn't even notice the sun disappear behind the thickening black clouds. She also missed the tapping on the plate glass windows. The tapping got louder as the wind increased. Katie looked up to see hail bouncing on the sidewalk and up against the glass. She stared blankly for a moment, mesmerized by the frozen white pellets dancing and twirling around. The rushing locomotive sound didn't register immediately either. When it did, Katie was terror-stricken. The rumbling grew louder as the wind picked up. The streets became littered with debris. Trash cans spilled their contents and rolled along the sidewalks. Papers, leaves, and dirt swept down Main Street like a cresting wave. The wind shifted and the hail, now golf-ball size, pounded angrily at the store windows. Then Katie heard the tornado warning sirens. Screams rose above the other sounds. People started running, banging into shelving and into each other. Stock fell from the shelves and rolled across the aisles. Katie searched frantically for her mother and father. She started yelling for them, but her voice was lost in the commotion.

Suddenly Steve Nylen's powerful hands gripped Katie's shoulders and jerked her backwards. The notebook flew out of her hands and rolled repeatedly in the air until it crashed against the bookracks.

"Come on, Katie," Steve yelled, "we've got to get out of here—fast!"

"I've got to find my Mom and Dad," Katie demanded, "I don't know where they are."

"There's no time for that now!" Steve pulled at her arm. "Don't worry about them. They know what do. They'll be fine." Katie yanked free and turned toward the center of the store, but before she could move, Steve wrapped his arms around her and held her tight.

"I'm sorry, Katie, but you have to get to the basement now or you'll get killed!" Katie struggled to break free but it was useless.

"Let me go Steve," she shouted, "I have to find them!"

Steve dragged Katie out into the main aisle. People from throughout the store rushed toward the stairwell. Others from outside poured in to seek shelter. The tidal wave of people, shouting, screaming, and shoving moved steadily toward the basement staircase. Katie was powerless to fight the current that carried her and Steve along as it spilled down the stairs and into the basement below. All the while Katie screamed for her parents.

The lights went out, and everything went black. Katie's eyes adjusted to the darkness. She could make out the top of the stairs and the ceiling of the store above. She saw Rachel Evens running toward the staircase with her husband, Cyrus, right behind her. The whole building moaned with the sounds of twisting metal and shattering glass. Cyrus looked to the front of the store and froze. Then his eyes bulged and his face distorted grotesquely. A look of horror overtook Cyrus as he realized what was going to happen next. Rachel turned around and screamed for her husband. Cyrus broke into a sprint, his arm reached out in front of him as his hand grasped at the air, but before he could take another step, a large jagged section of plate glass severed his outstretched arm. As Rachel looked in horror, her husband's blood sprayed out from his shortened limb and filled the air. The ceiling twisted, contorted, and finally gave way. A tremendous rush propelled Rachel down the stairs and onto the people below. Cyrus reached the top of the stairwell but could go no further. The ceiling collapsed on top of him, and he disappeared under the rubble. The only remnant of him was his blood streaming down the stairs.

It ended as quickly as it began. The open sky at the top of the stairs turned bright blue and calm, and sunlight poured into the basement below. Katie, Steve, and the others cautiously made their way up the stairs, over the crushed glass, bits and pieces of store merchandise, gypsum dust, and Cyrus Evens' blood.

The search for survivors started immediately. Local police and fire officials provided basic search and rescue training, assigned volunteers to teams, and supervised the operations. They made no effort to identify relationships between potential victims and rescuers. Several hours later, as Katie's team lifted a section of ceiling away, they exposed a woman's hand and forearm. On the woman's wrist, Katie recognized the bracelet she had given her mother for her thirtieth birthday. It was costume jewelry, not particularly fashionable, but Elizabeth had worn it every day since, no matter what the destination or occasion.

Someone yelled, "Her fingers are moving," and Katie stopped breathing for a moment when she saw the faint twitching. The team carefully lifted a large section of steel and mansard roofing lying atop Katie's parents. Elizabeth was lying face up underneath her husband. A massive I beam lay across Jim's back. It took eight rescuers to lift it. Once they did, they saw the impression it left from where it shattered his spine. A long metal lighting fixture lay across Elizabeth's head. When the team lifted it off, it exposed an ugly open gash on her forehead. Dried blood had dyed her hair red and pooled beneath her. More blood seeped from the side of her mouth and trickled down her colorless face. Katie knelt down and gently nudged her mother's shoulder. To her horror, her mother's skin was cold and rigid.

"Mom, Mom, it's Katie. Can you hear me? Oh God, Mom, please, please, can you hear me?" Tears ran down Katie's face, off her cheek's, and onto her mother. Elizabeth's eyes were open and Katie peered into them, trying desperately to connect to the most important woman in her life, but she was gone.

The hand movement Katie had seen was simply the muscles twitching in response to the removal of pressure. Once the pressure was relieved, the hand settled into its final, immovable position. Her mother's eyes, once so warm and alive, were vacant and fixed. Elizabeth lay wrapped in her husband's lifeless arms. In her own arms, she clutched a McCall's sewing pattern for designer jeans.

13

The weakest tornados have winds under 100 mph, diameters of 300 feet or less, travel less then a mile and last only a few minutes. The strongest can be more than half a mile wide, last for more than an hour, pack winds over 300 mph, and dig a crevasse over fifty miles long.

That evening, newscasters tried to explain what had happened. The category 4 tornado formed suddenly and without warning just outside of town. It moved quickly across the busy main street section before heading back out into the fields and dissipating. In its wake, it left a quarter-mile wide stretch of devastation and eleven people dead or missing. Ironically, the movie theater was untouched, and after the storm had passed, the matinee showing of "Twister" was still playing. While the reports contained detailed information about what had happened, they offered little explanation as to why there was so little warning.

Elizabeth's sister, Edna, and her husband, Jeff, took Katie in with them and their three children. Shortly after, Jeff left his construction job so that he and Edna could take over the day-to-day operations of the farm that Katie now owned. To maintain the business, they moved into the large farmhouse previously occupied by Katie's parents. Once again, Katie was in her own bed at her own home, but without her own family.

Edna and Jeff braced themselves for Katie's crash, for the falling grades and deteriorating personality, as the full realization of her loss settled in, but the crash never came. Katie had always been an excellent student; in her senior year, she became an outstanding one. First in her class, Katie excelled in math and science, became editor of the school newspaper, won several awards for journalistic excellence, and chaired the graduation yearbook committee.

Long active in student government, Katie easily won the election for class president. Her valedictorian speech received an enthusiastic standing ovation. All of the local papers reprinted it. Katie received acceptance letters and scholarship offers from all her first choice colleges. She chose the University of Chicago because of its strong program in her chosen field of study: meteorology. That came as a surprise to her aunt and uncle. They expected that she might major in business or animal husbandry or another field connected with owning the largest farm operation in the state, if not the country. However, they were comfortable managing the business. They also realized that something was missing in Katie, as if part of her was lost with her parents the day they died. They agreed to give her the opportunity to find it in her own way and time.

Even at the University of Chicago, Katie remained at the top of her class. That made Edna even more confused at Katie's decision to transfer.

"Katie," Edna said, making one final effort at persuading her niece to change her mind, "you said you like it at Chicago and you know that by graduating near the top of your class you could pick wherever you want to go next." Katie gave an understanding nod while packing. "And you've told me your courses and professors are excellent." Again, Katie nodded in agreement. "You're even considered a leader on campus, and that's no small feat. So I don't understand, dear, what could you possibly hope to gain by transferring to -- what's it called -- Nadowa College, out in upstate New York?"

"It's the Hudson Valley region," Katie finally spoke up, "and that's hardly hick country, Aunt Edna. General Electric has its management training center in that same area. That's pretty significant."

"Maybe so," Edna replied, "but from what I know, you're not planning on joining G. E., you're majoring in meteorology. What could Nadowa offer you that you can't get at Chicago?"

"Honestly," Katie stopped packing, turned around, and faced her aunt, "the ability to customize my curriculum so that I can concentrate my time in a very narrow field of study." Edna was hoping to avoid that discussion. They had been over that ground before. "I thought that you were going to discuss the matter with your professors. You said that they're very accommodating."

"And they have been, at least as much as they could be without completely ignoring the rules just for me. But I need more, and I know from my conversations with the people at Nadowa that I can get it there."

"You realize that even if you get your customized program, they might not have the funding to carry it out. Up until a few years ago, you couldn't find this Nadowa with a map."

"That's changed. Their research funding per student is more than Chicago's."

Edna looked up at the clock and rose slowly from her chair. "Well dear, I can see that there's nothing I can say that's going to change your mind." Edna hugged her. "We're going to miss having you around here. For the life of me, I don't see how we're going to find anyone nearly as reliable at supervising the early morning milking. I still don't understand how you could be up and out at five every morning without ever setting your alarm." Then Edna hesitated, her eyes glistened with wetness. She looked into Katie's pale blue-green eyes and brushed her hand through Katie's hair. "You look so much like your mother." Edna kissed Katie on the forehead. "I wish you the very best of everything, dear. You seem to know exactly where you want to go in life, though for the life of me I don't know where that is. I only hope and pray that this move helps you get there."

Katie was exhausted when she finished packing, not so much from her five a.m. chores, or even from the conversation with her aunt, but from staying up late reading the night before. Her uncle had already taken most of her things to the car. Katie picked up the subject of her late-night research and glanced at it before stuffing it into her carry-on: "Grant Award: Prediction of Sudden Onset Tornados: Development of an Early Warning Computer Based Tool Utilizing Geographically Diverse Physical Measurements, Advanced Instrumentation, and Macro-level Mathematical Modeling. Awarded by the National Oceanographic and Atmospheric Administration to Nadowa College, Professor Bertrand Myers—Grant Administrator. "

Uncle Jeff was honking the car horn outside. Katie looked at the clock and then picked up her pen to make her last entry into her journal.

Katie peered at the pen for a moment. In place of the traditional barrel, it had a sharp metal letter opener. It wasn't a feature that Katie needed or even preferred, but it was her father's pen. He and her mother were opening the mail with it the morning the tornado struck. Katie carried it wherever she went. She picked up her journal and made one last entry:

Off to Nadowa College and Professor Myers. Nothing left to do now but to do it. To be continued...."

14

Watch: When referring to severe weather (e.g. Hurricane, Flood, Tornado), indicates there is a chance this type of event will happen. A watch may extend over a large area for an extended period.

It took almost a month to restart the work at 34 Lakota Drive, but four and a half months later the renovations were complete. The walls and woodwork showed off their fresh new paint. New hardwood, carpeting or tiles covered every floor. The kitchen and bathrooms were fully functional, and fresh draperies adorned every window. The house looked and smelled brand new.

Ted Reggerio, the job foreman, made one last run-through prior to closing out the project. He had overseen hundreds of jobs in his career, including many on Nadowa's campus, but this was the oddest of them all.

No matter what use the building was meant to serve or how many people it was going to house, Ted couldn't understand why a house its size needed 400 amp electrical service. He also questioned the need for 100 runs of data cable, all terminating in that new room on the second floor. Sure, it had all sorts of electronics, but it was much too cramped to serve as a regular classroom.

Then there was the secret room inside it, the one he and his men couldn't even enter. With its bare studs and no wallboard on the outside, wires hanging from dusty old electrical boxes, the crib and that eerie wall clock on the inside, the room gave Ted the chills.

There were also the sensors hidden behind the walls and all the antennas in the attic. Maybe they were going to host foreign dignitaries and spy on them while they were here. Even if they were, no one would ever hear it from Ted. He had worked on his share of classified projects in the past. This was the first time he had to do it for a college, but it was clear from the onset that no one, not even his wife, was ever to know the kind of work he had done here, and no one ever would. These kinds of specialty projects were the most lucrative, and one slip up, one tiny leak traced back to him, and he could lose it all.

The front door opened; it was Bert Myers. A refreshing breeze followed him in, feeling more like fall than late summer.

"'Afternoon Professor," Ted greeted.

"Ted, the place looks great." Bert surveyed the final transformation.

"Yep, I'd be inclined to say so myself. She's all yours now." Ted handed Bert the keys. "All of the paint and spare parts are stored in the basement. I had the boys sweep it out and put up shelves to keep things neat and tidy. We came across these old cans of paint down there. The dumpster is gone but, I could put them in the back of my pickup and take them to the trash if you want."

"Sure thing," said Bert. "Thanks."

As Ted lifted the first two cans, something caught Bert's attention. "Hold on a second, Ted." Bert looked down at the cans on the floor. He noticed some wording scribbled on one of them: *Baby's Room*. Bert lifted the can and took a closer look.

Ted noticed the label, "Well, I'll be damned."

"What is it, Ted?" Bert asked.

"Oh, sorry Professor, but it looks like the last painter they hired for this place was one cheap bastard."

"What do you mean?"

"Well look at this," Ted pointed at a label on the can. "This stuff's from state surplus." Bert looked at the label. The color was crossed out with a magic marker—Baker-Miller Pink. "Guess you never heard of this stuff. Being from the trades, I guess the news stories just sort of caught my interest."

"News stories?" Bert asked. "For a paint?"

"In the '70s this color was famous. It cost a fortune then,

too. It was supposed to have some sort of psychological effect on people. The administrators down at the prison bought trailer loads. Can you imagine painting a whole prison cellblock pink? It was the craziest thing I ever heard of, and it made the national news."

"If the paint was so expensive, what makes you say the painter was cheap?"

"The surplus label. As near as I can remember," Ted scratched the back of his head as if trying to dig the memory out, "something went wrong and the prison stopped using it. For a time you could buy as much of this paint as you wanted for fifty cents a gallon."

"That's very interesting. Thanks for the history lesson."

"Don't mention it." Ted grabbed two more cans of paint and started for the door.

"Just a minute, Ted. On second thought, I'd rather you returned those cans to the basement. Please store them in a separate section so it will be easy to tell them apart from the new ones."

Ted hesitated for a moment, "Whatever you say, Professor." He was clearly not happy with the change in plans. He had already let the men go, and it was a much longer trek to the basement than to his pickup. He thought about asking the professor to give him a hand but before he could speak, Bert was bounding up the stairs to the second floor.

At the top of the stairs, Bert surveyed the new landscape. It had undergone a transformation. He looked straight ahead to his private apartment, small but adequate for his overnight stays. To his left was the door to the women's dormitory with separate rooms for each occupant. To his right was the same layout for the men.

Bert stepped onto the landing. Turning around, he admired the project's premier accomplishment—the new research room. It covered the entire front of the house and was spacious enough to accommodate Bert and the team. Most important, it completely enclosed the "pink room," as the team called

Amanda's room, allowing them unfettered access to the room's interior and exterior surfaces.

The area directly below the pink room was now a storage area with no ceiling. That allowed direct access to the open rafters above. The insulation above the room had been removed when the workers installed the antennas. Even the exterior walls were now removable facades.

Closed-circuit cameras monitored both the inside and outside of Amanda's room. Original plans called for making all the recordings from within the research room, but electronic signals wouldn't pass beyond Amanda's walls. The team constantly monitored and verified readings from all of the equipment. Bert hesitated a moment longer and smiled: We actually pulled it off. Then he walked around the stairwell and entered the research room.

"Hi, Bert," said Katie. Working together on the house renovations, Bert and Katie had become more colleagues than student and teacher. When it came to meteorology and physics, she was equal or better than most of the experts Bert had ever known. She was not only adept at tracking and forecasting weather, but she was also a whirlwind in her own right.

"Hi Katie."

"Sorry," Katie interrupted, "but I've really got to go." She was spinning around the room while she talked, straightening out paperwork, putting items on shelves, and stuffing things into her purse.

"I'm due for broadcast prep in fifteen minutes and Chris will have a stroke if I run late. I told Ted about the leak under the sink and his men fixed it this morning. They also nailed down the loose carpeting in the meeting room. There's a fresh pot of coffee brewing. The bookcases came, but the books are still on the floor. Chris and Drew installed the new equipment last night. Drew can fill you in on their progress." Katie glanced down at her watch. "Oh my God, Chris is going to kill me!" Before Bert could say another word, Hurricane Katie poured down the stairs, across the lawn and into her rusty Jeep

Wrangler.

Bert smiled, "And it was a pleasure talking with you too, Miss Jarvis."

"'Afternoon Professor," Drew looked up from his writing. With all the commotion, Bert hadn't even noticed Drew sitting at the long table in the center of the room. "I just finished the log entries for last night."

"Anything new?" Bert said, although he already knew the answer.

"No, just more of the same. We thought we might have had some variations in the temperature and light levels but it was just that we hadn't finished calibrating the new equipment. Once we did, the readings were the same as before."

After months of testing, the most telling aspect of the project was its sameness. Nothing about the room changed – ever! Moreover, they were no closer to explaining the cause of the phenomenon. Bert was concerned they were losing focus and was considering expanding the team to stimulate new thinking. Drew and Tess seemed disengaged, and Chris had competing interests. As Bert contemplated the dilemma, he had no way of knowing that all of that was about to change.

15

Warning: Means that a severe weather event is already occurring or is likely to occur soon. Warnings are issued for more precise geographic areas and shorter periods.

"Well, nice of you to grace us with your presence, your highness," Chris said as an announcement rather than a greeting. All around him, people were making last minute preparations for the 6 p.m. broadcast: doing microphone checks, adjusting light levels, updating storyboards, and tweaking computer projections.

"Sorry, Chris," Katie apologized as she removed her jacket. "It took longer than I thought to finish my work."

"Well, maybe you forgot, but this is your work too. Now get yourself into makeup." Chris's attempt at bravado couldn't mask his nervousness. With Katie, however, much of it was unwarranted. Off-site Katie tapped into multiple weather databases. She was always prepared and uploaded her reports to the station well in advance of arriving. On air, she delivered her reports flawlessly, having rehearsed them repeatedly in her head. And while she might run slightly behind occasionally, Katie never missed a camera call.

Much of Chris's anxiety grew from his fixation on his personal goals. Someday he was going to manage the news operations at one of the broadcasting giants like ABC, NBC, CBS, or maybe even CNN. Being at Nadowa was a huge step in that direction. Campus media had all of the amenities of a major production company. Thanks to large endowments from the tribal council, the college had an expert faculty and a reputation for solid programming from entertainment to documentaries. The star of their lineup, however, was the news.

Nadowa's programming spent little time on local news and most on state, national, and international events. The students involved participated in a grueling curriculum. In the last two years of the program, they were held to industry-wide standards. Those in front of the cameras were poised and professional and the highest performing of them became the news and weather anchors.

Money spent on programming produced a significant return on the investment. The campus studio gained a reputation for comprehensive, objective, and accurate reporting. The lobby display case, filled with awards and trophies, gave testimony to the quality of the operation, as did the sizable grant awards won for everything from equipment to travel. And Chris was just where he wanted to be, right at the center of it all.

News and weather were broadcast at 6 a.m. and 6 p.m. on a local cable TV network and simulcast over the internet and FM radio. The campus news and weather reports reached not only the student population, but also many local citizens and businesses. Thanks to Katie's skills and the outstanding facilities and faculty, Nadowa's weather forecasts were as accurate and comprehensive as the best of the commercial stations. So, twice a day students and parents, anglers and farmers, local business owners and senior citizens, tuned in for the latest news and weather reports from Nadowa College's station, WNMS.

Everything on the sound stage grew quiet. Only Chris's low, authoritative voice broke the silence. "And we're on in three, two, one." Chris pointed his finger at the announcer, Jerry Finn.

Jerry's deep, resonant voice filled the studio, "Right here, right now, news and weather at the sixes with news anchors, Kevin Casperin and Janet Johansen and meteorologist, Katie Jarvis. And now, here's Kevin Casperin."

"Good evening. At the top of the news tonight, word from Iraq that..." Kevin's voice faded in the distance as Katie sat at the weather desk, off camera. She was nowhere near the official designation of a meteorologist, but no one challenged the introduction and Chris was happy with the label.

Katie was busy comparing her planned presentation with the data streaming in from sources across the room and across the country. Up until the moment the cameras switched to her, she scanned and assessed her information sources, always ready to revise her report, always vigilant not to overlook any significant piece of information. Then she organized the most relevant data to present a clear, accurate picture of the current weather and the long-range forecast.

The college had its own Doppler radar system and a weather instrument cluster on the studio roof. There were similar clusters on other buildings throughout the campus and, thanks to cooperative agreements with local businesses, from similar installations mounted on buildings throughout the Hudson Valley. Katie scanned the live feeds from the better-known sources like the National Weather Service, and the U.S. Naval Observatory, but found nothing significant there. She also kept track of feeds from the more exotic reporting agencies like the National Hurricane Center and the National Severe Storms Laboratory. None of them showed any significant events on the horizon. She also had hot links to all the major media sources as well other government, university, and commercial weather information sites. There were no significant bulletins or alerts from any of them. Overall, it was a quiet weather day. Katie did not believe in exaggerating the weather in order to make it newsworthy. Then, the temperature data caught her attention. She went back to the data feeds and sat motionless for a while, her brow wrinkling as she eyed the documents.

Katie's actions caught Chris's attention. Occasionally, if her reading of the data led her to a different conclusion than the one provided by the computer models, she would add her own "Katie's Comments." These little diversions from the script were always a source of anxiety for Chris. Despite his concerns, Katie's minority reports often proved to be more accurate. But even when they didn't, listeners were delighted with her homespun anecdotes, editorial asides, and winning personality, all delivered with her signature, Midwestern drawl. Katie's reports proved to be a major contributor to the station's listenership. This, in turn, reflected well on Chris in the eyes of the administration and more importantly, future employers. Chris had simply learned to tolerate Katie's sixth sense.

Suddenly, Katie was a flurry of activity. She rushed from one database to another, shifting papers and looking as though a UFO had just landed in the center of the studio. Chris looked at the clock and scribbled a quick note. Then he eased his way to Katie's desk. Katie glanced at the note in Chris's hand, "Slow it down or you'll distract the news anchors. You're on in five."

Katie looked up and nodded. Chris glanced at the screen Katie was looking at and was surprised to see that while the month and day were correct, the display was for the weather patterns of a year earlier. He gave Katie a puzzled look as she reached over and pressed the print button. The laser printer in the soundproof booth off-stage came to life and started spitting out reports. Chris braced himself for a tempest, but it never materialized. To his delight, Katie delivered her pre-planned report verbatim.

"Now, back to Kevin and Janet with more of the news," Katie finished.

"Now, that's the way I like to see it done," said Chris as Katie breezed by him.

"Sure thing, Chris," Katie grabbed her jacket and the papers from the laser printer and rushed out of the studio door. As soon as she exited, she reached for her cell phone.

"Hello, Bert? Are you still at the house? Good. Could you please wait there a few minutes longer? I have something I need to show you. I'm sorry. I know it's getting late, but I'm certain that you are going to want to see this. I'm already on my way over. There's a lot more going on then we ever dreamed. Yes, that's right. We've just been looking in the wrong places. Bert, it goes way beyond the house itself, and I've got the data to prove it."

16

Given the number of variables involved, and contributing factors that are too small to observe, the current limit for an acceptably accurate weather prediction for a localized area is about two weeks.

Evelyn Simpson couldn't stop talking to herself. She looked up at the clock and fumed, *A quarter to ten, this is unbelievable.* She slammed the dirty dinner plates, one on top of the other, just short of shattering them. *You'd think he'd at least have the decency to call.* She added the dessert plates. *To top it all off, then he goes and shuts off his cell phone.* She wanted to say, "Damn phone," or better yet, "Goddamned phone," but she wasn't one to curse and was especially careful not to take the Lord's name in vain. She added the coffee plates to the pile. *I bet if I did this to him, he wouldn't talk to me for a week.* She reached for the coffee cups but thought better of it and piled the silverware on top instead. As she picked the stack up to head to the kitchen, she looked back at the four coffee cups and the clean, unused place setting at the head of the table. *Bastard!*

A few months earlier, she would have been frantic with worry, but that was before late nights became the norm rather than the exception. It was another two hours before Bert got home. By then she had erased all traces of the botched get-together, except for the cold roast beef sandwich and some vegetables sitting on the kitchen island. While she was putting away the silverware, she stopped to pick up Stephen's picture. She rubbed her fingers across the outline of his face and then across the surface of the brass booties attached to the frame.

Stephen was supposed to be their miracle baby. After two miscarriages, they had decided not to try again and busied themselves with traveling and their careers. Then they were expecting again. The pregnancy was difficult from the start and many times looked as though it would end like the others, but Stephen seemed determined to be born.

Evelyn came from generations of strong, prominent Catholics. Bert was a spectator in his Jewish faith, so he didn't object when she said she wanted Stephen baptized. For a time Bert even considered converting and took religious education courses at her church. He found the church's social agenda appealing, but when it came to issues of faith, he remained ambivalent. He wasn't a confirmed atheist like many of his colleagues, but he still questioned the existence of anything outside of the scientifically quantifiable realm. If God existed, Bert surmised, he did an unreasonably good job of disguising himself. Then there was the church's emphasis on Christ's being the one and only way to salvation. After learning that only a priest could forgive transgressions, Bert realized the impossibility of his conversion and quietly withdrew himself. He was, nevertheless, comfortable with their decision to bring Stephen up in the Catholic faith.

What irked Bert from the beginning, however, was Evelyn's insistence on keeping her maiden name when they married. He understood the arguments that they were both professionals and that it would be cumbersome for her to convert all of her documents. He also sympathized with her feelings of having to give up a part of who she was to satisfy some outdated cultural norm. However, he couldn't separate himself from what he saw as her rejecting his role as head of the family.

If that's how she wanted it, then so be it. Bert eliminated any mention of "wife" in his public life—on his Facebook page, in his professional releases, and in his college-related materials. Whenever someone asked him about Mrs. Myers, he simply replied, "There is no Mrs. Myers." Over time, Bert became increasingly anxious that Evelyn might insist that Stephen take her last name or a hyphenated combination or, worse yet, a random new one picked out of a book. He prepared himself to do battle so that the Myers' name continued in his progeny, but

Evelyn assured him that she wouldn't think about depriving Bert of something so important.

Evelyn endured the months of bed rest, the bland diet, and the endless back pain. She never complained. In the end, it would all be worth it. However, even in the delivery room, it was clear that something was wrong. The three short days Stephen lived were filled with tests and tubes, machines and medications. Evelyn paid the costs of pregnancy but received none of the benefits. There was no infant to nurse and no baby to balance on her broadened hips. Her once slim waist carried six pounds of stubborn baby fat, but there was no child to encircle it or look up and say, "Mommy, I love you."

Even more haunting were the emotional scars. The long, empty days, and the nights filled with images of Stephen trapped in a net of tubes and wires, so small, so helpless, struggling to live, but in the end…

There were also images of Stephen lying peacefully in his casket, and for a long time afterwards, frequent thoughts of joining him. She and Bert discussed adoption, but Evelyn wanted nothing of it. Besides, he was now a full professor and she was a bank vice president. They were living the good life—first class plane seats, five star hotels, garden party invitations and boards of directorships. They had made it to the "A" list. To the outside world, their lives were rich, full, and satisfying. But when it came to children, fate had worked against them.

Evelyn's womb ached each time the subject came up. There was a brief consideration of divorce, as if it would somehow lessen the pain, but they opted for counseling instead and worked through it. Part of the resolution was to escape the sadness of the memories and accept the support of loved ones, so when John Thompson offered Bert the position at Nadowa, close to Evelyn's parents, he accepted.

Evelyn lovingly replaced Stephen's picture atop the server and then reached up to wipe her tears.

The jingling of his house keys alerted her that Bert was home. As he reached to insert the key into the lock, the front door swung open. Hunched over with his armload of papers, Bert appeared more like a cartoon character than a person.

"Hi, Evie," he squeaked.

"Don't Evie me!" she said in a pinched voice. "Your sandwich is on the kitchen island. Arnie told me to tell you that you missed a great dinner and, believe me, you did. There, now I've said it." Bert laid his papers on the coffee table and tiptoed to the kitchen for his leftovers. Evelyn sat in the front room watching the recording of that morning's Oprah. Since the topic was not "Inconsiderate Husbands," there was a lot of fast forwarding. Bert walked into the living room and eased himself into the recliner.

"Are you going to stay mad at me for long?" Bert pleaded. Pouting was not something Evelyn was good at, a quality for which Bert was repeatedly grateful.

"No," she said. "Although I'd really like to try," Evelyn took in a deep breath, and then paused before continuing. "I had a really hard day, Bert. I ran late getting home from work and then had to rush to cook dinner. I was counting on your help. When you didn't show up, I just figured you were delayed at work again so I settled on having you home for when Arnie and Sandra arrived. It was embarrassing not being able to tell them where you were or why you were late. Then, when you didn't call and didn't even answer your cell phone, Bert, it was humiliating. So, yes, I was angry and I'd plan to stay that way if this wasn't so out of character for you. You never miss an engagement without letting me know. Couldn't you at least have called?"

Bert was tempted to prepare a defense, but Evelyn's sincerity was disarming. He knew she was right to be upset. He looked into her eyes, red and still glistening. "I can try to explain Evelyn, but there's no adequate excuse. I was wrong not to be here and doubly wrong not to have called. I'm really sorry." It was a sincere apology, not perfect but perhaps adequate.

"Then what did happen tonight, Bert?"

"I was just getting ready to leave when I got a call from Katie." Evelyn bristled, but Bert continued without noticing. "She asked if I would wait for her at the house so that she could show me some new data she had discovered at the studio."

Evelyn couldn't contain herself. "Katie, huh? Seems to me it used to be 'one of my students', or maybe 'Katherine so and so,' but all of a sudden it's just 'Katie.'" There was something new in Evelyn's voice, an uncharacteristic biting sarcasm. The insinuation caught Bert off guard. After everything he and Evelyn had been through, the notion that another woman might threaten Evelyn surprised him. He also took Evelyn's reaction as a compliment. Katie Jarvis was nearly half his age, and the prospect of her being interested in him seemed remote.

"Evelyn, are you jealous? I know I've been preoccupied with work lately, but do you actually think I'd cheat on you, and with one of my own students?"

"Oh, come on, Bert. I wasn't born yesterday. Of course with one of your own students—some fresh young thing with raging hormones who thinks that you're the greatest intellect since Einstein. Do you really expect me to believe that she doesn't stroke your ego? I just can't help wondering..."

Bert's eyes narrowed. The wrinkles on his cheeks deepened as if pulled by weights tugging at the corners of his mouth. "Evelyn, I love you. After everything we've been through, I wouldn't throw all that away on some one night whim."

"Honestly, Bert, I don't know what to think lately. You said yourself that you feel distracted by your work. Then there are all of these late nights and the secrecy about that room."

"The room?"

"Yes, Bert, the room, the one with the light that comes from nowhere, with perfect temperature in all kinds of weather without heating or air-conditioning, the one that gives you a shoe shine on the way in and doesn't charge you a dime. That room."

"You know about the room?" Bert was embarrassed that he was even asking. "How?"

"Dorothy Thompson, or do you think John doesn't share things with his wife either?" Evelyn didn't realize it, but her revelation broke the chain of silence that until that moment had held Bert captive. Bert understood for the first time that he had not told his wife about the room, not because he didn't want to, but because he couldn't. He had asked the students not to tell anyone about the room and agreed to do the same. Now, he realized that he was powerless to break that commitment, even to his wife. The prospect alarmed Bert almost as much as it fascinated him. His mind flashed back to his meeting with Dean Thompson on that icy March evening. Bert realized that if Thompson had not come to the house, he would have kept the room a secret until the auditors or the police arrived instead. Bert resolved to undo any commitments he and the students had already made and to monitor any future ones from this point forward. Then, Bert reflected back on his conversation with Katie—the one Evelyn was still waiting to hear about. It underscored for him how little any of them knew about what they were dealing with and, for the first time since the odyssey began, Bert added fear to his mix of feelings about the room.

17

Bands of equal atmospheric pressure (isobars) on a weather map are helpful in predicting the interaction of high and low pressure systems. They appear like elevation couture lines on a topographical map. The closer the lines, the steeper the gradient, and the higher the likelihood of severe weather.

As Bert reviewed the sequence of events at the house, Evelyn shifted from attentiveness to skepticism to borderline disbelief. More than once, she interrupted with, "You've got to be kidding," but Bert wasn't trying to be funny.

"I had just finished reviewing the latest readings and was preparing to leave when Katherine Jarvis, one of my students, called." Bert emphasized the name to make it clear that he heard and understood Evelyn's concerns.

"I explained to her I was expecting dinner guests," Evelyn bristled again when he said 'I,' not 'we.' She decided to leave that for a future conversation. Bert continued, "She said it was crucial that I see what she found so I told her I could spare twenty minutes. She agreed and was at the house in ten. I expected to finish and be home in plenty of time for dinner, but that was before I saw the data. Once I did, I lost all track of time. By the way, cell phones don't work in the room. We've run extension cords to power our instruments, but electronic signals can't enter or leave the room. It wasn't that I wasn't taking calls - the room wasn't." Evelyn's mouth curled in a frown.

Bert spread a map across the coffee table. "This is a map of the local area. The numbers across it represent the high temperature readings for today."

"Yes, Bert, I know, I've seen them a thousand times on the evening news."

"Yes, but there's something peculiar about this one."

Evelyn studied the map and shrugged her shoulders. "I just see a map with random numbers on it, and I'm in no mood for guessing games." Bert picked up the pace.

"That's what I saw, too." The pitch of Bert's voice rose along with the level of his excitement. "And Katie—uh, I mean Miss Jarvis—"

"Bert, just tell the story."

Bert explained that Katie wouldn't have noticed anything either if she hadn't just finished reviewing the data at the house before going to the studio. The big weather story was the anniversary of the heat wave that broke the record for the hottest recorded temperature on this date. While Katie was preparing her report, she remembered it was a year ago today that she and Drew had measured the temperature at the house, which was more than two degrees higher than what was reported anywhere else in the county.

Evelyn rocketed from interest to outrage, "Are you saying that the reason you stood up our friends, humiliated me, and ruined our evening was because some undergraduate noticed a couple degrees difference on some weather map! Do you know how ridiculous that sounds?"

"Not just some map, Evelyn, every map, every day, for the last five years, and that's only the beginning. Once Katie found the discrepancy, she added the readings from all of the campus monitoring stations to the maps."

Bert spread another map dated December 21, over the first one. A series of concentric circles were drawn in, all centered on 34 Lakota Drive. Evelyn gave a cursory glance at first and then looked more intensely. Not certain that she could believe what she was seeing, she moved repeatedly from one map to the other. The temperature at 34 Lakota Drive was about five degrees higher then the surrounding area and dropped off steadily in every direction as it moved further away from the house.

Bert explained, "Think of it like this. Suppose you threw a

rock into a pond. Waves would go out from where the rock entered the water. The biggest waves would be near the center, and they would get smaller as they moved away. The same kind of thing is happening at the house."

"And you say it's been like this for years? Then why hasn't somebody discovered it until now?"

"For several reasons. The first is that the effect is local. By the time you get a couple of miles away from the house, the differences are so slight you might not even notice them. Three miles out, the effect disappears completely. The second reason is that if you don't put the house at the center of the map, the readings look random, especially if you don't include all of the college's reading stations. The third reason is where things really get bizarre."

"More bizarre than this?"

"Yes, because the readings change over time. For whatever reason, the temperature at the house gets a little higher each day until you get to around December 21. This next map is a day later."

Bert spread out another map, and Evelyn studied it carefully. "Can this be right?"

"Absolutely. The map shows that instead of the house temperature being five degrees hotter than the surrounding area, the next day it was five degrees colder, and got progressively warmer as it moved away."

"And this has been going on for five years."

"At least. Katie ran maps back that far, and they all show the same pattern. Around June 21 of each year, there's no difference between the temperature at the Lakota Drive house and the surrounding area, but the temperature at the house rises a little bit each day until it peaks about December 21. Then we go from five degrees hotter to five degrees colder just like that," Bert snapped his fingers. "It continues to get a little hotter every day until about June 21, when we're back where we started. In the meantime, the temperature inside the baby's room never changes. Evelyn, it's as though that room is like some black hole, and it's sitting in the center of its own private universe."

It was past midnight when Bert and Evelyn finished talking. Evelyn went upstairs to prepare for bed while Bert paced in the living room. He was a stew of exhaustion and exhilaration. The void created by pouring out months of secrets filled immediately with puzzles and possibilities and, for the first time, Bert realized the size of the moat he had excavated between himself and Evelyn. She had borne it all with grace and patience, and he loved her for it.

As Bert entered the bedroom, Evelyn was coming out of the bathroom. The steam, still lingering from her shower, muted the light. It shone through her wispy nightgown, illuminating her torso and hugging each line, each curve of her body. It was almost as if he were seeing her nakedness for the first time. His eyes moved down her torso, from her auburn hair and olive eyes, to her long smooth neck, down the lines of her soft white shoulders and welcoming breasts, down the curves of her waist and hips to her long, slender legs and delicate feet. Then he followed the glow of the light up the inside of her legs until it disappeared between them. Evelyn was standing next to the bed. It was obvious that Bert was staring, which was not a common behavior for him, especially lately.

"Bert, are you all right?"

"I'm fine, Evie," he said as he approached her, "better than I have been in a long, long time." He spoke in soft, measured tones, kissing her neck between words. The skin of her bare shoulders tingled under the sensation of his warm breath. Bert's hand glided softly along the outline of her body, so gentle that she could feel the goose bumps where her skin tried to rise up to meet it. It had been a long time since he caressed her in that way and Evelyn shivered delightfully under his touch. Bert's downward caress ended at her lower thigh. Then his hand traveled across to the inside of her legs and moved slowly upward, taking the nightgown with it as it did. The cool evening air breezed softly up inside her nightgown. Evelyn grew light-headed as his hand reached the top of her legs, and his fingers probed gently. His other hand reached around her and cupped her bare bottom. Evelyn let out a low moan and started to go weak. Bert lifted the nightgown off her body and eased her down onto the bed. He lifted her arms above her head and explored her breasts with his mouth. Then he entered her. Like the secrets he had kept for so long, the pent up tension in Bert's body longed for release. His lovemaking was forceful and urgent, almost violent. Evelyn took it all in, longing, demanding more from every ounce of passion he could rally. In the end, they lie together, still, spent, and satisfied. Sleep came, long and deep.

Across campus, Katie tossed frantically in her sleep as she relived the day her parents died. She heard the soft, almost unnoticeable tapping. She saw the tiny ice crystals bouncing off the sidewalk. She felt the rumbling of the locomotive and experienced the terrifying realization that it wasn't a locomotive at all. She heard the sirens and the screams.

As Katie thrashed in her bed, Steve Nylen's powerful hands grabbed her and jerked her backward. She heard Steve's voice, "Come on Katie, you've got to get out—fast! There's no time Katie. Don't worry about them. They know what to do... They'll be fine...." Over and over, those words repeated in her head.

Once again, Katie was in the dark Sears basement looking up the staircase as Cyrus Evens tried desperately to make it to safety. There was that look of horror in Cyrus's eyes as he realized that he was about to die. Katie woke to the image of her mother's eyes, fixed, vacant, and dead.

Katie sat up straight in bed. Her nightgown was soaked through, sticking to her slim frame. She looked at the clock, 3:55 a.m., the same time it had displayed every morning since the one after the events of her dream; a dream she could never recall. Katie striped off the wet nightgown, removed the soaked sheets from the bed and calmly placed them in the hamper with the rest of her laundry. Then she took her shower. By 4:45, she was in her car on her way to the station for the 6 a.m. news and weather report. She was never late.

18

Before computer modeling, the primary means of weather forecasting was "Pattern Recognition." Forecasters searched for well-established historical patterns that closely matched the current conditions, assuming the patterns would repeat themselves. This method is still used to improve short range, machine-generated forecasts.

Bert woke to the aroma of fresh brewed coffee. By the time he finished getting dressed, the smell of bacon sizzling on the griddle was escaping from the kitchen. It was an infrequent aroma in their home. Evelyn was very health conscious and not prone to eating big breakfasts. Oatmeal or an English muffin was more typical.

"How would you like your eggs?" she asked as Bert pecked her on the cheek. "The morning paper is at your place."

"What's this?" Bert picked up an envelope with his name on it sitting beside the paper. "Dorothy Thompson asked me to give it to you. It's from John." Bert took a sip of orange juice and opened the envelope. Inside were copies of two newspaper clippings with a note from John Thompson, "Professor Myers. My assistant was re-organizing some archive files and asked me where to put these. I thought they might interest you." Bert glanced at the first article's headline, took a gulp of coffee, and started to read.

Reynolds Corp. to Close for Two Weeks Following Tragic Loss

The Reynolds Corporation, manufacturers and exporters of luxury cabinet hardware, took the unusual step of closing for an extended period during the Christmas holidays. The company's one hundred and thirty five employees will stay home until January 7 following the tragic death of three-month-old Amanda, the only child of Gareth and Cynthia Reynolds. Gareth Reynolds is the corporation's owner and founder. Union representatives questioned the move but recanted when they learned the company is paying employees for the furlough. This marks the first time in the company's 17-year history that the business has closed its doors for longer than the weeklong Christmas holiday break. Mr. Reynolds and his wife were unavailable for comment.

Someone had penned the date, December 23, 1990, across the top of the page. Bert frowned, sat back in his chair, and reread Thompson's note. Evelyn caught the expression on his face. "Something the matter?" she asked.

"I don't know. I'm just trying to figure out why Dean Thompson thought this article would interest me." He took another gulp of coffee and glanced at the second article.

Nadowa College to Receive Gift of House

Nadowa College got some welcomed news earlier today regarding its expansion plans when college officials learned of the generous donation of a large home and ninety-five acres of land. College officials have been in negotiations for several homes and land parcels on the western edge of the campus along Sunset Terrace. Officials had approached the Reynolds Corporation of Cincinnati, Ohio, owners of one of one the largest and most prestigious homes in the valley. College administrators already had commitments for several other homes in the area. They were hoping to negotiate a favorable purchase price for the house at 34 Sunset Terrace. The home, abandoned for over 17 years, is in need of extensive repair. "I have to admit that we were a bit shocked when they turned around and asked us if we would like to have it as a donation," said John Thompson, the college's president. "Of course, we immediately said yes."

The home was the previous residence of Gareth and Cynthia Reynolds. Mrs. Reynolds was prominent for hosting frequent social gatherings at the house that raised considerable sums of money for local charities. Gareth Reynolds owned the successful company which bore his name and which operated in the valley until 1992 when the company moved its operations to Cincinnati.

Two years earlier the couple lost their only daughter to a sudden illness. The house has remained vacant ever since. Over one hundred and thirty employees were idled when the company left. "Hopefully through our efforts at educating the future workforce of the area," Thompson said, "we can mitigate some of the negative history associated with the company's move."

Bert reread the first article's date, December 23, 1990. Then he looked again at the house's address.

"Evie, do you remember what Lakota Drive was called before it was renamed?"

"Sunrise or Sunset something," she said.

"Sunset Terrace?"

"Yes. That's it."

For a scientist accustomed to dealing with ambiguity, Bert was increasingly searching for solid ground.

The next day, Bert and the team sat huddled on the rug in Amanda's room surveying Katie's maps and Bert's newspaper articles.

Chris challenged, "So you're telling us that some kid's ghost is causing all this?"

"Absolutely not," Bert answered. "What I said was that her death seems to correlate to the temperature shift that occurs each year and even that correlation may be weak or nonexistent. At this point, all we have is an intriguing coincidence. We have to be careful not to jump to conclusions. We might even find evidence of the opposite: that the temperature shift contributed in some way to Amanda's death. Like any good reporter we need to verify our sources and get sufficient corroboration before we're ready to go to print."

Chris grinned at Bert's feeble attempt at journalese.

"This whole thing is kind of creepy," said Tess. "I mean we started off with a room that did a bunch of odd stuff, but it was still just a room. Now we're talking about dead babies and messing with the weather for miles around. I think the whole thing is way too weird."

"So where do we go from here, Professor?" Drew asked. Bert was pleased to see Drew take the lead on getting back to work. The new information seemed to rekindle his interest in the project, which Bert wanted to encourage.

Bert explained that Katie had only tracked data for temperature, and they needed to know if the phenomenon extended to other variables like barometric pressure and relative humidity. He asked Tess and Katie to gather weather data from the twentieth to the twenty-second of each month for the past twenty years and then plot the data on maps for each of those days. Tess's eyes opened nearly as wide as her mouth.

"It's really not all that much work," Katie reassured Tess. "Most of the information is already in our computer system, and it shouldn't be too difficult to download the rest from other sources. Since Amada died eighteen years ago, by going back twenty years we'll be able to determine if the correlation predates her death or was somehow associated with it."

"Dead on, Katie!" Bert jumped in so excitedly that he didn't even realize the pun until he caught the expressions on his team's faces. "Oh. Sorry about that."

The whole entourage broke out laughing, which helped to relieve Tess's anxiety.

Bert asked Katie to superimpose her circle grid on each map.

"What about us?" Drew asked.

Chris elbowed Drew's ribs, "What do you mean *us*?

Bert ignored Chris's gesture and answered Drew, "I need your computer expertise." Bert asked Drew to link the campus's weather monitoring system into the research room and to provide online access to the same kinds of historical data Tess and Katie were generating, but for the future. Drew's program would track the changes at least by the minute, preferable by the second, so they could pinpoint exactly when the December shift occurred.

"I've ordered a Doppler radar installation for the house," said Bert. "It'll be installed in the next couple of weeks. You'll need to tie that and some other new equipment into the system. Finally, I'd like you to install this and set up the workstations to access it from within the research room and Amanda's room." Bert handed Drew a set of computer disks.

Drew looked down at the label: *NOAA Data Input and Analysis Module for Prediction of Sudden Onset High Impact Events.* "Sounds pretty heavy, Professor."

"Yeah," Chris laughed, "what are we hunting for, earthquakes?"

Bert shot Chris a disapproving look. "No, sudden weather changes and violent storms: thunderstorms, hurricanes, tornadoes, things like that."

"Whoa. Whatever," Chris ended, then clapped his hands together. "All right everybody, looks like it's time to get to work."

"Not so fast, Chris," said Bert. "You're not off the hook yet. I need you to track down a story."

Chris's face lit up. Now this might be an assignment worthy of his talents. Bert asked him to find out everything he could about the house and its occupants, particularly about the circumstances surrounding Amanda's death.

"Now," Bert ended, "maybe we can finally start to make some sense of all this."

19

Doppler radar beams a microwave signal toward a desired target and monitors its reflection. It analyzes how the target's motion alters the frequency of the returned signal. This produces highly accurate measurements of the target's velocity.

Five weeks later Drew called Bert, Katie, and Tess into the research room for a demonstration. They stood in front of the large data monitor, speakers, and strobe lights mounted on the end wall of the room.

Drew held a wireless keyboard in his hands, "You asked for it, Professor, you got it."

Drew hit a key and the large screen came to life. It showed a satellite view of the area with the house at the center and an overlay of the current weather patterns. Katie's concentric circles linked the numbers scattered on the screen. "You can cycle through the parameters by hitting the function key." Drew pressed the key several times and, with each stroke, a new set of data populated the map. "I also set the triggers so that they'll sound the alarms."

"Alarms?" asked Katie.

"The system monitors all of the available weather data," explained Bert, "and searches for any trends that would signal the onset of severe weather. If any of the key indicators reach a preset threshold or change too quickly, the system alarms."

"It's a pretty sweet setup," said Drew. He explained the five levels of alarm in each of several categories including thunderstorm, tornado, and hurricane. "The screen changes color to correspond to each level: green is calm, blue is alert, yellow is for watch, orange means warning, and red signals an immanent threat. An audible alarm goes off at the 'watch' level and gets louder and faster as the threat escalates." Drew explained that there was an identical setup in the pink room.

"I've programmed in a simulation. Take a look." Drew pressed a key and the screen cleared and then zoomed out until the entire Earth was in view. A disturbance in the south Atlantic formed midway between Africa and the United States, then quickly escalated into a tropical depression, and then into a hurricane. As it moved toward Florida, continuous readouts showed its size, speed, location, and strength. When the storm headed north toward the middle-Atlantic states, the screen background changed from green to blue and the word 'hurricane' appeared in the hazard category box at the bottom of the screen. The threat level moved to yellow as the storm drew nearer. When the hurricane veered westward and approached New York, the monitor's background turned orange and began emitting a series of beeps. As the storm grew closer, the alarm grew louder and more intense. When it finally entered the Hudson Valley area, the threat level changed to red, the speakers emitted a piercing siren, and the strobe lights started flashing. The onlookers put their hands over their ears to protect themselves from the deafening noise. Drew hit a key and the chaos ended. "Pretty impressive, don't you think?" Everyone nodded in agreement. Drew handed Bert a stack of papers, "And these are the reports you asked for. The printed reports kick off automatically at 11:00 p.m. on December 20, and run through 1:00 a.m. on December 23 each year. All of the data is also accessible online and," Drew said as he was completing his demonstration, "this is something extra." Drew pressed a key and the monitor showed a tranquil Earth floating in the blackness of space. At the bottom of the screen sat a window with a flashing cursor followed by the words, "cell phone number."

"What's this?" Bert asked.

"Just a little icing on the cake," said Drew. "I used Google Earth, a GPS system, and a cell phone tracking program, and then I superimposed your weather mapping system on top of it.

Watch this. Katie, is your cell phone on?"

"Yes."

"Good." Drew typed Katie's cell phone number into the box and hit enter. The Earth rotated to North America, and then zoomed in on New England, New York, the Nadowa campus, Lakota Drive, and finally onto the house they were standing in. Superimposed on the image was the weather information.

"Nice," Katie said.

"Would it show us where Chris is now?" Tess asked.

"It should if he's got his phone on and if he's in an area with coverage," said Drew. "Let's find out."

Drew typed in Chris's cell phone number. The program spanned out to a view of the northeast, then zoomed back into Pennsylvania and onto an interstate highway.

"There he is," Drew said. "He must be in his car. He's traveling west on I-84 going in 68 degree weather, in a light drizzle with southwest winds at 15 miles per hour."

"That makes sense," said Bert. "He was headed to Ohio for some research."

"Wow," said Tess, "kind of Big Brotherish, isn't it? Is this like some kind of spy camera in a satellite?"

"No, nothing that elaborate," Drew answered. "Now, if we're out in the field you can match our location with the associated weather and pinpoint what's happening down to within a few feet. Anyway, it was fun making it."

"Very impressive, Drew," said Bert.

"And what about you two?" Drew addressed Katie and Tess. "I've shown you mine. Now how about showing us yours?"

"Tess and I would like a couple more days to plot the last of the data," said Katie. "We can settle on a meeting date as soon as Chris gets back."

Katie and Tess worked together for the next two days producing the weather maps Bert requested. As they did, Tess confided to Katie how much she loved Chris and how she longed to be a wife and mother, but she was afraid to tell Chris for fear of scaring him off. Katie listened attentively, but wasn't able to provide much advice. She often found the direction of Chris's emotional compass varied wildly, and lately she had the uneasy feeling that it was sometimes pointing toward her. The best she could offer was for Tess to be patient and look for signs of reciprocal affection.

She also didn't share with Tess the unsolicited text messages she received at least weekly from Chris. His "progress reports" were long on bravado, short on specifics and always started the same way:

HI K T CAT
R U NAKED?

The messages triggered Katie's memory of her first meeting with Chris on the day she arrived at Nadowa. In a move to be progressive, Nadowa had set up mixed dorms for men and women with separate bath facilities on each floor. Katie was sweaty and tired from her trip so she had headed to the shower right after settling in. She was standing under the spray lathering her hair when Chris arrived draped in a towel. He stopped and stared for a moment. Then he said, "Are you naked?"

Katie was surprised and annoyed but unruffled, at least as much as she could be under the circumstances. "No superman," she said, "it must be your X-ray vision. I always shower with my clothes on. And what are you doing in the women's shower room?"

"The name's Chris and I was about to take a shower. By the way this is the men's shower room, or maybe you missed the urinals on the way in."

Katie looked into the toilet area and was mortified at seeing the urinals. Chris caught the look on her face, despite being otherwise distracted. "Oh, you must be a newbie. It's a standard joke they play on new arrivals. They switch the signs on the bathroom doors."

Katie remained calm. "Well, if you don't mind, I'd like to

finish showering."

"No problem," Chris reached down to remove his towel.

"Alone, thank you!" Katie ordered.

"Sure thing. I'll even stand guard." Katie didn't let him see her smile as she watched him go. There was something endearing about the brash little narcissist. Once outside, Chris returned the signs to their proper doors. He was still standing there when Katie exited. She smiled and thanked him. She didn't learn until days later that it was Chris who had originally switched the signs.

The other thing Katie didn't share with Tess were her thoughts about Bert, how her affection for him had deepened over time, how it went beyond the student-teacher relationship and even the collegial one, into something more. She realized he was significantly older than she was and wondered why someone of his age and stature wasn't married. Did he have a bad relationship early on? Was he divorced? Was he gay? Did he live at home with his mother? She had gently probed the issue when they were alone, but his answers always seemed evasive. She finally got the answer she was seeking one afternoon when Bert arrived at the house wearing one black sock and one brown one.

"You're not quite up to your GQ standard this afternoon Bert," she said. "I guess Mrs. Myers forgot to check your wardrobe before you left."

"There is no Mrs. Myers," Bert answered. Katie turned away and smiled.

Katie wanted to confide in Tess and get her feedback, but it felt awkward and the timing never seemed right. Perhaps she would broach the subject soon, maybe today.

The two women were putting the final changes on their printed reports when the call for Tess came in. She and Katie were in the research room so Tess's cell phone was working. As Katie looked on, Tess's expression went from serious to somber. She didn't speak much. She nodded her head to, "Yes…uh uh…OK," and ended with, "I'll see what I can do… Yes... Thank you," and hung up.

"Is everything all right?" Katie asked.

"Not really," said Tess. "That was my aunt. My mother is in the hospital and it's not good; they don't expect her to last more than a couple of days. We haven't spoken more than a few words to each other in over a year. I'm still angry with her but I don't want her to die with that being the last feeling I have for her. I don't think I could handle that."

"Do you know what you want to do?" Katie asked.

"I'm not sure, but whatever it is I think I have to be there. I have to go home."

The next day Tess flew to Indiana. Drew and Katie gave her a ride to the airport. Chris was in Ohio and couldn't get back in time to see her off. He said he would keep in touch.

For the next couple of days things were very quiet at the research site. They got even quieter when Drew told Bert and Katie that he would be taking a few days off to study for his upcoming computer certification exam. Katie worked alone for long stretches. She continued working on her reports in her quiet solitude and she thought. She thought about what Chris might be uncovering about Amanda's room. She thought about what might lie ahead for Tess and Chris as a couple. She started to think about what might lie ahead for her and Bert and just as quickly dismissed it. Mostly she thought back to Tess's account of her childhood and wondered what ghosts Tess might be unearthing in Indiana.

20

A Drought is the result of a prolonged period of less than normal precipitation. If it lasts long enough, it can have catastrophic effects.

As Audrey Campbell lie in her hospital bed struggling to breathe, she tried feebly to fight off the demons that nipped at her soul trying to grab on, waiting for that last gasp, waiting to drag her down into hell with them. She could no longer lie to herself. She could no longer deny what had gone on between Ralph and her daughter or pretend that Tess was somehow partially to blame. As each breath became progressively shallower, Audrey could feel the flames closing in on her. Soon they would consume her.

"Mom," like some divine wind, her daughter's voice swept over the flames and beat them down. Audrey opened her eyes and saw Tess standing at the foot of the bed. She mustered enough strength to raise a hand and beckon her daughter closer. Tess approached and clasped Audrey's hands. Tess could feel her mother's bones protruding through her paper-thin skin. For Audrey there was no time for small talk.

"Tess," her voice was barely audible, "I'm sorry. I knew and I didn't try to stop it."

"Shhh, Mom. Save your strength. We can talk about this later."

"There is no later, Tess. You have to know it wasn't your fault. I was weak. I needed him and I was terrified about losing him. I looked the other way. I blamed you for something that I did. Can you understand that? For your own sake, you need to put it behind you and forget it. Can you ever forgive me?"

Tess had hoped to be gentle but her mother's questions made her furious. "I'll never forget it, Mother. I couldn't no matter how hard I tried and I don't intend to try. I want to remember because I'm never going to let anyone have that kind of control over me again. And no, I don't understand how you could know all those years and do nothing. I don't know what could make a mother abandon her own child like that."

Tess could feel the tremor of Audrey's hand and see the quiver in her mother's lips. Audrey looked helpless and abandoned and in spite of all that had happened, Tess still loved her. "But I didn't live your life, Mother. I have to believe that you at least wanted to stop him but couldn't. I have to believe that you loved me at least that much. So yes, Mom, I forgive you."

The weak grip Audrey had on Tess's hand loosened even further. Audrey's head sank back into her pillow as she repeated something inaudible. Tess stooped over and placed her ear next to her mother's mouth. She could barely make out the words.

"Thank you, Tess… Thank you, Tess… Thank you…" Audrey Campbell slipped away from life. From the peaceful expression on her face, it looked as though perhaps in her last moments on Earth, in her last breath, her God had finally found her after all.

The heart monitor flat lined and an alarm sounded. Two nurses rushed in. One of them asked Tess to step out of the room. Tess looked back at the flurry of activity knowing that it was for nothing. Her mother was gone. She waited on a bench opposite the nurse's station. A doctor passed by and entered the room. A few minutes later, a nurse emerged from the room and approached Tess. "Were you related to Mrs. Campbell?"

"Yes," Tess said, "I'm her daughter." Tess noted the name badge, Margret Simpson – Shift Supervisor.

"I'm sorry for your loss, Miss Campbell. Your mother seemed like a nice lady."

"Thank you. What will happen to her now?"

"We'll bring her body downstairs to await pick-up. Will you be handling the funeral arrangements?" Tess hesitated. She hadn't thought that far ahead.

"Well, if it ain't the prodigal daughter returned." Tess's shuddered at the chillingly familiar voice behind her and turned around to face him.

"What the hell do you want, Ralph?"

"Now, is that any way to greet your father, Tessie?" said Ralph.

"The name is Tess, you're not my father, and if I greeted you the way you deserved, the police would be here already."

Supervisor Simpson retreated to her nurse's station.

"That's my Tess," said Ralph. "Still as feisty as ever. I always liked that about you."

"I'm not your Tess and there's nothing I like about you, not now, not ever; so why are you still standing here."

"I came to look in on your mother, but it looks a little late for that now. The real question is, 'What are you doing here.' We ain't seen neither hide nor hair of you since you went off to that fancy school of yours." Ralph's folksiness hung on him like an oversized suit.

"Aunt Sarah called. She told me how sick Mom was."

"That she's been," said Ralph. "Poor thing's been in awful pain these past couple months. With all she's been through, she hasn't been able to be much of a proper companion, if you get my drift. Now that she's gone on to her reward, God rest her soul, maybe you and I should sorta pick up where we left off. I think your mom would be happier knowing that her kin stayed close."

Tess was sick to her stomach. She wanted to vomit, but her anger kept the bile in check. "You sick bastard. My mother isn't even cold yet and all you can think about is trying to get your disgusting paws on me."

"Now listen here, you disrespectful little bitch," Ralph raised his level to match Tess's, "you best keep in mind which side your bread is buttered on. Your mama was the one who thought you needed to go off to some fancy college. Personally, I always considered it a waste of good money so you'd do well to keep in mind where all those monthly checks come from. Without me, darling, you ain't got a pot to piss in. So if I were you, I'd worry a lot more about how you're gonna compensate me for my generosity."

"I'll compensate you, you ignorant ass." Tess swung to slap Ralph's face but he caught her hand midair as Nurse Simpson stepped up to the two combatants.

"I'm sorry, but you are in a hospital and this kind of behavior is unacceptable. I'm going to have to ask you both to vacate the floor immediately or I'll have to call security."

Tess yanked her hand free of Ralph's grasp. "I was just leaving." She turned in a huff and started walking off. Then she stopped, swung around, faced Ralph one more time, and yelled, "You and your filthy money can go straight to hell, you little prick. And if you so much as come near me again, so help me God, I'll kill you."

When Chris called that night, he expected Tess to be upset about her mother's death but he was unprepared for the onslaught of emotions.

"I don't know what to do Chris," Tess's voice quivered in between her sobbing. "I can't handle this. How am I going to finish school? How am I going to live? There's nothing left Chris, nothing."

"Tess, it may not be nearly as bad as you think. Your mother must have had some assets, a savings or checking account, a life insurance policy, maybe even a trust fund. And then there's the house. You're an only child Tess. That means that all of your mom's assets pass directly on to you. Sure they'll be some probate…"

"No, they don't," Tess interrupted. "He gets it all."

Chris was confused, "Who?"

"Ralph Campbell, my stepfather."

Chris was flabbergasted. His thoughts raced back to that first night in the room and Tess's revelations about her stepdad. "But you said he wasn't alive."

"No, I said he was a dead man, and to me he was. I can't

stand the thought of his existing—taking up air, forcing his way back into my life."

Tess described Ralph's plan for compensation in exchange for his continued support and explained that if she didn't go along, she couldn't afford to continue school. As fond as Chris was of Tess, he had no illusions about her academic prowess. A scholarship was not a realistic option.

"I'd have to drop out and support myself like my mother did. She spent most of her life waiting around for some pond scum like Ralph to rescue her. I can't end up like that; I'd rather die first. I hate him Chris. I hate his guts. I wish he were…"

The phone went quiet. Chris waited for a moment but heard nothing.

"Tess. Are you still there?"

"Yes, Chris." Chris was stunned by the sudden change. Tess sounded calm and composed, almost cheerful.

"Are you alright?" he asked.

"I'm really tired. It's going to be a hectic next couple of days with the funeral and all. I'll give you a call when it's all over. Good night Chris."

There was a click and a dial tone.

Chris sat quietly and thought about the conversation. He thought about Tess, how upset she was, and about how much he cared for her. He thought about how he loved her, more than he had let her know, more then he realized himself. Then he thought about how far he would be willing to go to help her.

21

The King of Thunderstorms, a Supercell, can measure ten miles or more across, extend up into the lower stratosphere, and cause enormous damage.

Ralph Campbell picked up the keys he had fumbled and frantically rummaged through them again trying to find the right one for the front door to his house. Once inside he flung the wet raincoat over the living room couch and headed upstairs. In the bedroom, he quickly undressed and headed for the shower. The hot water chased away the chill that had stayed with him since the cemetery. As the warm water washed over him, so did the memory.

Ralph had tried to get close to Tess all morning, but there were always so many people around. At the funeral parlor there was the constant procession of Baptists who wanted to offer their condolences. Then at the church his sister-in-law and her whole family perched themselves next to him in his pew. Afterwards they piled into the limousine with him as Tess drove her own rental car to the cemetery. Then, praise God, the rain came. It started suddenly and without warning so there was no tent set up by Audrey's gravesite. Everyone huddled together under umbrellas for protection. Tess stood up front next to the casket. It was only natural for the husband and daughter to stand close together for support so Ralph stood behind Tess with his raincoat draped over his shoulders and snuck under the back half of her umbrella. He placed one of his huge hands on her shoulder for comfort. As the minister took the tiny congregation through the valley of death, Ralph rested his other hand on Tess's hip. He was worried that she might react negatively as she had at the hospital but that didn't happen. Tess turned her head, placed her lips close to his ear, and whispered, "Later, at your house. After the dinner."

Ralph rushed through his chicken, potatoes, and peas. He would have skipped the dessert if it hadn't looked so tasty. Tess was not at the dinner, but that didn't matter. He just wanted to get it over with to keep his rendezvous with her at the house. However, the Baptists just hung in as if they had nowhere else to go. When they had finally finished eating, every one of them felt obliged to express their condolences all over again.

After his shower, Ralph put on his fake Rolex day/date watch and checked the time: 3:41. Then he opened a package of new underwear, put on a fresh pair of socks and picked out just the right pants and shirt. As he rummaged through the bedroom closet for the perfect outfit, something struck him as odd but he couldn't quite put his finger on it so he turned his attention to making up the bed. He was splashing on his eight-year-old aftershave when the doorbell rang. Ralph glanced out the bathroom window. It was gray, dark, and raining hard. The doorbell rang again.

"I'm coming, I'm coming," he shouted as he came down the stairs, as giddy as Scrooge on Christmas morning. A lightening flash stopped him cold. The thunder shook the house. Thunder and lightning terrified Ralph, and this storm was worse than most. Another flash, another clap, and the house went dark. Ralph was temporarily blinded. He fell back against the stair treads. He wanted to turn and run upstairs for cover, but his lust overcame his fear. Ralph felt his way down the remainder of the stairs. Knocking replaced the silenced doorbell.

"Hold your horses!" he shouted, "I'm almost there."

The only light in the foyer peeked in through the half-moon window at the top of the front door. Ralph was still speaking as he opened it, "Tess, you're gonna be so glad you…"

A blinding flash, a deafening thunderclap, and with it, the thick blade sliced through Ralph's ribs and deep into his gut. The force of the strike chipped pieces of bone on the way in and knocked Ralph down onto the hallway rug. His arm flailed out onto the hardwood floor. His wrist slammed against the floor shattering his watch crystal and freezing the display at Aug 16 - 3:59.

Everything went blurry. Then he felt the blood gushing up into his throat and tasted its saltiness in his mouth. The light from the street lamp dimmed and then faded away completely as the front door closed slowly and quietly. Ralph looked down toward his stomach. He could just make out the glove wrapping itself around the thick hilt of the knife. As everything faded to black, Ralph watched in horror at the slow twisting of the blade.

22

Supercells are responsible for almost all of the hail bigger than golf ball size and nearly all of the most violent tornados. They also produce extreme winds and are frequently the cause of flash flooding.

Sitting alone on the rug in Amanda's room, Katie finished her latest journal entry.

August 16, 2012

This room can really be addictive. No matter how stressed, lonely, or confused I am, being here sweeps away the clutter and helps me to think clearly.

What's your secret Amanda? I wonder: are we supposed to be guarding this place for safekeeping or sharing it with others? Do you even know the extent of the gift you've given us?

Our team members were always supportive, but now we have become even closer and despite our differences, care deeply for one another. I don't think there's anything we wouldn't do for each other. You seem to have affected our personalities too. I don't think any of us had a problem making friends but now we seem to attract them like magnets. Even Drew who used to be shy around new people has become downright gregarious. Chris is quickly becoming famous. The campus radio and television programming has been so effective that last week one of the national networks contacted Chris and asked him to come in and interview with them. Can you imagine? They contacted him!

Then there's Tess. The more I get to know her, the more I value what a wonderful and special person she is. While her mom's illness is distressing it looks as though it might just give her the opportunity she needs to finally reconcile and put some of those past hurts to rest.

Katie stopped for a moment and shuffled closer to the

window for better light.

There are also things that affect us as a whole. We won reelection to the student government with almost no work at all. Speaking of work, suddenly, studying and class work have become so easy it's almost effortless. The school may have to develop a new standard for awarding multiple valedictorians. To be honest, it's a little scary.

As far as my personal life goes, this has been one of the most fulfilling periods I have ever known. I still miss Mom and Dad; I know I always will, but I'm optimistic now that a big part of that void is slowly being filled. I've always respected and admired Bert for his intelligence and accomplishments but as I've worked more closely with him these past months my admiration has changed into something more: something deeper.

Katie's handwriting, normally fluid and elegant, was becoming more erratic as she began rushing her entries. The damp chill was beginning to make her shiver.

I haven't worked up the courage to tell anyone else, or for that matter to fully admit it to myself but, well, I guess it's true: I think I'm falling in love with Bert Myers. From the way he looks at me, and acts when we're together, I'm fairly certain that he loves me too!

The enormous thunderclap shook the window in its frame and the lightning flash blinded Katie. When the rumbling subsided, she could barely distinguish the system alarm from the ringing in her ears. She looked up at the monitor. Between strobe-light bursts, she made out the unmistakable pattern of a funnel forming around the house. Suddenly, she was back in Kansas, in the hot, dark, crowded Sears basement looking up to the top of the stairs and into the eyes of Cyrus Evens. She blinked, and she was looking into her mother's eyes. Katie trembled uncontrollably. Thoughts swirled in her head like the vortex outside.

The vortex! Katie was sitting directly beneath the open

window. She grabbed for her diary and dove under Amanda's crib for cover.

+++

Bert had left his house at 3:15. He tossed his things into the car and aimed it toward 34 Lakota Drive. He rested his arm in the window opening. Breathing in the afternoon air and feeling the warmth of the sun on his arm, he questioned his decision not to modify the GTO into a convertible.

Less than a half mile from the house Bert tired of the political pundits on talk radio and reached down to press the button for the oldies station. Bobby McFerrin's one-hit wonder, "Don't Worry, Be Happy," filled the passenger compartment. When he looked up again he was in a torrent. Even before he could roll up the window, his arm was drenched. The suddenness and ferocity of the storm surprised him. He stopped the car and looked back. Behind him, he could still make out the sunlit sky beyond the rain. In front, there was only bleakness.

Bert put the car in reverse. The view out the back window brightened with each inch traveled. He stopped again when the sound from the roof jogged something in his memory. He edged the car back and forth several times until he unlocked the recollection—the Mobil station's brushless carwash. Its huge tunnel would pass back and forth over his car, rinsing, washing, and waxing. The jets at the wash were only inches away from the car's body and directed in a straight line. Like the carwash, Bert could easily make out the dividing line between dry and rain on the car's roof. Looking around, the view through the driver, passenger, and front windows was still dismal and obscured by the deluge, even with the wipers on high. At the same time, bright sunlight poured in from the back windows and curled around the sides until it met at the dividing line.

Bert backed up until all of the GTO was basking in sunlight and then exited the vehicle to survey the surroundings. Up and behind the car he saw only wispy white clouds hanging in the still blue sky. That was to be expected. Looking forward he was still gazing on the same tranquil scene. In light of what he had just experienced, that didn't seem possible.

Bert walked to the front of the car and continued to where he thought the rain curtain should be. He jumped back when he felt the cold wetness on his face. When he reached up to wipe it, his face was dry. Then he turned and looked at his car—completely dry! Bert extended his hand into the invisible barrier. The sensation was that of the window in Amanda's room. While his body soaked up the warm afternoon sunshine, his hand was drenched in a chilling rain. Yet, when he withdrew it, it was completely dry again. He took a deep breath and stepped through the barrier.

On the other side, Bert found himself in a deluge. As he looked up, he shielded his eyes from the pea-sized raindrops that pelted him. The rain curtain bent outward as it rose. He stepped further into the storm and saw that at some point the barrier slanted back in again. Charcoal storm clouds swirled clockwise and rammed against the invisible bulkhead. Rain spiraled down in rivulets but the demarcation line remained razor sharp.

Bert tried to determine the size and shape of the storm. It was easier to see than believe. The leading edge formed a gradual but perfectly formed sphere. He was inside some giant invisible snow globe. As if shaken by an unseen hand, the storm raged inside it, churning clouds, bulleting rain, blinding lightning strikes, and explosive thunder. He was soaked through and could no longer control his shivering. He stepped back out through the curtain.

Immediately, he was warm and dry again. At the same time, he noticed the quiet. There was no sound at all associated with the storm raging only inches in front of him.

Questions crowded his head. He wondered when it began and what precipitated it. He needed to know how far it extended and in what directions. The equipment at the house could answer the questions. Bert jumped back into the car. As

McFerrin's voice on the radio lyrically advised not to worry and be happy, Bert drove back into the storm.

Hail the size of golf balls pelted Bert's car as he exited in front of the house. Saint Elmo's fire spewed from the treetops and, like a giant wave, surged across the grassy lawn. The air hissed around him. Atop the fountain, Saint Michael glowed as blue flames shot heavenward from the tip of his sword. Bert closed the front door of the house behind him, grateful for the relative safety of being inside. He took in a couple of deep breaths and then rushed up the stairs.

As he entered the doorway to Amanda's room, Bert yelled for Katie, but there was no response. The ferocity of the wind was driving rain and hail into the window and soaking the badly soiled rug. He rushed in to close the window. As he turned around, he spotted Katie under Amanda's crib.

He knelt down, "Katie?" There was no response, "Katie, are you alright?"

An earsplitting clap of thunder followed another flash. Katie recoiled, and then shuddered at the sound. Bert extended his hand and touched Katie's shoulder. She screamed, "Leave me alone Steve!" Then she lunged at Bert.

Katie pummeled Bert with her fists. "I've got to find them, do you hear me?"

Bert grabbed Katie's arms to stop the beating, but the tighter he held, the more she struggled to break free.

"Let go of me, damn you," Katie shouted. "Let me go. I've got to find them!"

Bert wrapped his arms around Katie and held her tight.

"Shhh," he whispered, "it'll be all right, Katie. It'll be all right."

"They won't be all right, Steve, damn you, they won't be all right!" Then Katie broke down and cried bitterly.

As quickly as it began, it was over. The digital readout on the screen flipped from 3:59 to 4:00. The cold dark room was suddenly bright and comfortable and the drenched, soiled rug was once again clean and dry. Outside the window, the clouds evaporated into nothingness, leaving behind them only clear, blue sky. The monitor reflected the change on the screen as the bands of pink, white, and green shriveled and then disappeared altogether. The strobe light stopped and the alarm became silent again. Even the racing of Katie's heart stopped as the peaceful tranquility and soft pink glow returned. Moments after the horrific episode ended, it seemed as though it had never happened. Bert's preplanning was already producing results. The research room came alive with beeps and tiny motor sounds as its computers processed data and its printers generated reports on the storm's brief lifecycle. Some data, however, remained hidden. Katie's emotional response and the memories that triggered it once again retreated into her subconscious, and she had no recollection of what she had said or done or what it was that drove her terror. All she could recall was her last journal entry prior to the storm. Katie straightened and sat up. Bert loosened his embrace and asked if she was all right.

"I am now," she said. "I heard it, Bert. I heard the thunder, I saw the lightning flash, and I felt the wind, rain, and hail coming through the window."

"I know. I did too, but from what we know about the room's environment that doesn't seem possible."

"Not unless it shut down for a time."

Bert considered the possibilities. "Katie, you didn't disturb anything, did you: disconnect an outlet cover or adjust the clock time or...?"

"No," Katie interrupted. "I didn't touch a thing."

"Then what do you think could make it do that?"

Katie wasn't ready to divulge her theory about Amanda. If she did, she would also have to explain her feelings for Bert, and she wasn't ready for that to come out yet.

"I honestly don't know," she said.

23

In 2006, the National Weather Service unveiled the Enhanced Fujita (EF) Scale for rating the relative strength of tornados in the United States. The scale has six rungs. An EF-1 tornado has winds of 86 to 110 miles per hour, enough to overturn mobile homes.

For the next several hours, Katie and Bert surveyed the area surrounding the house and then reviewed the data in Amanda's room.

"OK, then," said Bert. "Let's summarize what we've found." Katie sat with her laptop as Bert began.

"The external monitors recorded the first noticeable changes at 15:41 and 50 seconds."

Katie nodded as she scanned her copy of the printout highlighted in yellow, then added, "But the room's integrity wasn't lost for another 5 minutes and 21 seconds."

"Exactly," Bert agreed. "The duration of the event was 12 minutes, 36 seconds. During the first phase the temperature dropped 6 degrees, the barometric pressure lost .11 inches of mercury, and the wind speed went from .6 to 11.1 miles per hour."

"But then," Katie continued, "once the room's integrity was lost, in the span of 7 minutes, 15 seconds, the temperature dropped from 72 to 48 degrees, the barometric pressure dropped to 29.06 inches of mercury, and the wind speed went from 11.1 to 87.2 miles per hour."

Katie stopped typing and looked up at Bert, "That's the equivalent of an F1 Tornado."

"With one glaring exception," Bert added. "North of the equator, cyclonic storms revolve counterclockwise. This one revolved clockwise."

Bert continued, "Prior to the start of the event, the relative humidity was only 57% but by the time it ended we received 1.35 inches of rainfall."

"But only for a distance of a couple thousand feet out from the room," Katie added. Looking at the data, Bert and Katie determined that the storm had formed a near perfect circle centered on the room.

"Doesn't it seem odd," asked Katie, "that for such a highly organized storm system in such a small area there was no visible funnel, and that the wind speed didn't go any higher?"

Everything about the storm was odd to Bert, including that it happened at all. There were no significant atmospheric conditions present to cause the storm to form in the first place. "It's a good thing it didn't get any stronger," he said, "or you and I might not be sitting here right now."

When they exhausted their lists, Bert accessed the NOAA database to view the historical satellite images for the region. He was anxious to see the storm's signature in the upper atmosphere and wondered what the national weather trackers were going to make of a half-mile wide plug spinning in the center of an otherwise calm sky.

"Look at this," Bert motioned Katie over to the screen. Katie was accustomed to the images that moved across weather maps and then suddenly jerked back to the beginning and repeated themselves. What was odd about these images, however, was their normalcy.

"I don't see any disturbances," Katie said.

"There aren't any. There are just a few light clouds passing over the area with nothing out of the ordinary."

Katie placed her finger on the screen where the storm should have been, "It looks like outside of the bubble the storm was invisible. Maybe Tess was right. This is creepy."

They quit for the evening about seven. Bert started for the door but then hesitated for a moment. Katie smiled and assured him that she would be fine. As he exited the building, Katie picked up her diary and made one final entry.

Amanda, are you jealous?

Katie spent her free time the next day at the student center and then took in an early movie. She needed to be around other people, people not involved in the research. She also needed some space from Amanda. When she returned to her room that evening, she retrieved Tess's phone message.

"Hi, Katie. You asked me to call when I made my return flight arrangements. I should be landing tomorrow afternoon around two. Thanks for offering to pick me up, but I talked to Chris earlier and he said he could get me on his way back from Ohio. See you soon."

Katie smiled appreciatively. Picking Tess up would have required her to cut a class. Since it was also Drew's certification exam day, she would have been driving to the airport alone.

Tess's mention of Chris left Katie wondering how his research was going and where he was now. Then she had an idea. She walked up to one of the monitors and clicked on Drew's weather GPS program. A picture of the Earth filled the screen. She clicked on the window at the bottom of the screen and entered Chris's cell phone number. The image of the Earth rotated to the United States, and then zoomed into the northeast. To Katie's surprise, however, it didn't go to Ohio. The image continued to zoom in to the eastern seaboard, then to New Jersey, and finally to a cloudless Atlantic City boardwalk. She wondered why Chris offered to pick Tess up when he had already left Ohio. He certainly wouldn't leave Tess stranded at the airport. And why would he drive so far out of his way when Katie had already agreed to pick Tess up? Katie repeated Tess's message in her mind and was certain that she understood it correctly. On impulse, she highlighted Chris's information, and replaced it with Tess's cell phone number. When she hit enter, the program zoomed back out to the whole Earth and then zoomed in once again. It landed on the exact same spot as it had for Chris.

24

Summer Solstice (Northern hemisphere) – The first day of summer and the longest day of the year. The sun reaches its furthest point north, stops, and shifts direction southward.

Winter Solstice (Northern hemisphere) – The first day of winter and the shortest day of the year. The sun reaches its furthest point south, stops, and shifts direction northward.

Drew returned the next afternoon. Chris and Tess arrived a couple hours later, but no meeting took place. Chris wanted to finish his report, and Tess was exhausted from her trip and needed to rest. She also had to take care of some personal things the next morning, but said she'd be available by midafternoon. Everyone agreed to meet at 3:30 p.m. on Friday.

Drew and Katie had no classes Friday so they met earlier in the day. Sitting on the rug in Amanda's room, Katie relayed what had happened, leaving out the part about her journal entries. Drew was fascinated with the storm's sudden development and loss of the room's integrity.

"Drew," Katie asked, "do you wonder if maybe there's more to this than we know?"

"More? As in more than light and energy without a source, or more than an invisible barrier for sound, light, even dirt, or maybe more than your own personal tornado generator?" He paused for a moment, "No. I guess that's enough for me."

Katie pleaded for him take her seriously.

"All right," he answered, "but then you'll have to do better than 'more.'"

Katie asked if he ever questioned if Amanda never left, if she wasn't the one behind everything that was happening.

"We've all wondered that, Katie, except for maybe the

professor. I think he's still looking for some sort of physical explanation. Personally, I go with the Amanda theory myself."

"And do you ever think, maybe she's here right now, listening to us, evaluating what we say and do?"

"Amanda was only three months old when she died. I wouldn't expect much evaluation from a baby."

"But that was eighteen years ago. That would make her about our age now."

"You think she would have grown and matured like us during all that time?"

Katie nodded. "Something like that."

Lacing his fingers behind his head, Drew sat back against the wall. "I guess I never thought of that. That would mean she'd have to learn and understand from other people and to do that she would have to leave the house. How would she do that?"

Katie admitted she didn't know. "But do you think it's possible? Do you think that maybe Amanda could have intentionally caused that storm Wednesday?"

"After more than a year in this house, I believe almost anything's possible."

Bert arrived shortly before noon. Katie and Drew joined him in the research room. Down the hall, the clicking of Chris's keyboard gave way to the hum of his inkjet printer. Then there was silence.

"All right Drewski, that's enough work for one morning. My report's finished, and it's time to play."

Drew turned around to see Chris standing in the doorway looking like a poorly designed ad for "Sportsman's Guide." He wore a floppy angler's hat complete with flies and hooks, a camouflaged life vest over his tan safari shirt, and baggy jeans. He had a tackle box flung over his shoulder and was holding two fishing poles.

"Chris, you've got to be kidding," said Drew.

"Not on your life, Santiago. I'll bet that oversized pond out back has monsters just waiting to jump onto our hooks."

"Nice thought, but I doubt the professor would agree. Tess's been out for a week, you've been gone forever, and I just got back myself."

"Our meeting isn't until 3:30. We can make our quota of fish and still get back here in plenty of time. After being gone so long, I'm sure the professor can survive a couple more hours without our company." Chris turned to Bert, "So what do you say, Bertie? Can Drew come out to play or is his repartee so witty you can't live without him?"

Chris's attempts at humor were often lost on Bert and today he seemed especially grating. Still, Bert realized there was nothing else he needed from Drew prior to the meeting and if Chris's diversion cleared his head for work then it would be worth it.

Then Bert remembered Chris's report. "Wait a second Chris. How about leaving a copy of your report so I can review it and prepare some follow-up questions for when you return?"

"Nice try Professor, but the contents of that report are top secret until our meeting, at which time everything will be revealed."

"If that's the way it's got to be..." Bert wanted the team's full attention at the meeting. He hadn't told anyone yet, not even Katie, but he had decided it was time to involve others in the research. As aggravated as he was with Chris's secretiveness, he could see that Chris was genuinely trying to connect with Drew and he wanted to support that.

"Actually, Drew, Katie, and I should be able to finish the meeting prep with no problem. I hear you've been pushing pretty hard lately, and with outstanding results, so the R and R will probably do you good."

"Whoa. What results are we talking about here?" Chris asked.

"Sorry, Chris," Bert answered. "It's really not my place to say."

"Say what?" Chris looked at Katie. Her smile confirmed what he suspected. He was the only one in the room without a clue.

"All right, Drew, enough stalling, cough it up."

"It's really no big deal. I just aced the Network Security Certification Exam." From the frown on Chris's face, it was obvious that the accomplishment was lost on him.

"No big deal?" said Bert. "According to Professor Nervesky, in the seven years that exam has been given worldwide, you're only the third person to have ever aced it. He expects recruiters to be hounding you before the end of the week."

"Way to go, Drewski," said Chris. "Now can we get the hell out of here?"

Drew still hesitated. Katie asked what was wrong.

"To tell you the truth, I'm not that great a swimmer."

"Chris," said Katie, "maybe this isn't such a good idea."

"Hold on there a second, Katie." Chris turned back to Drew. "Listen, I'll bet that pond isn't more than six feet deep at any point. I can't swim a stroke and it doesn't scare me a bit. That's why they make life vests. In fact, here, you can use mine." Chris removed his camouflage vest and handed it to Drew.

"Then what are you going to wear?" Drew asked.

"Don't worry about me. There are plenty more in the boat."

Drew turned to Bert. "Well, if you don't really need me for the next couple hours..."

"No problem," Bert answered. You're probably our best chance at getting Chris back in time for the meeting." Drew smiled and the pair started for the door. At the last moment, Chris turned back and addressed Bert.

"Just one thing before we go," Chris paused for dramatic effect, "remember this: being in the pink isn't necessarily good for your health. See ya."

Chris shoved Drew out the door and they disappeared down the stairs.

Once again, the room was quiet and Bert and Katie were alone.

A half hour later, Bert commented on the report that Katie and Tess had generated. "Other than the storm on Wednesday and the two other dates you and Tess uncovered, there's an absolute elegance to these patterns."

Katie looked confused. She and Tess didn't see any new patterns in the data they had provided. In fact, to Katie it looked chaotic. The time of the December switchover varied every year. Some years it even occurred on a different day altogether, and there were similar problems in June.

"That's because you were looking for a fixed time instead of a fixed event," said Bert. "What time is that cat clock showing?"

Katie didn't have to look up. "About 7 minutes after 10."

"And we know the temperature shift occurred on December 21, 1990. Do you know what the significance of 10:07 p.m. on that date is?" Katie tapped her fingers and concentrated, but could not discern the answer. Bert continued.

"It's the exact moment of the winter solstice. If you compare your data on the December temperature shift to the seasonal movement of the sun, you'll find that the shift occurs every year at precisely that moment."

"Of course. That makes perfect sense."

"And the June data…" Bert started.

"…corresponds exactly to the summer solstice!" Katie finished.

Both of them beamed with excitement.

In the meantime, Chris and Drew had removed the Coleman canoe from the car, packed it with gear, and carried it to the shoreline. As the water came into view, Drew hesitated, "I thought you said this was a pond."

"Yeah, I know what you mean," Chris answered. "Anywhere else they'd call this a lake, and a big one at that, but check out this scenery. Is this a Kodak moment or what?"

Drew understood. Like the canvas of a skilled artist, the reflection of the tree-covered hillside melted into the surface of the water. It was nearly impossible to determine where the land ended and the water began. Only Drew's anxiety blocked his appreciation of the effect.

"I thought you said we had extra life jackets." Drew was

foraging through the canoe.

"Sort of," Chris answered. "You said you weren't a great swimmer and I said that's what life jackets are for. These seat cushions are life preservers. If the canoe flips, I can grab one of these, hold on to the straps, and ride it to shore like a surfboard. Comprende amigo?" Drew frowned but didn't bother to pursue the matter further.

Back at the house, Bert flipped to another matrix. "Take a look at this one, Katie. We already knew about the pattern for temperature differentials, but look at these other parameters."

Even before he finished, Katie understood. The spreadsheet tracked weekly weather changes from 1988 to 2012. It listed temperature, barometric pressure, relative humidity, wind speed, and other parameters, showing the differential readings for each over time. Most told a similar story. On the date of the summer solstice, the differential for each reading was zero. A week later, there was a slight difference. Each week the readings changed by exactly the same amount until the winter solstice, at which time the pattern peaked and then reversed itself. The changes continued until the following summer solstice when they zeroed out and began again. Except for a couple of anomalous dates, the spreadsheet showed the same pattern every year.

Bert sat back in his chair. "We used to think that everything in the universe was chaotic. Now we know that underlying most - maybe all of it - are patterns that give it coherence and meaning. I swear there's a message in here somewhere. I can't help feeling that these numbers are telling us something. I just don't know what yet."

"Or maybe who," said Katie. "I don't think it's the numbers that are trying to tell us something, Bert. I think it's Amanda."

Bert smiled. While he was certain there was a root cause that would explain everything, he was equally certain that the explanation would fall within the natural realm. Katie remained steadfast. Until a better explanation surfaced, she would stay with Amanda.

25

Downbursts: Potentially damaging horizontal winds that emanate from where a thunderstorm's downdrafts meet the surface.

"Hey, Drew," Chris reached into his windbreaker and pulled out a stack of papers, "take a look at this."

Drew didn't hear Chris's words. He was too immersed in the moment. His body moved in unison with the boat's bobbing. His ears attuned themselves to the birds singing, the leaves rustling and the waves lapping against the hull. His skin responded to warmth of the sun on his face, and the hint of a breeze softly brushing against his cheeks. And his eyes caught the reflection of the sunlight, shattering into a million facets that glistened on the water.

"Earth to Drew," Chris's voice penetrated the peacefulness with all the subtlety of a bulldozer in a flower garden.

"What?"

"I said, take a look at this. Believe me, you're gonna love it." Drew realized that there was no sense trying to hold on to the experience any longer.

"What is it?"

"It's my research on the room; I want your opinion before I show it to Bert."

"I thought you wanted to fish."

"Yeah, but I'm too antsy right now. You'll see why once you've read it. Take my word for it; you're not going to believe what's in it."

"Pretty unbelievable, isn't it?" Bert asked Katie about his analysis.

"Yes," said Katie, "I guess so." Although it was obvious

from her response that she hadn't heard the question.

Bert stopped talking and waited. Katie finally looked into his eyes and smiled.

"Welcome back," he said. "Did you notice some error in my calculations?"

"No," she smiled. "I was just looking at the tinge of gray in your sideburns. I think it's kind of cute." Katie leaned in toward Bert and rubbed her finger on his sideburn.

Bert swallowed hard, "Thank you Katie." He hesitated to express how taken he was with her—the way the light reflected in her eyes and the tiny dimples that appeared whenever she smiled. As distracting as her facial features were, Bert tried to maintain his focus. It was too dangerous to think about the rest—the soft curvature of her breasts, her petite hands and wrists, her tiny waist, and the way her hips gently sloped out below it. Bert shook his head trying to regain his concentration. "I was just thinking," he said, "I've never worked with anyone quite like you before." He leaned in a little. Katie responded in kind. "It's more than just aptitude," Bert could feel her breath against his face. "It's almost as though you read my thoughts and have the answers ready even before I ask the questions." Their faces were almost touching. "You really are truly amaz—" Katie's lips pressed gently against Bert's, soft and moist. Bert returned in kind, momentarily forgetting about anything or anyone else. He reached up to embrace her and then caught himself.

"I'm sorry," he said, and pulled his arm back.

"I'm not." Katie smiled and brushed her hand against his cheek. Then she got up and walked away into Amanda's room.

"This is amazing," Drew said as he finished the final notes of Chris's report. "Where did you get all of this stuff?"

Chris beamed. "Everywhere. I interviewed anyone who would talk to me: former neighbors, people at the hospital, even Amanda's dad. I researched police reports and even spoke to a warden at the prison. Where I really kicked-ass was with a friend at Children and Family Services. I've put myself on the line for him plenty, so he looked into Amanda's case file for me.

"So this is all true?" Drew asked. "Even the adoption?"

"Yep, I'm still waiting on that one piece. I don't know how relevant it's going to be, but they keep those records in a separate file so my CFS contact is looking into them for me as we speak. He's supposed to call me by three with the last piece of information. That's why I wanted to hold off the meeting till then."

Drew lowered the report to his lap. "I have to hand it to you; it reads like you witnessed it all first hand. It's pretty incredible."

That was incredibly stupid! Bert murmured to himself. He worried about Katie's reaction. Was she embarrassed, angry, frightened? He took a few moments to organize his thoughts and then started for Amanda's room. He began talking even before he reached the door. "Katie, if I stepped over the line with that..."

The scene in front of him stopped him short. Katie was kneeling on the floor facing the door. She had stripped down to her black panties and her unbuttoned blouse. The pale smooth skin down the center of her chest lay partially exposed between the swells of her breasts. The only other thing she wore was a smile.

"I've never been good at lying, Bert. I've been attracted to you since the first time we met, and I'm sure you feel the same way about me. I'm in love with you, Bert." She gently pulled her blouse open and let it slip off her shoulders and onto the floor. Bert was too euphoric to speak. Katie's youthful body was even more beautiful than he imagined - and he had imagined it a lot. His fixation on Katie made him oblivious to the storm gathering outside.

As Drew prepared to ask the first of several questions, Chris interrupted. "So did you hear about Tess's stepdad?"

"What about him?" Chris handed Drew a newspaper clipping and Drew scanned the story, "I thought Tess said the guy was already dead."

"I think we all wondered if Tess was stretching the truth when she said that. I'm surprised the room let her get away with it."

Chris's cell phone rang. He looked down at the screen, "This is it," he said. "Hi, Jerry, what have you got for me?"

Deep furrows dug into Chris's brow as he listened. The intensity of his focus on the conversation made him oblivious to what was going on around him. Drew looked over Chris's shoulder toward the shore. "Chris," he said. The alarm was evident in his voice.

Chris looked up at Drew, "Just a second, Jerry. Drew, what's the matter? You look like you've just lost your best friend."

"Maybe we both have," Drew kept gazing over Chris's shoulder.

"For God's sake, Drew, not the dramatics again." As he spoke, Chris turned to look back at the shore behind him, "Oh shit!"

Gunmetal gray clouds exploded toward them, swallowing the hillside and blocking out the sun. Wind gusts bent the treetops and ripped huge swatches of leaves from their branches. The forest disappeared behind a cloud of leaves. Wind and rain boiled the water as the storm moved offshore and headed toward them. Behind the rain, thunder roared as lightning flashes fractured the blackness above.

"We've got a situation here, Jerry," Chris yelled into the phone. "I'll have to get back to you. What? All right then, just give me a name." The boat rocked as the swells deepened but Chris sat motionless, "What? Are you sure?"

"Goddamn it Chris!" Drew yelled.

"I've got to go." Chris hung up the phone and jammed it into his dry bag.

They were less than a quarter of the way out on the pond. It looked like more than a mile to the other side. The rain was on them and the swells threatened to swamp the boat. Their only chance was to head back in the direction they came from—into the mouth of the maelstrom. "We've got to start rowing, Drew. We've got to row like hell!" Drew was soaked through. The report dropped into the watery bottom of the canoe as he stood to retrieve his oar. "No, Drew, don't stand up or you'll…"

Drew cut Chris short, "Holy shit!" Chris ripped around to see the funnel coming toward them, sucking up the lake, and sending it skyward.

Bert knelt down facing Katie, but instead of elation, his face froze into a sad smile.

"What's the matter?" Katie asked, "Did I say something wrong?"

"Not at all," Bert said as he lifted her blouse and placed it back on her shoulder. "What you said was perfect, Katie. You just said it to the wrong person."

"I don't understand." Her voice quivered from his reaction and from the sudden cold. "Don't you have feelings for me?"

"Believe me, it's not that. I think you're one of the most beautiful, most fascinating women I've ever met."

"Then what?"

As he answered, Bert began closing the front of Katie's blouse. "I'm sorry, Katie," his hands moved toward each other, "but this is impossible for me. I just can't do this…" As he moved toward the center, the backs of his fingers brushed slowly, softly against Katie's breasts, "…to my wife."

The room plunged into darkness. The icy wind blowing through the window carried with it heavy rain, dust, and leaves. A lightning bolt tore through a tree in the front yard while the thunderclap rattled the windows. Katie screamed above the noise, not out of fear, but anger.

"Your wife! What the hell do you mean, your wife?" Katie slapped Bert hard. An intense clap of thunder underscored her rage.

Then as if awakened from some nightmare, it was over as quickly as it began. Bert and Katie once again found themselves in a clean, dry room and bathed in its perfect pink glow. The room's emotional calm and peacefulness also returned. However, it did nothing to eliminate Katie's feeling of betrayal. She spoke as she dressed while Bert gazed out the window, "Bert, how could you? I trusted you."

Bert struggled for words to explain away his deceit, but he couldn't. He knew it would be a lie. The only deflection he could muster was a question, "You really didn't know, Katie?" If they were not in Amanda's room that would certainly have earned him another slap, but Katie remained composed.

"Of course not! You've never worn a wedding ring. You've consistently avoided any reference to being attached—let alone married. And even when I asked you directly, and I've given you plenty of opportunities, Bert, you've denied it outright! Are you ashamed of it, or is it just that it would have jeopardized you chances to get a free feel?" Katie was stating what they both knew, that Bert brushing against her was not accidental. "We've worked side by side for almost two years, Bert. You and I both know that I've been more than a student to you. And I think you know me well enough to know that if I even suspected you were married, I never would have let it get this far. I don't deserve this."

Bert could see the tears welling up in Katie's eyes. "I'm sorry, Katie, you're right. I've been stupid and selfish. I couldn't even begin to describe how much I admire you and value your friendship. I'd be lying if I said that the attraction wasn't mutual. I guess I tried to fool myself into believing that somehow I could have you and keep my marriage. When faced with the choice, I realized how impossible that was. I was so focused on what I wanted that I didn't stop to think about how it might affect you, or my wife. I'm truly, truly sorry."

Katie finished dressing, "Thanks for the feeble attempt at an apology, Bert, but right at the moment it just doesn't cut it." She brushed by him and left the room. Once she did, the grief overcame her. As she exited the front door, she was crying uncontrollably.

Bert started to leave the room, but then he hesitated. The real Bert was on the other side of the doorway, and right now, he didn't like or respect that man. He stopped, sat down against the wall in Amanda's room, and tried to remember the person he once thought he was.

26

There are two types of Waterspouts. The weaker convective type can occur in fair or foul weather, can rotate in either direction, and typically has winds less than 65 miles per hour. The tornado type occurs when a tornado moves from land to water. It has the same characteristics as a true tornado.

Something was wrong. The blaring of a siren was a rare sound on Nadowa's campus, especially on the fringes like Lakota Drive. As Bert exited the house, however, he met a chorus of them. They were too far off to see, but from the sound, he estimated that a procession of emergency vehicles was rushing along Taconic Lane, formerly Shore Road, which led directly to the pond. He got in his car and drove in the direction of the convoy.

Police tape blocked the street a couple of hundred feet from the road's end. He got out and walked the rest of the way. A fleet of rescue vehicles floated in a sea of flashing emergency lights. He walked to the front of the first fire engine and surveyed the scene. Several uniformed police were huddled around a stooped man with a scraggly salt and pepper beard. As the old man talked, his wiry silver hair whisked about his head in the afternoon breeze. Bert recognized him as Ben Jansen who lived in a shack on the pond for as long as anyone could remember. The Indians had once offered Ben five times what his place was worth, but he refused to leave. He was a loner and liked it that way, so now it seemed out of place for him to be the center of attention. Down by the water, two men in wet suits were loading gear into an inflatable boat. Bert caught a passing firefighter, told him he worked at the college, and asked what was happening.

"Old man Jansen called in a report that a couple of fishermen might have capsized out on the pond."

Bert's heart sank. "Do you know what kind of boat they were in?"

"They're looking for a green canoe, probably the plastic kind, about sixteen feet long." The description matched Chris's Coleman. Bert started toward the huddle.

"Sorry Professor," the fireman stopped him, "but this area is for emergency personnel only."

Bert explained, "I've been working at 34 Lakota Drive at the top of the hill. I'm fairly certain I know who those fishermen are."

The firefighter escorted Bert over to Ben Jansen's entourage. As they entered the circle, Bert caught Ben's old Yankee twang.

"Couple of damn fools if you ask me; any idiot who's been out on the water more than ten seconds knows you don't stand up in a canoe." Bert could smell the alcohol on Ben's breath. The firefighter placed his hand on the shoulder of a tall police officer standing off to the side and pointed toward Bert. The officer, whose hair matched the silver bars on his uniform, approached Bert.

"Professor Myers, isn't it?" Bert nodded.

"I'm Captain Davis. I understand you might know the fellows who were out on the pond."

Bert could see from his uniform that the Captain was a member of the campus police. It surprised him that the local cops would allow a campus officer to take a lead role on such a high profile incident. "Yes. A couple students of mine left about an hour ago to go fishing; the description of the boat you're looking for sounds like Chris's."

"I see," the captain started to write in his note pad, "and what were their names Professor?"

"Drew Richardson and Chris Matthews."

Davis paused for a moment and tapped his pen twice on the page, then continued. "And do you know where they live?"

"Yes, they live at the house."

"At 34 Lakota Drive?" The raised pitch of the question indicated that there was something significant in Bert's answer. The captain continued.

"Seems kind of off the beaten path for campus housing, doesn't it?"

"Well, it's more than that."

"In what way?" Bert felt his body temperature rising. He had to work at slowing down his breathing.

"Chris and Drew were officers of the student government. The house also serves as their headquarters."

"And what's your involvement?"

"Excuse me," Bert asked. "Is this relevant to your investigation?"

"Why don't you just let me be the judge of what's relevant, Professor. Now, what did you say was your involvement?"

"I'm the student government advisor." Bert realized that answer wouldn't justify a significant presence on his part. "And I head up a research project at the house."

"Really? What kind of research?"

"Weather."

"Weather. Now that's interesting."

"I don't follow you."

"Well Mr. Jansen claims that your students were caught in one hell of a storm out there. Second one in the last couple weeks," Ben interrupted.

The captain continued, "According to Ben this one was pretty nearly a hurricane. Funny thing is that our station is just on the other side of the campus—can't be more than a couple miles from here—and yet we didn't get so much as a raindrop. Strange, don't you think?"

"There was a storm, and it was fairly intense." Bert rubbed the back of his neck. He could feel the sweat forming along his shirt collar.

"What time was that?" Davis asked.

"About thirty minutes ago."

"Hmmm, that's just about the time the call came in."

"And don't forget about the spout!" Ben yelled.

"The what?" Bert asked.

"The water spout, you damned fool. You sure ain't too bright for a college man."

Davis took back control of the conversation. "According to Mr. Jansen, a funnel formed up on the hill and turned into a waterspout out on the pond."

"Must have been a hundred feet high." Ben wrestled back the lead, "Damnedest thing I ever seen. Them boys must of seen it, too. That's when one of them stood right up in the boat. The other one was waving his arms like crazy, like he was probably yelling to sit down or something, until he turned round, and then he must of seen it, too. That's when I lost sight of them."

"Why was that?" Bert asked.

"Cause of the spout. One second it was swirling right next to me. I though it was gonna suck me right up. But then it just took a beeline right for them boys, almost like it was aiming for them. It stirred up the water something awful. You couldn't see the boat or them boys, or nothing. Next second, it was gone and so were they—damnedest thing I ever seen. It was like some giant vacuum cleaner sucked up the spout, the wind, the clouds, everything, and the next thing you know, it's just as bright and sunny as you please, and all that's left is water and no sign of them fellers or their boat—damnedest thing I ever seen."

"That sound about right to you, Professor?" Davis asked.

"I can't speak to the funnel," Bert answered, "but the storm did end abruptly."

"Ben," the captain asked, "where were you standing when you saw all of this?"

"Come with me and I'll show you."

As they walked westward along the shore, Davis leaned in toward Bert, "I can't ever remember a report of a twister in this area, always struck me as too hilly for one to touch down. What do you make of Ben's story?"

"It seems pretty obvious that he's been drinking," said Bert. "I'd have to wonder if the alcohol hasn't amplified his recollection of what happened."

After walking a couple of hundred feet, Ben stopped and looked out toward the water. Bert and Davis gazed inland instead, at the 50-foot wide chasm carved out of the dense forest. It looked as though a team of bulldozers had laid waste to the trees, pushing them off to the sides of the crevasse. Looking straight up the middle of the ravine Bert could see the antenna mounted on the roof of Amanda's room.

"Then again," said Davis, "maybe Ben understated what he saw."

Davis searched Bert's face as if looking for something. Maybe it was because Bert sank into his own quiet coma. Ben's words kept reverberating in his head, "Almost like it was aiming for them."

The search was called off an hour later. A heavy rain settled in and continued on and off for the next three days. Gusty winds and frequent lightning strikes made it too dangerous for the divers. Volunteers combed the shoreline. They found Chris's tackle box on the far side of the pond. One of the seat cushions bobbed nearby. A piece of paper was stuck to it, but the inkjet printing had dissolved. Other than that, there was nothing.

The college contacted Drew's mother. She told them she was too ill to travel but asked to be kept informed regarding the search. Chris's parents were on an extended vacation in Europe and Asia. They had arranged to correspond via e-mail every other week, but they had just checked in from somewhere in Turkey so when they found the boat a week later the police called Bert. Captain Davis met him at the campus station. As they walked around to the back of the station Bert asked, "The pond doesn't seem that big. Once the rain stopped, why did it take them so long to find the boat?"

"They didn't find it in the pond," Davis answered. "A couple of hunters came across it three miles east of the spillway."

"The spillway?"

"The pond is fed by springs and tributaries. When it rains

heavy, the spillway empties the overflow into a stream. In the dry season it's not much more than a trickle, but after a hard rain like the last few days, it can be a real surge. It's been known to take down sizable trees."

"So are they searching downstream for Chris and Drew?"

"They are, but it's not likely they'll find anything soon, if ever. Eventually that stream empties into the Hudson. Besides, they didn't find the boat in the stream."

"I'm not following you."

Davis pulled back a large tarp exposing what used to be a boat. It was mangled and broken, cracked everywhere, and almost bent in half. "Is this Matthew's boat?" Davis asked.

Bert looked at the name, Coleman Ram-X, 16', and nodded affirmatively.

Davis ended, "They found the boat about a mile from the stream, wrapped around the trunk of a tree, thirty feet in the air. We hadn't searched that far out so after we found the boat, we brought out the dog teams and searched the area. That's when we found this." Davis removed the remainder of the tarp exposing a life vest.

Bert looked down at the camouflage vest. Half of it was stained red.

"Does it look familiar?" Davis asked.

"Yes," Bert answered, "the last time I saw him, Drew was wearing this."

"The stains are blood," Davis explained. "Since the boys were living at the house, I'd like to look at their personal belongings. We should be able to use their DNA to determine whose it is."

"Of course," was all Bert could say. When the DNA results came back, they only confirmed his worst fears. It was Drew's blood. Bert's nerves were shot. He couldn't get the sight of Chris's boat out of his mind, or the thought of Chris and Drew's bodies rotting away somewhere. He drove to O'Rourke's Tavern in Cairo. Along the way, questions he desperately tried to avoid kept pushing their way into his consciousness. If the nearly indestructible canoe looked that bad, what would Chris and Drew look like when they found them? If their parents were still unavailable, would the police ask him to identify the bodies?

Bert had only been to O'Rourke's twice before. The last time was after finals when a group of graduating seniors dragged him into their celebration. It wasn't that he objected to bars; he just normally preferred places where he could get something decent to eat as well as drink, and everything at O'Rourke's was deep-fried.

On a sunny afternoon, the bar's interior was as dark as a confessional. The only illumination came from the neon beer signs, the light above the pool table, and the outdated song list on the jukebox. Customers paid no heed to smoking restrictions so even when the air purifiers were all working—which they seldom were—what little light there was came filtered through a thick haze of cigarette and cigar smoke.

The bar catered mainly to two kinds of clientele: transients looking to get drunk or lucky, and regulars who no longer remembered or cared why they were there. Bert ordered a double scotch straight up. He drank it so quickly that, for a moment, he could not breathe. Then he ordered another one.

Bert knew why he was there, for absolution, the kind dispensed in two-ounce glasses, the kind that would let him forget the images: the look of anxiousness in Drew's eyes as he left to go fishing, the emaciated remains of Chris's boat, and the old Yankee's description of the waterspout, "almost like it was aiming for them."

Most of all Bert wanted to forget the pained look on Katie's face, that look of betrayal in her eyes, and the indignation masking the hurt in her voice. Then Bert thought about Evelyn's eyes: sometimes calm, sometimes cross, always trusting. Then he thought about how that look would change forever if she knew.

Bert downed the next scotch. The images were still there, still clear.

Finally, he thought about the religious education class on confession at Evelyn's church, *Father, forgive me for I have sinned.* Bert settled into his stool and ordered another drink.

27

Latitudinal bands of global winds, named for the direction from which they flow, surround the Earth. The area surrounding the equator lies between the Northeast and Southeast Trades. Here, winds are so light and variable that ships can be caught for days or weeks without enough wind to power their sails. The common name for this band is the Doldrums.

Standing tall and proud at the living room entrance, the grandfather clock dutifully obeyed its programming and finished its last chore for the evening. For a few moments, it filled the house with its resounding Westminster chimes. Then it hammered out eleven rich, resonant tones before falling asleep for the night, except for breathing out its soft, rhythmic tick tocks. Still, there was no sign of Bert.

Evelyn sat on the living room sofa. She had dispensed with her solo dinner and disposed of the plastic ware and paper plate. The only thing left to do was worry about her husband, not about some accident or catastrophic illness but about his mental and emotional health.

This wasn't the first time Bert had lost a student, or for that matter, more than one. There was a car accident at MIT that cut short the lives of three juniors from his class and the suicide of Carl Dunlap, a gifted senior whom Bert liked and admired. But this time was different. Bert had never taken a loss so deeply, so personally. True, Nadowa was a much smaller campus, and he had worked more closely with Chris and Drew than with other students, but even that failed to explain the debilitating impact of their deaths. Bert hadn't taught a class or taken a shower since the accident, nor had he returned to the house. He hardly ate or slept. When sleep did come, it was restless and punctuated with nightmarish images that tormented him back to wakefulness. His normally meticulous appearance gave way to a three-day stubble and rumpled clothing. Now he was out on the second day of a marathon drinking binge. Evelyn realized that Bert needed time to heal, but it had been long enough, maybe too long. She would talk to him tonight.

Another set of chimes sounded. This time it was the doorbell. Evelyn opened the front door to find Bert slumped in the middle of a young couple, his arms drooping over their shoulders. He looked like Dorothy's scarecrow just liberated from the cornfield. "Oh Bert," Evelyn sighed.

"We met Professor Myers at O'Rourke's Tavern," the young woman said, then hesitated, struggling for the right words.

Her partner broke the silence, "The bartender said he'd been drinking for quite a while and really shouldn't drive himself home so we gave him a lift."

"Please come in." Evelyn directed the trio to the couch. Bert reeked of sweat, smoke, and alcohol. "Let me give you something for your trouble?"

"No thanks. It was on the way." The couple exited the house.

Evelyn sat on the couch and rested her husband's head on her lap, "My poor Bert," she said as she softly brushed his hair with her hand. He was groggy and exhausted but he could still see the tears trickling down his wife's face. He needed to purge his sins, to explain somehow.

"I screwed up Evie. They're dead and it's all my fault." There, he had said it. He had finally admitted it to someone. He had finally admitted it to himself.

"Shhh," Evelyn gently continued stroking his hair. Her voice was low and soothing. "There's no need to talk, just rest for now." By the time she finished her sentence, he was sound asleep.

Bert roused again as the Westminster chimes worked their way into his consciousness. From the volume, he realized he was on the living room couch instead of in his bed. He counted the gongs that followed: one, two—his head pounded with each strike—eight—nine—ten. From the light spilling in around him, Bert knew it was morning. Could he really have slept that late? The aroma of fresh brewed coffee drifted in from the kitchen, but as Bert sniffed it in, it mixed with the foul stench of his own body. He lifted his frame from the couch and went into the bathroom for a shower and some aspirin.

Forty minutes later Bert was halfway through his second cup of coffee. The combination of aspirin and caffeine had kicked in sufficiently for him to join the conversation Evelyn had already begun. While he was now clean, comfortable, and feeling rested after a full night's sleep, she was nearly exhausted. She slept poorly and was up and out of bed at five. She took a sip from her third cup of coffee as she formulated her question.

"Bert, last night you said something strange before you fell asleep. You said that Chris and Drew's deaths were your fault. Do you remember?" Bert nodded in agreement. "What did you mean by that?" she asked.

The previous evening, under the influence of half a quart of Scotch whisky, Bert was a firm believer that confession was good for the soul. He was ready and willing to bear everything to Evelyn, including his indiscretion with Katie. Now, in his sunlit kitchen, and dealing with the aftermath of his excesses, he realized how devastating his self-serving honesty would be. He resolved that the Katie part of the story would have to stay between him and his conscience.

He took another gulp of his coffee, "There may be even more going on at Lakota Drive than I thought—something conscious, something capable of controlling the weather."

"Including the pond Chris and Drew were fishing on?"

"Yes, including the pond."

"Are you suggesting that that room somehow caused Chris's and Drew's deaths?"

His voice was subdued, "I'm not sure what to believe anymore."

"Even if it could, and believe me, I'm not suggesting I go along with that theory, it still doesn't make it your fault."

Evelyn's statement led to the issue Bert was trying to avoid. His fingers tensed at the memory of their brushing against Katie's breasts. For a moment Bert was back in Amanda's room, kneeling next to Katie, feeling the icy wind sweep in, seeing the lightning flashes cut through the dark clouds, and hearing the deafening thunderclaps.

"Bert," Evelyn's voice sounded far away. "Bert!"

He was back again. He looked around at the familiar surroundings. He was sitting in the safety and quiet of his own kitchen. He looked up at his wife and smiled weakly, "I'm sorry."

Evelyn continued, "I said that still doesn't make it your fault."

"Maybe not entirely, but I'm the expert physicist. I'm the one who's supposed to know, or at least be able to estimate the potential risks involved and I didn't. I feel responsible." It wasn't a lie. It might not have been the full truth, but it was as far as he dared go. He hoped it was far enough.

Evelyn leaned against the kitchen counter and took another sip of her coffee. "Bert," she said, "I think it's time I saw this room for myself."

28

Spring (Vernal) Equinox – (March in the northern hemisphere) First day of spring. The sun crosses the equator traveling northward. There are equal periods of day and night.

Autumn Equinox – (September in the northern hemisphere) First day of autumn. The sun crosses the equator traveling southward. There are equal periods of day and night.

Reverend Eugene Foley, or Gene as the students called him, had been resident chaplain at Nadowa for over seven years. The college was large enough to support a modest congregation yet small enough for him to get to know most of the students on campus.

Gene fit in well with the student population. With his smooth complexion and straight dirty blond hair, he looked younger than his thirty-six years. Some students, like Tess and Katie, were regular members of his congregation. He offered a single service each Sunday at 9:00 a.m. It was standard practice to host coffee and conversation afterwards, and Gene made a special point of seeking out new attendees at these events. That's how he met Chris and Drew. It was the first service that Tess and Katie had dragged them to, and probably would have been the last if it weren't for Gene's gift for conversation. He was friendly and outgoing, a die-hard Yankees fan and a master at getting people to talk about their favorite subject: themselves.

Gene took note of Chris's role in leading the campus media. Conversations that started over coffee and pastry in the chapel hall continued over pitchers of Bud draft at O'Malley's, just off campus. Gene pitched the idea of a weekly call-in show dealing with faith related issues. Chris was skeptical but he liked Gene and took the idea up with his faculty advisor who quickly signed on. Gene immediately co-opted Drew into providing technical support for the program.

It was an instant success. Gene dealt with thorny issues like parent/student relationships, sex and dating, war, civic responsibility, civil disobedience, and even suicide. He explored topics, not only from a religious viewpoint, but also from moral, political, and philosophical perspectives. Over time, the group of five became close-knit friends. It was Gene's formal role, however, that prompted the call from Dean Thompson, the one requesting that Gene contact Chris and Drew's families and tell them about their missing sons.

Gene reached Drew's mother directly. He was surprised and a bit dismayed by her emotional detachment. He was even less successful with Chris's parents. Their extensive travel throughout Asia and the Far East included many regions that lacked modern communications. Gene's message arrived two days after their last contact. A week later, Chris's parents contacted Gene after receiving his message. Gene had to break the news to them over the phone.

Carl and Gail were seasoned travelers and had long ago accepted the reality that life would go on in their absence. Before embarking on a long trip, they met one-on-one with aged relatives and close friends knowing that it might be the last time they would see them. However, they were unprepared for the unthinkable, that one of their children would die in their absence. Gail took the news hard and had to cut the conversation short. By the time they called back later that day, Carl had arranged for them to return to the States.

Gene told them he was planning for a joint memorial service but didn't want to set the date until he heard from them in the event that they might like to attend. Carl said their response would have to wait until after their return. Agreeing to the service felt tantamount to accepting their son's death, and neither of them was ready for that.

Another week passed before Carl responded. The couple had seen the pond and searched the area around it, talked to the police, and even tried to contact old man Jansen, but the recluse didn't respond. The police cautioned them not to push further. Jansen had a reputation for fending off intruders with a shotgun. They finally accepted the inevitable and said they wanted to participate in the memorial service. Before the call was finished, they had set the date.

Gene asked Tess and Katie for assistance in disseminating information about the service. Then he called Bert and told him about the arrangements. As Bert hung up the phone, he realized that he couldn't stall returning to the house any longer. In addition to being their research site, it was also Chris and Drew's home. Someone had to gather their personal effects together for their parents. Katie was the Residence Assistant, but under the circumstances, he thought it best not to contact her. Tess was the only other person he might have contacted, but he felt it might be too difficult for her to go through Chris's things. He accepted that if someone had to box up the personal belongings, he was going to have to be the one.

Bert hesitated at Drew's door on his way to Chris's room. He carried unassembled boxes under his arm and a packing tape dispenser in his hand. He placed several boxes in the hallway outside of Drew's room. Drew had fewer interests than Chris and was a consummate neatnick, so Bert anticipated that packing Drew's things would go quickly. As he looked in on Drew's bed, he realized it was going to take longer than he planned. On the bed was Drew's handheld Mario Brothers game. The jingle started playing in Bert's head. It was playing the first day they had met. Running late to class from a meeting that went on too long, Bert had almost knocked the game out of Drew's hands as he brushed by him on the way into the classroom.

"Hey," Drew said without looking up, still concentrating on his game, "why don't you watch where you're... Oh, sorry, Professor." Drew shoved the game into his pocket, the melody still beeping away and offered a hand. Thanks to their work on Amanda's room, their relationship had grown into a genuine friendship.

Bert stepped into the room and reached for a framed photo from the top of Drew's dresser—it was a picture of him and the four students. He flashed back to the day Drew had taken it, so proud of his setup with the tripod and automatic timer. It was, as Chris was so fond of saying, a real Kodak moment. Bert reviewed their faces, all smiling and full of life. Bert looked back at the boxes and considered how everything that defined who Drew was at Nadowa would soon be sitting in a few cubic feet of cardboard - everything except one small item. He put the frame in his pocket.

Bert moved down the hall into a room that could hardly have been more different. Drew's room could pass muster at West Point while Chris's looked like the inside of a quarterback's locker. Drew's walls were almost bare and, where there were items, they were neatly organized in symmetrical arrangements. Chris's walls were randomly covered floor to ceiling like a modern art collage. Bert started removing items and placing them in the first box. New York Yankees memorabilia covered much of the wall's surface. Like Gene Foley, Chris was a rabid fan. Centered directly opposite the entrance was a Sports Illustrated pinup calendar. It had taken the place of the totally nude Miss August after Tess and Katie objected to Chris's blatant sexism. When Bert removed the calendar, he found Miss August still hiding au-natural. Bert noticed several more pages underneath. Leafing through them, he discovered Miss January to Miss July.

"Why, that lying little shit," Katie's voice echoed from the doorway. "He said he had gotten rid of those."

Bert was a confused mix of emotions—part happy at the sound of Katie's voice, and part embarrassed and remorseful at the way their last meeting had ended. He struggled for words. "Katie I, uh, I wanted to…"

"It's all right, Bert. I'm not going to bite you."

"I don't know what to say," Bert tripped over the words. "I was stupid, and, uh, selfish." He couldn't formulate anything else coherent to say except for the question that lingered in his head, "Are you still angry with me?"

"Of course I'm still angry. You played me and that's not something you get over right away. I don't know if I can ever fully trust you again."

"I understand," Bert hesitated a moment, "but, then, why are you here."

"I live here, remember?" Bert was embarrassed at the absurdity of his question. Fortunately, Katie continued. "But I also figured that we've all put a lot of work into this project and Chris and Drew deserve to have that work finished and be recognized for their efforts."

"Then you're going to stay on?"

"For the time being. We'll just see how things go from here."

Katie offered to pack up Drew's things. A half-hour later, she returned to assist with Chris's belongings. She had a book in her hand.

"What's that?" Bert asked.

"'Pillars of the Earth.' Drew said it was his favorite book. I didn't think he'd mind if I read it. It's kind of a way to remember him."

"I think he'd be very pleased with that."

They worked in almost complete silence. Occasionally, Katie requested clarification as to where to store a particular item. Then Katie paused before packing one of Chris's things away.

"Bert, have you seen this?" She held out a black soft cover book similar to the kind she used for her diaries.

Bert scanned the notebook's contents. He recognized some of Chris's outlines for stories printed in the campus newspaper or aired on the TV or radio broadcasts and ideas for Gene's call-in show. The last few pages, however, captured Bert's attention. The opening date corresponded to the initiation of Chris's research into Amanda's room. A few moments later Bert sat on the edge of Chris's bed, rereading pages and analyzing individual lines.

7/13/12 – Pink Room – Lakota Drive

7/20/12 Warden Frank Capshaw – Fishkill Corr. Inst. - P-618 BMP

Commander Miller / CWO Baker – U.S. Naval Correctional Center,

Short-term impacts, Corr., M.H., Schools, Football Teams

Long-term impact? – "Ed effect," termination, disposal

Finley's blood?

Amanda Reynolds

Born - 3:06 am - 9/23/90 - Albany Memorial Hosp - Autumn Equinox?

Gareth and Cynthia Reynolds

Pronounced - 11:52pm - 12/21/90 - Hudson Valley Medical Center

Pediatrician - Dr. Phillip Grey (Died – 1993)

7/27/12 Dr. Charles Miller - Emergency Room Doctor - cur. Albany

Medical Group, COD - S.I.D.S.

8/3/12 Winona Seivers - Tom's River, New Jersey, PPD?

Gareth - suspicious?

Adoption?

Police Report 12/23/90 - Investigating Officer Charles Davis - Hudson Valley Police Department - Estimated TOD 12/21/90, 7:30 - 11:15 pm

10:07 - 12/21/90 - Winter Solstice?

Cynthia Reynolds – cause - croup / colic ???

Suit - Dr. Grey, Dr. Miller, Hudson Valley Medical Center

Official COD - S.I.D.S.

RVW Adoption Services - Catskill - No comment

Jerry Berman - DCF

Records sealed, off the record, confirmed two

8/10/12 Gareth Reynolds - arrogant SOB

8/17/12 final report to Bert

Most of Chris's notes read like gibberish to Bert. That Chris had linked the events of Amanda's death and even her birth to the solar cycles intrigued him. But his main attention was fixed on the final line of Chris's notes (*8/17/12 final report to Bert*). Bert remembered that Chris's final report was ready on August 17, the date of the accident. Somewhere there had to be a full copy. Bert looked at Chris's computer. Katie had shut it down and unplugged the monitor. "Katie, hold on a second. I think we need to take a closer look at that computer."

They reconnected the hardware and turned it on. When it came to the log-on screen, however, a password request stopped their entry. For the next forty minutes, Bert and Katie tried to guess at every possible combination of words and numbers Chris might have used. Bert stroked, clicked, and cursed at the computer without success. Finally, when his patience ran out, he unplugged the useless pile of technology and relegated it to the last of the cardboard boxes.

29

Tsunamis, once called Tidal Waves, are long, high sea waves caused by a sudden, massive displacement of water.

At Tess and Katie's insistence, Gene had secured the campus auditorium for the memorial service. Nevertheless, he remained skeptical about the need. It was a month since the accident and the first week back after summer break. Gene thought most students would be too distracted settling in to attend. Katie made certain that people would at least be informed. She put a notice of the service in the campus and local newspapers and announced it on her radio and television broadcasts. The response was overwhelming. As Tess had predicted, nearly the entire student population turned out, but even she and Katie were unprepared for the flood of participation from the community at large.

The two girls positioned themselves at the entrance doors and supervised the handing out of the service programs. Gene thought he had erred on the high side by printing 600. At first, every attendee received one. A half-hour before the start, programs were given to every other person and people were asked to share. Fifteen minutes before the service was to begin, they ran out completely. The auditorium had seating for 800. By the start of the service, there was standing room only.

Early on, Katie reached out to hand a program to the next pair in line. Bert stretched out his free hand. Katie didn't recognize the woman on his arm, but it wasn't hard to guess. Bert introduced Katie to Evelyn. There was a tinge of nervousness in his voice. Evelyn looked prettier and softer than Katie had imagined. She didn't look like the kind of woman whose personality might drive her husband to cheat on her.

"It's nice to meet you, Katie," Evelyn extended her hand. "Bert's told me a lot about you." Katie extended hers and Evelyn took hold. "I don't suppose he's told you nearly as much about me." The question had the precise effect Evelyn had intended. There was a long line of people waiting to get in, so Katie had no time to generate an elaborate ruse.

Katie's response was short and to the point, "Not really." Evelyn let go of Katie's hand, smiled, and moved on. Katie kept the couple in her sight until they disappeared into the crowd, then leaned over to Tess and whispered in her ear, "She may be cute as a kitten, but that cat has claws."

People from throughout the valley and beyond packed the auditorium. Some came out of curiosity. Others wanted to express their sorrow for two lives full of promise, cut short. Many more came to say goodbye in person to the face on the television, or the voice on the radio, that had become their virtual friend and companion. While Chris was naturally outgoing and extroverted, his aspirations were always to work behind the scenes. However, the size and budget of his operation dictated otherwise. He was the pinch hitter for every head cold or case of cold feet, for every bout of test anxiety or unexpected visit from friends or family. Then, Kevin Casperin self-destructed.

Kevin was supposed to be the delivery instrument for one of Chris's greatest brainstorms. While watching "Good Morning America" one morning, Chris had an epiphany: Why not produce a local version of the popular format right on campus? He recruited Kevin to co-host "Good Morning Nadowa." Casperin had effectively anchored the evening news broadcast so Chris assumed he'd be perfect for the new show. While Kevin was a natural at reading off the teleprompter, however, in Chris's estimation he lacked the creativity and personality to connect with his audience in the more informal setting. The show was instantly popular, but Kevin's stutters, stammers, and stalls grated on Chris until he finally decided to unseat Kevin and fill in himself until he could find a suitable replacement.

That's when the magic happened.

Chris's personality broke through the barriers of the radio speaker and television screen and projected itself directly into people's lives. With his easygoing manner and quick wit, he soon became the voice on the shelf in the barbershop, the companion to lonely souls in the rest homes, the friend over coffee at breakfast tables, and at the lunch counter at the Chief's Diner. The programming added to the show's popularity. Chris made certain to address news of national interest. He encouraged the administration to invite speakers to the campus whose opinions were front-page news and then contacted the presenters to appear on the show before or after their speaking engagement. Chris became a superstar and the nemesis of Kevin Casperin, who was convinced that he'd been set up for failure in order for Chris to forward his own career. Kevin was not alone in that assessment.

During the service, people from a wide spectrum of backgrounds gave testimonials of both Chris and Drew, but the bulk of the praise went to Chris. His mother, Gail, was overwhelmed. She knew Chris was a strong, self-confident individual but never imagined the depth of the impact he would have on the lives of so many. She cried through most of the service, at first for the loss of her son, then with swells of pride at the man he had become and the way he had used the time he had. Several rows behind her Kevin Casperin sat rigidly, clenching and unclenching his fists.

During the reception that took place in the auditorium lobby, Tess and Katie helped serve beverages and pastries. Tess was handing out coffee when Gene brought Carl and Gail to meet her. Gail didn't need to say anything. She looked into Tess's eyes, saw the reflection of the lights glistening in their wetness, and took Tess into her arms. The two women stood in silent embrace, gently swaying back and forth and absorbing each other's shudders.

Eventually the crowd thinned and the bereaved parents went outside. As arranged, Bert was there to meet them. He parked his GTO in front of their car. As the two men transferred the contents, Bert said, "Mr. Matthews, I just wanted you to know what an honor it was to have known Chris." It was an overstatement, but under the circumstances, it seemed justified.

Carl answered, "Thank you Professor. You probably knew him better than I did. And it's Danford actually."

"I'm sorry?"

"My last name, it's Danford. It's a lot to go into so I won't bore you with the details."

As Carl and Gail drove away, Tess watched from inside the lobby. Then Tess turned her thoughts to what she had not shared with them, that she had not flown home as planned, that Chris had picked her up in Indiana and driven her back instead, and that they drove to Atlantic City, got a room on the boardwalk, and made love until dawn. Then she reached up and fingered the chain around her neck. As it twisted and twirled, the diamond ring shown at the edge of her blouse. Tess stared at it and recalled how Chris had given it to her the next morning when he asked her to marry him.

Outside, Bert placed his hand in his coat pocket and retrieved his vibrating cell phone.

"Hello, Hank. Yeah, have you finished? What do you mean not exactly? I know—I know. I'm sorry. I just finished saying goodbye to Chris's parents. I guess my nerves are shot. Can you at least show me what you have? Great. Thanks. I'm on my way."

Then Bert considered the piece of information he had not shared with Chris's parents: that he had removed and replaced the hard drive from their son's computer.

30

Modern forecasting is based upon data, instrumentation and, increasingly, on powerful computer programs. An individual can still make useful predictions regarding weather patterns and changes, but only if he or she knows what to look for and how to accurately interpret it.

Hank Nervesky, the head of Nadowa's computer sciences department, was building his own computers while his friends were still playing with G. I. Joes. He was also a longtime friend of Bert Myers. Bert's recommendation was the deciding factor in the college's decision to hire Hank, so when Bert asked for help hacking into Chris's hard drive, Hank was eager to oblige. Since it was Sunday, Hank had no classes. He also had no social life to speak of, so while Bert was at the service, Hank was digging for data.

"Please tell me you found the report," said Bert.

"Like I told you on the phone, Bertie, yes, and no." Hank spoke in a mix of Polish accent and Brooklyn slang. "Getting at the file was easy, getting into it wasn't."

"I don't understand."

"I put the hard drive in another computer and used its operating system to boot up. That way I could navigate directly to the root directory and this is what I found."

Bert looked at the file structure displayed on the screen. He scrolled through the files until he came upon one titled "Pink Room." "That's got to be it!"

"Yeah, from what you told me that's what I figured too, but then I opened it, and this is what I got." Hank clicked on the file. A moment later, the screen filled with technical gibberish.

"What the hell is this?" Bert shouted.

"Whoa, you've got to calm down, Bertie, or you're going to give yourself a stroke. This is what you get when you encrypt a file."

"Well, don't you have special programs to decipher it?"

"I do, and I've tried them all, but this kid really knew what he was doing."

"That's impossible. Chris was a communications major. He was only interested in what a computer could do for him. He didn't have the faintest idea of what made them work."

"Well, somebody sure did."

"Drew! I'll bet Chris got Drew Richardson to install an encryption program for him."

"Drew?" Hank reflected on the possibility for a moment. "Well, if Drew Richardson installed something on this computer, we've got a real problem."

"Was he that good?"

"Bertie, I've been teaching this stuff for as long as I can remember, and in all that time I've never met anyone who could program as fast or as well as that Richardson kid. If he installed something to keep you out of this kid's business, then we're going to need more resources than I've got here to crack it."

"Is there anyone who could?"

"The FBI's got some pretty good stuff. A few of my past students work at the bureau. They might be willing to help, but we'd need one hell of an excuse to get them involved. Just how important is this?"

While the information was vital to Bert, he reasoned that it probably wasn't going to have much significance to law enforcement. Anyway, how would he explain that the report was about the room of a kid that died eighteen years ago and who some of his students believed just might be able to control the weather from the grave?

"Thanks, Hank, but I don't think we should go that far, at least not just yet."

"Well, I'll check with a few of my buddies to see if they have anything better, but I wouldn't get my hopes up if I were you."

Bert reached into his coat pocket and retrieved Chris's notebook, the last item he had withheld from Carl and Gail Matthews. He leafed through the pages and thought about his next steps. "Thanks for your help Hank, but I think for now I'll try a different approach."

What was left of the team resumed work after classes the following Monday. Each member had a different reason for continuing. Bert desperately needed to resolve, at least in his own mind, the link between his indiscretion and the loss of his students and friends. While he logically concluded that it was just coincidence, emotionally he couldn't disconnect his feeling of guilt from the event. He needed proof that he wasn't responsible for Chris and Drew's deaths.

For Tess, the work kept her connected to Chris. The emptiness of his room pained her each time she walked past and, at her request, the door remained closed. However, Chris was still present in the work and that presence comforted her, so she dove back into the research.

Katie remained philosophical. Chris and Drew had put the last years of their lives into the project and it was important to her that their efforts were not wasted. Chris had confided in her about the altercation between Tess and her father at the hospital, but Katie kept that to herself. She remained largely unaware of the deeper motivations that drove her. She still awoke each night soaked with sweat, from a fear she could not face, a dream she could not remember.

Neither Katie nor Bert gave any indication to Tess of what had transpired between them, so when Evelyn arrived that evening, Tess was unprepared for the exchange that followed.

"So this is Amanda's room," Evelyn said as she stood in the doorway. Her statement was not sarcastic. Rather it was reflective and carried with it the kind of respect given to a shrine or house of worship.

"Pull up a seat and join us, Evie," Bert pointed to an empty spot on the rug. Evelyn took her place and glanced at the papers strewed across the floor. "We've been reviewing the data generated around the time of Chris's and Drew's… around the time of the accident," Bert said.

"Are you finding what you hoped for?" she asked.

"The data verified the presence of the waterspout," said Tess. "Chris and Drew had installed solar-powered monitors on the north side of the pond shortly before the accident. The readings are consistent with the formation of a funnel."

Bert added, "And the timing of the funnel corresponds almost to the minute with the collapse of the room environment."

"We still haven't uncovered the triggering mechanism for the storm," said Katie. "There were no fronts, low pressure systems, or other anomalies that would account for that kind of phenomenon."

"Any theories?" Evelyn asked the group in general.

Bert shuffled uncomfortably and stuttered at a response, but Katie spoke first, "We're still generating possible scenarios but haven't come up with anything plausible yet." From Katie's perspective, the answer was an honest one. She did not ascribe to Bert's fear that their interaction was connected to the accident. She didn't believe Amanda was capable of viciousness. There had to be a better explanation, but they hadn't found it yet.

From Bert's perspective, however, the only true answer amounted to a confession. Again, he started to formulate a response, but Evelyn intervened.

"Bert, why did you take my Volvo this morning instead of your GTO?"

"Did you forget? I'm supposed to drop it off for service tonight. I'll call Lenny and see if he can leave the keys in a loaner for me. Then it won't matter when I get there."

"No need. I can drop it off on my way back from my mother's house."

As they exchanged keys, Evelyn noticed the faraway look in Tess's face. "I gather you and Chris loved each other very much."

Tess smiled in appreciation of Evelyn's sensitivity and nodded in agreement. "We had just gotten engaged." Evelyn could see that the news came as a surprise to Bert and Katie.

"I'm so sorry." Evelyn lightly stroked Tess's arm as she talked and then turned her attention to Katie. "I understand this room has a calming effect on people."

"That's the word we've all used to describe it," Katie answered.

While she spoke, Bert could see something in Evelyn's expression, something foreign to any of the other occupants.

"Are you all right, Evie? You look strained?"

"You don't feel it, do you, Bert?" she asked.

"That feeling of calmness? Of course I do. It affects everyone in the room."

"Not everyone, Bert. I definitely feel something, but calmness is the last word I would use to describe it." Evelyn turned back to Katie, "Bert tells me that it is impossible for people to lie in this room."

Katie thought about what Tess had told them about her dad's being a dead man. While people might not be able to lie outright, it was apparent that they could still hold different interpretations of the truth, but this was not the time to get into that discussion. "That's been our experience," she answered.

Evelyn paused and then looked directly into Katie's eyes, "I love my husband very much, Katie. Are you sleeping with him?"

Bert stopped breathing. Tess's eyes opened the size of dinner plates. Katie simply smiled.

"No, Evelyn, I'm not. I offered to, but he turned me down because he said it would hurt you, and he couldn't do that to you."

"I see," Evelyn leaned back against the wall and exhaled deeply. "Thank you Katie."

This was the second time Evelyn had laid a trap for Katie. Katie's mother had taught her early on: *Fool me once, your fault;*

fool me twice, mine. This time she was ready.

"But," Katie looked directly at Bert and then back to Evelyn, "that was *before* he told me he was married." Tess shook her head to make certain she wasn't dreaming.

Katie's meaning was not lost on Evelyn. She waited a moment, looked directly at Bert, and then back to Katie, "And how long ago was that?"

"A little more than a month," said Katie. Evelyn returned her gaze to Bert. Even in Amanda's room, she could see the rest of the answer in his face.

She turned back to Katie, "You're every bit as remarkable as Bert said you were. Thank you, Katie." Tess fell back against the wall in exhaustion.

"Bert," Evelyn asked as she rose up to stand, "can I speak to you outside for a moment?" Bert swallowed hard and followed his wife out into the research room.

"You've got a lot of explaining to do," Evelyn said as soon as they exited.

"I know I do, Evelyn." Bert was somewhat relieved that the truth, or at least that part of it, was finally out. "But you have to know that I really do love you and I..."

"You can try to explain yourself later. What you need to know right now is that you may be a genius when it comes to physics, but there's more going on here than you could possibly imagine."

"Evelyn, I've been working here for over a year now. You've been in the room for all of ten minutes! Where do you come off saying something like that?"

"Because, Bert," Evelyn's eyes started to water as her voice broke, "no one else here has lost a baby."

Bert's anger welled into rage. "What the hell are you talking about? You don't think I lost Stephen, too! You don't think I loved him every bit as much as you did?"

Evelyn could see the hurt in her husband's eyes. As she rubbed her hand against his face, she could feel the wetness on his cheek. "I'm sorry Bert, that's not the way I meant it. I know you loved him just as much as I did. You would have made a wonderful father." Evelyn took in a breath to regain her composure. "But Stephen was a physical part of me. We shared the same space, the same food. If I heard a loud noise, we both jumped. When you go into Amanda's room, you feel the peace and calm of a newborn's world. I felt some of that, too. But you're not feeling the rest of it, the fear, the pain, the anger hidden just beneath the surface. And the frustration, Bert—the aggravation that comes from screaming but not being heard. Please Bert," she squeezed his arm as hard as she could, "you and your students have to stop this before it goes too far. You've got to leave it alone."

Bert thought about the room and its environment, about the December temperature shift less than three months away, about the research and the storms, about Chris and Drew out on the pond and the waterspout that was aiming for them, and the thousands of other things he didn't understand. Then he thought about how important it was that someone, somehow finally understand, and he knew what he had to do. He would continue. There was no doubt about that. He would share Evelyn's concerns with Tess and Katie. They had a right to know. However, he was equally certain of what their decision would be.

"I'm sorry, Evelyn, but I can't stop now. We're just now scratching the surface. If you fully understood how important this is to us, to everyone who could benefit from it, for Chris and Drew, even for Amanda, you wouldn't be asking me to stop."

"You're not hearing me, Bert," Evelyn loosened her grip on Bert's arm. "I think it's Amanda you need to fear."

Evelyn kissed her husband, softly at first, then more passionately. As she moved her face away from his, Bert could see the tears streaming down her face.

"I need to go." Evelyn walked down the stairs, out of the house, and into the safety of the unpredictable, chaotic, violent world outside.

31

The National Weather Service labels winter storms the 'Deceptive Killers,' because most deaths are not directly related to the storm. About 70% of the deaths associated with ice and snow occur in automobiles.

Bert stayed in the research room after Evelyn left. He ran diagnostic checks on the system, including the monitors in Amanda's room and the inputs from the remote monitoring stations. With the winter solstice only weeks away, he wanted to ensure that everything was working perfectly. Tess and Katie emerged from Amanda's room.

"Katie and I are ready to call it a day," said Tess. "Maybe you should too."

Bert looked down at his watch, "Maybe you're right. If I leave right now I can probably catch the monster matinee at the campus cinema and still be home in time for dinner." All of them chuckled. It felt good for Bert to laugh. It had been a long time since he had.

As they made their way to the door, something caught Katie's eye. It was an unusually quick change on one of the monitors. Bert noticed Katie's sudden stop, "What is it?"

"Look at the monitor," Katie pointed to the screen. Where moments earlier the screen displayed only clear skis and gentle breezes, it was now filling with clouds and clusters of rain. "That's the area of Stony Clove Notch."

"Isn't that near Phoenicia?"

"Sort of. Phoenicia is at the southern tip of 214."

"It's also where Evelyn's mother lives." Bert dialed Evelyn's cell phone. As he did, the clouds on the display began spiraling. Lightening strikes appeared, at first sporadically, then more frequently. "Come on, Evie," Bert pleaded into the phone, "pick up."

The readouts for the house monitors changed. The wind speed picked up while the temperature and barometric pressure started dropping. The same thing was happening at Stony Clove Notch. Outside the windows of the research room, the sky blackened as it filled with swirling storm clouds.

Katie started shaking uncontrollably, "Oh my God, it's happening again."

Tess wrapped her arm around her friend, "It'll be all right, Katie. Everything's going to be fine." For a moment, Katie thought she was in Steve Nylen's arms again, hearing him saying, "They'll be all right Katie," and she primed herself to lash out and scream. Then Tess's soft, soothing voice floated into Katie's consciousness, "It'll be all right, Katie. Everything's going to be fine." Tess's hand softly stroked Katie's arm as she caressed Katie's head. To Katie, it felt like her mother's embrace, and she felt herself calming, focusing, and returning to the present, a present in which Bert was trying desperately to save his wife.

"Hello, hello!" Bert yelled into the phone. Evelyn picked up.

"Evie, where are you?" Bert was almost shouting.

"Is everything all right, Bert?" she asked. "You sound panicked."

Bert took a deep breath, "I'm fine Evelyn." He calmed himself as best he could. He didn't want to alarm his wife needlessly. "I was just wondering if you were still at your mother's."

"I'm on my way back now. I was just going to call you. It's a good thing this car is going into the shop. Your brakes need adjustment; they're very spongy. It's bad enough driving around in this kind of weather with good brakes."

"What kind of weather Evelyn?"

"It's really getting bad out here, dark and windy, and it's just starting to rain."

While Bert and Evelyn talked, Katie regained her

composure and remembered Drew's program. She smiled appreciatively at Tess, then turned on the monitor, and handed Bert a note: *What's Evelyn's cell phone number?*

Bert wrote down the number and Tess typed it into the program. The Earth rotated on the screen and the image zoomed in. When it finished, it showed a red dot representing Evelyn's car. She was just north of the top of the Stony Clove Notch on a sliver of a road that barely etched its way between Hunter and Plateau mountains.

Evelyn had already passed Devil's Tombstone state campground. She was now on the steep downward slope of the mountain, the end of a range known to locals as the Devil's Path. Early settlers described Stony Clove as a terrifying place to be in a storm, where thunder and lightening tossed back and forth from one mountain to the other, turning the narrow pass into "the very gates of hell." As the team looked at the screen, the conclusion was unmistakable. Evelyn was at the center of the storm they were tracking.

Tess pointed her finger to the temperature reading on the storm screen. Stony Clove Notch was showing 50 degrees and clear only moments earlier. Now it was 28 degrees, with heavy precipitation. Katie turned to Bert, "Ice!"

"Evie," Bert said, "listen carefully. You need to pull over and stop the car."

There was a pause, "What's wrong, Bert?"

"Probably nothing, but you need to stop the car right away… please."

Another pause, "All right, Bert, but I don't like the sound of this. I see an overlook up ahead. I'll pull in there."

Bert waited. When Evelyn's spoke again, her voice was thick with panic.

"Bert," she sounded far away. Bert realized she must have put the speaker on and tossed the cell phone onto the seat. "Bert, the brakes aren't working. The car's not slowing down!"

Tess picked up the phone and dialed 911.

"Are you in the overlook, Evelyn?" It was a stupid question.

Of course she wasn't. Bert couldn't think straight.

"No. No. I was going too fast."

Bert started sweating profusely. His mind raced. "Evelyn, downshift into second gear!"

"I'm scared, Bert. What if I lose control?"

"You've got to try, Evie. It'll slow you down."

"It's not working!"

"Force it, Evie!"

There was a clunking sound, then, "It worked, but I'm still going too fast. Oh God, there's a switchback coming up."

"Just ease into it Evie," Bert tried to control the panic in his own voice. "Don't try to take it too sharp."

Evelyn screamed. Then there was silence.

"Evie… Evie!" Bert couldn't think of anything else to say.

"Oh God, oh God Bert, I'm so scared," Evelyn was crying but she had made it through.

Katie pressed on Bert's shoulder and pointed at the screen of Drew's GPS monitor. Bert recognized it too.

"Evie, listen. There's a runaway truck ramp coming up on your right. You need to steer the car onto that ramp."

"I don't see it. I can't Bert. The car's speeding up again. I'm going too fast. I'm going to roll over, or crash or…" Bert looked at the next switchback on the screen. It was an outside hairpin turn. If Evelyn didn't stop before it, she was going fly off the side of the mountain and nothing would prevent it.

"Listen to me, Evie. You've got to. Do you understand? There's no choice. You have to do it."

"Oh God Ber-" Evelyn's signal was breaking up "I'm so… just can't-" The only other noise was the intermittent sound of Evelyn's screaming. Then there was silence.

"Evie, Evie!" Bert screamed into the phone, but it was no use. Her phone's signal was gone. Bert looked at Drew's screen as the red dot flickered, faded, and then disappeared. Bert collapsed onto the stool. He bent over the table, put his head in his hands, and cried. Tess and Katie rested their hands on Bert's shoulders as tears streamed down their faces. Suddenly, Bert shot up. His eyes blazed with fury. His angry expression was etched in steel. Tess and Katie stepped away as Bert rushed to the tool cabinet, withdrew a crowbar, and started toward Amanda's room.

Katie stepped in front of him, "Think Bert," she pleaded. "Amanda wouldn't do this, she couldn't." Katie was certain it was true, but didn't know how or why.

"Get the hell out of my way!" The crazed face in front of Katie didn't belong to Bert. She feared that if she didn't move, he might use the crowbar on her. Katie reluctantly stepped aside.

As he reached the door, Bert's cell phone rang. He froze. Then it rang again. Bert dropped the crowbar and reached for the phone.

"Evelyn?"

"Yes, Bert." He could tell she was crying.

"Thank God. Are you all right? Are you hurt?"

"I'm fine, but I'm afraid your car is pretty banged up."

"To hell with the car. Where are you?"

"On that truck ramp you told me about. How did you know it would be there?

"Drew Richardson," he answered. "I think Drew just saved your life." There was no reply. "I'll explain it when I get there. I'm on my way." Bert rushed out the door.

Tess tapped Katie on the shoulder, "Look," and pointed out the window. The storm was gone. Katie scanned the monitors. There were no signs of severe weather anywhere. The sound of Katie's text message alert interrupted their concentration. Katie opened the phone and stared in disbelief.

HI K T CAT
R U NAKED?

32

A great deal of information can be gathered through direct observation with little or no instrumentation (e.g., Upper air wind speed and direction can be determined from cloud shape and/or movement, and plane contrails indicate moisture in the upper troposphere). Careful observations taken over a sufficient period can yield a useful and fairly accurate local forecast.

Katie stared at the number; it was from Chris's cell phone.

"Write him back," Tess squeezed Katie's arm so hard it almost welted.

Katie winced but Tess ignored it. "Now!" she insisted.

Katie typed,

CHRIS WHERE R U? EVERYONE THINKS U R DEAD

The screen remained blank. Tess yanked the phone from Katie's hands and typed,

CHRIS, ITS TESS. R U HURT? TELL US WHERE U R AND WE'LL GET U

Still no response.

PLEASE CHRIS. I NEED U

There was a long pause, then one final message:

SORRY, NO CAN DO. C U L8R
C

Tess dialed Chris's number and hit the call button, but the phone just rang. Tess hung up and tried repeatedly without success. Then Katie turned to Tess, "Wait a second, there's something we can do." Katie ran to Drew's cell phone GPS system and typed in Chris's number. The two women stared intently as the image of the Earth rotated, then zoomed in on the United States, the northeast, New York, and the Nadowa campus. As it zoomed in further, Katie and Tess went from elation to shock. When the program stopped zooming in, its crosshairs rested directly above Amanda's Room.

Bert returned to the house the next day. Evelyn was recuperating at home. She was badly shaken, but not seriously hurt. Bert drove up in his GTO. He planned to put it up for the winter, but it looked like the Volvo's repairs might take a while.

When Bert shared Evelyn's concerns with Tess and Katie, as he anticipated, neither wanted to quit. The freak storm and Evelyn's near fatal car trip only strengthened their resolve. Then they told Bert about the message from Chris and the strange results from Drew's program. They tried calling Chris for the remainder of the day and well into the next morning without success. None of them could understand why he was being so evasive. It didn't make sense. Bert suggested that since Chris had contacted them once he would do it again. They would just have to be patient and wait for the next message.

"Till then," Bert said, "I suggest we follow up on Chris's notebook." They opened the book and tried to make sense of the entries.

"P - 618 BMP, I know I've seen that before," Bert said. "I just can't place where."

The three of them reviewed the notes and identified priority items for follow-up. Friday Tess and Katie would go to Albany to seek out Doctor Charles Miller. At the same time, Bert would go to the Fishkill Correctional Institution.

But first, Bert suggested they report Chris's message to the campus police. "I don't know if there's anything illegal about disappearing, but it seems they should at least be informed." Katie concurred. Tess reluctantly agreed.

Bert and Katie met with Captain Davis on Thursday afternoon, right after Bert's last class. Davis hadn't fully closed the door to his office before Katie asked the first question. "I'm curious, Captain. The nameplate on your door says Captain C. E. Davis but you introduced yourself as Ed."

"Edward's my middle name," Davis answered. "After growing up as 'Charlie,' I guess you could say I wasn't thrilled with my given name, so at some point I just switched to Ed. Now, what can I do for you folks?"

Bert had missed the nameplate on the door. He wondered if Nadowa Campus Police Captain Ed Davis and Hudson Valley Police Officer Charles Davis were one and the same person. That would mean Chris might have interviewed Davis only weeks before the accident. If he had, it would go a long way toward explaining Davis's interrogation of Bert at the pond. However, Davis hadn't said anything about knowing Chris, or about the house and its history. Even before Bert had fully considered the possibility, Katie started to explore it.

"We're conducting research on the history of 34 Lakota Drive and Chris Matthews..."

"Katie," Bert interrupted her, "let's not bore the captain with old news. Why don't you just show him your cell phone?" Bert's interference startled Katie, but she had worked with him long enough to trust his instincts. She opened her phone and handed it to Davis.

"What am I looking at here?" Davis asked while peering at the screen:

HI K T CAT
R U NAKED?
C

"Are you reporting some sort of sexual harassment?"

"It's from Chris Matthews," Katie said, "yesterday."

"You mean it's a hoax."

"I don't think so," said Katie. "The C is the way Chris signed his texts. That phrase was something that only he used. I never told anyone else about it."

"That's a bit of a stretch, don't you think?" Davis moved his gaze from Katie to Bert.

"The number is from Chris's cell phone," said Bert. "He had it with him the day he disappeared."

"Then where's he been all this time, and why all the secrecy?"

"We have no idea," said Bert. "That's why we came to you. I was also thinking about contacting his parents."

"Hell, no!" Davis ordered. "If this turns out to be a prank it could devastate them." Davis wrote down the cell phone number. "Give me a day or two to coordinate with the local PD and make some arrangements. In the meantime if you hear from him again, get back to me immediately."

Bert and Katie agreed to the plan. As they readied to leave, the vibrator went off on Bert's cell phone. "Excuse me," he apologized, "this is important."

While Katie and Captain Davis finished, Bert spoke into the phone, quietly at first then louder as his anxiety grew.

"Are you certain? But how? Can I drive it again? I see… All right, I'll be right over."

Bert's face was ashen. He swallowed hard before he spoke, "That was Lenny, my auto mechanic. He was supposed to have my car ready for pickup today. He's convinced that someone rigged my brakes to fail."

"Call him back right now," instructed Davis. "Tell him not to touch a thing. I'm coming with you."

Less than an hour later, Bert, his mechanic, and Ed Davis were all standing under Bert's Volvo at the A-Plus Service Station.

"What do you see?" Bert asked as Davis examined the undercarriage of the Volvo.

"Take a look," Davis was shining the flashlight at the suspect part, "check out this cut."

Bert looked at a slice in the liquid-soaked hose entering the wheel housing. "Couldn't that just be from fatigue?"

"Not this, the edges are too long and ragged. This line was intentionally cut. Besides," Davis flashed his light on another similar looking hose, "you wouldn't normally see two brake lines rupture at exactly the same time." Bert started feeling lightheaded. Davis moved to another wheel, "And then there's this," he shined his light at a third hose. It looked to Bert like a wad of green gum covered the gash.

"Whoever did this was planning on someone hitting the brakes hard when they started to go, like you might do on a mountain road. If your wife were driving around town when the brakes let go she might have gotten away with a fender bender or nothing at all, and we'd be almost certain to find evidence of tampering. But, if she'd have gone off a cliff in that storm, I doubt anyone would have taken note of the brake lines at all; that is, if there were much of the car left to examine. How many people knew your wife would be driving it on that road that afternoon?"

"No one, Evelyn wasn't even supposed to be driving it that day. She has her Ford. I was supposed to bring the Volvo in for service so I could start driving it again, and put my GTO away for the winter. When I forgot, she offered to bring it in for me."

Davis addressed the mechanic, "Don't touch another thing on the car. The guys from the crime lab will be down later." Then he returned his attention to Bert, "And Professor, you'll need to visit the police station. They'll have plenty of questions for you. This is out of my jurisdiction now. At this point, it's an attempted murder investigation."

33

I came into a place void of all light, which bellows like the sea in tempest, when it is combated by warring winds.

Dante's Divine Comedy - The Inferno

It took several calls for Bert to secure an appointment with Warden Frank Capshaw. The warden's secretary insisted the meeting take place at 11:00 a.m. Bert downloaded information on Fishkill and studied it over hash and eggs at Koch's restaurant in Leeds. As he sipped his black coffee, Bert delved into the institution's history.

Fishkill Correctional Institution began in 1886 as the *Asylum for Insane Criminals*. The following year it was renamed Matteawan State Hospital, where doctors prescribed a program of "moral treatment." The institution gradually became known as "the madhouse atop Asylum Road."

Eventually "newer" treatments were introduced. By 1949, they included electric and insulin shock therapy and lobotomies. Chronically ill patients were held until the warden deemed them fit to leave. Inmates committed for relatively minor infractions were sometimes confined for thirty to forty years. A series of court cases ended the practice, and, after 1972, Matteawan held convicted patients only.

In its latest configuration, Fishkill was a medium security facility with a work release program, a maximum security cellblock, and a regional medical unit. The more Bert read about Fishkill, the less he understood what possible connection it could have to 34 Lakota Drive.

After breakfast, Bert took the New York State Thruway south to Newburg where he picked up route 84 eastbound. While he enjoyed driving the GTO, he was growing increasingly weary of possible winter weather. In addition to the damaging effects of road, sand, and salt on its meticulous paint finish, the GTO's traction on icy roads was no match for the Volvo, which was still at the crime lab, and he wasn't sure for how long.

As Bert crossed the Newburg Bridge, he gazed out over the Hudson and wondered if Drew's body had floated past on its way to Long Island Sound. Would it ever be found? And what had happened to Chris to send him into hiding? Bert was so lost in thought that he forgot his destination until he crested a mound, and the sight of the institution jarred him back to reality. The term Correctional Institution reflected the facility's last iteration, a period when people believed that inmates could be counseled back into law-abiding behavior. To most of the locals, however, it was simply "The Prison." The expansive brick buildings and chain-link fences covered the pastoral landscape like a dried scab over an open wound.

Bert parked in the designated lot and walked toward the central administration building; a gothic fortress, buttressed by towers, and fitted within a walled city. The barbed steel bands that topped the chain-link fencing slashed at the passing breezes. Entering through the main gate, reminded Bert of Dante's voyage into hell: *All hope abandon, ye who enter here.*

Bert sat on the hard wooden bench outside of the warden's office, as uncomfortable mentally as he was physically. He thought about how far afield he was from the environments he knew and understood. To him, the complexities of the cosmos paled in comparison to those of the abnormal human psyche.

"Professor Myers," Bert looked up to the outstretched hand above him; it was the size of a Thanksgiving ham. He rose from his seat while extending his own hand, which quickly disappeared inside the warden's. He was grateful Capshaw didn't emphasize a tight grip.

Bert noted the similarities between Capshaw's office and John Thompson's. Both contained massive executive desks facing miniature visitor chairs, Capshaw's desk was larger and his visitor's chair smaller. Both featured photographs of the occupants with prominent political figures, Capshaw's had more. Both displayed degrees and certificates, Capshaw's had less. And both offices had large windows through which the CEO could survey his domain. Thompson's looked out on a verdant landscape stretching into the serene campus courtyard. Capshaw's looked out on the blacktop exercise yard encased in galvanized fencing and stainless steel razor wire. Each of the offices seemed intentionally designed to make visitors feel small and powerless. In that regard, Capshaw's succeeded magnificently.

"My secretary said you wanted to follow up on my interview with Christopher Matthews," said the warden.

"Yes, that's right."

"Nice kid, that Matthews. I get interviewed a lot. He's got a better style than most. How's he doing?"

"I'm afraid he's missing."

"Really? What happened?"

"A boating accident." Bert waited for the follow-up questions that inevitably came after that kind of statement.

"That's too bad. Well, how can I help you Professor?" Capshaw brushed aside the news of Chris's disappearance as easily as he would bread crumbs from the dining room table. It was a chilling reminder of the kind of world Capshaw inhabited, and Bert was grateful not to be a part of it.

"Actually, anything you can share about your conversation with Chris would be helpful."

The warden frowned, folded his arms, and said nothing. Bert realized that a healthy level of suspicion was probably necessary for survival in Capshaw's world. "I'm sorry. I should explain. Chris was doing some critically important research and was scheduled to share his findings the day he disappeared. He had the report on him at the time of the accident, and as far as we can determine there are no other copies. Other team members are following up on other aspects of his research." Capshaw's face softened. Bert decided to continue.

"Chris did leave a notebook behind outlining some of his interviews. Two names were listed under yours, a Commander Miller and Chief Warrant Officer Baker at the U.S. Naval Correctional Center in Seattle. Do you know them?"

"Not personally, but I certainly know of them."

"Chris also included a number reference: P-618 BMP."

"That makes sense," Capshaw pressed the intercom for his secretary. "Veronica, look up the file on the interview with Christopher Matthews and run off a copy of the Schauss article for Professor Myers."

Capshaw returned to Bert, "P-618 refers to a paint mixture for a shade of pink Schauss was experimenting with. He was a researcher in the state of Washington and he was convinced that this one particular shade of pink had a significant, measurable effect on people's behavior, especially aggressive behavior. He tried to convince administrators to let him do a study in their jails and prisons. Can you imagine asking a warden to let you paint his jail pink? They practically laughed him out of the state. But he was also teaching at the time for Washington's Justice Training Commission. I guess that's where Miller and Baker heard about his idea and decided to conduct a little experiment of their own. They painted one of their admission cells with it. Schauss was so impressed he named his color after them - BMP - Baker-Miller Pink."

Bert thought back to the can of paint Ted Reggerio had shown him at the house. At the same time, the warden's secretary returned with the report: "The Physiological Effect of Color on the Suppression of Human Aggression: Research on Baker-Miller Pink."

"Does it really work?" Bert asked.

"That's why I told Veronica to schedule our meeting for eleven. We have some admissions coming in from the city—street thugs trying to work their way up in the Brooklyn drug gangs. For them going to prison is like earning a college degree. Come with me."

Capshaw led Bert down a long yellow cinder block hallway.

It looked to be the main corridor into the prison. All around him, Bert heard the clanging of gates opening and closing. The sound reverberated off the concrete. Men dressed in prison uniforms avoided eye contact with the warden while staring at Bert. At last, they came to an iron gate where a guard granted them egress. Bert followed Capshaw down a narrow hallway into a small, vacant room. Its only features were the two windows along the far wall, with a small speaker and intercom switch below each one. Capshaw closed the door and turned off the overhead lights. Bert could just make out Capshaw's outline from the light spilling in through the window glass.

"These are one-way mirrors," Capshaw explained. "We can see out, but they can't see us. The room to the left is our admissions area. The barred one to the right is the holding pen where the inmates wait until we call for them.

Bert immediately noticed the color of the admission room. The walls and ceiling gave off that same pink glow as Amanda's room. The floor and metal furniture were a drab gray. Capshaw pressed one of the two intercom buttons. "All right Baxter, send them in." Moments later two guards appeared with three men in street clothes. The prisoners looked to be in their mid-twenties. The first was short, slight and looked dazed. Bert couldn't tell if he was high on drugs or terrified. The second man was the biggest, a full head higher than the other two, in jeans and a black T-shirt. His skin was a tattoo artist's billboard. His right upper arm displayed the grim reaper and the words *Life Sucks; Then You Die.* The final man was in constant motion, shifting weight from one foot to the other, darting his eyes around the room as his hands twitched, like a boxer waiting for the bell.

One of the officers unlocked the barred gate. "All right, gentlemen, wait here until that door opens." The officer pointed to the door separating the pen from the other room. "The admissions officer will call your name." The first two men swaggered into the room but the boxer held his ground.

"Move in, Vanders," the second officer said. "We haven't

got all day." Bert could just make out the name *Baxter* on the officer's uniform. Vanders started to move forward and then took a quick step back into Baxter's outstretched hand. The inmate whipped around and faced the officer.

"Get your fucking hands off me, pig. I ain't your motherfucking bitch." In his secure room, Bert swallowed hard but the officers didn't flinch. Years of training and experience triggered their automatic responses. The two officers closed ranks in front of the unruly prisoner. A third officer positioned outside of the bars lifted his two-way radio, primed to call for backup.

The face on the formerly placid Officer Baxter turned to stone as he looked directly into the eyes of his challenger, "You've got one second to move, or we'll move you."

Vanders entered the room and turned as the gate slammed behind him. "Fuck you, bitches."

Warden Capshaw leaned over to Bert. "Under normal circumstances, Vanders would be headed for the hole right now but the officers are soft peddling because of our demonstration."

As the officers left the area, Vanders addressed the other inmates. "Did you see the look on that pussy's face? He was shitting his pants. He knew if he touched me again I was gonna fuck him up."

"Didn't fucking look that way from here," the tattooed man said. "Looked like you crawled in on all fours before they could put you in a world of hurt."

In a flash, the boxer was on him. He got off three rapid punches before the other man even moved. The last was an elbow to the nose.

Tattoo man was bruised, bleeding, and in shock. "Back off, man. Get the fuck off me!"

Bert didn't even notice the door open, but as soon as the last blow landed, the two officers had Vanders in their grip.

"That's it, Vanders," Officer Baxter said. "You've overstayed your welcome." He had Vanders' arm twisted upside down with his palm facing upwards in Baxter's hand. His other hand was pressing down on Vanders' elbow. From the pained expression on Vanders' face, the grip was effective. The other officer unlocked the door to the admissions room, and Baxter shoved Vanders through. Once inside, the officers slammed the door behind them, cutting them off from the other inmates. The smallest prisoner was crouched up in the corner rocking back and forth. Bert was now convinced the expression on his face was one of panic. Tattoo man sat wiping the blood from his nose with his T-shirt. Inside the admission room, the two officers pushed Vanders down onto a metal bench against a table.

"Cool your heels, Vanders," Officer Baxter said. He and the other officer exited the opposite door.

Vanders shot up from the seat and shouted at the closed door, "You fucking pussies. You think you're hot shit with your fucking Kung Fu cause you got me from behind. Try that when I'm looking, and I'll knock your motherfucking lights out." Bert wished there were a seat in the room. He was feeling light-headed and starting to sweat.

Capshaw leaned over again. "Standard operating procedures would have been to bring Vanders straight to segregation, but I wanted you to see this." Bert continued to watch. Vanders paced back and forth furiously. He tried to lift the benches and table but everything was bolted to the floor. Then the change became evident. Vanders slowed his pacing, slightly at first, then significantly. Within a couple of minutes, he had stopped shouting. For the next several minutes, he murmured expletives to himself and periodically hammered at the walls and furniture with his bare fists. Then the aggressive behavior stopped completely.

"This shit sucks." With that, Vanders sat down on the floor. Ten minutes after being confined, Vanders lay quietly on his back staring up at the pink ceiling. The warden pressed the other intercom button.

"All right, Officer Driscoll, you can process him." Seconds

later, Driscoll entered the admissions room, crossed over to the table, and opened a folder filled with forms.

"Mr. Vanders, please have a seat." Without saying a word, Vanders approached the table and sat down. Driscoll pulled out a pen, "Your full name is Eric Vanders?" he asked.

"Eric Anthony Vanders," was the reply.

Capshaw turned to Bert, "I think that should be sufficient to make the point."

As they walked back into the warden's office, Capshaw's secretary intercepted him.

"Mr. Benwell from Prison Industries called. He said he got caught in some traffic, but he should still be here on time."

Capshaw looked at his watch. "Good. Buzz me when he arrives. Professor, I've got about another five minutes before I have to prep for my next meeting."

Bert wondered if there was another meeting or, for that matter, a Mr. Benwell. It really didn't matter. "That's fine. I only have a couple more questions. Chris made notes about corrections, mental health, and schools. I assumed he meant applications for the Baker-Miller Pink. But he also made a note about football teams."

Capshaw laughed, "That's right. At one point some coach out in Iowa State got the notion that he could get a foot up on the competition by having the visitor's locker room painted Baker-Miller Pink."

"Did it work?"

"Don't know. But the Western Athletic Association put a stop to it. They actually instituted a rule that both home team and visitor locker rooms couldn't be different colors."

Bert joined in the laughter. "Chris made note of the 'Ed Effect.'"

Capshaw stopped laughing. His face grew stiff, even stern as he spoke into the intercom, "Veronica, hold my calls till I get back to you." Then he looked at Bert.

"Ed Lowman was a veteran correctional officer with almost thirty years of service. He was also one of the finest officers who ever worked here. Everyone liked and respected him, even the inmates. For his twenty-five year mark, the staff petitioned to designate it "Ed Lowman Day" and held a huge party for him. They cut attendance at 250 because that's all the hall could hold. As Ed approached retirement, he was reassigned to admissions. It's considered one of the gravy jobs in the institution. Ed had earned it, the administration figured no one could do it better, and for a time that was how it worked out. Then Ed began complaining about the color of the room. Nothing major, but from Ed any criticism was unusual. Anyway, after a while he said something about the color was getting to him—headaches, temperament and such—and he wanted out. The warden, Tom Dennis, instructed the shift supervisors to arrange the switch. They started a review immediately and figured they could line up a substitute within a couple of weeks. But before it happened, Ed stormed into the Captain's office one day, threw his badge on the desk, and said he was quitting. I was a new lieutenant at the time, and the shift supervisor asked me to go to Ed's home and find out what set him off. When I got to his house, Ed was already dead, along with his wife and teenage daughter. He had shot the other two before he turned the gun on himself. It was a hell of a mess, and only four days before Christmas. Ed was devoted to his wife, and his daughter was his pride and joy."

"And you think the color had something to do with it?" Bert asked.

"We knew that the calming effect wore off after a time. There were some rumors early on about potential negative reactions, but they were proved wrong. In fact, this color has been used for decades in schools and other applications across the country without so much as a hint of trouble."

Bert sensed that Capshaw was holding back, "But you do think there was a connection."

"This is strictly off-the-record," said Capshaw. Bert nodded in agreement. "At one point, Warden Dennis was considering painting the entire cell block that pink color. He never followed through, but the head of the paint crew got wind of it and figured there wasn't enough paint on hand for that big a job, so he decided to make it stretch by mixing it with another color. He had some God-awful off-white that he and his crew had made up with leftovers from various jobs. They had used it to paint parts of the medical wing where the insulin and electroshock therapies were administered and the operating room used for the lobotomies. Many of the inmates seemed to go off right after they entered that wing. I'm sure the doctors took it as added proof that the treatments were necessary. Even after the color was changed and the negative reactions decreased, I don't think anyone made a connection. Anyway, that was the color the paint crew mixed into the Baker-Miller pink."

"So you think the combination of colors changed the characteristics of the paint?"

"I'm no scientist, Professor. All I know is that nothing else explains what happened to Officer Lowman."

"And what about Finley's blood?"

The normally stoic warden visibly jerked at the question. Capshaw's volume increased noticeably as he answered, "I never said anything to Matthews about Finley. If he put that in his notes, he was listening to rumors. I never put any stock in that story, and neither should you."

"Fair enough, Warden, but I'd appreciate hearing it just the same."

Capshaw calmed slightly, "Like I said, it's just a rumor. We used to have an inmate here named Simon Finley. Everyone called him Snakes because that was pretty much his personality, and his hair made him look like Medusa. He was in for child molesting, but while he was here, the state prosecutors were building a case against him for a series of unsolved child murders. He never got to trial. In prison, molesters and baby killers are at the bottom of the food chain. Most of them know enough to keep a low profile, but Finley was an asshole with a big mouth. The other inmates hated his guts. We found his body in a laundry cart. From the look of things, he'd been cut and bled out, real slow. The funny thing was we never found the blood. We eventually caught the guys who did it, but they would never say what they did with the blood. Personally, I figured they just washed it down some drain, but because they worked on the maintenance crew, the rumors were that they mixed the blood into the paint."

"I could see where that kind of rumor could seriously affect the way people reacted to the color."

"I guess Warden Dennis figured the same thing. He scrapped the idea of using the paint elsewhere and had the admissions room repainted blue. It wasn't until five years ago that we tried Baker-Miller again, only this time from a new batch mixed according to the manufacturer's specifications. Our policy requires that we pull an officer at the first hint of a negative reaction, but thus far there hasn't been so much as a hiccup."

"I see." That was all Bert got out. Capshaw's finger was on the intercom button.

"Veronica, tell Mr. Benwell I'll be with him in a minute." Capshaw extended his hand. "I hope I was of some help, Professor."

"Yes, very helpful. Thank you."

Capshaw gave Bert a firm handshake. Bert winced from the pressure. "Just one last thing, Warden; what became of all of the contaminated paint?"

"Warden Dennis planned to have it destroyed, but before he got the memo out, the head of maintenance had already sent it all off to State Surplus."

34

Fog: A thick cloud of water droplets suspended at or near the Earth's surface, obscuring, or restricting visibility.

As Bert was traveling to Fishkill Friday morning, Tess and Katie were driving in the opposite direction for their meeting with Doctor Charles Miller at the Albany Medical Group.

Doctor Miller tried to resist the meeting. First, he said he had already shared everything he could with Chris. Then he spoke about doctor/patient confidentiality. Finally, he said he was just too busy to take the time, but that still didn't deter Tess. Chris was gone, and his research was all she had left of him. When she broke down and told Miller the story of Chris's death, he suddenly agreed. She withheld mention of the subsequent text messages. Dr Miller said he could meet with her and Katie at 11:30.

They arrived twenty minutes early. As soon as Tess and Katie introduced themselves, Dr. Miller turned flush. When he extended his hand, Tess could feel the wetness on his palm. He was perspiring.

"I'm sorry," said Tess, "we got here earlier than expected. We didn't mean to upset your schedule. We can go across the street for a cup of coffee and come back later."

"No, don't do that." Miller rushed his answer, "Please come in." Miller scribbled a name and phone number on a note, and handed it to the receptionist.

"Sandra, please call Mr. Iverson and tell him my 11:30 appointment arrived early. I'll see him as soon as I've finished with them."

"But doctor…"

"Just tell him it's important. He'll understand. And hold my calls, please."

Inside Miller's office, Tess initiated the interview.

"As I explained on the phone, Chris Matthews was writing a report for our research team. On the day he was supposed to present his findings he disappeared in a boating accident and the report was lost with him."

"Chris left behind a notebook with an outline of his research," Katie explained, "and your name was referenced in it."

"I see," Miller said. "And when did you say this accident happened?"

"About a month ago," Tess answered.

"And what exactly does this research entail?"

Miller's tone caught them both off guard. It was beginning to feel as if he was interrogating them instead of the other way around. They had no way of knowing what Chris had told him, but they doubted it was that they were trying to find out how Amanda's spirit might still be occupying her home. If they answered wrong, Miller might become suspicious and refuse to answer anything further. Katie took the lead. "We've established a research facility at Nadowa College in a home that was once occupied by the Reynolds family. According to Chris's notes, you were the Emergency Room physician the night Mr. and Mrs. Reynolds brought in Amanda."

"That's correct."

"And the diagnosis for the cause of death was S.I.D.S.?"

Miller relaxed. Katie surmised that she had guessed correctly.

"That much is a matter of public record. As I told Mr. Matthews, anything further is protected by doctor/patient confidentiality."

"We understand," said Tess, "but if you could provide some generic information regarding the diagnosis, that would greatly aid in our research."

"SIDS stands for Sudden Infant Death Syndrome, doesn't it?" Katie asked.

"Yes, that's right. It's a disease that affects infants from birth to about one year old." Miller sat back and relaxed. "It peaks from two to four months. As to cause, that's a matter of debate."

"Could you explain?" asked Katie.

"The syndrome refers to the sudden, unexplained death of an otherwise healthy infant. There are dozens of cause theories from low birth weight, bacteria, lack of breast-feeding, premature birth, and toxic mattress gasses, to plush bedding materials, child abuse, even bedbugs and secondhand smoke. No one has identified a definitive cause yet. The best the field has produced to date is a list of risk factors and mitigation steps."

"You mentioned child abuse," said Katie.

Miller adjusted his seat position. His body tightened noticeably. "Yes. Initially people were reluctant even to consider that a parent would take the life of their own child. Then a mother was caught on videotape suffocating her baby. It made national news on all the major networks. She was arrested and convicted, and so were many other mothers of SIDS victims. That was probably an overreaction, and a number of those cases were subsequently overturned. Still, in the interim the number of reported SIDS cases decreased sharply. Some researchers predict as much as 5 to 20 percent of SIDS diagnoses are actually cases of infanticide."

"So children were being murdered by their own mothers," Tess said in cold condemnation.

"Or fathers," Miller added. "But before you rush to judgment, you might try going without sleep night after night, listening to the constant coughing or screaming of a child who can't tell you what's bothering them, and see how well you hold up."

"Is that what you think happened to Amanda Reynolds?" Katie asked. Miller's body stiffened as his jaw locked in an angry frown, but before he could react, the receptionist's voice came over the intercom.

"Doctor Miller, I'm sorry to disturb you, but Mr. Iverson is here."

"Send him right in."

The sudden interruption surprised Tess and Katie, but Miller continued to answer the question. "As I told you when you first came in, that is a matter of doctor/patient confidentiality. That's what I told Miss DiPetro when she called. It's also what I told Mr. Matthews when he interviewed me over the phone two months ago." A tall man in a sport jacket and Dockers walked in, accompanied by two uniformed police officers. Miller raised his voice, "And it's what I repeated to Matthews when I talked to him in person last Wednesday. I don't know what kind of game you students think you're playing, but you've stopped playing it on me."

"That's impossible!" said Katie.

The Dockers man spoke, "Ladies, I'm Inspector Iverson. Why don't you two come down to the station and clear this whole thing up for us."

"This can't be happening," said Katie. She looked at Tess who just stood motionless and dazed. Katie turned back to Miller. "Doctor Miller, what did Chris Matthews look like?"

Miller sneered defiantly.

"Please," Katie begged.

Iverson advised, "You might want to answer her, Doc. It may save you some paperwork."

"Then this is the last question I'm answering. After this, every one can speak to my attorney." Miller didn't look at either of the women. He directed his answers to Iverson, "He was thin, a little taller than me, in his mid-twenties I'd guess. He had a sort of baby face, blue eyes and, oh yes, straight blond hair."

Katie's jaw dropped. The description matched Chris exactly. She looked at Tess, but Tess just paced back and forth, her hands tightly clenched, repeating to herself, "Yes," and smiling. It was the crazed smile of someone unable to think.

35

Wind normally refers to horizontal airflow, but the vertical movement of air is a critical component of weather. When there is very little vertical movement of air, the atmosphere is considered "stable." It's considered "unstable" when there is a lot.

"I see," Inspector Iverson wore a puzzled look on his face as he balanced the telephone between his chin and shoulder, "and you're absolutely sure of the date and the student's identity?" He was scribbling as he spoke. "You do? Yes, that could clear things up completely. How soon could you fax that over to me? Great, thank you, Reverend."

As Iverson hung up the phone, he turned his attention back to Tess and Katie. "Reverend Foley corroborates your story. I don't know which is crazier: you two going on about some dead guy who's really alive, or this guy running around ahead of you when he's pretending to be dead." He walked over to a small refrigerator in the corner of the office and opened the door. "Would you like something cold to drink?"

The station house was hot and dry. "That would be great," said Tess. "Do you have a Coke?"

"Diet OK?"

"Terrific."

"Same for me," added Katie. Iverson took out a can, poured it into two glasses, and handed them to the women.

They each took several sips of their drinks before continuing.

"Believe me inspector," said Katie, "you're not half as confused as we are."

"Unless," Tess said, "Chris didn't die in the accident after all."

"In that case," said Iverson, "he's either really scared of something or really messed up."

"Bill, these just came in on the fax for you." James Sanders, one of the officers who had accompanied Iverson to Doctor Miller's office, handed the inspector several sheets of paper.

Iverson scanned the papers, "Well, this is it. It's a copy of your campus newspaper and it backs up your story. Since Matthews' picture seems to match Doctor Miller's description, it looks like you may be correct, Miss DiPetro. In that case, it's a matter for your local police to handle. Anyway, you're both free to go."

"Inspector," Tess asked, "is there any way you could call Doctor Miller and clear things up with him?"

"I might if I thought it would do any good, but Doctor Miller was adamant. He's through answering any more questions from you. By the way, Miss DiPetro, are you originally from around here?"

"No, this is my first time in Albany. Until I came to Nadowa, Ohio was the furthest east I'd ever been."

"Strange. For some reason I could swear I've seen you before."

Katie chimed in, "Now certainly a man with your experience could come up with a better line than that. Besides, Inspector," she giggled, "don't you think you're a little old for her?" Iverson's face reddened.

"Quiet, Katie," Tess laughed. "I'll let you know when I need rescuing."

"All right, all right," Iverson said with feigned sternness, "that'll be enough from you two. Now get out of here before I think up something I can pin on you."

The two women exited the station, giggling as they did. As Tess went through the front door, she turned, smiled, and waved back to Iverson. He waved in return. As he brought his hand down, he picked up a tissue, lifted Tess's glass by the rim, and carefully placed it into the plastic bag on his desk, the one he had scribbled her name on during his conversation with

Gene Foley. Then he placed the other glass in a bag with Katie's name on it.

"Jim," he called to officer Sanders, "run these down to the lab for me. Ask Niles to see if he can lift some prints from them and then run them against the NCJRS database. Tell him there's no rush, but I want him to call me if he gets a hit."

Iverson was finishing his last report when the phone rang. He looked up at the clock: ten to five. Lately all of his conversations with Pam ended in an argument. It seemed that no matter how well things were wrapping up, something else surfaced just before he had to leave. He quickly scanned the desk—no notes, no messages, no follow-ups, and less than ten minutes until he walked out the door. He took a deep breath and answered, "Inspector Iverson."

"You sound very official, Inspector."

"Hi, hon. How's it going?"

"Pretty good today. I had a nice lunch with your sister. She said to say hello and to tell you that your mom's foot is healing nicely. Jamie got a ninety-five on his math exam and he's the starting pitcher for tonight's game. Did you want to meet us at the field?"

The phone fell silent. Iverson could feel the tension on the line as Pam waited for the disappointing news of another broken promise, another night alone. At the same time, two images flashed through Iverson's mind. The first was the smile on Jamie's face as he looked up into the stands and saw him sitting there. The other was Tommy Arnone's mom, who worked in the concession stand during the game. She was well endowed and habitually wore deep-cut, loose-fitting tops. Most of the children were too young or too short to notice, but their fathers relished the thought of her leaning forward to push an order through the serving window.

Iverson snapped himself back to attention, "Yeah, hon. That sounds fine." He could hear his wife exhale as she relaxed at his answer. "What's for supper?"

"Meatloaf with oven brown potatoes and corn, and

blueberry pie for dessert."

Iverson was stunned. Meatloaf was his favorite dish. He loved potatoes and corn, but Pam always said that it didn't make sense to serve two starches together. And she'd been complaining for weeks about his expanding waistline, "Are we expecting company?"

"No. Jamie's invited to sleep over at Nick's house following the game, so we're alone for the whole evening. It seemed like the perfect night for me to show you what I bought at Jan's house party."

"Jan's party?"

"Yes silly. Remember, you wanted to come too—the Naughty Nightie Party."

"Oh, yeah, that party; I'd love to see what you bought there."

"Good. I'll show you right after my bubble bath. See you at the game."

Iverson hung up the phone, shoved the last stray items from his desktop into his center drawer, and started to leave. From his years of experience, he should have known better than to look at anything but the exit door. Out of habit however, his eyes roamed to the Wanted Board as he walked past it.

There was a pencil drawing of Tess DiPetro. Iverson approached the board and ripped off the notice.

Wanted: Person of Interest in connection with the murder of Ralph Campbell of Franklin Indiana - Theresa Campbell, formerly of Greenwood, current residence unknown.

As he continued reading, Iverson picked up the phone and dialed. "Niles? Good, you're still there. You know those prints I sent down earlier? Yeah. I need you to put a rush on them. I know, I know. Me too, but this is urgent. Yeah, I'll wait here for the results." Iverson finished reading the notice.

For more information, contact Inspector Clive Bowman at …

Iverson picked up the receiver again and looked up at the

clock, five after five. By placing the next call he'd put in motion a string of events that, once started, would have to be seen through to completion. He was in for a long night. As he held the receiver to his ear, he thought about the disappointment in his son's face as he looked at the empty seat next to his mother. He thought about Pam's anger and frustration; about Tommy Arnone's mother's tits; about cold meatloaf, potatoes, and corn; about unbaked blueberry pie and the unseen, unworn Naughty Nightie. As he dialed the number, Inspector William Iverson though about how much he hated Tess DiPetro.

36

As long as the temperature of a rising parcel of air remains warmer than its surrounding, it remains unstable and keeps on rising. As long as the temperature of a falling parcel of air remains cooler than its surrounding, it remains unstable and keeps on falling. As long as air remains unstable, it continues to provide fuel for a storm.

Bert stood in O'Malley's doorway adjusting to the change in light. The long, ornate bar along the right side came into focus, followed by the red upholstered booths running down the left. Finally, he saw Tess, Katie, and Reverend Gene in the round corner booth at the back.

O'Malley's had a much different feel than O'Rourke's. Being just off campus, it bustled with college students. During the week, most of them used it to hang out. It had a small dance floor and an elevated platform where local entertainers performed on weekends. The booths were larger, more comfortable and better lit, and the menu offered homestyle meals. It was known for its beef stew and corned beef and cabbage. It also offered the *Diablo* burger. If you could eat two, the third was free. To Bert's recollection, no one had ever successfully met the challenge. The bar also served as the team's off-site conference space. A pitcher of beer and glasses were on the table.

"So how did you two make out?" Bert asked Tess and Katie as he poured himself a draft.

Tess and Katie spent the next half hour filling Bert in on what happened in Albany, and then Tess asked, "Bert, do you think Chris could have survived the waterspout?"

"From the way the canoe looked and the fact that they found it thirty feet in the air, I would have guessed not. But with the text message and now Doctor Miller's account, it's certainly beginning to look like maybe he did."

"Then what do you make of all this lurking around?" asked Katie.

"I wish I knew."

Bert filled the trio in on his experience at Fishkill. "So I think we can safely conclude that the feelings of calmness and well-being you get from being in the room are at least partly attributable to the paint color," he ended.

"Maybe so," Tess challenged, "but what about the light and temperature control and..."

"Slow down Tess," said Bert. "Let's just continue to take things one step at a time. Right now, following up on Chris's notebook has been our most fruitful course of action. I suggest we maintain that investigation while continuing our normal research at the house." All agreed.

"I'd like to help if I can," Gene offered.

Bert opened Chris's notebook and the team laid out its next steps. Bert summarized the plan of action. "Tess and Katie, you'll research if Officer Charles Davis and Captain Ed Davis are the same person. Either way, you'll see what additional information he can provide regarding Amanda's death. Gene will get a copy of the original police report and interview Gareth and Cynthia Reynolds. They're probably going to be the hardest to get to talk, but hopefully they'll open up to a minister easier than they would to one of us. And I'm going to follow up with Winona Seivers of Tom's River, New Jersey. I don't know who she is or how she's tied into this, but hopefully she can be of some help. We'll all reconvene here next Friday night and update each other. Sound like a plan?" Everyone concurred.

As Bert approached his car and started for his keys, he reached instead for his ringing cell phone and then stopped dead as he read the message:

HI BERTIE
U'VE BEEN A BAD BOY
IT WOULD HAVE BEEN A SHAME IF THE MRS HAD

DIED FOR YOUR SINS
STAY AWAY FROM KATIE
C

37

An inversion is a deviation from the normal change of an atmospheric property with altitude, such as temperature increasing rather than decreasing with height. It can suppress convection by acting as a "cap," trapping the air below. If the cap ruptures suddenly, convection of the moisture present can erupt into violent thunderstorms.

Gene was as excited about talking to Gareth and Cynthia Reynolds as Bert was reticent. The core questions that needed to be answered involved what happened to Amanda and that went down a path Bert was not comfortable taking. Gene was more comfortable than Bert regarding matters of the soul, so on Wednesday afternoon Gene visited the offices of Reynolds Corporation in Cincinnati, Ohio.

Gareth insisted on starting the meeting by giving Gene a tour of the plant. It was an immense operation. Gene couldn't tell whether the purpose of the tour was to impress or intimidate him. He didn't have to wait long to find out.

"So you're a priest, are you?" Gareth asked as they reentered his office.

"A minister, actually. I'm the chaplain at Nadowa College."

"And what interest would a college chaplain have in me?"

Gene knew the question was at least partly disingenuous. A person—even one who owns a large corporation—doesn't donate a mansion and not remember the name of the school. Gene didn't make an issue of it. He believed in using confrontation sparingly.

"It's about the house you donated to the college."

Gareth had his back to Gene as he poured himself a drink. "Scotch?" he asked.

Gene looked at his watch: 2:30. "No, thank you."

"So what is it about the house that interests the campus minister?" Gareth's references to Gene in the third person were getting old. It was time to even the playing field.

"It's what's in the house I'd like to discuss, Mr. Reynolds, or more precisely *who* is in it."

Gareth froze for a moment at the mention of *who*. He downed the first scotch, poured himself another, and sat down facing Gene, "And who is it that you think is in the house."

Gene had Gareth's undivided attention, "Your daughter, Amanda."

Gareth's grip tightened on the scotch glass. His knuckles whitened. "Go on," he said.

For the next twenty minutes Gene traced the history of 34 Lakota Drive, at least as best he knew it. He included the deaths of Chris and Drew both to impress upon Gareth the seriousness of the situation and because he knew the most about that event.

"And you believe that my daughter's spirit is still occupying the house?" Gareth asked.

"We don't know, but nothing else explains everything that's happened."

"Sounds like you should be performing an exorcism."

From the mocking tone, Gene understood the emptiness of the suggestion. "That's a Catholic rite. Besides, it's for casting out evil demons, and I don't believe your daughter is a demon or evil. Do you?"

"You said yourself those two boys are dead."

"So far as we know, but that doesn't mean that Amanda caused it."

"Reverend, this conversation is getting irritating. I can't believe you're actually sitting here telling me that a three-month-old baby who died almost twenty years ago is not only haunting our house, but also controlling the weather. What could I possibly add that would make any difference at all?"

"You could tell me how your daughter died."

"It's all in the police report. You can read it for yourself."

"I have read the report and if I believed it was all in there, I wouldn't be here now."

"What are you getting at?"

The biting sarcasm was still there, but so was something else. Gene could see it in Gareth's eyes—a need, a yearning to communicate. "It would be very helpful to understand the circumstances surrounding Amanda's death."

"And have you spoken to my ex-wife about this?"

"No. I left several messages, but she hasn't returned my calls."

"And she won't," Gareth got up and poured himself another drink. "Cynthia had a complete nervous breakdown several years ago. She's as good as dead."

Gene was stunned. "I'm sorry for your loss," he clenched his jaw at the awkwardness of his response. She wasn't actually dead.

"Loss? Not hardly," Gareth answered. "Cynthia and I haven't talked since our divorce, not that we had that much to say before it." Gareth downed the scotch and sat down again. "Listen, Reverend, Amanda was sickly from birth. For three months, we spent half our lives in doctors' offices. When she got the croup, our idiot doctor said she'd be all right if we kept the humidifier going. The walls in her room had water running down them from all the moisture and she still coughed and whimpered for three days. It would have been better if she had screamed. At least that would only have been annoying. But she just moaned like an injured puppy. Do you know what that's like?" Gareth didn't wait for a response, "It was like she was pleading for help, begging for us to stop the pain, and there wasn't a thing we could do."

Gareth sat motionless, staring at his glass.

Gene leaned forward resting his arms on his knees, "Mr. Reynolds, I'm an ordained minister. Whatever you say to me in confidence is protected communication between a client and his counselor. You can tell me. Did you hurt your daughter?"

Gareth got up, walked to the bar and with his back to Gene,

poured himself another scotch. As he did, he smiled.

"Padre, this interview is over."

38

A stationary front is a boundary between two air masses, neither of which is strong enough to overtake the other. They can remain stalled in the same area for an extended period.

Before leaving for Cincinnati, Gene secured the police report concerning Amanda's death and forwarded a copy to Bert and Tess.

On Wednesday evening, Tess and Katie sat on the rug in Amanda's room going over the report and highlighting the pertinent data.

- Officers Charles E. Davis and Benjamin Solaris filed the report on December 23, 1990.

- The call from the Hudson Valley Medical Center came into the station at 1:21 a.m. on December 22.

- Amanda was pronounced dead at 11:52 p.m., December 21, after resuscitation attempts failed. The actual time of death was estimated to be between 7:30 and 11:15 p.m.

- Officer Davis interviewed Gareth Reynolds at the hospital at 2:05 a.m., on December 22. According to Mr. Reynolds, when his wife, Cynthia, checked on Amanda at about 10 p.m., the baby had turned over and was lying face down in her crib. The soft bedding was surrounding her face and she was not breathing.

- The couple drove the twenty-two miles to the hospital instead of waiting for an ambulance.

- Mrs. Reynolds was too upset to be interviewed.

- At 10:45 a.m. on December 23, Officers Davis and Solaris went to 34 Sunset Terrace and found the room and bedding as Mr. Reynolds had described. Nothing at the scene appeared to contradict Mr. Reynolds' description of the events.

- The case was officially closed January 7, 1991.

According to Gene's additional notes:

- Officer Solaris left the force August 11, 1991. He and his family moved to Florida. His current whereabouts are unknown.

- Officer Charles E. Davis was promoted to sergeant August 17, 1991. He became a lieutenant September 21, 1993, and captain March 13, 1997. He retired from the force after 20 years in March 2009.

- Davis currently works for the campus police department at Nadowa College.

Katie contacted Captain Davis and arranged for her and Tess to meet with him.

"So what can I do for you, ladies?" Captain Davis asked.

"When Professor Myers and I were here," Katie started, "we didn't realize that you were the same Charles Davis who used to be with the Hudson Valley police department." Katie went on to explain about their research on the history of 34 Lakota Drive and Chris's involvement.

"Chris had just finished his research when the accident happened," she said. "From the notes in his diary it appears that he interviewed you.

"I remember Matthews. It's too bad. He had a nice way about him." Tess smiled and nodded in agreement.

"Could you share with us what you told him about the house and, in particular, about Amanda Reynolds?" Katie asked.

"He wanted to get more details about the night the Reynolds girl died. I'll suggest the same thing to you as I did to him. Get a copy of the police report."

"We've already read the report," said Tess. "It wasn't very helpful."

Davis leaned back in his chair and folded his arms. "Well, if it wasn't very helpful, since I'm the one who wrote it, I don't see how asking me more questions is going to get you any further."

"It's just that it still left a lot of questions unanswered," said Katie.

"Whatever I uncovered I put in the report so you should have everything you need, or at least everything I can tell you." The more evasive Davis was the more heated Katie became.

"Not really," she said. "SIDS is fairly broad diagnosis with a wide variety of potential causes, including child abuse, but there's no mention in the report of exploring that or any other possibility. In fact, you never even interviewed Mrs. Reynolds."

"There was no need to. Mr. and Mrs. Reynolds were two of the most respected members of the community, and Mrs. Reynolds was devastated by her daughter's death. She was too upset to talk."

"Then why didn't you interview her later, when she was less overcome?"

"Miss Jarvis, don't you think that you're a little out of line here."

Katie ignored the question and asked another. "Didn't it strike you as a bit odd that the Reynolds drove 22 miles to the hospital instead of calling for an ambulance?"

"No, it didn't strike me as odd," said Davis, "and I don't much like your tone of voice."

"I understand that you took your twenty-year retirement from the force in March of 2009."

"That's right. What of it?"

"That would mean that when you investigated Amanda's death, you had only been with the force for a few months." Katie was in overdrive.

Tess was transfixed. She didn't know what Katie was doing, but it felt like trouble. She could not think of an effective way to intervene. Like a passenger on a runaway train, all she could do was sit and brace herself for a wreck.

"Are you questioning my abilities?" Davis' face flushed and his neck turned bright red.

"No, I just find it curious that six months after you and

Officer Solaris filed your report, you made sergeant, and he moved to Florida. Sergeant in six months is pretty fast, isn't it?"

"What are you getting at, young lady?"

"What aren't you telling us, Captain?"

"That's it you two. End of discussion! And if I were you Miss Jarvis, I'd leave the investigative work to the professionals and get my ass back into my school work."

"My ass is just fine, thank you," Katie returned.

Katie and Tess walked halfway back to their car before Tess broke the silence, "That went well, don't you think?"

Katie smiled, "I guess I kind of lost it, huh?"

"My ass is just fine, thank you. You think?"

"I know. I know," Katie apologized, and then suddenly stopped short.

"What's wrong?" Tess noticed the worried look on Katie's face.

"Did you hear that?" Tess listened carefully as Katie scanned the parking garage. "Like rustling leaves."

"All right, enough of that, Katie. You're starting to scare me."

Katie thought she saw something move in the trees, although she wasn't certain and didn't feel a breeze. She listened a second longer, "Sorry. My imagination I guess. Anyway, something in my gut tells me our captain is hiding something. I can feel it."

"I don't know about that, but I can tell you one thing for sure. From now on you'd damn well better stay within the speed limit when you're driving on this campus."

As they exited the garage in Katie's Wrangler, neither of them noticed the leaves swirling feverishly in a dust devil, right beneath where Katie had parked her car.

39

Relative humidity is the percentage of water vapor currently in the air to the maximum amount it can contain. The warmer the air is the more water vapor it can hold. When a parcel of air contains all the water vapor it can (100% relative humidity) it becomes "saturated."

Friday morning Bert pulled off the Garden State Parkway in Tom's River, New Jersey. All he felt was discouragement. Gene called Wednesday with the disappointing results from his meeting with Gareth Reynolds and the even more dismal news of Cynthia Reynolds' breakdown. On Thursday, Katie described the disastrous meeting with Captain Davis. Whatever rapport Bert had established with Davis was now gone. He was bitterly disappointed in his team, but even more so in himself. What did he think he was doing anyway? He was a physics professor, not a private investigator.

Investigating Chris's notebook was getting in the way of the basic research at the house, of Bert's spending time with his wife and friends, and even of his ability to think straight. Now he was pursuing another tangent—one that seemed certain to lead to a dead end. He didn't know who Winona Seivers was or how she fit into it all, and Chris's notes were of little help. The only good news was that there was only one listing in Tom's River for a Winona Seivers.

Maybe Bert had overestimated Chris. Maybe the report was nothing but fluff. It would certainly be more in line with Bert's original expectation. Maybe he only wanted it to mean something—to make sense out of his being on a senseless treadmill. Then it hit him. Sitting alone in his car, he began yelling, "I never called her! Why the hell didn't I tell her I was coming? She might not even be home!" Bert pulled into the drive for Spring Lake Village. The sign at the entrance read *A Community for Adults 55 and Over*. Bert's diatribe escalated.

"It's a fucking retirement community! She might be dead for all I know. Four hours on the highway, and it could all be for nothing." Bert couldn't stop himself. "This is it. This is the last useless trip, the final wasted hours. I'm quitting this stupidity. If she's not home, I'm getting the hell out of here, calling the others, and putting an end to this lunacy!"

As he pressed the front doorbell, Bert counted under his breath. When he reached ten, he didn't bother to press it again. He just turned and headed for the car.

"Yes, what is it?" The tiny voice behind him had the ring of a crystal bell.

He turned and looked down at a smiling face beneath the neatly combed silver-blue cloud.

"Winona Seivers?"

"Everybody just calls me Winnie." In her white dress and matching vest, she looked as if she might have just come home from church.

Bert went into fast forward. "I'm sorry, I should have called. I'm following up on some research a student of mine was conducting and he had your name listed in his journal. I'm assuming the address 34 Lakota Drive has no meaning for you."

"No, I'm sorry it doesn't."

"And I'm guessing the letters PPD don't mean anything to you either?"

Winnie remained tranquil, but started moving back and slowly edging the door closed. "I'm sorry again but no they don't."

"I didn't expect they would. And I'm guessing you've never heard of Gareth or Cynthia Reynolds either. I'm sorry to have bothered…"

Winnie opened the door wide again, "Cynthia Reynolds? Why yes, Cynthia is my sister."

Bert stood dumfounded, "You're Cynthia's sister?"

"Last time I checked," Winnie chuckled softly at her own

joke. "Cynthia's maiden name is Seivers. I've never been married myself. You said you were following up on a student of yours. Would that be Christopher?"

"Yes, Christopher Matthews."

A delighted smile lit Winnie's face, "Then you must be Mr. Myers. Christopher's told me so much about you. Please come in."

The inside of Winnie's condominium appeared as neat and orderly as she did. The white lace window curtains matched the doilies on the furniture.

"Please make yourself comfortable. I'll make us some tea," Winnie was already heading for the kitchen, "or would you prefer coffee. All I have is decaf."

"That won't be necessary. I'll only take a few minutes of your time."

"Nonsense, it's no work at all. I also have some fresh Jewish Coffee Cake. A friend of mine baked it and it's very tasty." Bert opted for the tea.

As Winnie worked in the kitchen, Bert took in the surroundings. A pad by the phone listed Winnie's neighbors. He noted that condominiums 7 and 12 once listed couples, but in each case, the husband's name was neatly crossed out. Number 2 listed Father William O'Brian. A church bulletin on the coffee table listed the times for weekday masses and William O'Brian as Pastor Emeritus. Maybe Winnie really had just come home from church.

Winnie suggested that they have their tea in the dining room. As Bert reviewed pictures arranged on the sideboard, Winnie joined him.

"This is Cynthia," she picked up a pewter framed wedding photo and stroked her finger across her sister's face. "And this was her husband, Gareth." The sweet innocence that typified Winnie's voice was suddenly missing. "He was a different one, that Gareth, although he didn't start out that way."

"Different?"

Winnie picked up another picture, "This is the two of them

at Cindy's junior prom. Isn't she beautiful?" Bert nodded in agreement. Cynthia was strikingly pretty.

"They practically grew up together. She was a year behind him in school. He didn't take much notice of her until the prom. After that he couldn't get enough of her."

Bert asked what happened. He enjoyed listening to Winnie as much as she seemed to enjoy talking.

"I think it was that darned business of his. Excuse my language, but I just get so angry when I think about it."

Over tea and cake, Winnie described how Cynthia put Gareth through college and then worked with him to start the business.

"They seemed really happy at first, but the business took so much to get going. They worked all hours until Cindy just couldn't keep up. She's always been frail, you know. Gareth was the strong one. When the bills started piling up, Cindy's nerves got the best of her. She wanted him to quit, but Gareth wouldn't hear of it. He worked day and night, and I have to give him credit, he made it work."

Winnie described how even after the business was going well, Gareth couldn't stop. No matter how big or strong the business became, he just kept on working. Then Cindy got pregnant.

"With Amanda?"

"With the twins."

Bert shook involuntarily. He sat silently for a moment trying to decide if he should quit and run or delve further. Winnie handed him another photo. "This is Amanda. Wasn't she the most precious thing?"

The baby in the photo was adorable. Bert flashed for a moment to Stephen. Then for the first time since the odyssey began, he felt something new—a connection to the child who once occupied the room at 34 Lakota Drive. "Could you tell me a little more about the twins?"

Winnie hesitated for a moment. "Give me just a second," and then she disappeared into another room. She returned holding a large scrapbook. "You might say that I'm the unofficial family historian." There were pictures of Winnie's family, of her and Cynthia growing up, and the history of Cynthia and Gareth's marriage and business. Several newspaper clips chronicled the growing enterprise, while other photos revealed the mounting strain in the couple's faces. The weariness was even more evident in Gareth. His eyes had sunk deep into their sockets, as if they were trying to retreat from the world.

"What about this one?" Bert asked. The photo showed Gareth, Cynthia, and another man standing next to a prestigious looking automobile.

"Oh, that's them and their driver standing by their Rolls Royce. As you might imagine the business was doing very well by then, and this was their summer home in Quissett Harbor. That's on Cape Cod in Massachusetts, now Cindy lives there year round."

Bert pointed to another photo, "This is house I was talking about, 34 Lakota Drive."

"Oh?" Winnie looked surprised, "I remembered it differently."

"You're right. It was originally 34 Sunset Terrace."

"That's it."

Winnie paused over the next picture as a cheerless gaze crossed her face. The photo showed Cynthia pregnant, but looking anxious. "This was when Cindy was five months pregnant," said Winnie. "It was a difficult pregnancy. Cindy was confined to bed rest for weeks at a time. We had just gotten back from the doctor's office. Her sonogram showed she had the twins, a boy and a girl. Sometimes I wish I hadn't been there that day. Something changed in my sister that day—she was almost hysterical. She made me promise not to tell Gareth about the boy."

"Did she explain why?"

"She said she couldn't, and begged me never to ask again, so I didn't." Winnie sat silently for a moment, then took in a breath, and forced a weak smile before continuing. "When Gareth got home, she told him it was twin girls and she couldn't possibly care for two children. She even mentioned abortion, but we were raised strict Catholic and she knew she couldn't go through with it. Anyway, Gareth would never allow it. She said she wanted to give them both up for adoption. I've never seen Gareth so angry."

Winnie described the terrible argument that ensued. She wanted to leave but feared for her sister's safety so she left them in the front room and waited in the kitchen. Hours later, Cindy finally agreed to keep one and give the other up for adoption.

"I think Gareth might have been all right with that if they kept the boy. He had always hoped to involve a son in the business and pass it on to him someday. Gareth couldn't imagine a daughter, especially one of Cindy's, being strong enough to manage it. He hated the idea of keeping one girl and giving up the other. But Cindy was adamant—it was one or none at all. Gareth finally gave in to Cynthia. When they came into the kitchen, Cindy asked me to help make the arrangements. Gareth just stood against the counter and stared. I'll never forget the way he looked at her." Winnie fell silent again, and then perked, "I could use another tea, how about you, Professor?"

As Winnie refilled their cups, Bert continued scanning the album. Amanda's birth brought a temporary lift to Cynthia. For a time her smile returned. Gareth was not present at all. If Bert didn't know better, he might have concluded that Cynthia was a single mother. In time, the strain returned to Cynthia's face, and then Bert came to a blank page.

"There are no more pictures of them. Amanda, poor thing, died. Gareth divorced Cynthia, and my sister wouldn't allow anyone to take her picture after that."

"And what happened to the boy?" Bert asked.

"I helped my sister find an adoption agency. She and Gareth arranged it so that neither of them ever saw the other baby. Gareth never learned he had a son. Cindy delivered cesarean. When she woke up they had Amanda, and the boy was gone."

"So none of you ever saw him again."

Winnie sat back in her chair. "My sister's had a nervous breakdown, you know."

"Yes, I only heard about that recently. I'm sorry."

"She never recovered from giving him away. She was so despondent that she had difficult caring for Amanda. Post partum depression was what the doctor called it."

"PPD," Bert said to himself, "of course."

Winnie explained how she tried to have Cindy move in with her, but even after being divorced for so many years, Gareth blocked it. He claimed Winnie would be unable to provide for her sister's needs, and Cynthia was too weak to fight him. Instead, Gareth arranged for a home aid worker to fix meals and keep the house clean, and a visiting nurse to make weekly checks. Winnie made frequent calls, but Cynthia spoke very little. "Most of the time she just sits at home alone without a person in the world to talk to." Winnie's eyes began to water.

"I'm sorry. If I had realized this would be so upsetting, I never would have bothered you like this."

"Actually, I've appreciated your company. It's been nice to have the chance to talk about it. You see, as part of helping with the adoption, I had to promise Cindy that I would never tell another soul, not even my priest in confession. But now that she's almost gone…" Winnie dabbed her eyes with a handkerchief. Bert reached over and rested his hand on her wrist.

"I hope I can trust you to be discrete," she said.

Winnie turned the next page. "This is him." The picture was of a boy about five. The caption read, "Robert's first day of school."

"So his name is Robert?"

"I don't know what his real name is. Robert was my father's name and it helps me to think of him that way. A dear friend of mine ran the agency I found. We went to school together. I know these kinds of things are supposed to be kept secret, but I promised her that I wouldn't try to contact him."

Winnie said that each year on Robert's birthday, she would give her friend money to send to him, simply saying it was from an anonymous benefactor. "I just wanted him to know that he wasn't alone in the world. I guess it did some good. My friend said he referred to me as his fairy godmother. Every now and then, the agency would receive a picture of Robert, and she would send it along to me. Cynthia and Gareth never knew."

"So he wasn't adopted?"

Winnie explained that the couple who was supposed to adopt Robert was killed in a car accident, and there was no other family to take him in. He was also colicky, which scared many people off. Robert became a ward of the state. He had multiple foster placements, but never for very long.

"And where is he today?" Bert saw the tiny tremors in Winnie's hand as she answered.

"My friend told me she is under strict orders never to divulge any information about him so she's never offered, and I've never asked. Every now and then, he sends her a picture and she forwards them on to me so I can add them to my book. The last one I got was his final year in high school. I haven't heard anything since." Winnie stood up suddenly. "I'm sorry, Professor, but I don't think I can manage talking about this any more."

"I understand. Winnie, could I borrow a couple of your pictures? I'd like to make copies of them, and then I can return the originals."

Winnie picked up the album and handed it to Bert. "Cindy and I are all that's left of the Seivers. Gareth was an only child, and he and Cindy had no others, so that boy is all that remains of our family. I think Robert might like to have this someday, to know where he came from. If you find him, I'd like you to give it to him. He may also be able to help you find some of the answers you're looking for." Bert nodded his thanks.

"Professor, if you do find Robert would you please tell him

his fairy godmother loves him very much, and please tell Christopher I said hello."

Bert didn't want to add any more pain to Winnie, so he decided not to tell her about the accident. "Of course," was all he said.

As Bert was driving back north on the Garden State Parkway, Katie was treating herself to a tour and lecture at the Museum of Modern Art, so the phone rang in Gene Foley's office.

"Gene, it's Tess," she sounded frantic. "I need help and I can't reach Katie or Bert."

"Of course, Tess, what do you need?"

"I'm not sure," she was crying.

"Tess, are you all right? Where are you?"

"I'm at the police station. Gene, I've been arrested."

40

When a parcel of air becomes saturated, its rate of temperature-change-with-altitude reduces. It remains warmer as it ascends and cooler as it descends. That promotes greater instability, more vertical air movement, and more powerful storms.

Something in Bert had changed. Regardless of what they learned about the room or its affect on the weather, he wanted to know all he could about Amanda Reynolds. After talking to Winnie, he needed to know how and why she died.

He was impatient to share his findings with the others. Rather than wait until seven to meet at O'Malley's, he asked Katie to call Tess and Gene and meet him at the house at five. When he arrived, he found Katie sitting alone on Amanda's rug and immediately launched into a description of his meeting with Winnie. He didn't even notice Tess and Gene's absence until Katie stopped him.

"Bert, Tess isn't coming."

"That's all right. We'll just update her at O'Malley's."

He slowed as Katie looked down and tightened her lips. In another setting, it might have gone unnoticed, but in Amanda's room, it was a firestorm of emotion.

"So this is the room." Gene stood just inside the doorway. He looked around and then went over to Amanda's crib and rubbed his hand on the railing. He gazed with puzzlement at the equipment and computer screen. He smiled at the cat clock, its hands still stuck at 10:07. Then Gene walked over to the open window, put his arm through, and giggled like a youngster as he moved his hand in and out. Finally, he closed his eyes and stood in silence for a moment as if he were on a deserted beach soaking up the afternoon sun. Then he smiled and joined Bert and Katie on the rug, "It's everything you said it was."

"Katie was just starting to tell me that Tess couldn't make it," said Bert.

"Oh? Then she hasn't told you why yet." Gene filled both of them in on the details concerning Tess' arrest.

"And they're saying she lied about being at the house?" Bert asked. "That can't be good."

"I'm afraid not," said Gene. "I don't think Tess was thinking straight when they interviewed her. I tried to get her to stop talking until we called a lawyer, but she couldn't seem to control herself, and the more she talked, the worse it sounded."

"You don't honestly believe Tess could do something like that," Katie asked, "do you?"

"I don't know," said Bert. "If she wasn't trying to hide something, why did she lie about being at his house the night he was murdered?"

Katie couldn't answer.

"Anyway," said Gene, "it doesn't really matter what we think."

Katie answered, "It matters to me."

Gene nodded sympathetically, "I called an attorney friend of mine. He agreed to represent her. He's with her now."

"Can we visit her?" asked Katie.

"Yes, but we should do it soon. They've scheduled a hearing for Wednesday morning on extraditing Tess to Indiana."

After finishing their discussion about Tess, Bert brought out Winnie's album. Katie sighed over the pictures of Amanda. Bert explained the complex relationship between Gareth and Cynthia Reynolds and the secret of Amanda's brother.

As they flipped through the pages, Bert answered questions about each picture until Katie asked, "Am I seeing what I think I am?"

The same picture had stopped Bert at Winnie's house. "You are unless we're both wrong."

"That would make three of us," Gene added.

Bert smiled. He anticipated their reaction. "Well, if you find that picture interesting, I wonder what you might make of this one," Bert flipped to the next page.

"Oh my God!" said Katie.

"You might not be far off," said Gene. "I think God himself might find this intriguing."

"Then that settles it," said Bert. "I know where we'll be going tomorrow."

Saturday was Bert's perfect storm. It began at the front stoop where the morning's paper should have been. Instead, it was on the lawn halfway to the curb. Dressed in his slippers and bathrobe Bert trudged through wet grass and early morning frost to retrieve it. He threw the paper on the kitchen table and brushed off the chill as he reached for his coffee. That's when he realized he'd forgotten to put up a fresh pot the night before. He tossed the stale grounds into the garbage and refilled the pot, but even before the coffee finished brewing, the phone rang. It was 7:15 a.m.

The phone almost never rang that early on weekends. When it did, it was usually bad news. The last time it was about Evelyn's father after his long battle with cancer. The only other calls came when someone found Bert's home number and phoned in a panic to explain why he or she was going to miss an assignment deadline. If that were the case, he or she was about to feel Bert's wrath. Bert picked up the phone and braced himself for bad news or battle.

"Professor Myers," said John Thompson, "what the hell is going on at Lakota Drive?"

"I'm sorry, John; I'm not clear on what you're talking about."

"You're not clear? Haven't you read this morning's paper?"

"No, actually I was just getting to it."

"Read it! Then call me back." The phone went dead.

Bert poured himself a cup of black coffee and opened the paper. He didn't have to look any further than the lead headline:

Is Nadowa Dorm Haunted? Two Students Dead; Another Arrested for Murder

Bert gripped the paper and started reading:

The normally quiet Nadowa College has been rocked in recent weeks by a series of events revolving around one of the campus dormitories. The unit at 34 Lakota Drive is more than four miles from the main campus and houses only four residents, all officers of the student government. Recently fate seems to have hunted down three of them. On August 17, student Vice President Christopher Matthews and Program Chair Drew Richardson disappeared in a boating accident on Crazy Horse Pond. They are presumed dead. According to police reports, the two men were caught in a freak storm that came out of nowhere and vanished just as quickly. One eyewitness claimed the men and their canoe were taken up in a waterspout. The battered canoe was found in a tree a week later. Neither of the men's bodies has been recovered.

Yesterday, student treasurer, Theresa DiPetro, was arrested for the murder of her stepfather, Ralph Campbell. Campbell's body was found stabbed to death in his Franklin, Indiana, home. Miss DiPetro was in Indiana at the time attending her mother's funeral. She is being held on $250,000.00 bond pending an extradition hearing on Wednesday.

The history of the house is almost as perplexing as the fate of its residents. It was previously owned by prominent valley residents Gareth and Cynthia Reynolds, but was abandoned twenty years ago after the sudden death of the couple's three-month-old daughter. In 1999, they donated the house to the College. It was subsequently renovated as part of the college's expansion program. The mansion-size home sits on a 95-acre estate that could easily house at least two dozen students, but it has been used exclusively as headquarters for the student government offices and has never had more than the four residents. Now only student president Katherine Jarvis still remains.

The recent incidents have raised questions about the property and its uses. According to Campus Police Chief Edward Davis, the storm that killed Matthews and Richardson was not an isolated incident. He confirmed reports of strange, localized storms centered near the Lakota Drive property. "Our station is less than four miles from the house but on the dates these storms were reported we didn't receive any indication at the station. That seems very odd." Davis also said that DiPetro and Jarvis had been in to talk to him recently about the history of the house and its occupants, but wouldn't elaborate further.

Meanwhile, curiosity about the house has raised concern in the student population. "Its kind of creepy," quoted one student. Another student, campus news anchor Kevin Casperin, was more critical. "I think Dean Thompson and the college administration have a lot of explaining to do about the money expended on the house, the way the building has been used, and about the operation of the student government. And what are all those antennas and weather instruments for?" Casperin asked. "I think they know a lot more about what's been going on than they're telling." Physics Professor Bertrand Myers is the student government advisor and overseer of the dormitory. He's been conducting weather-related research at the house for more than a year but few students have been involved. Some in the student population have dubbed him "Professor Frankenstein." Calls to College President John Thompson for comment were not returned.

Bert picked up the phone, dialed John Thompson's office, and steeled himself for the next onslaught.

"So you've finally gotten around to reading it." Thompson's sarcasm accentuated his anger.

"I only found out about Tess's arrest last evening."

"And after Matthew's and Richardson's deaths and an attempt on your own life, you didn't think it was worth telling me that another member of your team had been arrested for murder?"

"I should have. I'm sorry."

"Sorry isn't good enough. My phone is ringing off the hook. I have the press and the auditors asking questions about what's going on in the house and where all of the money has come from for doing research there. I've got a ton of explaining to do."

"You mean we do," Bert said, trying to share the burden.

"No, Professor, I do," said Thompson. "I'm shutting you down. You've got till the end of the semester, then I want Katherine Jarvis out of that building and I want all of your research activities ended."

"But John, we're so close to a breakthrough..."

"A breakthrough? Is that why Jarvis and DiPetro have been going around making wild accusations against our campus police chief? I was under the impression that you were conducting scientific research, not ghost hunting."

"I regret the way Tess and Katie conducted themselves with Captain Davis." Bert tensed further as he thought about Gene's encounter with Gareth Reynolds.

"It's too late for regret. You and your team are out of control. I want you out of that house by Christmas, and then I want your operation shut down. Good-bye."

The first press call came in a half hour later and the next immediately after. By nine a.m., Bert stopped answering the phone and let the machine take messages—there were more than twenty by noon. The last one was not from the press. Bert gave a weary smile at the sound of the voice, but that disappeared as he continued to listen.

"Professor Myers, this is Winnie Seivers. I just heard some distressing news on the television. They said one of the students living in Cindy's home had been arrested. They also said Christopher Matthews was killed in a boating accident several weeks ago. It's a shame about Christopher; he was such a nice young man. However, even more disturbing is that when you and I met, you knew Christopher had died but you hid that from me. I value honesty very highly, Professor, and your lack of truthfulness is upsetting. I think it would be best if we didn't talk any further. Thank you and have a nice day."

Bert was convinced the day couldn't get any worse. That's

when his cell phone rang. It was a number he guarded closely and very few people knew it. He looked at the screen—it was Evelyn.

"Bert, it's horrible," she said. "You're all over the news—in the papers, on the radio and television. How are you holding up?"

Bert was surprisingly calm, even to himself. "I'm OK, Evie."

"I wish I could say the same for John," said Evelyn. "I just got a call from Sandy. She said he's very nervous about the auditors and funding issues. Sandy said he's even worried about his job." Bert didn't respond.

"Are you hearing me, Bert?" Evelyn asked.

"Yes, hon. I'm sorry. It's been an intense day. John ordered me to stop the research,"

"Well, that's the best news I've heard in a long time. John and Sandy have been very good to us. I only hope we can repair the damage. They cancelled out on the Paul Winters concert. This will be the first time in seven years that they haven't attended the winter solstice concert with us."

"The what?"

"The winter solstice concert. Haven't you heard anything I've said? Bert," Evelyn pleaded, "don't you see what this is doing to you, to us, to our friends and everyone around us. You have to stop this. People are getting hurt, people are dying."

"I will, Evelyn. I will." Bert was thumbing through the pages of Winnie's photo album.

"When, Bert?" Evelyn was angry, forceful, and desperate. "For God's sake Bert, when will you stop all of this?"

Bert paused at a photo of Amanda before answering. There was a determination in his voice that seemed impenetrable. He answered with the icy, calm resolve of a glacier. "I'll stop when I know the truth."

41

Light from a lightening strike travels virtually instantaneously. Sound travels at 343.2 meters per second. Counting the seconds between the lightning and the resulting thunder (one kilometer for every three seconds of delay) will yield an accurate estimate of the distance.

At 2:45 Saturday afternoon, Bert and Katie entered the campus police station. Davis was sitting behind his desk.

"Professor, I'm surprised to see you." Davis didn't acknowledge Katie's presence. "I would have thought you'd be preoccupied today with more pressing business."

"No, Captain, you pretty much head the list."

"If you're here to apologize for your students' behavior, I've already forgotten that incident. Besides, it looks like Miss DiPetro has more urgent matters to attend to."

"Actually, in retrospect, it seems they weren't so far off after all."

"Oh no, don't tell me you're going down that same road? Don't you think it's time that you and your students just dropped this whole conspiracy thing and get back to physics or weather or whatever it is you do?"

"No, I don't, at least not until you can help me understand things like this." Bert tossed a photo on the desk. Davis picked it up and examined it.

"Where did you get this?"

"Let's just say it's from a mutual acquaintance. I assume you recognize it."

"Of course. It was the day Gareth Reynolds brought home his new Rolls."

"And did he drive it home himself?"

"I don't like to play games, Professor. If you have this picture, you know perfectly well who drove the car home—his driver, me."

"For a man who doesn't like to play games, you led Tess and Katie to believe you hardly knew the Reynolds."

"It really wasn't any of their business, just as it's none of yours."

"It must have been pretty handy to drive for a man who was also the head of the police commission. So, exactly whose business is it when a crime is covered up?"

"Here we go with the conspiracy theories again. Well I've entertained about enough of this. Unless you walk away from this right now you're going to..."

Bert tossed another picture on the desk. Davis closed his eyes and shook his head from side to side in exasperation. Then he grabbed the picture and continued, "Don't say I didn't warn you, Professor," Davis glanced at the picture and tossed it back down on the desk. "A high school picture of me at the pool is hardly compelling evidence of anything." Davis pressed the intercom "Sergeant, I've got a couple people in my..."

"It's not of you," said Bert. "It's of Amanda Reynolds' fraternal twin, your son."

Davis sat transfixed, staring at his younger self, smiling back at him from the picture; only it wasn't his face. It belonged to the son he had never known. As Davis stared at the photo each missing year, month, and second seemed to plow new furrows into his brow, until his whole face sagged under the strain.

"Are there more?" Davis's voice broke as he asked. Bert nodded affirmatively.

"Is he all right?" Davis's eyes glistened in the afternoon light.

"So far as we know. The trail ends when he left high school."

"What's his name?"

"I don't know. We call him Robert."

"There seems to be a lot you don't know," Davis challenged.

"What I know for certain is that Cynthia Reynolds's son looks strikingly like you and nothing like Gareth Reynolds. So, perhaps you could educate me, unless you'd rather I ask Gareth."

Bert had gotten through. Once the wall of silence fractured, it quickly crumbled and fell. Davis talked about Gareth's preoccupation with the business and Cynthia's growing loneliness. He described her solitude for long periods, and how he became her sounding board and confidant. With each secret shared, their attraction grew until one night, just before Christmas 1989, it became too overpowering for them to resist.

The affair was short-lived. Cynthia was racked with guilt and by February, it was over. Soon after Cynthia discovered she was pregnant.

"I wanted to end it right away, but Cynthia wouldn't consider an abortion. She just hoped it would be a girl. She was certain that if it was, she could convince Gareth it was his. But if it were a boy, well you can see that problem for yourself."

"So that's why she insisted on giving Robert up for adoption," said Bert. Davis nodded in agreement. "And Amanda's death?"

Davis said he needed to distance himself from Cynthia. With Gareth's help, he got into the Hudson Valley Police Department. "I was a just a rookie at the time, so I was pulling the night shift when the call came in. As soon as I heard the address, I called dispatch and said I'd cover it."

"And then what?" Bert was pushing hard. "What happened to Amanda?"

"What are you hunting for, Professor? It happened over twenty years ago. What does it matter now? For God's sake, can't you just let it go?"

"No, Captain, I can't." Bert could see the desperation in Davis's face: the fear of acknowledging what happened mixed with the anguish of holding it in for too long. "Whatever happened that night triggered something that's still impacting people right now. Two of my students are dead, another is being held for murder, and somehow they're all connected to Amanda Reynolds. I need to know how. Why are you protecting him? Why are you letting Gareth Reynolds get away with murdering his daughter?"

Davis looked up at Bert and let out a nervous laugh, "Is that what you think? You think I'm covering for Gareth Reynolds?" He paused, and then stared directly into Bert's eyes. "Listen carefully, because I'm only going to say this once, and if either of you ever push it, I'll deny I ever said it. Given your current standing in the community, there is no way on Earth you would ever be able to prove it. Gareth Reynolds didn't kill Amanda—Cynthia did."

The next evening, Bert, Katie, and Gene met in Amanda's room. Bert and Katie reviewed their meeting with Ed Davis. Then Bert related his phone conversation with John Thompson.

"So that's it," said Katie. "We're shut down, just like that?"

"It's hardly 'just like that,' Katie," Bert answered. "Dean Thompson has a lot of explaining to do, and right now the mere existence of this project is highlighting some thorny issues that he'd rather just disappear."

"Maybe so, but to stop everything now, after so much time and work..." Katie couldn't continue. Like Bert and Gene, she understood the futility of her arguments. Even after more than a year of study, it felt as though they were just beginning to make headway, and even that was more of a feeling than a reality. Katie sat back, rubbed her hand against the soft clean surface of Amanda's rug, and let her head fall against the wall.

"Even if you're barred from continuing to work at the house," said Gene, "that doesn't have to stop our pursuing Chris's findings."

Bert expected Gene's comment. While he would have preferred not to address it, he had steeled himself for this moment. "I don't think that's a good idea, Gene."

"Is it because of Dean Thompson, Bert, or is there

something else?"

"Gene," Bert gazed downward, "what would you have done if Gareth Reynolds had taken you up on your offer and confessed to you that Cynthia had killed Amanda?"

"I..." Gene stumbled as he realized what Bert was getting at. "I wouldn't have had a choice. I would have honored the client/counselor relationship and maintained his confidentiality."

"Exactly, and we would have been worse off than before you met with him. Let's face it; none of us are trained investigators."

"I am." Bert and the others looked up to see Ed Davis standing in the doorway.

Bert invited him in, "Are you offering to help?"

Davis joined them on the rug, "I've been thinking a lot since your visit yesterday."

Katie looked at him sheepishly, "I guess I owe you an apology."

"Not at all. You said I was being evasive and you were right. My wife and I have two girls of our own. I never told her about Cynthia or the other children. I thought I could keep it buried forever. Obviously, I was wrong. It's a funny thing about secrets. Sometimes the more you try to contain them, the larger they become and the more energy they consume until at some point they devour your whole life. Well, now my wife knows."

"How did she take it?" Gene asked.

"She's angry, and she has a right to be. We have a lot of work to do. I'm trying to get her to agree to counseling. Right now, my main concern is Robert. He's been abandoned by everyone he's ever known."

"Then we continue searching?" Gene posed.

"I have to agree with the professor, Reverend. Interrogation is very different from counseling, especially when people are out to deceive you. And even you, Professor, although your performance has been decidedly better than the others, even you missed some fairly obvious clues."

"I did?"

Davis tossed Robert's high school swim meet picture on the rug. "Take a look at the background behind Robert."

Bert and the others peered at the photo. Mounted on the pool wall was an out-of-focus banner. Only a portion was visible, but Bert could make out some of the letters, "Looks like 'avier' over his right shoulder and 'ays' followed by a diamond shape over his left."

"It could be a kite," Gene said. "It's got a tail on it."

"Not bad," said Davis. "It's a stingray."

Katie leaned over the picture and squinted, "I see it."

Davis continued, "Given the size and placement of the letters, I'd bet that full sign reads "Xavier Stingrays." Since Robert is at a pool, that's probably the name of the high school swim team. If you look carefully just below his left belt line, you can just make out the word 'Captain.' Robert was born September 1990 and the picture was taken his senior year. That means this picture was taken sometime around 2007. Since he was a ward of the state, it's a safe bet that he went to high school within a few hundred miles of here. How many Xavier High Schools with a swim team named Stingrays do you suspect there are within a 300-mile radius? And how many students do you think were the swim team captain for that school in 2007?"

"Captain Davis," Gene said with admiration, "I think you've made your point." Then Gene sat back against the wall and let out a quiet sigh.

"Are you OK, Gene?" Katie asked.

"I'm fine. I was just enjoying playing my part on the team for a while. I'll miss that."

"Don't jump ship just yet," said Bert. "There's a crucial role for you to play right now and one for which you are perfectly qualified." Gene forced an amused smile, but Bert was serious, "Tess needs your help."

"Maybe there are more connections here then we realized," said Katie. "Maybe what happened to Cynthia is related to what's happening now with Tess."

"How do you mean?" asked Bert.

"Look at that officer at the prison who killed his wife and daughter and then himself. You said he worked in a room that was finished using the exact same paint as this one."

"That's right."

"Cynthia and Tess were both in this room and both of them were under strain: Tess from her abusive father and Cynthia from her post partum depression and a sick child. And so far as we know, Ed Lowman killed his family at or very near the time of the winter solstice."

"Exactly as Cynthia did," Bert finished.

"Hold on just a second," said Gene. "I was going along with your theory for a while, but let's remember that Ralph Campbell was killed in mid-August, no where near an astronomical event.

"What was the date he was killed?" Katie asked.

"August 16," said Bert, "why?"

Katie opened her journal and thumbed through the pages until she reached the entry for August 16. She reviewed what she had written, taking special note of her sloppy penmanship and recalled why. "August 16th was also the date the room's environment died for a time."

"Katie," said Gene, "don't you think 'died' is a little personal. You're talking about this room as though it were a real person."

"To be honest, Gene, I believe that Amanda and this room are somehow tied together and that a lot of what's been happening here has to do with her trying to communicate with us. I think she uses the weather and the room's environment as her means of warning. After all, the same kind of thing happened the day of the boating accident and when Evelyn was almost killed in Bert's car. I think Amanda's been trying to tell us all along how and when she died."

"While I don't necessarily go along with the spirit thing," said Bert, "it does seem as though there are definite connections between the weather anomalies, this room's environment, and the related events. And for whatever reason, many of these events are somehow tied into astronomical phenomena." Bert looked up at Amanda's crib. "From everything we've learned to date I think we can safely conclude that Amanda Reynolds was suffocated by her mother in that crib at the precise moment of the winter solstice in 1990."

"I can understand that kind of statement coming from Katie," said Gene, "but I'm surprised hearing it from you, Bert. Don't you think that's a bit more superstition than science?"

"Maybe so Gene," said Katie, "but then how do you explain the clock's hands being stuck on..." She stopped in mid-sentence. "Oh my God," Katie froze while looking up at the clock as did the others when she described what they all saw. "The clock's hands are moving again."

42

Multi-Cell Thunderstorms: As the first thunderstorm matures, its downdraft seeds the development of a new, up-wind cell. As long as the flow of warm moist air and instability remain, cells can be self-propagating. Clusters of individual storms can form into narrow bands called Squall Lines. They can stretch for hundreds of miles and last more then ten hours.

Hudson's Columbia County Courthouse is small by comparison to its big city cousins, but the gray stone edifice with its copper-domed rotunda, Corinthian columns, and sculptured pediment can still make a sobering impression on those adjudicated there. Gene and Katie arrived just before the start of the hearing and slid into the wooden bench behind Tess and Brian Rosenthal, the lawyer secured for her by Gene. As they sat, Gene placed his hand on Tess's shoulder and she turned around. The ashen look on Tess's face brightened and a glimmer of hope filtered into her otherwise gloomy demeanor. She had been held since her arraignment pending the extradition hearing. The door to the left of the judge's bench opened. The bailiff called everyone to attention and read off the case number and purpose for the hearing. Judge Harvey Singleton called on the prosecutor, Salvatore Conti, to explain the state's position.

"Your honor, the state requests Miss DiPetro be extradited to Indiana to stand trial for the felony murder of Ralph Campbell of Franklin, Indiana, Miss DiPetro's stepfather."

Attorney Rosenthal looked up at the word 'felony', and then wrote something in his note pad. Judge Singleton asked Rosenthal to state the defense's position. Rosenthal hesitated for a moment. He had been preparing a defense for first-degree murder. Felony murder meant that the homicide was committed in connection with another crime. "Your honor, the state of New York currently has no jurisdiction to execute offenders convicted for capital offenses. The state of Indiana does and has put two offenders to death by lethal injection as recently as 2007."

"Mr. Conti," Judge Singleton asked, "how many people has the state of Indiana executed in the last hundred years or so?"

"Eighty-nine since 1900, your honor."

"And how many of those were women?"

"None, your honor."

"The state's motion is accepted." Judge Singleton addressed Tess's attorney, "Mister Rosenthal, I warn you in the future not to waste this court's time."

"Your honor," Conti interrupted, "the state also asks that Miss DiPetro be held without bail until her arraignment in Indiana."

"That hardly seems necessary, your honor," said Rosenthal. "Miss DiPetro is a college student with a part-time waitressing job. Her current bond is set at $250,000, which is an exorbitant amount of money for a person in her position. She's an honors student at Nadowa College and has no prior convictions."

"Miss DiPetro represents a significant flight risk, your honor," Conti returned. "Two days after Mr. Campbell's murder, Miss DiPetro deposited $175,000 in two separate bank accounts in Atlantic City, New Jersey."

Katie turned to Gene. From his expression, it was obvious that he was as surprised as she was. Of even greater concern was the surprised look on Brian Rosenthal's face as he leaned over to scribble something in his notebook. But Conti wasn't finished.

"Miss DiPetro also has in her possession an unused airplane ticket. She had purchased a round-trip ticket from Albany to Indiana to visit her dying mother. Her boyfriend, Christopher Matthews, apparently met her in Greenwood. After her stepfather's murder, the couple drove to Atlantic City where they stayed overnight while she opened the accounts and made the deposits."

Gene turned to Katie with a look of bewilderment. Katie looked downward. She had kept Tess and Chris's excursion to Atlantic City a secret. It now looked as though that decision might have been a mistake. Once again, Gene and Katie could see the same confused anxiety in Rosenthal who seemed at a loss to say anything.

Conti continued, "Supposedly, Mr. Matthews was killed in a boating accident last month, but we understand from Hudson Valley Police Department that friends of Miss DiPetro have received text messages from Mr. Matthews since then. He has since been identified as a person of interest in the case. Given the gravity of the charges against her, the unknown whereabouts of her accomplice, her access to considerable funds of money, and her demonstrated ability to quickly orchestrate alternative travel arrangements, we believe Miss DiPetro represents a significant flight risk."

"I'm inclined to agree with you, counselor. Motion accepted." Singleton raised his gavel. "Miss DiPetro will be held without bail until her arraignment in Indiana." The judge brought the gavel down with resounding finality, "Next case."

Sitting across from Tess in the holding pen, the tone of Gene's conversation was out of character for the normally composed minister, but seemed necessary to save Tess from herself.

"All right Tess, that's it. No more stories, no more lies. This isn't a game. You're on trial for your life. You've lied to the police—to your friends—even to your attorney. You're going to spend the rest of your life in prison. Is that what you want?"

"Of course not," Tess was talking through the tears streaming down her blotched face. Her nose was running as fast as her tears, and the taste of salt sat on her lips. Brian sat stoically. He had been blindsided in court. Tess had lied to him, hidden information, and made him look like a fool. If Gene couldn't get through to her, she was going to trial in Indiana with another attorney.

"Then why all the lies?" Gene pleaded. "For God's sake, Tess, what's the truth?"

"You'll hate me if I tell you."

"Nobody will hate you, and it doesn't matter what anyone else thinks. If you didn't kill your stepfather, the only thing that matters is the truth."

Tess looked up, "Do you think I killed him?"

"Honestly, at this point I'd have to say yes."

Tess wiped her eyes and nose and sat up straight, "I stole the money."

Rosenthal moved forward and entered the conversation, "How Tess? When? And don't leave out a thing."

Back in the Catskills, Ed Davis sat opposite Bert at the Chief Diner. He said, "Andrew Irving."

Bert finished sipping his coffee, "Not Robert?"

"No. According to his guidance counselor, his friends called him Andy. She said he was extremely bright and was quite an athlete. He was the only sophomore in the school's history to be named as the swim team captain. In his senior year, a scout spotted him at a swim meet and offered him a full scholarship to Saint John's University."

"Did you find anything else?"

"More than I wanted to. He had eleven foster placements. Most of them lasted only a few months. In between, he attended four different schools and had three institutional placements. He also spent six weeks in the hospital when he was twelve." Bert could see in Davis's face that there was more to the hospital story. "He only had three placements that lasted for any length of time. At five, they placed him with a family here in the valley for more than two years. At eleven, he had a placement that lasted for a little over a year. During that one, he went to the hospital after four months with a broken arm. Supposedly, it happened when he fell off his bike. Eight months later he wound up back in the hospital in a body cast and his prick foster father went to prison." Davis gripped his cup hard while tightening his jaw. Bert pictured the foster father's neck in place of the cup. Davis continued, "Then at fourteen he got a placement that stuck and he stayed with them clear through high school right up until the time of the accident."

"Accident?"

"Yeah," Davis's face looked beaten and drawn. "Andy was in a car accident midway through his senior year. A drunk driver hit him head-on. His face was badly cut up. Fortunately, the person that hit him was loaded—a plastic surgeon. In addition to covering the medical expenses, Andy ended up with a huge settlement. Then he fell below the radar and vanished. He moved out on his own and changed his name before taking off for college. It seems he wanted to start over completely and had enough cash to make it happen."

"So what's next?"

"Several things. I checked with the station house about the calls between Matthews, you, and Katie. I'd like to put a trace on both your phones so that when he calls again we can try to get a fix on his location. I gather from Katie that it doesn't look very promising, but it's a start. Maybe we can also decipher some clues from his messages."

"Kind of Big Brotherish, isn't it?" Bert asked.

"I agree, but there was that thing with your car."

"You think Chris might have had something to do with that?"

"I don't know, but it's too much of a coincidence to overlook. Are you OK with this?" Bert's mind flashed back to the last message he had received from Chris:

IT WOULD HAVE BEEN A SHAME IF THE MRS HAD DIED FOR YOUR SINS

STAY AWAY FROM KATIE

C

He shivered at the thought of others reading Chris's text. It could look even worse than it was, and what it was, was bad enough. Then he thought about how close Evelyn had come to being killed. No amount of embarrassment was worth putting her life at risk. "I can't speak for Katie, but as long as you're sure the monitoring will be limited to calls to and from Chris…"

"You have my word on it. I'll talk to Katie. There's one other thing." Davis slid a piece of paper across the table. "This is the name and address of Andy's first long-term placement. If you're willing, I'd like you to find out what you can from them."

Bert smiled and nodded, "Of course."

"Thanks. I'll talk to the people from his last placement. I want to know as much about my son as I can before I meet him."

43

The eye of a hurricane is a region of mostly calm clear weather found at the center. The eye wall, a ring of towering thunderstorms, surrounds the eye and is where the most severe weather of the storm occurs.

As Katie reached the stair landing, she peered over to the stack of cardboard boxes sitting in front of her room. At first, she thought she might like moving into a regular dorm and mingling with the other students, but that was before the questions began. There were the questions about the mysterious house on Lakota Drive, about the secret room, the freak storms, Chris and Drew, and most of all about Tess. Then there were the ones about her and Bert. Were they lovers, did his wife know, was he good in bed? Katie avoided answering. Others took that as evasiveness, and the questioning only intensified. Now she dreaded leaving the safety of her cloistered world.

She went into her room, retrieved her diary from the top drawer of her nightstand, and walked into Amanda's room. As she entered the door, her pressures and anxieties melted away. Katie rested on the soft clean rug, closed her eyes, and let the room's peacefulness envelop her like a protective blanket. After a time she sat up, picked up her journal and began to write.

October 11, 2012

Hello Amanda,

I'm lost and confused. I don't understand. I sit here feeling safe and calm while I know that outside of this room, a storm is brewing and I feel powerless to stop it.

It all seemed so perfect at the start. You seemed like an invisible friend, maybe even protector but now I'm not so sure. If you really cared for us, if you had some sort of control over our lives, how could you let events get so out of hand; how could you let such terrible things happen to people you care about, or are you just playing with us? Is this just some cruel game?

Even as I write this, I don't believe that. You couldn't be so callous, yet fill us with these feelings of warmth, and ... love, yes love. I can't help it but that's the feeling I get sitting here. I feel loved. So maybe you don't have very much power over us after all. Or is it that you didn't love Chris and Drew as much? Some people think that you actually caused their deaths. Did you? Could you? I don't believe it. We all felt the same way in here.

So what is it, Amanda? What are you trying to tell us, and what about Tess? I know her stepfather was a real SOB but I can't believe she's capable of killing anyone, even him. And Chris, what's going on with him? Everywhere I turn someone else has seen or heard from him. If he's alive, then what's all the mystery about? What is he hiding, and why? I don't understand Amanda. Where's it all going?

Now, only Bert and I are left and even we seem to be under attack. Dean Thompson shut down the research. Even he is in trouble. I have to leave by Christmas. It's like everyone who's had anything to do with you or this house is being punished, but for what? I wish you could talk to me, let me know what you need or want.

I'm going to miss you, Amanda. I'm going to miss being in this room and feeling your presence. It's not going to be easy for me; there are too many questions I can't answer. Now people are even beginning to ask questions about Bert and me. I want to tell them there is no Bert and me but God forgive me, I know that just isn't true. I know he's married. I've met his wife and she seems nice. I can tell that she really loves him and I can see that he really loves her too. But I can't help myself from thinking about him, about what it would be like to be with him.

Katie stopped writing. She listened carefully for any sounds and looked around her. She glanced out the window for any signs of unsettled weather. It was bright and clear outside and the room remained perfectly quiet and comfortable. Katie smiled weakly, relieved that at least one concern evaporated.

She returned to the diary.

I'm glad I was wrong about your being jealous.

If you can, Amanda, please help Tess. I don't know what you can do, but she really needs the help. It doesn't look good for her right now.

I hope I can get back here after we move, at least to visit you. I feel so close to you I can't even imagine not having you in my life.

I hope you feel the same.

Katie closed the book, shut her eyes, and sat back. She immersed herself once again in the room's perfect atmosphere. As she did, she felt something new. Katie tried to tell herself it was only her imagination, but she couldn't dismiss the physical sensation. She felt arms wrapping gently around her, as if she were being hugged.

Katie breathed deeply, grabbed the diary, and exited the room. As soon as she cleared the doorway, the tears started streaming down her face.

Meanwhile, across the valley, Bert arrived at the house Ed Davis had asked him to visit. He rang the doorbell of a ranch house that looked pretty much like every other in the neighborhood. It was typical of the developments that defined middle class for the baby boomer generation. Each 1200-square-foot starter home had three bedrooms, one-and-a-half baths, and a fireplace. Over time, people added touches like better entrance doors and outdoor light fixtures. Beyond that, only the color differentiated one house from the others.

Bert did not repeat the mistake he had made when he visited Winnie Seivers. This time, he had called ahead. The door swung open to a neat, slim woman as modest looking as was the house. Tinges of gray ran through her chestnut-brown hair.

"Professor Myers?"

"Bert is fine. Mrs. Samuelson?"

"Roslyn, please." She invited him in.

Like the outside of the house, the interior was unpretentious. Whatever it lacked in opulence, it made up in warmth. Neatly clustered pictures adorned the walls and hallway. There was something else, too. Like Winnie's, the house had a decidedly feminine feel about it.

"Will Mr. Samuelson be joining us?"

"No, Professor, I mean, Bert. Richard has been dead for more than twelve years now."

"I'm sorry, I didn't know."

"That's all right. I'm the one who should apologize. I intentionally didn't share that information on the phone. I was afraid that if I had you might not have come, and I would have missed the opportunity to talk about Andy." She spoke in a soft, almost admiring tone.

"It sounds like you cared very much for him."

"More then I could say. Let me show you something." Roslyn walked Bert to the start of the hall connecting the living room to the bath and bedrooms. She pointed to one photo in a collage of pictures. "This was the day Andy first came to us." The photo showed an overjoyed young couple kneeling to either side of five-year-old Andy. Richard was a huge man with a warm smile and at least fifty excess pounds. Roslyn and Richard lovingly wrapped their arms around the boy, although his remained stiffly against his sides. The boy's face reflected a flat, almost autistic affect. Roslyn guided Bert through the series of collages that lined both sides of the hallway and, in sum, chronicled Andy's thirty-month stay with the couple. As the months passed, Andy's expressiveness grew, as did his obvious affection for his foster parents.

"This was our vacation at Lake George," Roslyn said as she pointed to a photo of Andy holding a fish almost half his length. Richard stood beside him helping to support the catch and smiling proudly. "Andy was seven then. He and Richard loved fishing. Most days, Andy did the catching. My husband was a terrible fisherman. It didn't matter though. Andy idolized Richard, and believe me, no father ever loved his son more than Richard loved that boy. It was during that vacation that we decided to adopt Andy."

"But he was only with you for a few more months." Bert felt the judgmental tone in his voice. While it wasn't intentional, he could see the pained expression in Roslyn's face. "It was my fault," Roslyn pointed to one last photo showing Richard and Andy standing in a grassy field. Andy was wearing a catcher's mitt on his right hand. Richard held a softball. "This is the last picture I have of them. They loved tossing that stupid ball back and forth. Richard had to special order that catcher's mitt and believe me, it cost him a pretty penny."

Bert nodded, "Because it was left-handed."

"Yes, how did you know?"

"I'm a lefty, too, and a baseball buff. In the whole history of the game, there have only been a handful of left-handed catchers. The last one to catch in the big leagues was Benny Distefano for Pittsburgh, and he only caught for three games back in the late eighties." Bert looked at Roslyn, "Oh, sorry for boring you with all this baseball drivel."

"Not at all," Roslyn became animated. "Benny Distefano was the signature on the glove."

"Really? A decent left-handed catcher's mitt is rare enough. An autographed one has to be exceptional. No wonder it was expensive."

Roslyn looked back at the picture and described how sometimes Richard and Andy wouldn't come in until it got so dark out that they couldn't see the ball anymore. That was how it was the night Richard died. After dinner, Richard went into the living room and sat on the recliner, the same one Bert had been sitting on earlier. Richard never got up. The doctor said it was a massive heart attack.

"Please understand, Bert, I wasn't at all prepared for that. Richard was so young and alive. Neither of us had even considered anything like that. We had no real savings to speak of, very little insurance, and virtually no equity in the house. After the funeral, I found myself with no husband, no money, and a mountain of debt. I guess it was just too much for me. The bank threatened to take the house. I had to work two jobs just to meet expenses. I went into a deep depression, and I let the house go. After a while, I just wasn't thinking straight. Everything got overwhelming and I couldn't cope. Finally, I snapped. I don't even remember how I did it, but I was in my car in the garage with the engine running. The empty bottle of sleeping pills was on the seat next to me. I would have died if Andy hadn't gotten home from school when he did. He found me, turned off the engine, and called 911. As I was recuperating in the hospital, DCF got the police report. The social worker came back with a sheriff and they took Andy. I never saw him again. That's why when you called, I hope you understand, I just had to… I needed to talk about him."

Bert sat in his car for a long time before starting the engine and thought about Andy Irving. As Ed Davis had said, eventually, everyone in Andy's life abandoned him.

44

Unstable conditions produce clouds with higher development and a piled-up appearance. Clouds with a high proportion of ice crystals appear white and translucent. Those with a higher percentage of water block the sun and can appear dark and foreboding.

While Brian Rosenthal's arguments didn't prevent Tess's extradition to Indiana, he did manage to get a change of venue to Kokomo, an hour north of Greenwood. He also petitioned for and secured a speedy trial. Meanwhile, the prosecution amended its charge from felony murder to murder. Katie decided to support Tess by attending the trial, even if it meant seeing her GPA plummet in the process; but that didn't happen. What did was something she could not have anticipated or even imagined.

When Katie told Kevin Casperin she was attending the trial and would not be around to do her weather forecasts, Kevin reacted immediately. The "Good Morning Nadowa" incident had turned out to be a life-changing event for the previously mousey announcer. He resolved to do battle for every future opportunity. Following Chris's boating accident, Kevin not only recaptured his seat on the popular show, but he also lobbied for and secured the position of Student Media Administrator. It didn't take him long to establish his credentials. He bolstered his reputation as a hard-hitting reporter with penetrating investigative reports, which he integrated into the morning show. Unfortunately, for Bert and Dean Thompson, the focus of much of his initial reporting dealt almost exclusively with the financial peculiarities associated with the Lakota Drive property and the rumors about the strange events that surrounded it.

Kevin mapped out a strategy for Katie to cover the trial for the campus media and pitched it to the media faculty advisor. Several days later, he presented the approved plan to Katie. At first, she had mixed feelings about profiting from her friend's struggles. She changed her mind when she realized that, with the right approach, she might actually be able to do Tess a great deal of good. She accepted Kevin's offer.

Katie covered the courtroom proceedings and did an entire series on the background story as well. Who was Ralph Campbell? What was he like? What did his neighbors think about the crime? What were the strategies for the prosecution and defense? Katie provided in-depth interviews and broadcasts from the site. Kevin integrated concise reports into the six a.m. and six p.m. newscasts, and broader segments as part of "Good Morning Nadowa." Katie also continued to provide her morning and evening weather forecasts. A mobile broadcast studio and a two-man crew accompanied her. The truck contained satellite communication facilities for transmitting the live reports and for tapping into weather related databases. Each student attended classes via teleconferencing. Faculty granted extra credit for life experience that more than offset any missed assignments.

As unprepared as Katie was with Kevin's proposal, she was even less so with the firestorm of interest her reports generated. Virtually everyone on campus tuned in. Several professors incorporated the case into their course curricula. Even outside the campus, life in the valley came to a virtual standstill three times daily.

Katie provided a graveside report on Audrey Campbell. She interviewed Audrey and Tess's minister and members of their congregation. She talked to Tess's teachers and fellow students. She also featured court analysts who dissected potential prosecution and defense strategies for the trial and gave Brian Rosenthal as much airtime as he wanted. Local talk show hosts on both sides of the argument made the case a central issue of their programming, and it soon became a prime topic of discussion on Facebook and Twitter. Kevin posted feeds of

Katie's reports on the campus web site and media blogs. The major networks and the Associated Press picked up the reports. By the completion of Katie's third broadcast, each of the major networks had sent its own crews to Indiana. Vowing to prevent a media circus, Judge Harry B. Pendleton prohibited any cameras from entering the courthouse.

By the start of Tess's trial, the murder of Ralph Campbell was a cyclone of national news, Kokomo was in the vortex, and Katie stood in the eye of the storm.

The trial took place in courtroom 2A on the second floor of the courthouse. The judge's bench and jury box were higher than the level of the spectators' seats. A row of windows to the judge's right extended from just beyond the bench to the rear of the courtroom. During the trial, Katie sat directly behind Tess. Jeff Shearing, an art major and the crew's cameraman, sat along the aisle of Katie's row. Jeff captured the courtroom drama in pencil sketches that Katie incorporated into her reports. Simon "Sy" Jenkins, the technical member of the team, manned the mobile studio that he had driven out to Kokomo.

Fortunately, the meeting with Tess and Gene after the botched extradition hearing prompted Brian to stay on as Tess's attorney. It was a good move for his firm. Win or lose, the publicity generated by the trial had already resulted in a flurry of new retainers.

The police did not find the murder weapon, but the evidence against Tess was substantial. In addition, Tess's lies and changing stories seriously undermined her credibility. Brian decided to go on the offensive. He called Tess to the stand at the very start of the trial.

"Miss DiPetro, why were you in Greenwood on the day Mr. Campbell was murdered?" From his first words, Brian sounded more like the prosecutor then the defense attorney.

"I got a call from my Aunt Sarah that my mother was very ill with cancer so I went to see her. She died shortly after I arrived and I stayed for the wake and funeral."

"Did you get a chance to talk to your mother?"

"For a few minutes."

"What did she say to you?"

Tess hesitated. Brian had prepared her for this line of questioning, but she wanted desperately to avoid it. Brian pushed.

"What did you talk about, Miss DiPetro?"

"She said she was sorry."

"We couldn't hear you," Brian barked. "Speak up."

"She said she was sorry."

"Sorry for what?"

"For letting my stepfather molest me."

Brian looked at the jury. Tess's statement had the desired effect.

"So your mother knew your stepfather was molesting you?"

"Yes."

"But she did nothing?"

"No."

"How many times did this happen? Once, twice, more?"

Tess looked at Brian confused, "I'm not sure what you mean."

"It's a pretty simple question, Miss DiPetro. How many times did your stepfather molest you?"

"I don't know. Hundreds, maybe."

"Hundreds? Over what period of time?"

Once again, Tess's response was inaudible. Once again, Brian chided her, "We couldn't hear you. Speak up."

Tess fought hard to hold back the tears, "About four years."

Murmurs traveled around the courtroom. Judge Pendleton put down his gavel. "Anyone who feels the urgency to carry on a conversation can wait for a recess or leave now."

Brian pushed forward, "So you and Ralph Campbell were lovers."

Tess was outraged. Brian had never prepared her for such an onslaught, "No, we weren't lovers. I hated what he did to me. I hated him."

"Then why didn't you just tell him to stop?"

"I couldn't. I didn't know how to."

"Didn't know how to? That hardly seems credible. A smart woman like you seems perfectly capable of communicating a simple message like 'no.' How old were you when you first starting having sex with your stepfather: fifteen, sixteen?"

Tess responded in barely a whisper.

"How old?" Brian's voice was suddenly soft and sympathetic.

"I was eleven." Tess couldn't hold the tears back any longer. She began to cry.

Brian looked at the jury again. The impact of Tess's answers was evident on their faces. It was time to switch the line of questioning.

"You said your mother apologized for not stopping your stepfather."

"Yes."

"What else did she say?"

"She thanked me for forgiving her."

"And then?"

"Nothing. That was the last thing she said and then she died."

"What happened then?"

"The nurses came into the room and asked me to wait outside. That's when my stepfather arrived."

"Right after your mother died?"

"Yes."

"And what did he say to you?"

"He wanted to pick up where we left off."

"You mean as a father and daughter?"

"As sex partners."

"Isn't it possible that you just misunderstood? That he had changed and just wanted you to share in his loss?"

"No," Tess shouted. "He wanted sex. My mother's body wasn't even cold and all he could think about was getting me back into his bed."

"The nurse supervisor will testify that she heard you

threaten him."

"He made it clear to me that if I didn't go along, if I didn't put out for him, that he would cut off my school funding."

"And what did you say?"

"I told him to take his money and go to hell, and if he didn't stay away from me I'd kill him."

"So you did threaten him."

"Yes, but I didn't mean it literally. I was upset. My mother had just died. They were just words."

The men at the prosecutor's table were scrambling through their notes, leafing back and forth in their legal pads, highlighting, underlining, and making notes in the margins. More than anything else, they were crossing lines out.

Brian looked at the jury again. He was not able to assess the impact of Tess's last statement. Pushing further would be risky. He changed direction again.

"And when was the next time you saw your stepfather?"

"Two days later, at the cemetery."

"You stood right next to him, didn't you?"

"He stood next to me, behind me."

"And what did he say to you?"

"Nothing."

"Then did he do anything?"

"It was raining hard and he stood very close behind me. He put one hand on my shoulder like he was consoling me, and he put the other on my hip."

"And how did that make you feel?"

"It disgusted me."

"Well, you have an odd way of showing it, because there are people here who will testify that you didn't seem bothered at all. In fact, instead of looking disgusted or even upset, they will say that they saw you talking to him and that you were smiling as you did. Now, how could that be?"

"Because I wanted him to think I was playing along with him."

"Why bother? Once your mother was dead you could have

just left and never seen your stepfather again."

"Because I wanted to throw him off guard so he wouldn't suspect that while he was at the funeral dinner, I would be taking my money from his house."

"Your money?"

"Yes, my mother slaved for that man their whole married life and made certain that he set aside enough money to pay for my college education. She wanted to put the money in a trust fund for me, but Ralph said he didn't trust banks so he kept it hidden in the bedroom closet. All I was doing was retrieving my own money."

Brian scanned the prosecutor's table and caught a glimpse of Eliot Mason. He didn't like what he saw. By raising each of Tess's suspicious behaviors during his interrogation, he had hoped to rob the prosecution of their most lethal weapon—getting the jury to distrust the truthfulness of Tess's testimony. Looking at Mason smiling, it was clear to Brian that he had missed something. The thought unnerved him for a moment. He shook it off and continued.

"And did you take the money?"

"Yes."

"But you told the police you were never at the house."

"I lied. I was trying to cover taking the money. When the police questioned me, I didn't know my stepfather had been killed."

"How much did you take?"

"I didn't know until I arrived in New Jersey and counted it. $175,000."

Gasps rose from the spectator seats and the jury box. It was a bad sign, but it was going to come out eventually and Brian preferred it to come out on his watch.

"So you took all the money from the closet."

"No. The money was in several layers of shoeboxes. I took the money from the bottom layers and left the one at the top full. That way he wouldn't immediately notice the money was gone."

"What did you do next?"

"I went back to my motel room and waited for Chris."

"Chris?"

"Chris Matthews, my boyfriend. He was picking me up to drive me back to New York."

"And did you see your stepfather at all?"

"No. The house was still empty when I left."

"And what time was that?"

"About one or one-thirty."

"And what time did Matthews arrive to pick you up?"

"Between three-thirty and four."

"Over two hours later, more than enough time to go to your stepfather's house prior to picking you up."

Tess stared at Brian. He hadn't prepped her for this line of questioning. "But he wouldn't go to my stepfather's. There was no reason for him to."

"Didn't you talk to Matthews the night before the murder?"

"Yes."

"And hadn't you previously told him about your stepfather molesting you?"

"Yes, but..."

"And didn't you tell him about what your stepfather said to you at the hospital?"

"Yes, but Chris would never..."

"And that if you didn't give into his demands he would cut you off financially?"

"You're twisting everything around..."

"And how much you hated Ralph Campbell? And how you wished that he were dead?"

"Yes, but..."

"Did Christopher Matthews love you?"

"Yes."

"Are you sure?"

"He proposed to me. He told me he wanted to spend the rest of his life with me."

"And you loved him?"

"Of course."

"Enough to lie for him?"

"I… I don't know."

"You don't know or you won't say?"

"Chris would never… Chris could never hurt anyone."

"But you don't know that for certain, do you?" Brian shouted again, "Do you?"

Tess broke down and cried. Judge Pendleton called for a recess, and the prosecution team stormed out the back of the courtroom.

After the recess, Brian continued extracting details from Tess, mostly against her will, on Chris's potential involvement in the murder. He emphasized how Chris had lied to Katie about picking Tess up at the airport, how he proposed to Tess and then suggested they celebrate their engagement in Atlantic City, and how he even helped Tess set up the bank accounts in both their names. By the time he finished, Brian had achieved his goal of explaining away Tess's presence at the murder scene, her suspicious and sometimes contradictory behavior, and even her lying to the police. More importantly, and more disturbing to Tess, he had succeeded in planting doubt in the jurors' minds by proposing an alternate perpetrator in the murder of Ralph Campbell: Christopher Matthews.

45

High pressure systems tend to be more spread out, with weak winds near the center, increasing in speed as they move further out. The weather is normally clear with blue skies and little or no precipitation.

"Reporting live from the Howard County Courthouse in Kokomo, Indiana, I'm Katie Jarvis, WNMS news."

"That's a wrap Katie." Jeff gave her a thumbs-up. The 6 p.m. report was done.

There was no doubt that Katie was an accomplished weather forecaster, but she surprised everyone—including herself—with her forceful reporting of Tess's murder trial. Like the rest of the on-site reporters, Katie presented the facts of the case clearly and competently, but there was something else—when Katie delivered her report, she did it in a manner that elicited an emotional response on the part of the viewers. Jeff's evocative sketches reinforced her verbal reports. They not only captured the physical tension of the scene, but also the human drama etched in the faces and body language of the participants. The combination mesmerized her viewers.

Katie's report after the first day's testimony barely hid her excitement. Reporting the results of the next two days proved much more challenging. The prosecution did not cross-examine Tess immediately. They started by calling members of the local police who had investigated the crime scene. The police conceded that Chris could well have been at Campbell's house, and may have even participated in the murder, but quickly posited that it didn't automatically rule Tess out. She could just as easily have murdered Campbell by herself or in concert with her lover. They had only her word that she had left before

Campbell arrived. She had no witnesses to place her at the motel at the time of the murder, and she had already demonstrated her propensity for lying to the police. She also had more of a motive than Chris to want Campbell dead. Even more plausible was that the murder was a burglary gone wrong. Campbell could have arrived earlier than expected and caught her—or both of them—in the act of the theft. There was also the fact that only Tess's fingerprints were found at the crime scene.

While Brian's offensive strategy worked well, it couldn't erase the emotional impact of hearing the testimony directly from the witnesses themselves. Nurse Supervisor Simpson trembled as she recounted the threats Tess hurled against her stepfather. Relatives and friends showed their indignation as they described how Tess and Ralph carried on at the gravesite, especially when Tess smiled and whispered in Ralph's ear. The Atlantic City bank manager recalled Tess and Chris's calm demeanor as they opened two joint accounts.

"And did they explain to you why they wanted two accounts instead of one?" prosecutor Mason asked.

"Yes, because they were still under the impression there was a $100,000.00 limit on FDIC insurance. They wanted to be certain that all of the money would be protected."

Brian could hear the murmuring. He scanned the juror's faces. It didn't look good.

Next, Mason put Olga Simms on the stand.

"Mrs. Simms, could you please state your address for the court?"

"I live at 717 Peony Way in Greenwood."

"And where is your house in relation to Mr. Campbell's?"

"Right across the street."

"Please tell the court what you saw on the afternoon of August 16, 2012."

"I was looking out my front window when I saw that woman go into Mr. Campbell's house."

Mason addressed the court stenographer, "Please note that

Mrs. Simms is pointing to the defendant, Teresa DiPetro."

As Mason spoke, Chris's parents entered and seated themselves at the rear of the courtroom.

"Mrs. Simms," Mason continued, "what time did Miss DiPetro arrive?"

"It was twelve minutes after noon."

"How can you be certain of the exact time?"

"I was waiting for the mail to come. The mailman almost always arrives just before noon. He was running late that day so I was keeping my eye on the clock."

"Did you also see the defendant leave?" Simms answered yes.

"And what time was that?"

"A quarter past four."

When Judge Pendleton called the lunch recess, Carl and Gail walked forward, but went to the prosecution's table instead of Tess. After a brief conversation, they handed Mason a large manila envelope. When they turned to leave, Tess tried to get their attention, but they avoided eye contact and quickly left the courtroom. Gail was crying. At the prosecution's table, Mason was reviewed the contents of the envelope and began to grin widely.

On cross-examination, Brian established that while Mrs. Simms had a clear view of Tess going into the house, it was raining heavily when she came out. Mrs. Simms insisted that the person she saw leaving the house looked the same as the one who entered, had the same height and build, and was wearing the same raincoat.

At the end of the day, Mason spoke up, "Your Honor, we have one more item we want to enter into evidence."

Brian objected because the defense had not received the evidence beforehand, but Mason explained that he only received it this afternoon. The judge called both lawyers to the bench. After a brief discussion, the judge said he'd allow the inclusion and both attorneys returned to their respective tables. As Brian reviewed the document, he was visibly disturbed.

The prosecution waited until the last day to put Tess on the stand.

"Miss DiPetro," Mason started, "you attend Nadowa College in upstate New York, don't you?"

"Yes."

"That's a four-year college, isn't it?"

"Yes, it is."

"And what year are you in?"

"I'm a junior."

"So you only have one more year to go."

"That's correct."

"And you testified that you stole the money from Mr. Campbell to pay for your education expenses."

"Yes." Tess could see where this line of questioning was heading and she started to perspire. Brian looked at Mason's face and caught the same smile he saw earlier.

"How much does it cost to go to Nadowa miss DiPetro?"

"I'm not sure. There are lots of different expenses."

"Then let me refresh your memory." Mason approached the prosecution table. His co-counsel handed him a pamphlet. Mason opened the document.

"This is a copy of Nadowa's current course catalogue," Mason handed it to Tess. "Would you please read the amount listed for the current full-time tuition?"

"$23,500."

"And room and board, including the deluxe meal plan?"

"$2,500."

"And how much would you say you pay for books and lab fees per semester?"

"I don't know. It varies from year to year."

"Well we do. We've done the math for you." He handed Tess another piece of paper. "This is a list of your current course load, Miss DiPetro. Does it look complete to you?"

Tess scanned the document. "Yes."

"We've listed the required books and lab fees next to each course. Does it look accurate?"

"I think so."

"Would you please read the figure for the total cost? It's underlined at the bottom."

Tess found the figure and read it off, "$1,175."

"And since you can't really survive without some incidentals like gas for your car, a cell phone, birth control pills…"

"Objection," Brian shouted as he stood.

"Sustained," said the judge. "Mr. Mason, drop the smear tactics."

Mason continued, "Well, Miss DiPetro, we've allocated an additional $10,000.00 a year for your incidentals. Would you say that would be sufficient to cover your needs?"

Tess wanted to refute Mason's assertion but realized like everyone else in the courtroom how grossly he had overestimated the amount. "Yes it would."

"And have we missed anything at all in the way of your expenses?"

"None that I can think of."

"Good. Then let's do a little math, shall we?" Mason handed Tess a final sheet of paper. On it were listed each of the expenses the prosecution had listed and Tess had agreed to. Mason reviewed each one again for emphasis and got Tess's verification.

"Miss DiPetro, would you please read the total expenses underlined at the bottom of the page."

Tess read off the figure, "$37,175."

"For the sake of simplicity we'll just round it up to an even $40,000. Now, you're just about at the end of your current semester so you have half a year to go and all of next year. That would come to a total of $60,000, but let's not be stingy. We'll add another $10,000.00 for inflation to bring the grand total to $70,000."

Mason walked over to the jury box. He rested his hands on the railing and faced the jurors as he asked the final question. "Refresh our memories if you would, please. How much was it that you stole from Mr. Campbell's home before you murdered him?"

"Objection," Brian yelled.

"Sustained," Pendleton answered angrily.

Mason corrected himself, "Before he was murdered."

"$175,000," Tess answered.

A persistent murmur rose in the courtroom.

"But, I told you," Tess yelled. "I didn't count the money right away. I didn't know how much I had until after I had left."

"That's right, you did say that." Mason picked up a copy of the first day's testimony. "You also said this." Mason handed the transcript to Tess. "Please read the highlighted section."

Tess read the section, "My mother slaved for that man their whole married life and made certain that he set aside enough money to pay for my college education. She wanted to put the money in a trust fund for me, but Ralph said he didn't trust banks so he kept it hidden in the bedroom closet. All I was doing was retrieving my own money."

Mason walked over to the prosecution table, retrieved a document from his co-counsel's outstretched hand, and addressed the bench, "Your Honor, we'll be addressing people's exhibit 21. We'd like to point out for the jury that this material was not retrieved from Mr. Campbell's home. It was discovered among the personal effects of Christopher Matthews, Miss DiPetro's lover." Then Mason returned to Tess and placed it in front of her.

"Miss DiPetro, have you ever seen this document before?" Tess went pale. "And let me remind you that you are under oath."

"Yes, I have."

"Would you please describe for the court what the document is?"

"It's a prenuptial agreement between my mother and my stepfather."

"Please read for us the highlighted section." Tess swallowed hard and hesitated. "Please, Miss DiPetro."

Tess read the passage, "Both parties recognize that Ralph Campbell will provide a monthly allotment to his wife to use in whatever manner she chooses, including her daughter's support and education. Audrey DiPetro acknowledges that this does not constitute a binding contract, and in the event of the separation, incapacitation, divorce, or death of either party, this will in no way constitute a responsibility on the part of Mr. Campbell or his estate, now or in the future."

"So, Miss DiPetro, when you stole that $175,000 from Ralph Campbell, you knew that you weren't taking your own money after all, didn't you?" As Mason turned from the jury box, Brian could see the smile on his face.

"No further questions, Your Honor," said Mason. "The state rests."

46

Low pressure systems are more compact, with higher winds that strengthen as they approach the center. They produce cloudy skies, higher and more variable winds, and often, intense precipitation. The fiercest storms are associated with low pressure systems.

The prosecution had succeeded in creating an image of Tess as an unfeeling opportunist who was easily capable of committing murder. It wasn't a portrait that Katie recognized, but she had no choice. It was one she had to share with her viewers. Kevin provided her with double her allotted time during the 6 p.m. segment to cover the closing arguments. Katie broadcasted her report live from the courthouse steps.

The parking lot was a sea of mobile broadcast vans from virtually every news network. Satellite dishes rose skyward from each creating something akin to a high-tech trailer park. Many of the major stations recognized Katie's uncanny draw and contracted with Nadowa to carry her live as part of their coverage. As Katie prepared to deliver her report, she stepped into a nest of microphones while cameras focused on her from every angle. Drivers turned up their car radios, people planted themselves in front of their televisions, bars across the northeast switched from sports channels to the news, and life in the Hudson Valley came to a virtual standstill.

Jeff cued Katie, dropping his fingers in sync with his narrative, "OK, Katie, we're live in three, two…" The country tuned in to hear a farm girl from Kansas report about a student from upstate New York on trial for the murder of a man from Indiana.

"Good evening," Katie started. "I'm standing on the steps of the Howard County Courthouse where earlier today the prosecution rested its case against Theresa DiPetro. Miss DiPetro was on trial for the murder of her stepfather, Ralph Campbell, of Greenwood Indiana."

In the van, Sy switched in canned videos of the crime scene and local shots of Greenwood while Katie narrated. Next, Katie reviewed the trial highlights while slides of Jeff's pencil sketches moved across the screen.

"In his closing arguments, Chief Prosecutor Elliot Mason painted a picture of Tess DiPetro as a cold, calculating killer bent on stealing her stepfather's life savings and taking his life to prevent him from turning her into the police.

"Defense Attorney Brian Rosenthal presented a very different image. He described a young girl, sexually victimized by Campbell, who rose above her abuse to become an honors student, an active church member, and a mature, responsible individual whose only crime was escaping the clutches of an incestuous pedophile.

"An eyewitness placed DiPetro at the scene during the time of the murder, but the defense cast doubt on the reliability of the witness's testimony. Although the police never found the murder weapon, Prosecutor Mason says that he is confident of a guilty verdict. Rosenthal, on the other hand, says the state has failed to prove its case, especially in light of the fact that DiPetro's fiancé, Christopher Matthews, also had the means and motive to commit the crime. Matthews disappeared in a boating accident, but his body was never recovered. Now, there is mounting evidence that he may still be alive.

"In charging the jury, Presiding Judge Harry B. Pendleton cautioned them not to speculate regarding Matthews and stick to the facts of the present case only. Can they help wondering, however, like so many others, that while they are deliberating a verdict for Miss DiPetro, the real killer may still be roaming free? For now, at least, Theresa DiPetro's fate rests in the hands of the twelve jurors. Reporting live from the Howard County Courthouse, I'm Katie Jarvis."

Jeff gave the cut signal and Katie exhaled deeply, "I'm so

glad that's over."

"Not quite yet," said Jeff. "You've still got the verdict to report on."

Katie became silent. In her mind, she reviewed the trial and the evidence for and against Tess. She recalled the closing arguments and visualized the faces of the jury members. Putting herself in the place of a juror, she had to admit that the situation looked dire. Katie feared for her friend.

The vibration of her cell phone broke Katie's concentration. What little color had returned to her face quickly drained away again as she looked at the screen.

HI K T CAT

R U NAKED?

WAY 2 GO!

I XPECTED TESS 2 TOSS ME UNDER THE BUS 2 SAVE HER OWN SKIN BUT U SURPRISED ME

U R ALL SO QUICK 2 BELIEVE THAT ONLY CHRIS IS WILLING 2 RID THE WORLD OF SCUM LIKE RALPH

VERY SOON THE TRUTH WILL OUT

C

With her morning weather reports completed, Katie took time to eat breakfast and soak in the sun. She sat at an outdoor table at the coffee shop across from the courthouse. For the third week in November, the weather was balmy. By 9 a.m., the temperature was already 68 degrees. Indiana, like many of the northeastern states, was experiencing Indian summer. The mild temperatures and mostly sunny skies produced near picture-perfect weather.

As the jury deliberations entered their fourth day, most of the major networks moved their camera crews to other stories, and the courthouse parking lot was mostly empty. Though a large contingency of reporters were still present, ready to respond to the verdict. Katie was finishing off the last of her toast when her cell phone rang. She noted the time: 10:40 a.m.

It was Jeff. "Better head on back to the courthouse, Katie.

We just got word that the jury's finished its deliberations." Katie's breakfast soured in her stomach and a wave of nausea passed over her. As she finished packing her things, she looked up at the graying sky. The sudden gloominess of the day seemed to match her disposition. She left money under her plate on the table and made her way across the windswept parking lot.

When Katie reached the courtroom, Tess was already sitting with Brian at the defense table. The windows provided very little light from the smoky skies outside so, in accordance with Judge Pendleton's instructions, the maintenance worker lifted shades to let in what little outdoor light there was. Jeff took up his position at the end of the bench, and several people filled in the seats between him and Katie. By the time the bailiff ordered, "All rise," the courtroom was full and buzzing with conversations.

Katie scanned the scene outside of the windows. In the parking lot, leaves danced in reels circling each other like a country hoedown. Sporadic shafts of light pierced through the blackened sky in the distance. Closer, there was only thickening darkness.

The judge's gavel brought the room to order. The bailiff rose and crossed over to the jury box. There he retrieved a piece of folded paper from the jury foreman. All eyes, except for Katie's, were fixed on the performance playing out at the front of the courtroom.

Katie looked through the windows to Judge Pendleton's right. Behind him in the distance, she could see the mounting billows of black clouds soaring skyward. Above that and extending forward above the courthouse, was the anvil top, the flat, leading edge of the cloudbank: a supercell was forming.

The bailiff walked the piece of paper to the judge's bench. Judge Pendleton opened it and read the note. His stoic expression gave no indication of its contents.

Still looking out the window, Katie made out the flashes of lightening in the distance. The rumbling thunder was barely audible in the courtroom. Had it not been for the silence surrounding the drama unfolding inside, even Katie might have missed it.

"Something's not right," Katie surprised herself when she realized she was speaking aloud. Judge Pendleton looked up momentarily, then looked down at the paper again, folded it, and returned it to the bailiff. As the bailiff returned to the jury box, Katie returned to the windows.

The leaves were no longer dancing. They were racing across the parking lot, joined by pieces of paper, twigs, branches, and larger debris. Katie mentally reviewed her morning forecast and contrasted it to the scene outside.

"This is wrong," she said, and then louder, "this shouldn't be happening." People stared at Katie and murmured. The rumblings in the courtroom quickly surpassed those outside.

The loud clap of Pendleton's gavel caused people near the front to jump. "Young lady, one more outburst like that, and I'll have you removed from this courtroom."

"I'm sorry, Your Honor."

"Don't be sorry, be quiet."

The bailiff left the note with the foreman and returned to his seat. Pendleton asked, "Ladies and gentlemen of the jury, have you reached a verdict?"

The foreman replied, "We have, Your Honor."

Pendleton addressed Tess, "Will the defendant please rise?" Tess rose unsteadily to her feet.

Katie didn't hear or see what transpired. She was listening to the tapping at the window and watching the parking lot turn from black to white as the beads of falling ice spread across the surface. Then she looked again past the judge and into the distance. She could make out the swirling mass of clouds—thickening, darkening, accelerating, and then hardening into the unmistakable form of a vortex.

"We have to get out of here," Katie shouted, "right now." She was talking more to herself then anyone else.

"Officers," Pendleton boomed at the uniformed staff at the

courtroom doors, "escort that woman out of this courtroom." The judge looked down at the bailiff and nodded for him to poll the jury.

As the guards descended upon Katie, the bailiff asked, "On the count of theft in excess of $100,000, how do you find?"

The jury foreman replied, "We find the defendant guilty."

A rumble of thunder punctuated the verdict.

The guards approached closer as the bailiff volleyed back, "On the count of conspiracy to commit murder, how do you find?"

The jury foreman responded, "We find the defendant not guilty."

The guards reached the end of Katie's row. The first one spoke sternly, "Come with us, Miss."

Katie looked out the window. The funnel was on the ground and moving toward the courthouse.

Katie yelled, "Everyone get away from the windows!"

"Guards," Pendleton yelled, "remove that woman immediately!"

The courtroom reverberated with conversation as others looked at the scene developing outside. Some people rose halfway from their seats and froze, unsure if they should leave or stay. Pendleton, oblivious to the scene unfolding outside, rapped his gavel frantically against the anvil and shouted, "Order! I'm warning you, come to order, or, so help me, I'll clear this courtroom."

Above the chaos, the bailiff shouted stubbornly, "On the count of first degree murder, how do you find?"

One guard grabbed Jeff by the arm and yanked him into the aisle. The other climbed in front of others toward Katie.

Katie stood but remained in place and only yelled louder, "Everyone move away from the windows. Now!"

Trees across the parking lot twisted wildly and bent low to the ground. Large branches broke off and took flight. Hail grew from pea-size, to golf ball, to baseball-size. A lightening flash lit the room accompanied by an enormous thunderclap. People screamed and ducked low or pushed away from the windows.

The jury foreman shouted above the din, "We find the defendant…"

The guard grabbed Katie's arm as she let out a piercing scream, "Tornado!"

The guard looked out the window and released Katie. Both of them dove for cover. Tess and Brian ducked down beneath the defense desk. The jury foreman yelled, "Guilty!" and sank down into the jury box.

Judge Pendleton looked to his right, dropped his gavel, and dove under his bench.

The funnel brushed against the side of the building and shattered the windows, starting with the one closest to the judge's bench and traveling to the back of the courtroom. A deafening roar combined with the explosions as clouds of glass dust and shards permeated the air.

The rumbling peaked, subsided, and finally ceased as the storm moved away. Slowly, tentatively, people rose to their feet, shaking the broken glass and wind blown dirt off as they did.

Pendleton rose from beneath his bench. As Katie stood, the guard reached out and grabbed her.

"That won't be necessary," Pendleton stopped him. Then the judge made eye contact with Katie and nodded slightly. "Ladies and gentlemen of the jury, thank you for your service. Officers," he addressed the guards, "remove the prisoner. Then come back as quick as possible to assist anyone who needs help."

Katie reached out and touched Tess's shoulder. Tess turned around. A stream of tears cut a path though the dust on her face. Katie hesitated for an instant but then pulled her friend toward her and hugged her tightly.

"I didn't do it, Katie," Tess could barely get out the words through her crying. "I swear I didn't."

"I know, Tess," Katie answered. "It's not over. Somehow, some way, we'll prove you're innocent. I promise."

The guards forced the women apart. As they escorted Tess

from the courtroom, Katie's cell phone started ringing. She opened it to the curt message:

K T
U BITCHES R ALL ALIKE
C

Katie had difficulty reporting the 6 p.m. news, not just because of the verdict, but because suddenly, Katie Jarvis was the news. With so much press coverage for the trial, networks across the country picked up her intervention during the tornado. She had prevented the injuries and possible deaths of scores of people, and a large number of them were news reporters. The story of her standoff with the judge overshadowed the trial itself.

Katie left Nadowa a student and returned a superstar. Everywhere she went people sought her autograph and asked her to recount the details of her ordeal. There was a beneficial spillover for Bert, John Thompson, and the college. With so much positive press for the last of the Lakota Drive residents, Kevin's investigative reports concerning the house and its occupants lost their power. People were much more interested in hearing about the Kansas farm girl's heroic exploits than they were in rehashing the negative accusations of fiscal improprieties and cover-ups. The dean calmed down considerably, and Bert and Katie were free to continue their research with less scrutiny.

One thing, however, had not changed. The project would end, and Katie would still have to move out following the Christmas break. Nevertheless, to everyone in the Hudson Valley, Katie Jarvis of Nadowa College was a heroine. To everyone, that is, except for Katie herself.

Sitting in the tranquility of Amanda's room Katie picked up her diary, but instead of writing, she leafed through her recent entries until she came to the page she was looking for:

I'm glad I was wrong about your being jealous.

If you can Amanda, please help Tess. I don't know what you can do, but she really needs the help. It doesn't look good for her right now…

I feel so close to you I can't even imagine not having you in my life.

I hope you feel the same.

Katie reread and then pondered the words. Whatever their meaning, whatever the relationship between what she had written and what she experienced in Indiana, Katie resolved that she would never again ask for Amanda's help.

47

Tropical Wave: Disorganized. Maximum sustained winds less than 25 mph.

Tropical Depression: Closed circulation. Sustained winds of at least 25 mph.

Tropical Storm: Shower and thunderstorm activity. Sustained winds reach 39 mph.

Hurricane: An eye forms in the closed circulation. Sustained winds reach 74 mph.

It started out as a tropical wave off the coast of Africa. Had it formed anytime before mid-October, it would hardly have been noticed, but this was the day after Thanksgiving. Tropical disturbances weren't supposed to form that far out in the North Atlantic that late in the year. Staff at the National Hurricane Center marveled at the anomaly. Some took it as further proof of global warming. Their assumption wasn't without merit. The late season heat wave had kept the waters of the North Atlantic and the Gulf Stream unusually warm. Within twenty-four hours, the wave had formed into a tropical depression and caught the attention of meteorologists across the globe.

Bert sat at his kitchen table sipping his morning coffee, reading the headlines and half-watching and listening to the news and weather on WNMS TV. At 6:10 a.m., he heard the familiar introduction, "And now for a look at how the weather is shaping up for tomorrow and the week ahead, here's Katie Jarvis."

The camera panned onto Katie standing in front of the blue screen. "Well it looks as though we are going to enjoy this summer-like weather for at least the next several days, so you might want to put away those snow shovels and break out the lawn chairs instead. But before we get to the local forecast, we'll take a look at the other side of the Atlantic for what's shaping up to be a fairly unusual weather event."

The map behind Katie scrolled across the Atlantic to a swirling air mass off the coast of Africa. "Yesterday this was just a tropical wave with fairly mild winds. In the last twenty-four hours, it's grown into a full-blown tropical depression. While that's common in summer, it's very rare for this late in the year. Right now the storm is moving westward at about twenty miles per hour. Meteorologists expect the storm to die out within the next couple of days but until it does, we'll be monitoring it for you and reporting on its progress. Now getting back to our local weather ...."

The meteorologists were wrong. Two days later, it was a tropical storm. By the end of the week, it was a category one hurricane.

The unusually heavy hurricane season had exhausted all of the letters for naming storms. Following tradition, the National Hurricane Center restarted with the letters of the Greek alphabet, so the new storm became Hurricane Alpha. When it strengthened to a category three, newscasters sought a more personal nickname. An Atlanta weatherman jokingly compared the storm to an ill-tempered date he once had. Someone posted the video on You Tube, and it went viral on the internet. Then the national networks picked it up. Within hours, every reporter in the country was referring to the storm by the shrew's name: Amanda.

The irony wasn't lost on Bert and Katie as they worked at the house. The reference amused Bert as he prepared to join a group of weather experts investigating the storm. For Katie, it held a deeper, more troubling meaning, "Bert, have you reached any conclusions about what might have caused Hurricane Amanda?"

"Not really. If I could answer that question with any certainty, I could probably start drafting my Nobel acceptance speech."

"Have you wondered if there might be a link, a relationship between Hurricane Amanda, and our Amanda?"

"If by link you mean, 'Do I think Amanda caused the hurricane,' the answer is no."

"Actually, Bert, I'm suggesting even more than that. I think maybe the only reason the hurricane continues to exist is because of Amanda."

Bert stopped working on his notes and looked at Katie, "You're serious, aren't you? All right, what leads you to that conclusion?"

"You have to admit that the presence of a hurricane this late in the season is unusual." Bert nodded in agreement. "Then, when it should have weakened, it actually gained strength."

"It's a unique storm all right, but we've also had a very peculiar weather pattern. I don't think there's precedence for the kind of water temperatures we've seen this late in the year."

"Maybe not, but do you really think they're high enough to fuel a hurricane, let alone a category three?"

"If it's a choice between lukewarm water temperature and Amanda's whim..." Bert could see the frustration in Katie's expression. "Let's look at this from the perspective of what we've observed here to date."

Katie brightened as Bert continued, "The weather we've associated with Amanda thus far has been localized to within two to three miles from this house. This hurricane developed over 4,000 miles away. The anomalies we've observed are invisible from the outside. This hurricane's been tracked by meteorologists throughout the world. And the systems we've studied are small. They're no more then five or six miles across. Hurricane Amanda is already bigger than Rhode Island and still growing. Even if I agreed that the observations we've made here at the house were somehow caused by Amanda, which by the way, I don't, why would she make such a huge departure from everything she's done so far?"

"Because I'm convinced she's trying to tell us something. I think she's frustrated that she hasn't been getting through to us and this storm is some sort of wake up call. I think that Amanda caused the tornado at Tess's trial, and that she's behind this hurricane too."

"Well, I certainly hope you're wrong, Katie. You said yourself—people could have been seriously hurt or killed in that courtroom. A hurricane is one of the most destructive forces on the planet. If Amanda wields that kind of power and isn't in complete control of it, then no one on Earth is safe."

48

The energy contained in a large hurricane is equivalent to about 500 trillion horsepower or that of exploding an atomic bomb about every ten seconds. If one percent of a single hurricane's energy were harnessed, it could meet the power, fuel, and heating needs of the United States for a year.

People in the Caribbean Islands breathed a sigh of relief when Hurricane Amanda changed her course. It had looked as though the mammoth storm was poised to cross directly over the islands on its way to Florida's east coast. With sustained winds of over 140 miles per hour and a storm surge in excess of fifteen feet, Amanda would be among the most devastating storms ever to hit the region. When the hurricane veered sharply to the north, the residents of Bermuda braced themselves. However, Amanda continued turning northeastward keeping her far out at sea and sparing the islands completely. Small craft advisories went up all along the outer banks. For the next several days, Amanda continued to follow the Gulf Stream and stayed well off the eastern seaboard. Meteorologists predicted the storm would weaken as she moved northward and dissipate completely long before she reached New England. Once again, they were wrong. By the time Amanda was parallel to Chesapeake Bay, she was a category five monster spanning more than 360 miles. Then midway between the Mid-Atlantic Bight and Georges Bank, Amanda stalled. Like a lioness stalking her prey, the storm crouched off the New England shelf for the next forty-eight hours. At first people remained vigilant but as the hours passed and followed into the next day, caution gave way to ambivalence, ambivalence to curiosity, and curiosity became fascination. People started flocking to the shores to catch a glimpse of the colossal surf. Dry-suited surfers rode swells the size of small mountains and gave television interviews comparing the waves to Hawaii's Pipeline. The entire region took on a festival atmosphere.

In the meantime, another low pressure system, nowhere near the size or strength of the hurricane, strategically positioned itself, growing steadily like a black hole, drawing parcels of higher pressure air into it, closer and closer to its epicenter, to where Katie Jarvis watched and waited—at 34 Lakota Drive.

The more Katie studied the developing weather systems, the more certain she was that Amanda was making them happen. Katie was sure that once she discovered what Amanda was trying to communicate, the potentially deadly hurricane would simply dissipate. But time was running out. Katie was equally certain that if she failed to unravel the mystery, Amanda would act, putting the lives of millions at risk.

Then Katie recalled her conversation with Bert and realized that this time things were different. This time Amanda was not hiding her activities within an invisible bubble. Katie looked at the swirling mass off the eastern seaboard and asked herself why. "That's it!" Katie pulled out her cell phone and hit the speed dial for Bert.

Bert was at the meteorology conference at Woods Hole in Massachusetts. Organizers had chosen that location so participants could closely monitor Amanda's behavior.

Bert sounded rushed. "I can only talk for a few minutes. We've had some significant developments and I'll need to get back soon."

"Sorry for the interruption, but I think I know what Amanda's been trying to tell us. I think she's trying to warn us that something's going to happen in the path of the hurricane."

"I see. And how did you arrive at that conclusion?" Katie chose to ignore the condescending tone of Bert's words.

"You said that there was no relationship between the

current weather patterns and the ones we've observed at the house. Well, now there is. The low pressure system centered over the house is clearly visible from the outside. That's the first time Amanda's allowed that to happen. Now that the hurricane has stalled, I'm sure that Amanda is trying to point us in the direction of something."

"Whoa, slow down a minute. Low pressure systems form all the time all over the country. The fact that one has formed in our area..."

"Not just in our area, Bert, right over the house."

"All right, all right, even right over the house. There's nothing particularly strange about that. As far as a weather system stalling, that happens all the time, too. You're making an awful lot of assumptions here."

Bert didn't say so, but it was much more than Katie's assumptions that troubled him. If she were right, it meant Amanda was somehow present in her room. That led to accepting the existence of spirits, which led directly to acknowledging the possibility of God, something Bert had abandoned long ago.

"But what if I'm right? What if..." Katie's phone rang. She looked down at the screen, "I've got a message coming in from Chris."

Katie pressed hold, checked the message, and then reconnected with Bert.

"What does he have to say this time?"

Katie skipped the standing joke about being naked and went right to the heart of the message:

GREAT MINDS THINK ALIKE
IT'S SHOW TIME!
TALK 2 U LATER
C

"Do you have any idea what he's talking about?"

"I don't know." Katie was as confused as Bert was angry.

"Well, I'm pretty damned tired of being jerked around. I

don't have time for this anymore. I don't know what kind of game Chris thinks he's playing but I, for one, have had it. At this point, as far as I'm concerned it's a matter for… Just a second," Bert put Katie on hold and returned seconds later.

"Katie, check out the Weather Channel. I've got to go." Bert hung up.

Katie switched on the Weather Channel and turned up the volume, "Now for that breaking news on Hurricane Amanda. We go directly to the briefing currently underway at the National Hurricane Center."

The camera switched to a spokesperson standing at a podium in front of the Center's banner. Her calm demeanor belied the seriousness of the situation.

> As of 3:21 p.m. this afternoon, approximately fifteen minutes ago, we confirmed that Hurricane Amanda has started moving again. The storm is 365 nautical miles due east of Fenwick Island near the Maryland—Delaware border and the storm is moving northwesterly at sixteen miles per hour. Given its current speed and direction, we expect the hurricane to make landfall near Point Judith, Rhode Island, at approximately 11:15 tomorrow morning. At present, the storm measures 410 miles across and has maximum sustained winds of 160 miles per hour. A hurricane warning is in effect for all of New York, Connecticut, Rhode Island, and Massachusetts. A hurricane watch is in effect for northern New Jersey, New Hampshire, and southern Maine. We'd like to point out that this is an extremely dangerous storm. All state and local officials responsible for residents in the path of the hurricane and in coastal and low-lying areas within a four-hundred-mile radius are encouraged to implement evacuation plans immediately.

Within minutes, the governors of the impacted states had declared states of emergency. Government officials asked residents to remain calm and stay tuned to their local stations for further instructions.

That evening Katie tuned in to CNN. The images were heartbreaking. Panic was widespread and growing, and there was sporadic looting. High winds and waves forced the suspension of ferry service. Traffic clogged the highways, bridges, and secondary roads. There were accidents everywhere, and some urban areas were in complete gridlock. The reports only confirmed the obvious—it would be impossible to evacuate everyone.

Some reporters, eager to cash in on the headlines, commented on the timing of the storm and suggested a link to December 21, 2012, the end of the Mayan calendar, and for some, the end of the world. Like the Santa Ana winds, their comments created a firestorm of speculation. Inland dwellers sent invitations over the web to join in "End of the World" parties. The humor was lost on people trapped in the path of the storm. Among them was Bert Myers.

49

As it is making landfall, the most dangerous part of the northern hemisphere hurricane is the right front quadrant.

For most participants, including Bert, the "Hurricane Amanda Symposium" was frustrating at best. The greatest scientific minds in the country had spent more than three days analyzing the potential causes for the storm. They were still no closer to an explanation than when they had started.

None of the commonly accepted principles applied. The Gulf Stream's water temperature was elevated but nowhere near the 80-degree threshold needed to fuel such a giant. Nor did the warm water extend to a depth of at least thirty meters, another critical requirement. And the storm should have lost energy as it moved northward, but it didn't.

For Bert, only one theory accounted for the hurricane's continued presence. He decided to test the waters by sharing Katie's hypothesis with Josh Gibbons, a math professor and trusted colleague from MIT. Josh sat, listened, and nodded as Bert traced the history from his first entry into Amanda's room to his latest conversation with Katie.

"Well, that's everything," said Bert. "What do you think?"

"What do I think?" repeated Josh. "I think you'd better have a really good second career to fall back on, because once you share that story, you won't be able to teach first grade science. It would make a great novel. But as far as this conference goes, you'd be committing occupational suicide."

"But no one's come up with a more plausible explanation."

"Maybe not, but we both know how ridiculous your story sounds, and I can't believe that you ever seriously expected me to support your idea about sharing it. So what's really up?"

Bert let out a sigh. "Josh, I've resisted any suggestion that there wasn't a purely scientific explanation for what we've uncovered, but damned if I can find one. I need a fresh pair of eyes on this, or soon I might start blaming it on God myself. What about it Josh? Would you be willing to come out and look for yourself?"

"I'll make you a deal, Bert. You keep this theory to yourself for now, and I'll plan on visiting the site and giving you a second opinion on it."

Bert reached out his hand and smiled, "Deal." Josh returned the gesture.

Another colleague from Chicago University interrupted the handshake, "Fellahs, you'd better come inside. They're making an announcement and they want everyone present for it."

"That sounds a little dramatic, don't you think?" asked Josh.

As Bert and Josh reentered the main meeting room, the moderator was asking participants to return to their seats. Bert grabbed a cup of coffee and rejoined his table. The moderator cleared his throat and began.

> Ladies and gentlemen, I have some rather sobering news to report. While we've been studying Hurricane Amanda, it seems the rest of region has been gearing up for her arrival, sometimes with unanticipated consequences.
>
> A little over two hours ago, while moving cargo to a safer harbor, a tugboat lost control of the barge it was piloting through the Cape Cod Canal. The barge broke free, picked up speed and crashed into the pilings of the Bourne Bridge, rendering the bridge unusable. Police rerouted traffic to the Sagamore Bridge. About an hour ago, a wind gust pushed a tractor-trailer coming off the Island into the on-coming lane. It collided with an oil tanker coming onto the island. The tractor-trailer flipped over, blocking all traffic lanes. The oil tanker punctured and spilled 8,000 gallons of home heating fuel onto the bridge's surface. Even under ideal conditions, it would take hours to clear the site. In the meantime drivers trapped behind the accident

> panicked and abandoned their vehicles. All access routes to the bridge are blocked for miles. We've just received confirmation that the bridge cannot be cleared prior to the hurricane's arrival. Travel by boat or plane is no longer an option and all of the available shelters are already at maximum capacity. Our only alternative is to ride out the storm in place.

A commotion filled the room, drowning out the speaker. The moderator shouted into the microphone, "Please, please, can I have your attention for a moment longer? There's more I need to tell you." The noise subsided.

Professor Niles Wittington, a thin, white-haired climatologist from Texas A & M raised a hand and stood, "We should make accommodations for other residents. There's plenty of extra space here."

"That won't be necessary." There was an abruptness in the moderator's response. A look of bewilderment crossed Wittington's face as he sat down. The moderator continued. "Amanda has shifted course again. At her present heading, the eye wall of the hurricane will cross directly over us with the eye to our west. The storm has shown no signs of weakening. The maximum winds are now 166 miles per hour. The storm has also accelerated. It's currently moving onshore at twenty-two miles per hour. At its current rate of speed, it will make landfall concurrent with high tide tomorrow."

The room went deathly silent. Everyone knew exactly what that meant. There'd be no need to make room for others, as this was the last place on Earth anyone would want to be. Woods Hole was going to be in Amanda's right front quadrant. That meant they would be sitting in the area of maximum winds. The speed of the storm's forward movement would add to the wind speed of the eye wall, creating an effective wind speed of 188 miles per hour with gusts even higher. That placed Amanda in the company of true hurricane monsters like Camille and Katrina. The greatest concern was the storm surge. Amanda would drive the ocean before her like a plow, and the wall of water in the right front quadrant would be the highest. Coming at high tide was the worst-case scenario. If the water became high enough, no building, no matter how sturdily constructed, could withstand its fury. Riding the storm out in place was tantamount to a death sentence.

Professor Whittington broke the silence as he rose again to speak, "Then it looks like we've got a problem to solve so I suggest we don't waste any time and get straight to work."

The participants ate their dinner amid a flurry of activity. First, they surveyed the campus and identified the most substantial multistory buildings, positioned as far inland as possible. Immediately after dinner, everyone relocated to the upper floors of the selected shelters. They left vacant the rooms on the windward edge of each building.

They brought their personal belongings with them along with stores of food, beverages, fresh water, and emergency supplies. Amateur radio operators set up ham radio stations in each building and established contact with each other and operators throughout the region. Computer experts established communications with the state's Emergency Operations Center and provided it with detailed information on their numbers, location, and status. Participants also taped and blocked all the windows.

It was well past nightfall by the time the preparations were finished. There was nothing left to do but wait. Rain came down hard. The windows shrilled as the wind swells rushed by. Few participants slept. Most of those who weren't actively involved in communications activities called home and engaged in hours-long conversations with loved ones. Bert had a lengthy conversation with Evelyn. He downplayed his predicament, but Evelyn knew better. Neither said it openly, but in their own way, they each said their goodbyes. Others read, more than a few prayed. Late into the night, some cried. It was worse in the dark without the benefit of visual cues as to what the storm was doing. With each passing hour, the wind grew fiercer as the rain bulleted the building. Finally, the black emptiness over the sea gave way to the first glimmer of light. By then Amanda was hitting the shoreline with sustained winds of seventy-three miles per hour and gusts over ninety. Bert stood well back from a taped window, sipping his coffee, and looking out into the predawn gray.

"So what do you think, Bert?" asked Josh. "I'm just a lowly mathematician. You're the weather expert. Does it really look like we're going to have front row seats to Armageddon?"

"I don't know, Josh. New England's never been hit by a category five hurricane. The nearest we've come was the Long Island Express in 1938, and that was a category three. It decimated the coastline, flooded towns thirty miles inland, and created the Shinnecock Inlet."

"Thanks for the real estate report. Not that I don't appreciate hearing how the storm affected property values, but how about the really juicy numbers. How many died?"

"Over 700."

"And that was a category three?"

Bert took another sip of his coffee. "Tornado hunters have an expression for an F-5 tornado. They call it the 'Finger of God.' A hurricane the size of Amanda could spin off a dozen that size. If an F-5 tornado is God's finger, then in a few hours we're going to get a firsthand look at His fist."

Beyond the administration building, the two men caught sight of something bouncing wildly in the surf just below the sea wall.

"Is that a boat?" asked Josh.

"Looks like a sailing yacht, twelve meters I'd guess."

"What kind of idiot would be out in seas like these?"

"I doubt anyone's on board. Most likely, it broke free of its mooring. We should tell the communications crew so they can alert the coast guard."

Before they turned to go, the boat disappeared into a trough. Then two enormous waves collided, and the water crested into a mountainous arc. Like an erupting volcano, the plume of water soared skyward pushing the yacht upwards. A wind gust catapulted it off the arc. The craft cartwheeled through the air like a giant plaything thrown in a tantrum, until it crashed into the side of the administration building and exploded into a cloud of fiberglass. The wave hammered down into the parking lot. When it subsided, the pavement was gone, replaced by a deep, open chasm. Bert and Josh stepped further back into the room as they heard glass shattering on the windward side of the building.

A couple of hundred miles to the northwest, Katie was also awake, but not for the usual reasons. When confronted with the tornado at the courthouse, she wanted to run. By staying, Katie had released the demons trapped in her subconscious. Since then, the sounds, images, and feelings that lay hidden in her dreams, overflowed into her daily life. At first, she was terrified. Eventually, she unlocked her emotions. She spent hours pouring her feelings out in her journal. She cried bitterly as she surfaced the anguish associated with her parents' deaths. Katie railed against them, herself, and God. Then she faced the loneliness and isolation left in the wake of the tragedy. Finally, she started the agonizing process of saying goodbye. The work of resolving her loss was not finished, but other concerns were immediate. She picked up her journal and pen, walked into Amanda's room, and sat down on the rug. She opened her diary and began to write.

December 13, 2012

Amanda,

Do you have any idea of what you are about to do? Do you even know what a category five hurricane is? I know that you're desperate to communicate something to us, to have us understand you, but this isn't the way. What you're doing could kill hundreds, maybe even thousands of people. Is that what you want?

Amanda, you need to understand what the impact of this could be. If this storm comes ashore, it will push a wall of water ahead of it that will slam into homes and tear them apart. It could drown nearly everyone on the Cape and be catastrophic for people further inland.

Katie paused for a moment as she thought about Bert and the others sitting directly in the hurricane's path. She took in a breath and continued.

Amanda, the water is only part of the danger. The winds near the eye of your storm are among the highest ever recorded. They will uproot trees, even massive ones, and break them apart. They'll fall on houses, people, power lines, and roads, making rescue difficult or impossible. Homes will be completely destroyed. Amanda, are you getting this?

Even the strongest buildings will be severely damaged. Their roofs will be ripped off, their windows shattered, and their interiors flooded. Debris will fill the air. Anyone hit by it will be severely hurt or killed. Many people will be trapped in the rubble, and many of those will probably die before they can be rescued. Heavy rains will cause rivers to overflow, flooding cities and towns, and destroying even more homes. Power will be cut just when people need it most. It may not be restored for days or weeks. Without light, heat, or refrigeration, people who survive the storm will face food and water shortages, contamination, and disease. And if the weather turns colder, they could freeze to death.

Amanda, I know there's something in the storm's path that you're trying to alert us to, but there just isn't time for us to figure it out. I'm sorry. I wish we could but it's just not going to happen. If it doesn't, is this what you really want? Is there anything so important that it would be worth inflicting so much suffering on so many innocent people? I'm begging you, Amanda, please, please stop now, before it's too late.

Katie closed the book and wrapped it in her arms. She hugged it tight to her chest as if that might give greater power to the words she had written. Katie closed her eyes and sat back against the wall. Then in the peaceful, perfect glow of Amanda's room, she started to cry.

50

Dividing the forward speed of a hurricane into one hundred provides the approximate inches of rainfall.

"Any luck?" Josh asked Bert as the two of them stood in the middle of the makeshift ham radio shack. The only light in the room came from two small lanterns and what little squeezed through the slits of the barricaded windows. People had stopped looking through the cracks. Huge chunks of the seawall were gone. Where it remained, the surf crashing against it sent sea spray a hundred feet into the air. The parking lot was awash, and waves lapped against the side of the administration building. The sea had already reclaimed what was left of the shattered yacht. When the main power went out during the night, the emergency generator came on-line for twenty minutes, and then stopped.

Bert looked down at his useless cell phone as he spoke to Josh, "Coverage went out about an hour ago. I've been trying to reach Katie though the ham radio net, but it keeps going directly to her voice mail."

"Well, it's confirmed," said Chet, an operator sitting at one of the ham radios. "She's slowing down, barely creeping ahead at four to five miles per hour."

"Good news or bad?" Josh asked Bert.

"The winds won't be as severe, that's good. But we'll also be sitting in the height of the storm for a longer time. That's bad. Then there's the rain."

"It's a little too late to build an arc." Josh had done the math. At the storm's reduced speed, they could expect a rainfall of twenty to twenty-five inches per hour.

"Fellahs," said Chet, "if you're planning on making peace

with your maker, now might be a good time. The winds have reached a hundred miles per hour, and they'll keep on rising for the next few hours. It won't be much longer…"

"That's it!" Everyone in the operations center stopped and looked at Bert. He turned to Josh. "I know who Katie was talking about, who it is that's in the path of the storm."

"I hate to be the first to break the news to you, buddy," said Josh, "but it's us."

Bert ignored the joke and handed Chet a phone number to dial. Bert donned a headset and waited impatiently, hoping, praying she would be home.

"Hello," Bert recognized the unmistakably sweet voice in his earphone.

"Hello, Winnie. It's Bert Myers."

"Oh," Winnie sounded alarmed, at least as alarmed as she was capable of sounding, "I'm sorry, Professor, but as I said in my message to you…"

"Winnie, there's no time to explain right now. This is critically important." The urgency in Bert's voice was enough for Winnie to stop protesting and listen. "You said your sister lived on the water in Massachusetts. I need to know where."

"I doubt you've ever heard of it, Professor," Winnie answered. Bert motioned for a pad and pencil as she continued. "It's really not a very big town. It's mostly government people out there, you know."

Bert tapped his foot nervously and dug the point of the pencil into the pad, "What town is it, Winnie?"

"Oh, I'm sorry, Professor. Sometimes I can't help myself from carrying on. The name of the town is Quissett Harbor. That's Q U I S S…"

Bert placed his hand on the mouthpiece and yelled out, "Does anybody know where Quissett Harbor is?"

"Of course, Bert," said Josh, "you passed it on the way here. It's the next town inland."

"Winnie," said Bert, "I need Cynthia's street address and phone number, please."

Bert scribbled frantically as Winnie dictated the answer. He thanked her, hung up, handed the new number to Chet, and paced nervously as he waited for the response.

"Busy signal," said Chet. "The phone lines are probably down."

"Then can you get me in touch with the police or fire service? I need for them to check on that address."

"I can get them for you, but it won't do you any good. They're running flat out with evacuations and, according to the radio traffic, they've already cleared that area."

"Then I'll have to go there myself." Bert ran to his room to retrieve his jacket and car keys. Josh followed.

"Have you lost your mind, Bert?" Josh pointed toward a barricaded window, "That's a hurricane outside. You go out there, and you're going to die."

"That's just it, Josh. If I don't go, we're all going to die." Bert started down the hall.

"Hold on," Josh retrieved his own jacket. "I can't believe I'm actually saying this, but I'm coming with you."

As the two men passed the ham shack, Chet stuck his head out and yelled, "Fellahs, before you go off to get yourselves killed, you might want to take a look at this."

Forty-five minutes later Katie opened her ringing cell phone. It was an unknown number.

"Katie?"

"Bert! Are you alright?"

"Yes, Katie, I'm fine. We're all fine. It's like a miracle."

"The storm dissipated," she said.

"Yes, that's right. We'll have to see what the data show, but the consensus is that once the storm veered far enough from the Gulf Stream, the sharp drop in the water temperature sapped the energy from it."

"Just about thirty minutes ago?" Katie asked.

"Exactly. Have you been tracking it on the monitors?"

"No, Bert. I'm not in the lab. I'm in Amanda's room."

"How could you be? You're on your cell phone. Katie, did

you do something?"

"I tried to communicate with Amanda, Bert. It seemed as though when I wrote to her in my journal, she understood what I was saying. I tried to get her to listen, to make her understand what she was doing, but it didn't feel like I was getting through to her."

"When did you start trying?"

"I don't know the exact time. Maybe three-quarters of an hour ago or so."

"Forty-five minutes ago is when the hurricane slowed down. Then it stopped completely. While it sat offshore for the next fifteen minutes, it started to dissipate. Then a half hour ago, it suddenly disorganized and evaporated."

"Oh, God," Katie began quivering. "Oh, God, what have I done?"

"Katie, I never believed I would say this, but I think you're been right all along. You may have just saved the lives of everyone at this conference, and maybe hundreds, even thousands more."

"I've got to go, Bert, I can't talk anymore."

The phone went dead. Bert pressed off the speakerphone and turned to Josh.

"I've got to see this for myself," said Josh. "I'll be up during the Christmas break."

Meanwhile, Katie cried hysterically with her back against the wall. Her cell phone rang again. She sat forward and opened it.

HI K T CAT
RU NAKED?
WAY TO GO SHERLOCK!
C

Katie peered at the screen through her watery eyes—WAY TO GO. It's as if he knows my every move—but how? Then she looked again—SHERLOCK, that's so cliché! Something about the message struck her as odd, but she was too drained to process it. She would revisit it later.

Katie shut the phone and fell back against the wall. Tears ran down her cheeks and fell onto the open pages of the journal. An icy wind poured in through the open window, but Katie didn't notice. To her right just above her elbow, the writing pen she retained from her father, the one with the letter opener, extended out perpendicular from the wall.

Unaware that Amanda had heeded her call to abandon the storm, Katie took the only action she thought she had left. The clock and crib no longer affected Amanda, and there was no time to experiment with other, less lethal options. In desperation, Katie imbedded the metal blade into the wall's surface, into Amanda.

Below the blade, a tiny drop of wet paint oozed out. It was not the same pale shade of Baker-Miller pink. It was a deeper, darker red. It was the color of blood.

51

When the wind dies down and the surface of the water turns smooth as glass, a sailboat can sit for minutes, hours, even days without moving, helplessly waiting for a reprieve from a dead calm.

Bert returned from Woods Hole to find Katie's letter opener exactly as it was when she plunged it into the wall. Since that moment, everything associated with the room was gone. There was no perfect pink glow or sound attenuation, no overwhelming sense of peace and tranquility, no weather anomalies. There was nothing out of the ordinary, nothing at all.

In addition to Hurricane Amanda's exit, the low pressure system over the house also dissipated. Weather patterns across the country stayed within their seasonal norms.

In light of the events that drove Katie's action, she and Bert discussed the pros and cons of attempting to restore the room's environment. Bert was convinced that Katie had found a way to communicate with Amanda, and that Amanda understood and stopped before Katie drove her letter opener into the wall. They also agreed that there was still much to learn, and the results could be profound. In the end, they decided the benefits outweighed the risks. They would attempt to repair the damage. Evelyn didn't share in that assessment.

"Have you completely lost your mind?" Evelyn couldn't believe what Bert was telling her. "After all you've been through, I can't believe you would even consider trying to restore that demonic room."

"Now, Evelyn," Bert was intentionally subdued, "don't you think 'demonic' is a bit over the top?"

"I don't know, Bert, let's see. There are two students dead, except that one of them still lives in your cell phone, another is in jail for murder, and we still don't know who tried to kill you and almost killed me instead. Then there are the periodic violent storms that come out of nowhere and most recently, let's see, oh, that's right, a category five hurricane that almost killed you, all of your colleagues, and a few thousand others on Cape Cod for good measure. No, Bert, I don't think demonic is over the top at all. If anything, it's a gross understatement!"

"When you put it that way…"

"My God, Bert, what other way is there to put it?"

"In terms of what we could learn, Evie. I'm convinced now that this room is some sort of portal into a power we can't even imagine. If we understood and could harness that power, we could change the world. How could we abandon our research after having invested so much time and work, especially now that Katie may have found the link we've been searching for?"

"The link? You mean by communicating with a dead kid through her journal? Do you hear yourself, Bert? You're an internationally recognized physicist, and you're talking about your student's effectiveness at conducting a séance. Can't you see that you're losing your objectivity?

Listen, Bert, my parents have invited us to spend the holidays with them in Florida. The break would do you good. It might even help you regain your perspective. And if you still feel the same way afterwards, at least you could start fresh when we come back home."

Bert looked down sheepishly, "I'm sorry, Evie. I can't go now. Josh Gibbons agreed to come up during the break to review our findings. Maybe he can catch something we've overlooked. I only hope Katie and I can restore the environment before he gets here."

"Then I certainly hope you and Katie will have happy holidays together."

"You'd go without me? Evie, even after Stephen—we haven't spent the holidays apart since we've been married."

"Well, Bert," Evelyn's voice faltered as her eyes welled up, "then I guess there really is a first time for everything." She turned, wiped the tears from her cheeks, and went to the bedroom to pack.

The next morning Bert drove Evelyn to the train station.

"Are you sure you wouldn't rather fly down?"

"No," she answered, "I could use the time to think."

Over the next several days, Bert and Katie consulted with construction and restoration experts and developed a plan to repair the damage. Like archeologists on a dig, they carefully scraped away the backside of the wall. When they reached the back of the paint layer, they drew the blade out and used surgical instruments to coax the drop of red—still wet—back into the opening. After closing the gap from behind, they reinforced the wall behind it, but the environment did not return. As a last resort, Bert retrieved the can of Baker-Miller Pink from the basement. They both held their breaths as they opened the can, fearing they would find a solid block of pigment, but instead, the paint was still liquid. Katie applied only enough to bridge the tiny scar. She and Bert sat back and looked at the tiny ribbon of moist pink against the dry wall. "That's as much as we can do at this point," said Bert. "Now we just wait and hope."

"Katie, no matter where I am or what I'm doing, please call me immediately if the environment returns."

"I'm so sorry, Bert."

"Don't be. If I had gotten through to you that night, I would have asked you to do exactly the same thing."

Katie nodded in understanding, "I'll call the instant there's any change."

After Bert left, Katie sat down on the rug next to the still wet patch and opened her journal.

December 19, 2012

I spoke to Tess today. She says she's holding up OK, but I can tell in her voice that she's lonely and scared. Brian has filed the appeal, but without new evidence, it's going to be difficult to get the verdict overturned. All we can do now is hope and pray.

Amanda, I'm sorry I didn't trust you enough. I thought you weren't listening and I was afraid for all those who might be hurt by the storm. I hope you'll forgive me.

Please come back Amanda, not for what we can learn, or for any of the benefits Bert thinks we might derive, but because I miss you. I know it seems strange, Amanda, but I feel closer to you than to any friend I've ever known. I've probably shared more with you than anyone else in my life and I can't help thinking that you feel the same way about me.

At last, Bert is convinced that you've been trying to communicate with us. I'm only sorry we hadn't fully understood how until now. If we had, Cynthia Reynolds might still be alive. I can't help feeling partly responsible.

If I had just left you alone, sitting offshore for a while longer, Bert might have gone to Mrs. Reynolds' house and found her in the car before the garage filled with fumes. Now even Bert believes that you were trying to signal what was happening so we could intervene. I only hope we'll understand better the next time, if there is a next time.

Please don't leave me, friend. Please come back to me, if only so that I can say a proper good bye, one that lets you know how deeply I care for you.

Love,
Katie

52

A single cell thunderstorm consists of a one-time updraft and one-time downdraft. The typical life cycle is less than an hour. At its mature stage, high winds, severe precipitation, and hail may develop.

The sound didn't register immediately. It came from a distance and got closer and louder until it broke through the fog of sleep. It was the phone ringing.

Bert's first impulse was to grab it before it woke Evelyn. She was an early riser, but loosing sleep sometimes put her in a foul mood. Then he remembered she wasn't there. He let out an involuntary sigh and forced his eyes open. It was still black outside. Bert reached for his cell phone as he tried to focus on the clock radio's dial.

"Bert, it's Katie. She's back! And she's doing something again."

Bert's eyes cleared enough to make out the time: 4:10 a.m. "What's happening, Katie?"

"The pressure is dropping rapidly and the temperature's gone down eleven degrees in the last half hour."

Bert thought to himself, "Does this girl ever sleep?"

Katie continued, "The rain started about ten minutes ago, and now the storm if forming into a cyclonic pattern around the house. The wind speed is seventeen miles per hour, but it's climbing steadily."

"I'll be right there."

As Bert opened the door to the garage, his cell phone buzzed. The text message stopped him in mid-stride.

HI BIRTY,
B 4 U GO 2 C K T
U HAVE GOT 2 C THIS!

MMIRL
DAMNEDEST THING I EVER SEEN!
C

Bert stared at the message, MMIRL - "Meet me in real life?" and wondered why Chris was suddenly willing to break his self-imposed isolation. But where? There was no rendezvous location, just that last cryptic line: DAMNEDEST THING I EVER SEEN! Then Bert recalled where he had heard those words before—from old Ben Jansen. Bert jumped into the GTO, pulled out onto the street, and sped off into the darkness.

Twenty minutes later the GTO made its way down the long dirt road toward the lake. The rain was torrential in the predawn chill. At the shoreline, Bert circled the car so that its hood was facing back up the hill. The sky was attempting to brighten, but thick gray clouds obliterated the sun. Bert started toward Ben's cottage, but stopped and turned back to the car. He opened the trunk and pulled out the tire iron. Then he took a flashlight from the emergency bag and tucked in his jacket. He held the lug wrench with one hand while he slapped the bent end against the other. "Yes, this should do."

He was surprised at how far the cabin was from the road. He had traveled almost a quarter mile before he came to the clearing for the house. It was more modern and well equipped than he would have imagined.

A covered porch jutted out ten feet along the front. A tall metal tower, topped with a ham radio antenna, stood forty feet away from the right side of the house. About two-thirds up on the tower, Bert recognized the familiar arrangement of a weather instrument cluster. Against the house on the left was a gas-powered generator. Further left, against the tree line, were several cords of neatly stacked firewood. Through the sparse winter foliage, Bert could make out the silver-gray surface of the pond.

Bert moved cautiously, remembering the gun Ben purportedly used to keep intruders at bay, but there was no detectable movement from the house. He stepped onto the porch, walked up to the front door, and knocked. There was no response. He knocked louder, "Mr. Jansen, it's Bert Myers from the college. I need to talk to you. It's very important." Still nothing. Then he called out, "Chris, Chris, are you there?"

Bert checked the windows on either side of the entrance. Shades blocked the ones to the left. To the right, he saw a corner desk and table with a ham radio rig, computer, and electronic equipment. QSL cards, used by ham operators to confirm successful communications between stations, papered the walls above the desk and around most of the room. From the looks of old Ben's "shack," the hobby consumed much of his time. However, there were no signs of activity.

Bert walked around the left of the house. The generator wall had no windows. As he continued around back, the rain grew steadier, and he began to feel chilled. A window in the back corner of the house looked into the kitchen, sparse but neat, but still no signs of life.

A small overhang protected the back door to the house. Solar panels covered the back roof and, in the corner, there was a small satellite dish. "To say that old Ben is self-sufficient would be an understatement." Bert wandered a few feet from the path and his foot sank ankle deep into a soft patch of earth. The wetness soaked though his sock and into his shoe. He lifted his mud-encased foot from the muck. As he shook it off, the rain intensified. He was shivering and ran to the back door for cover. The wind picked up and drove sheets of rain under the overhang and against him. He opened his cell phone and looked at the text message again - DAMNEDEST THING I EVER SEEN! Then he put the phone away, drove the chisel end of the lug wrench between the door and the frame, and pushed hard. The door sprung inward and Bert escaped from the icy deluge.

In the kitchen, Bert caught the first signs of life. A pile of dirty dishes and some dinnerware lay at the bottom of the sink. The refrigerator contained a healthy stock of beer and some leftover pepperoni pizza. In addition to beer bottles and soup cans, the garbage can held empty pizza boxes and salt and vinegar potato chip bags. Bert crossed through the dining room and made his way to the ham shack. A stack of QSL cards with Ben's name and call sign lay on the table. Sitting next to the cards was a one-page letter addressed to Ben from SKYWARN. Bert scanned the letter.

Dear Mr. Jansen,

Thank you for supporting the work of SKYWARN. Because of the assistance of ham operators like yourself, we can provide early warning of severe storm activity to people nationwide, and we greatly appreciate your input.

Unfortunately, as we have been unable to reconcile the significant differences between your submissions and those of major weather information sources and other reporters in your area, we are unable to incorporate your information into our database at this time. We suggest you contact your equipment and software suppliers for assistance in restoring the accuracy of your system. When you have ensured that the system is once again generating reliable, accurate weather data, we would be delighted to have you provide us with your input.

It was signed by the regional coordinator. Bert smiled to himself. *Poor Ben must have been beside himself with frustration. He didn't know what was skewing his weather data. No wonder he acted paranoid.*

He continued walking through a hallway toward the left side of the house. In the bathroom to the right, towels lay crumpled on the floor. Toiletries were piled haphazardly around the sink. It didn't match Bert's impression of the old man. To the left of the hall were two doors. The first opened to a storage area filled floor to ceiling with dusty old items. The other led to the bedroom. There was no light switch so he crossed to the far side of the room to lift the shade. As he did, he heard the creaking of the door behind him. Bert spun around to see a figure lurking in the shadows behind the door.

He brought the tire iron up high above his head and clenched it tight as he directed the flashlight at the silent figure. He was panting hard and sweating, but the specter didn't move. When the light hit its mark, he exhaled and lowered his weapon. The would-be assailant was Ben's hat and coat draped over a sewing manikin. As Bert shook off the tension, he noticed the opposite wall of the room.

A laptop sat atop an antique dresser. A network cable connected to the computer ran up into a hole in the ceiling and a stepstool lay crouched against the dresser. Starting at the ceiling a path of papers meandered their way down the entire height of the wall. Notes and news clippings accompanied the main paper trail. He stepped in for a closer look.

Bert touched the keyboard and the laptop's screen sprang to life. It displayed a camera image of the corner of a room, but no activity. He turned his attention to the stream of papers flowing down the wall. At first, it looked to be like a time line. Upon closer examination, it appeared more like a story outline. Once he determined the starting point, he examined the papers in detail. He pulled the stool closer, mounted it, and started reading from the top.

9/21/1990 – Amanda + brother DOB
Andrew - BBFN
AE

Next to the note was taped a news clipping announcing Amanda's birth. Bert pulled a piece of paper from his wallet. It was a listing of common internet acronyms and emoticons. He had downloaded it after trying to decipher some of Chris's cryptic phone messages.

He looked up BBFN – "Bye-bye for now." From the previous research with his team, he understood AE to mean Autumnal Equinox. He went back to the chart.

12/21/1990 – Amanda – CYA
Andrew – WGAF
WS

The next clipping described Amanda's death. CYA equaled, "see ya." Bert had penciled in the other acronym at the margin of his crib sheet, along with others he had seen in Chris's notes or heard used on campus: WGAF equaled "Who gives a fuck." Bert took WS to mean Winter Solstice.

6/21/1999 – Andrew – SNAFU
SS

Another news clipping accompanied the note. It was dated June 22, 1999. The headline read "Couple arrested for Child Abuse." Penciled next to the article was "child = Andy Irving"

Ronald and Samantha Niles were taken into custody this morning as they attempted to visit their foster child at Saint Mary's Hospital. Speaking on the condition of anonymity, a hospital worker said that doctors became suspicious when the nine-year-old child arrived at the hospital yesterday for treatment associated with a fall. Upon closer examination doctors found "numerous fractures and contusions" over much of the young boy's body and several older injuries that "looked like they could have been the result of cigarette burns." Andrew was treated at the same hospital less than a year earlier for a broken arm. His foster parents claimed he was injured when he fell off his bicycle. Both adults are being held on fifty thousand dollar bonds pending trial. In the meantime, the boy has been returned to the custody of the Department of Child Welfare.

The SNAFU acronym captured the hopelessness of Andrew's status—"Situation Normal, All Fowled Up." It was the SS, however,—Summer Solstice—that held Bert's attention. "Whoever assembled this is linking these accounts to astronomical events. Ben Jansen isn't doing this."

Bert thought he caught movement on the monitor to his side, but when he turned to look, it was gone. He stared at the screen for a couple of minutes and then returned to the outline. As he reviewed the structure of the notes, he recognized Chris's outlining pattern. Bert skimmed down several pages until another entry caught his attention.

9/23/2006 – Ronald – CYA
Samantha – BBFN
AE

The related news clipping, "Early Morning Fire Kills One, Leaves Another In Critical Condition," had the same date.

A fire at 221 Rosemont Avenue claimed the life of a local resident early this morning and left another in critical condition. Early reports indicate that the blaze apparently started in the first floor kitchen and spread quickly through the two-story wooden frame house. Ronald and Samantha Niles were taken to Saint Mary's Hospital. Ronald Niles was treated for third-degree burns over ninety percent of his body. He was scheduled to receive further treatment at the burn center at City Center Hospital but died of his injuries before he could be moved. Samantha Niles remains in critical condition with second-and-third-degree burns over thirty percent of her body. While the cause of the fire is still under investigation, police do not suspect arson…

Bert made a mental note, *It looks like it took Andy a while, but when he got even, he wasn't fooling around.* Then Bert moved to the next entry.

8/16/2012 – Ralph Campbell – CWOT - CYA

Bert looked up the new acronym: CWOT - Complete Waste of Time. The attached article recounted the gruesome details of Ralph Campbell's death. Bert recalled Chris's meeting with Tess in Indiana, their drive home together, their detour to Atlantic City, the rushed engagement, and the stolen money. Bert tried to push away the picture that was forming in his mind—a picture of a very different Chris—a portrait of a murderer, but the next entry only reinforced that image.

9/22/2012 – Chris Matthews – BBFN
Drew Richardson – :-< - CYA

AE

Bert looked up the figure next to Drew's name. Once he read the explanation, however, he looked at the figure sideways and it made perfect sense. It was the emoticon for sad. Chris was going away, but Drew's CYA was more permanent. Everyone else with that label was dead.

The next entry cemented into Bert's consciousness the image of, not just a murderer, but also of a serial killer.

12/13/2012 - Mom - CYA

Bert was familiar with the accompanying headline: "Prominent Socialite Found Dead in Garage."

The story recounted how the Quissett Harbor police found Cynthia's body in her car with the engine still running and a bottle of sleeping pills on the seat next to her.

Though the article referenced Cynthia Reynolds, Bert kept hearing the voice of Roslyn Samuelson as she recounted her unsuccessful suicide attempt. Cynthia died as Roslyn would have if Andy hadn't rescued her. *Did Chris kill her? Of course, that's what Amanda was trying to warn us about.* Bert reread the note.

Mom? Bert asked himself, *Are Chris Matthews and Andy Irving the same person? Could Chris have murdered his own mother?*

His mother? That made no sense. Chris came from a strong, well-to-do family. He wasn't even adopted—or was he?

Bert realized that it never occurred to him to ask the question. He took out his cell phone and looked up his contact for Chris's father. He called and got Carl's voice mail.

"Mr. Matthews, oh, I'm sorry, Mr. Danford, this is Bert Myers at Nadowa College—Chris's Professor. We met at the memorial service. Please forgive me for asking such a personal question but it's critically important. I need to know—was Chris adopted? Please call me back as soon as possible." Bert left his number and hung up. He wasn't even clear on what explanation he would give for asking the question, but that was secondary. Right now, he just needed to know the answer.

Bert rifled quickly through the remaining pages, trying to get a complete picture of the story they told. It was all there—the history of the house, of Amanda, of Andrew Irving and the portraits of the people, and even the things involved. It included information on Doctor Miller and articles on Baker-Miller Pink. It was Chris Matthews's missing report—the report he was supposed to hand in the day that he and Drew disappeared. However, this wasn't the work of a ghost. A living, breathing person had assembled this.

Bert was almost finished reading when his eye caught movement on the laptop again. This time he was ready and quickly moved his concentration to the screen. It was the image of Katie Jarvis. That's when Bert recognized the setting. It was the corner of the lab just outside of Amanda's room. Katie was walking back into the room. Instinctively, Bert started hitting the function keys. The F-10 key caused the picture to jump from the corner image to a wide-angle view of the entire lab. Hitting it again toggled to an image of Katie working at the monitor inside Amanda's room. It was being taken through the doorway from the wall opposite the room. "He's tapped into the room's cameras!" Bert said aloud, "What the hell is going on here?"

Bert opened his phone to dial Katie. As soon as he did, the monitor turned blue and filled with white letters. Bert started reading.

12/21/12 – 4:50 a.m.

Mr. Matthews, oh, I'm sorry, Mr. Danford, this is Bert Myers at Nadowa College – Chris's Professor. We met at the memorial service. Please forgive me for asking such a personal question but it's critically important. I need to know – was Chris adopted? Please call me back as soon as possible.

"What the…" Bert scrolled down the screen.

12/21/12 - 4:31 a.m.

HI BIRTY,

B 4 U GO 2 C K T

U HAVE GOT 2 C THIS
MMIRL
DAMNEDEST THING I EVER SEEN!
C

Bert scrolled down further.

12/21/12 – 4:10 a.m.

"Hello Bert, it's Katie. I'm sorry to call so early but you said you wanted to know..."

The text confirmed Bert's suspicions, Chris was secretly recording his and Katie's cell phone calls. "So that's how you knew our every move, you little son of a bitch!"

Bert closed the phone and dialed Ed Davis's number. He got Ed's voicemail. As the recording went on, it also printed on the computer's screen. Bert realized that Chris might be monitoring the same text from another location, but there wasn't time to worry about that now. He didn't want to wait and take the chance that Chris might destroy the evidence. At the beep, Bert gave his message, "Ed, this is Bert Myers. I'm at Ben Jansen's place. From the looks of things, Chris Matthews has been living here, probably for some time. I'm certain he was the one who murdered Ralph Campbell and from the looks of things, maybe several others, too. You need to get here as soon as you can."

There was one final page on the bottom of the wall. It was too dark to decipher. Bert pulled the flashlight from his jacket and shined it on the text. Then he stopped breathing.

12/21/2012 – Katie – :'-(- CYA
WS

Bert didn't have to look up the emoticon's meaning—it stood for crying.

WS - *Winter Solstice,* Bert was talking to himself as he beat the head of the flashlight into his hand, "The winter solstice occurs at 6:11 this morning. That's it! Katie - CYA. Chris is going to kill Katie at the exact moment of the winter solstice!" He took in a deep breath and looked at his watch: 5:15. He bolted out the front door.

By the time he reached the car, he was gasping for breath. He jumped in and gunned the GTO's engine. Even with its legendary limited slip differential, the tires spun in the waterlogged earth. He got out of the car and looked at tires buried halfway to the rims. "Damn!"

He looked at his watch - 5:35. He gathered rocks, tree limbs, and branches and stuffed them under the wheels until he was confident that the cradle would work. Inside the car, he gently pressed on the accelerator, "Come on baby, you can do this. Just ease up onto the wood."

The wheels caught onto the skids and lifted the back end of the car up and on top of them. Bert kept a slow, steady pressure on the gas pedal until the car's momentum started him up the long climb to the top of the road. As he moved forward, he accelerated gradually. The conditions kept him from fully utilizing the massive horsepower under the hood. Patches of icy leaves caused the car's tires to slip at one moment and jerk violently the next.

The clouds were ink black and beads of hail pelted the windows. Driving with one hand, he called Katie's cell phone with the other—it went right to voice mail. He left a message, "Katie, you've got to get away from the house. Chris is on his way over and you have to leave before he gets there. There's no time to explain, but for God's sake, leave now!" Maybe she would turn around and see the message light flashing in the doorway. Maybe she would step out of Amanda's room just long enough for him to get through. Bert hit redial. The phone rang once and then picked up. "Hello, this is Katie, sorry I can't...." Bert hung up and hit redial again.

The hail increased and the wind pushed the car from side to side. Then it all stopped—replaced by a disquieting calm. Bert tried to remain focused but couldn't stop drifting into thoughts about Evelyn and about what he was in jeopardy of losing—

their years together, the struggles they survived, even her inability to stay angry with him no matter how hard she tried. As Bert reflected on how much he didn't want to give that up, he was unaware that his speed kept creeping higher.

The ringing of his cell phone broke his daydreaming. He looked down at the screen. It was Carl Danford. At the same time, he saw he was passing the driveway. He swung the steering wheel hard, too hard. Wet leaves and ball bearings of hail covered the pavement. The car spiraled out of control. Bert tried to compensate with one hand on the wheel and his foot pressed hard against the brake pedal. The left front tire caught a patch of dry pavement and jerked the steering wheel from his grip. The GTO spun around and slammed against the concrete gatepost.

As his body smashed against the driver's side door, Bert heard the snap in his shoulder and felt the sting shoot up his side. A web of cracked glass formed where his head hit the driver's side window, and blood streamed down the window and the side of his face. The cell phone, still in his hand, mimicked the car window's pattern of shattered glass. The front of the car faced the road, and the headlights peered into the edge of forest beyond. The engine stalled and steam escaped from the hood. Bert turned the ignition switch—nothing. He tried to open the driver's door. Excruciating pain accompanied any movement of his left arm. The door wouldn't budge. Bert crept along the front seat and escaped through the passenger door. Steam billowing from the radiator filled the air with the sweet smell of hot antifreeze.

Bert lost his footing on the oily, icy ground and came crashing down on the blacktop. He screamed uncontrollably as the crack in his shoulder widened. His left arm sandwiched itself between the pavement and his stomach. Another snap alerted him to a cracked rib, and he could feel a shard of bone in his arm trying to slice its way to the surface. He started to faint, but then remembered Katie and fought blacking out. He looked up at the house a quarter mile in the distance and saw Katie's car parked outside. Then he saw another car parked against the side of the green house. Its location was chillingly clear—it was impossible to see from Amanda's room. There was something else, too. Bert wasn't certain, but for a moment, he thought he saw a figure standing in the shadows almost directly below Amanda's room. It appeared to be looking toward him. He forced himself to his feet. When he looked again, the figure was gone. Bert began inching his way down the long, icy driveway toward the house.

53

When molecular bonds are broken, e.g. melting and evaporation, energy (heat) is absorbed. When new bonds are made, e.g. condensing and freezing, the energy is released. It is called latent (hidden) heat because the material's temperature does not change.

After making the call to Bert at 4:10 a.m., Katie lingered in the research room checking on the monitors. None of the stations outside of the storm's perimeter picked up any of the unusual activity. The satellite and Doppler images showed clear skies. It was almost 5:30 a.m. when she reentered Amanda's room and checked that monitor. The map had zoomed in to the Hudson valley with the house at the center. A vortex of clouds circled around the house and for two and a half miles out. She toggled through the parameters. The temperature and pressure were still dropping, and the wind speed was increasing. The threat level had already moved from green to blue and was now at yellow. The monitor emitted a stream of low, steady beeps. "What are you up to now, Amanda? What are you trying to tell us this time?"

Then the room went dark. A blast of damp icy air shot through the open window and then quickly subsided. On the screen, the clouds and precipitation dissipated, then vanished. The temperature and other weather readings took on their normal random patterns. Behind her, Katie heard a slow, steady scraping at the doorway. Looking up, she saw the black silhouette on the wall, flashing on and off with the message strobe.

"Hello, Drew," she said without turning around. "I was wondering when you'd get here."

"Drew?" The voice from the doorway was followed by a

long silence, "You're amazing, Katie. When did you figure it out?"

"I've had my doubts for a while, but your last e-mail cinched it."

"Oh?"

"Sherlock, you called me Sherlock. It's terribly cliché, even for Chris. But if Chris was anything at all, he was a chauvinist. He never mixed his sexual references. He might have likened me to Bones, or Agatha Christie, but never to Sherlock Holmes."

"And then there was this." Katie reached for the item on the shelf in front of her. As she did, she saw the silhouette move and heard the footfall—Drew was moving closer. She quickly turned and tossed the leather catcher's mitt to Drew as she did. He stopped to catch it in his glove-covered hands.

In the diminished light, had it not been for their conversation, Katie might have thought she was actually looking at Chris. Drew's tight black locks were gone, along with his beard and heavy rimmed glasses. The man who stood in front of her was clean-shaven, baby faced, and had wavy blond hair. She also saw the blue tint of the contact lenses in Drew's brown eyes. However, even more striking than Drew's transformation toward Chris were the features that were there all along, the ones hidden beneath his beard, hair, and glasses—the unmistakable facial features of Ed Davis.

Katie also noted the huge knife Drew held in his left hand and the long, ugly gash on the wall next to the door. Even more alarming were the long streaks of deep red that leached out from the openings and trickled down the wall and onto the floor. Katie maintained her composure, "What are you doing, Drew?"

"I'm finishing what I started, Katie." Drew opened the leather glove, exposing the signature.

"Benny Distefano," said Katie. "According to Bert, that left-handed catcher's mitt is about as unique as your DNA. I couldn't remember where I'd seen it until I opened one of your boxes to return 'Pillars of the Earth.' I didn't think you'd mind if

I read it. After your phone message, I put it all together. According to Roslyn Samuelson, you really loved your foster father, Richard. He bought you that glove and, if he hadn't died, he would have adopted you. The main character in your book took on his father's name, too, so when you decided to change yours, Andrew Irving became Drew Richardson."

Drew gently dropped the glove to the rug, "Very good, Katie. You always were the best and the brightest of us, though I really thought I had you fooled this time."

"But why, Drew? Why all the mystery, the false identity, and all the rest? Why didn't you just come forward after the accident?"

"Accident, huh?"

For the first time Katie became alarmed. A tremble crept into her voice, "What are saying, Drew?"

"When I swung that oar Katie, I think I almost took Chris's head clear off."

Katie shuddered, "But you were friends."

"We were, and everything would have been fine if you all hadn't gotten so nosey. But then the professor had to assign Mr.-Sixty-Fucking-Minutes to look into my background. It was all there in Chris's report. Eventually, you would have found out what I did to my scum foster parents and Tess's stepfather."

Katie's eyes opened wide in astonishment.

"Oh, that's right. This is all new to you. Yeah, well Tess didn't know either. By the time I got to the hospital, her mother was gone. But the nurse filled me in on her fight with Ralph Campbell. You should have seen him at the cemetery, that decrepit slob. His hands were all over Tess, right there next to her mother's gravesite. I could see in his eyes what he was thinking. I would have preferred to wait until the timing was right, but he needed killing so bad. They weren't supposed to pin anything on Tess, and they wouldn't have if she had just stayed clear of his house. Chris didn't have the guts to do what I did for her. But that didn't matter to Tess. She still wanted him. She didn't even know I existed. Nobody ever does."

Drew's voice started quivering. "You know, my parents couldn't stand to have me around, not even for a single day. Amanda had three months. I spent my life being bounced from one funny farm to another, never good enough to be family to any of them. I was always too smart or too dumb, too loud or too quiet, too little this or too fucking much that for any of them."

A loud crash at the end of the driveway interrupted Drew's ramblings. Katie and Drew looked out the window to see Bert's GTO spurting steam into the cold winter air. Then the passenger door opened, and Bert crawled out, only to fall screaming to the pavement.

"Like a moth to a flame," Drew smiled. "In a way I'm sorry he made it. Now we'll have to end this, though I have to hand it to the Professor. He certainly knows how to arrive in style." Katie looked into Drew's face; his eyes glistened, and his cheeks were wet with tears. "Do you have any idea of what it's like to have your own mother wish you were dead: to wish you had never existed at all? No, you wouldn't, would you? You came from the Midwest fucking Waltons. Anyway, Cynthia said it would have been better if she had died in childbirth, so maybe I was a little late, but I finally granted her wish."

Katie felt lightheaded and braced herself against Amanda's crib. "You killed your mother, Drew? Is that what the hurricane was about?"

"When we discovered this room and Amanda still here, I thought for sure my own sister would accept me," Drew's voice grew angrier. "But that little bitch is no better than the rest of you. I tried to connect with her, but like everyone else, she turned her back on me.

"She was there when I killed Campbell. I thought she was there to help. But when the tornado hit the courthouse, I realized she was angry they convicted Tess instead of me. She never supported me. She just tried to warn people, just as she tried to warn you today. Well, now that little bitch can die, too." Drew raised the knife and clenched it tightly in his hand. Tears ran down his face. He brushed his running nose with his sleeve, and then looked at his watch—6:11. "I'm sorry, Katie. I really liked you. I wish things could have been different for us...."

"Drew!" The voice came from the doorway. Drew swung around, knife in hand, and faced Ed Davis.

Ed was out of uniform and holding a gun. "Drew," he commanded, "Don't say another word. Put the knife down. Don't make this any worse on yourself than it already is."

Drew let out a nervous laugh and dropped the knife. "Any worse? How could this get any worse? And who the fuck are you?"

"Drew," said Katie, "this is Captain Davis from the campus police. He's been helping us research Amanda."

"And her brother," said Ed. "Drew, do you remember Winnie Seivers?"

"Yeah, some old lady who sent me money. I saw her name and address on one of the envelopes. The social worker never said why."

"Because your mother's maiden name was Seivers, too. Winnie is her sister."

Ed handed Drew a piece of paper with two pictures taped at the top.

Drew studied them, "Pictures of me at my high school swim meets. I gave them to my social worker to send to the old woman. So what?"

"They're not both you."

Drew looked more closely at the pictures. In the one on the right, the logo on the swim trunks was for the 'Dolphins' rather than the 'Stingrays.' Drew's eyes darted back and forth across the pictures then he flipped them over. The date on the Dolphins picture was March 11, 1983. Drew stared at the photo.

"That was taken my junior year at Catskill High," said Ed.

Drew looked up at Ed and noticed the same features he saw in his own mirror.

"Gareth Reynolds is a powerful man," Ed explained. "He's also brutal. Your mother was terrified of him. She knew that if she tried to divorce him he'd leave her homeless and penniless."

Ed explained the affair between him and Cynthia, her pregnancy, and their cover-up. He told how Winnie found the adoption agency and how he arranged it so that that Drew was sent there directly from the hospital. "Gareth never forgave your mother for forcing him to give you away. Then again, he was never much of a sentimentalist and, in time, he forgot all about you, but I never have, Drew. When Katie and the professor told me about Amanda, I offered to help because I hoped it would lead me to you."

"All I ever wanted was to belong," Drew trembled uncontrollably, "to be connected to someone, anyone."

"I should have been there for you when you were growing up. I'm sorry I wasn't, but I want to help you now."

"You can't help me," Drew sobbed. He rubbed the tears from his cheeks with his shirtsleeve. "Nobody can. You don't know the things I've done. You'd hate me if you did."

"I don't care what you've done. I've loved you from the moment you were born, and I'll never stop loving you, no matter what. I know you're in trouble, Drew, but please, let me help. Let me be there for you now."

"Oh my God," Drew fell to his knees. Tears poured down his face. "Oh God, I'm sorry." Drew buried his face in his hands, "I'm so sorry."

Ed lowered his gun, knelt down next to Drew, and for the first time in his life, hugged his son. "It'll be all right. I promise. I'm going to do everything I can to make this right for you."

Outside, Bert reached the head of the driveway. He paused and looked up to Amanda's room. The message light pulsed through the open window. Bert's head throbbed in time.

Inside the room, Ed was still hugging his son as Drew repeatedly sobbed his mantra, "I'm sorry, oh God, I'm so, so sorry." Katie heard the change at the same moment as Davis. The words were the same, but not the emotion. "I'm sorry, Dad." The sobbing disappeared and the trembling stopped. Sarcasm and hatred filled the void. Davis stiffened and tightened his grip on the gun, but it was too late. The knife cut below his ribs and sank deep into his stomach. Ed's gun fell to the floor as the blade tore its way through his insides. He could feel his organs ripping apart as Drew straightened up and broke free of his embrace.

"I'm so sorry, Daddy Dearest." Drew rose to his feet bringing Ed with him. Then Drew turned, slowly raising the knife as he did, "but your heartfelt sympathy is way too little," Drew starting driving Ed backwards toward the window, "and too," Ed broke through the glass, "fucking," Ed's body poured out of the window, backed into the cold winter air and then started its decent, "late!"

As Drew's face vanished into the distance, Ed searched it for some sign of understanding, of forgiveness. All he saw was Drew looking back at him, laughing.

Bert, stooping half over from the pain and fatigue, looked up when he heard the crash. But unlike Ed, all he could see in the dim light was the wavy blond hair of Chris Matthews, peering down from the window, laughing. Bert couldn't hear the laughing above the wind. There was something in the wind.

Ed's body crashed onto the muddy lawn in front of Bert. A storm of wood splinters and glass accompanied it. The huge knife still protruded from his stomach. Red soaked his shirt and poured down his sides, turning the mud crimson. Bert knelt down. Ed gripped Bert's hand and moaned, "Too late, too late, too…." Ed's grip loosened and his hand fell to the ground.

Bert jerked himself upward and tried to stand, but shards of bone cut their way through his skin. Pain filled his body. Everything spun out of control. The pounding in his head exploded as his body crumbled below him. As blackness filled his eyes, Bert felt the life ebbing from him. He had failed. He was too late. This was where he was going to die, and his last action was going to be a fruitless one. He could not stop Chris from killing Katie. As Bert floated earthward, his mind retraced all he had done and all he had failed to do. He had time and energy for only a single word, "Evelyn!"

54

Absolute zero is calculated to be equivalent to -273 ° Celsius. It is the theoretical absence of all warmth.

Katie remained frozen by the scene that had just played out in front of her. She hadn't even noticed Ed's gun lying on the floor until Drew reached down and picked it up.

"Looks like Dad did you a favor, Katie," he said. "This way it'll be fast and painless." Drew focused so intently on his goal that he didn't even hear the wind howling around him. Katie did, and something she heard in it frightened her even more than Drew.

"But, Bert is on his way, Drew," Katie yelled above the gusts. "Everyone will know you're alive. Don't you see? You'll be caught for sure." As she finished, Katie caught the image forming in the monitor. The threat level jumped from green to blue, to yellow, to orange as the vortex swirled around them, small, swift, and violent. Lightning flashed everywhere. "Drew, look!" Katie yelled, but Drew stayed focused on completing his task.

"Bert?" Drew's shouting was barely audible above the roar of the storm and the thunder. "I'm counting on him, Katie. Drew Richardson is dead. Once Bert finds you here, everyone in the country will be searching for Christopher Matthews."

The threat warning went from orange to red. With the room's environment intact, the warning system would have been barely noticeable. The siren would have been a pleasant low whistle, and the lights only noticed if a person was looking directly into them. However, with the environment gone, the piercing scream of the siren pained Drew's ears and the strobe lights blinded him. Then the sound of a thundering waterfall overpowered the siren. As Drew tried to block the lights and dampen the pain in his ears, Katie dove under Amanda's crib. The image on the monitor confirmed her fears.

The tornado descended upon them. The room moaned as the wood frame twisted and splintered and the plaster walls cracked. From each crack, blood-red liquid spurted out and drenched the walls. Drew looked around him as the reality of what was happening settled in. He looked down at Katie who held her hand stretched out to him. He dropped the gun and reached out for Katie as the top of the room twisted, turned, and finally broke free. Then in his face, Katie saw the same expression as that of Cyrus Evens—the look of a man who knew he was about to die. His body lifted into the air and, for an instant, he seemed to float motionless. Equipment ripped free from the shelves and then the shelves themselves took flight, circling around his helpless body. Then Amanda's crib lifted and crashed into the screaming, helpless Drew. He and the crib spiraled upwards into the vortex and disappeared into the blackness beyond. Then it was gone. The wind died down, the clouds evaporated, and the morning sun shone through the crisp clear air.

55

Rainbows are created when sunlight is bent as it enters tiny droplets of water suspended in the air. The individual droplets act like prisms and mirrors. The light is reflected off the inside wall and is bent again as it leaves, separating the white sunlight into its component colors.

The sounds of the medical monitors were the first thing to get through to Bert's consciousness. Then his eyes cleared enough to make out the instruments themselves, and finally Katie's face came into focus.

"Katie? How did I, how did you get...?" Bert shook his head and tried to concentrate. "How long have I been here?"

"Whoa, slow down, Bert," Katie moved closer. "They brought you in three days ago. You did quite a job on yourself, a broken arm and collarbone, two cracked ribs, a ruptured spleen, and a concussion. The doctors said it was a miracle that you made it to the house."

"The house. I was kneeling next to Ed Davis. He kept repeating, 'Too late.' I thought he meant you. I got to my feet and that's the last thing I remember."

"You must have tried to move too fast," said Katie. "With everything that was broken, your body just shut down, and you blacked out. The doctors think that's probably when you ruptured your spleen. I found you on the front lawn and phoned the medics."

"Chris," said Bert. "I was trying to get to Chris before he...."

"It wasn't Chris. It was Drew. You were rambling about old Ben Jansen's place so the police checked it out. They found poor Mr. Jansen buried out in the back of the house." Bert looked down and remembered his foot being stuck in the soft mud and shuddered. When he looked up again, he saw Katie wiping a tear from under her eye. "They found Chris's body under the wood pile."

"Drew did that?" Katie nodded yes.

"So he used me," Bert thought about the police recording his call to Davis. He felt like a fool. "He planted the information there to make it look like Chris was behind everything."

Katie nodded in agreement, "He had it well planned; only he hadn't figured on Amanda."

"Amanda?"

"Before you blacked out, did you hear anything else, Bert?"

"I heard the wind."

"Just the wind?"

Then Bert recalled what he thought he had only imagined. "Almost like a young girl screaming?"

"So you heard it, too."

"If you hadn't asked, I would have guessed it was a hallucination. And Drew?"

"The tornado took him, along with everything else in Amanda's room, and in the research room. It's all gone, Bert," a sad smile crossed Katie's face, "everything but the clock."

"The clock?" Bert asked.

"When the storm ended, it was lying next to me on the floor, without a scratch on it. It was almost as though Amanda left it behind on purpose."

Bert let out a sigh, "Maybe she did, Katie. And even if everything else is gone, we're still here, alive." Then Bert stiffened, almost as if he were afraid to ask the question, "Evelyn?"

Katie nodded. "She's been here all night. She just stepped out for some coffee."

"And she's not going anywhere, mister." Evelyn stood in the doorway. She held two cups of coffee in her hands. As she made her way to the bed, she handed one of them to Katie and put the other down on the bed table. Then she sat on the edge of the bed and rubbed her hand through her husband's hair.

"I'll leave you two alone," said Katie. "Evelyn can fill you in on the rest. Besides, you've got a lot of catching up to do." She looked at Evelyn, and the two women exchanged knowing smiles. Bert looked up at his wife, confused.

"I'll explain it in a minute, Bert. First, I'll let you two say your good-byes."

"Good-bye?" Bert looked at Katie even more confused.

"Yes, Bert," said Katie. "I'm going back to Kansas. Did you know I own the biggest dairy farm in the state? My aunt and uncle have been managing it for me. I'm not quite sure what my plans will be, but it's about time I started making some. Besides, I found what I was looking for when I came here, although that may be a problem on the farm - I slept till noon today." Katie leaned over and kissed Bert's forehead, "Goodbye, Bert, and thank you." Katie walked out the door.

Evelyn looked into Bert's eyes. "Bert, do you think it's too late for us to adopt."

"No, Evie, but I'm surprised. We talked about it, and I thought you were dead set against the idea."

"I was, but I've been thinking. I realized that I was focusing on what the baby would do for us, as though it would be responsible to somehow make up for our losing Stephen. Lately, I've been thinking that what's really important is the love we could provide for the child."

Bert smiled and squeezed Evelyn's hand.

Outside, Katie stopped at a bench on the way to her car. She sat down and pulled out her journal.

December 22, 2012

What a beautiful day! The air smells so crisp and clear after this afternoon's shower. There's a rainbow in the distance and the late afternoon sun is casting one of those pinkish/golden hues that make everything look even better then it really is.

I'm looking forward to seeing Tess before I go home. After what the police learned about Drew, they've reopened her case. They've determined that the knife used to kill Captain Davis is the same as the one used on Mr. Campbell. Brian said there's DNA from both men's blood on the blade and he's certain Tess's conviction will be overturned soon. I've talked to Tess about coming to Kansas, at least for a while. I know a farm there that could use someone with good accounting skills. She said she's not the farm type, but she's agreed to come for a visit. I'd also like her to meet Steve.

Katie stopped writing for a moment and reached into her carry bag to retrieve a stack of letters. Five of them were from newspapers and television networks offering her work. She had scanned each quickly and placed them under the others for later consideration. The rest of the letters she had opened and read many times. Each of them was from Steve Nylen. In the early ones, he apologized for pulling Katie into the department store basement against her will and expressed his deep regret at the fate of her parents.

Katie finally wrote back after Tess's trial. She told Steve that she realized he had most likely saved her life and was correct in saying that her parents knew what to do. Once they didn't find her in the stationery aisle, they would have headed to the basement to look for her there. Had she gone looking for them, they might have missed each other and all died.

In his later notes, Steve shared his experiences at college, his future career plans, and most importantly, his long-held feelings for Katie. She in turn, expressed her feelings toward him. Katie returned the letters to her carry bag and resumed writing.

I'm not certain how I feel about a future at the farm. So much has changed, especially me. I need some time to think about my future and to select the options that feel right. For now, the farm seems like the best place for me to start.

It's a shame that so many people feared you, Amanda. As it turned out, you were more like a guardian angel to us. I hope you found peace. I owe my life to you and I'll never forget you.

Goodbye, Amanda. I'll miss you.

To be continued…

Epilogue

The house at Lakota Drive lay dormant for the next ten months, its fate uncertain. Throughout the spring semester, Bert's meteorology class took a host of weather measurements at the house, around the property, and for five miles out. Josh Gibbons came out to assist. None of the readings showed anything out of the ordinary. Bert's interest in the project waned after he and Evelyn adopted baby Stephen. Katie sent the couple a congratulatory note and an update. After her release, Tess visited Katie in Kansas and stayed on as the accountant for Katie's farm. It seemed as though the environment, and some of the farm hands, agreed with her disposition. Katie left the management of the farm to her aunt, uncle and Tess, and accepted a position as an investigative reporter at the Chicago Sun-Times. She included a picture of herself in her new office. In the photo, on the wall behind Katie, was the Kit-Cat Clock from Amanda's Room.

The new dormitories at Nadowa were up and supplied the college with all of the space needed to accommodate the student population. The incoming student government officers moved their offices back into the center of campus. John Thompson reviewed the damage to the house and decided that the cost for repairs outweighed the benefits of the restoration. Several people approached the college with offers to buy the property. Thompson declined the offers in favor of holding onto the land for future expansion, especially once he learned that, to everyone's surprise, old Ben Jansen had left his property to the college in his will. In the end, Thompson decided it was best to demolish the house. He allocated funds for demolition to begin in October. In the interim, the house deteriorated. Snow and rain poured into the open second-story rooms and soaked through the floors to the level below. Ceiling plaster cracked and fell, and walls bulged and crumbled. Maintenance workers boarded up the doors and windows to prevent would-be squatters from entering and being injured. That didn't stop the animals, however. Prior to the start of demolition, the building became home to a host of raccoons, squirrels, mice and, on the upper level, several nests of birds.

On a sunlit afternoon in late September a young robin ventured out of its nest before it was ready. It spread its wings but couldn't coordinate them for flight. The young bird flapped wildly but fell into a wall opening between the studs. A sudden wind gust slammed against the east side of the house. The inrush propelled a shaft of air upward between the studs that carried the bird aloft, landing it on the edge of its nest. The bird did not venture out again until it was strong enough to fly.

Right up to the moment of its demolition, the smell of death never again entered the house at 34 Lakota Drive.

Acknowledgements

Writing may be a solitary endeavor, but moving Amanda's Room from concept to completion was anything but. I am grateful first, to my wife Judy, who exercised a saint's patience dealing with my long and many mood swings and kept me focused on you, the reader.

Other than me, no one has spent more time and energy on Amanda's Room than my two daughters-in-law, Jennifer and Jolene, and my sons, Mike and Jason. Their detailed and substantive comments dramatically altered the final work. Mike's outstanding cover design captures not only the central setting for the book, but the feelings associated with it, and Jason's computer expertise kept me from drowning in technical overload. I am also indebted to Jo-Anne Lockard, who expertly edited many sections of the early drafts.

I have benefited greatly from my participation in the Osher Lifelong Learning Institute (OLLI) at the University of Connecticut's Waterbury campus. I am especially indebted to Director Brian Chapman, Assistant Director Rita Quinn, and President, Nancy Via. Many dedicated and talented OLLI instructors helped me to improve the craft of writing, especially, Jack Lander, Alvin M. Laster, Sandi Noel, Cindy Eastman, Philip Benevento, Robert Grady, Jeremy Joyell, and Dorothy Sterpka. I also appreciate the encouragement and input of the many OLLI members who traveled with me on this path toward self-fulfillment.

Much of Amanda's Room deals with the weather and I drew a significant amount of my information from the U.S. Power Squadron's Weather Course for Mariners. I am grateful to Ken Bell who expertly organized and co-taught the course and to the other instructors from the Meriden, Connecticut chapter.

As subsequent drafts were ready for review, others provided feedback that guided my revisions, validated that this was a story worth telling, and helped me to tell it in a more compelling way. I am grateful for the input and constant encouragement of many family members and friends, including: Cindy Cayer, Becky Chawner, Carmella Chawner, Ron Cormier, Lucille Donadio, Nick Donadio, Brian Durbin, Janet Ebert, Toni Escott, Fred Gagliardi, Joan Gagliardi, Attorney Scott Garver, Grace Grab, Dr. Carol Grant, Cathy Miceli, Dawn Miceli, Maria C. Montante, Doctor Chuck Motes, Lisa Niedermeyer, fellow author Matthew Plourde, Lorraine Rochefort, William Seymour, Pete Smith, (who encouraged me to keep going when I thought the end would never come), and Diane Smith. I also want to thank Woody Young and David Milburn of the California Clock Company for permission to use the "Kit Cat Clock" illustration on the cover.

There is specialness about the kind of spaces that are conducive to spending hours each day writing and rewriting, and consuming copious amounts of coffee. Some of those places while working on Amanda's Room included Annie's Diner, Denny's Restaurant, Grace's Restaurant, Fancy Bagels, the Pepper Pot Restaurant, Saint's Restaurant, and the Southington Public Library. I completed the final layout for this paperback version of the book while cruising aboard the Costa Romantica in the Mediterranean Sea. Talk about a special place for writing!

At the Connecticut Author's and Publisher's Association (CAPA), I share in a community of people who, like me, have stories to tell, need to tell them well, and desire to share them with the world. Through CAPA, I met Roberta J. Buland, whose expert editing of later drafts helped to produce the finished product you have before you.

Finally, I want to thank you, dear reader. After all, you're the reason I wrote this. I visualize you sitting in your recliner, or on a train, or at the beach, and smiling in satisfaction at a character, a bit of dialogue, or a particular scene. I also imagine you twitching or glancing around as you read something eerie. I have to confess a certain satisfaction at making you squirm. If I have succeeded in giving you a few hours of pleasure through reading this book, or robbing you of a bit of sleep because you had trouble putting it down at times, I am delighted. I welcome your feedback and your suggestions for future mysteries in this series. Thank you, and good reading.

About the Author

Much of Chuck Miceli's professional career has been in the field of criminal and juvenile justice. He was a Training Officer at a maximum-security prison, a Resource Center Coordinator for the National Institute of Corrections, and Chief of Curriculum at the Connecticut Justice Academy.

His text, "Fire Behind Bars," co-authored with Alton P. Golden, was the first book in the nation to deal with the issue of deadly fires in secure institutions. He has delivered programs and seminars on criminal justice, juvenile justice, and professional development topics throughout the U.S. and has been a consultant to government and professional associations across the country. He has authored professional journal articles, government profiles and nationally distributed lesson plans. Thousands of people have participated in his training programs, "Public Service Excellence," co-authored with Bonnie Delaney, and "Making the Most of Your Time, Work, and Life." He is a columnist for the WXedge.com weather information website and his poems and short stories have appeared in magazines and literary journals.

In addition to writing, he spends much of his free time involved in civic, social, and religious volunteer work. He is past Board Chairman for Every Dollar Feeds Kids (**http://www.edfk.org**), a non-profit organization that raises money to feed hungry children in the U.S. and abroad.

Chuck Miceli was born one of eleven siblings in the coal mining town of Pittston, Pennsylvania, grew up in the East New York section of Brooklyn, New York, and now lives in suburban Connecticut with his wife, Judith.

Connect With Me

Thank you for reading *Amanda's Room*. For questions, comments or further information refer to any of the following:

My website, which covers all aspects of my writing:
AuthorChuckMiceli.com

My Amazon Author's page (paperback and Kindle eBook):
http://www.amazon.com/Chuck-Miceli/e/B007ETDHF0

My Smashwords author page (for other eBook formats):
www.smashwords.com/profile/view/ChuckMiceli

My general information Facebook page:
http://www.facebook.com/authorchuckmiceli

My "Amanda's Room" Facebook page:
https://www.facebook.com/AmandasRoom

My tweets:
http://www.twitter.com/CharlesMiceli

My professional background information on LinkedIn:
http://www.linkedin.com/in/cmiceli

My blog posts:
http://somethingsignificant.wordpress.com/

My weather related articles:
http://wxedge.com/author/78

I look forward to hearing from you.

Chuck Miceli

Made in the USA
Charleston, SC
27 October 2015